P.D. CACEK

SECOND
CHANCES

This is a **FLAME TREE PRESS** book

FLAME TREE PRESS
6 Melbray Mews, London, SW6 3NS, UK
flametreepress.com

US sales, distribution and warehouse:
Simon & Schuster
simonandschuster.biz

UK distribution and warehouse:
Marston Book Services Ltd
marston.co.uk

Thanks to the Flame Tree Press team, including:
Taylor Bentley, Frances Bodiam, Federica Ciaravella, Don D'Auria,
Chris Herbert, Josie Karani, Molly Rosevear, Mike Spender,
Cat Taylor, Maria Tissot, Nick Wells, Gillian Whitaker.

The cover is created by Flame Tree Studio with
thanks to Nik Keevil and Shutterstock.com.
The font families used are Avenir and Bembo.

Flame Tree Press is an imprint of Flame Tree Publishing Ltd
flametreepublishing.com

A copy of the CIP data for this book is available from the British Library
and the Library of Congress.

HB ISBN: 978-1-78758-334-4
US PB ISBN: 978-1-78758-332-0
UK PB ISBN: 978-1-78758-333-7
ebook ISBN: 978-1-78758-335-1

Printed and bound in Great Britain by Clays Ltd, Elcograf S.p.A.

P.D. CACEK

SECOND CHANCES

FLAME TREE PRESS
London & New York

P.D. CACEK

SECOND
CHANCES

FLAME TREE PRESS
London & New York

To My Family:
Blood related or love related
you will always be in my heart.

1872

Hickory, Mississippi

Millie kept her hands behind her back as she walked down the center aisle that separated the older children from the younger. The four older, three near-grown boys and a gal about her own age, were working on arithmetic while the six younger, all gals, were busy practicing their letters on slate boards.

"Very good, Manda," Millie said. The child was only a little mite, but Lord was she bright. She knew her letters and how to count to fifty without having to think about it, but her penmanship still needed a bit of work. "Best not to hold th' chalk so hard or ya'll likely snap it in half, which'd be a shame after them nice Quaker ladies give it t'us. Just ease up on your fingers."

The little girl looked up with a smile bright enough to blind the sun. There were smudges of chalk dust on Manda's fingers and blue overskirt. "Yessum."

Millie reached out and tapped the board on the girl's knees and watched the child slowly spell out her name. She was still holding the piece of chalk as if it was a chicken about to escape the ax, but Millie nodded.

"There ya go," she said and continued down the aisle and back up the hay foot side of the classroom, pausing to bask in the warmth that rolled out from the woodstove near the coming-in door. The heat felt good against the scars that crisscrossed the palms of her hands. She'd gotten them when she was no older than Manda and in training to become a kitchen slave. The Ol' Missus caught her running her fingers across the linen tablecloth she was only supposed to carry out to the washroom.

"*What do you think you're doing? Mustn't touch! Mustn't touch!*"

The Ol' Missus was one for the switch and there were very few working in the house that didn't carry evidence of it on their hides. The Ol' Missus was a mean one and Millie hadn't been sorry when, after the bluecoats came and freed her and the other slaves, the old woman went off her head and shot herself with the Ol' Masser's pistol.

"*Thou should forgive, Millie.*"

Millie felt her cheeks grow warm. Mrs. Benezet, who'd taught Millie reading and writing and such, was one of the Quakers who had come to live in the Big House now that the war was over, and Quakers believed in forgiveness. Fact was, they were about the most forgiving people Millie ever hoped to meet.

And the kindest.

Mr. and Mrs. Benezet and a whole mess of their Quaker friends came all the way down from Philadelphia to turn the Big House into what they called a 'Way Station' for anyone, colored or white, who needed a place to stay or a hot meal or just a kind word; and fixed up the old quarters so any of the freed slaves who wanted to stay, like Millie, would have homes that were solid and dry.

Then they did something Millie wouldn't have thought possible in a hundred years – they fixed up the old harness shed into a school to teach those who'd never known anything beside the whip and cold and hunger and pain that there was more they could be besides some other man's property; that life could be good. And when she was ready, they made Millie the teacher. Mr. and Mrs. Benezet were the first white folks she didn't fear.

The first white folks she trusted.

God must have been watching the day she ran off to make sure they'd be the ones to find her.

She hadn't planned to run, thought never entered her mind even when the overseer had snatched her up when she'd come out of the smokehouse carrying some fatback for 'Liza, the cook. He was drunk on 'shine and said she was stealing the fatback and when she told him, "No sir, I gettin' it for the cook," he backhanded her across the side of her head a few times to take the fight out of her before doing what he wanted.

He'd about done her in so that she could barely walk, which got her another beating when she got back with the fatback all covered with dirt and leaves. She hadn't let go of it even while the overseer was rutting on top of her, but that hadn't stopped the Ol' Missus switching her half to death for being 'so utterly clumsy'. It was afterward when Millie'd finally crawled into the cabin and her mam was putting lard on her back and telling her she was lucky she was still too young to breed, that one of the field hands come running in, saying the bluecoats were right up the road and freeing every slave they came across, but that they all had to hide, because he'd heard that the Ol' Masser was coming with a rifle to kill all of them before he'd let the bluecoats take his property.

Millie remembered her mam screaming and snatching up the baby boy Young Masser got on her the spring before and telling her to run... *"run t'freedom, child, they's just up th'road, an' don't stop till ya find 'em!"*

So she ran and ran, but *just up the road* was a lot farther than she thought and she hadn't known about miles or distances back then. When her strength finally gave out Millie collapsed in a ditch by the side of the road and closed her eyes, knowing the next time she opened them it would be to the glories of Heaven.

Which was where she thought she was when she woke up in a bright white room, tucked into a feather bed beneath a thick quilt, and why she said what she did when a man with fair hair and a beard and gentle blue eyes leaned over her.

"Dear God, ya brought me home t'paradise. Praise be your name."

The man she mistook for the Lord God had laughed softly, thanking her for her innocent mistake, and then the world went black again and she slept. And slept, and when she finally was able to keep her eyes open for longer than a minute and sit up without her head swimming, the man came back and said his name was Benezet and that he was a Quaker.

He asked Millie if she knew what a Quaker was and she said it must be the name of an angel.

Millie could still remember the tears that filled the man's eyes.

"No, child," he'd told her, "I'm only a man."

Maybe so, but Millie suspected the Quakers were as close as a body could get to the Lord God himself and still be breathing.

The Quakers were good people. Not only did they take her in and heal her up, but fed and clothed her and taught her the magic waiting for her beneath the covers of books.

They taught her what freedom meant.

They taught her hope.

That had been eight years ago come summer and now she was a woman grown who could read and write and was teaching others the way she'd been taught. She had purpose and a place in the world.

Millie allowed herself a slow deep breath and a smile as she lifted the small lapel watch Missus Benezet had presented to her the day she finished up her teaching studies.

It was just a bit after two, but winter days were short and Millie knew the shadows would already be gathering under the trees. In an hour or so it'd be so dark along the wooded path that it'd be impossible for the children to get home without stumbling.

Besides which, Millie wanted to get home to finish up reading the book of poetry Missus Benezet had given her. The poems were the most beautiful things Millie had ever read, even if she couldn't recollect what some of them were going on about. But that didn't matter, it was the way the words floated around inside her head that made them as irresistible as molasses on fresh bread.

Letting the dainty little watch drop back against the top of her pinafore, Millie picked up the iron poker from its place against the wall and used it to open up the stove's metal grating. The poker felt comfortably warm in her hand, but she could feel it getting hotter as she stirred up the coals. No use in putting on another log if she was going to end class sooner rather than later. The coals would do to keep the schoolroom warm enough while they finished up.

After closing the door, Millie laid the poker back against the wall and clapped her hands together as she walked back to the big wooden desk Mr. and Mrs. Benezet had bought from a catalogue and cost a whole five dollars.

"A'right now," she said as the children looked up. "It's gettin' late and I smell snow comin' on the wind, so I'm gonna let y'all out early so set down your boards 'n' chalk an'—"

Millie planted her hands firmly on her hips and waited for the whooping and hollering and scraping of hobnails against the wood floor to end. The oldest girl noticed first and hushed the others.

"Shh! Miss Millie ain't done talkin'!"

Silence — or as close as it was going to get with the promise of going home still hanging in the air.

"That's better," Millie said and let her arms drop. "Now, I think we should end today by practicin' th' song we're gonna sing for Mr. Benezet's birthday this comin' Sunday after meetin', 'lessen ya'all'd rather just screech like hooty owls."

"No, ma'am, Miss Millie," Abraham, the second to oldest boy, said, "we wanna *sing* proper."

There was just a little seat-squirming as the rest of the children nodded in agreement.

"A'right, then. Now 'member, the boys start and gals do the answers and then everybody gonna do the chorus together. Ready? Fine, ev'one stand on up and take a deep breath in...." Millie took a deep breath and watched her students do the same. "An'—"

The children's voices came out as screams when a gunshot blast echoed into the classroom.

"Come on outta there!"

The children made other sounds now — softer, trembling sounds Millie remembered too well. She raised her hands.

"Hush up!"

They hushed, their eyes wide and scared, but quiet. It was the other voice, the one outside that continued.

"You deaf? I said come outta there!"

There was another shot, this one tearing a small chunk off from the top of the coming-in door. The screams erupted again and this time Millie's joined them.

"Guess they ain't deaf after all."

Laughter outside, crying inside.

"Miss Millie?"

"Shh!" Putting a finger to her lips, Millie motioned the children toward the peg wall where they'd hung their coats and scarves and hats.

"Get bundled up now, good and warm," she said, "and head out the back door. Hurry on home an' don't stop for nothin'...nothin'. Y'all hear me?"

"Yessum."

"But Miss Millie, those men—"

"Don't you be worryin' 'bout those men, hear? You older ones take care of the lit'l uns and tell Mr. Benezet 'bout this." Millie clapped her hands hard enough to make the old scars sing as if they were fresh. "Make sure you tell him what happened and ask if he'd please come on down t'th' school. Mr. Benezet'll take care o' those men. Now, 'member, don't none of you stop for nothin'. Hurry up!"

"We know you're in there, gal, you and all them little chicks. Come on out and maybe we'll let 'em go."

Millie herded the children out the back door that led to a narrow path between the two privies and out through the woods. It would be hard traveling to make it back to the Big House, but they wouldn't be seen by anyone at the front of the building.

"G'on now."

The oldest boy stopped just outside the door. "Ain't you comin', Miss Millie?"

"I'll be right behind you. Hurry up and mind the lit'l uns."

Millie wished the trees hadn't dropped all their leaves as she watched the children slip away, but the good Lord must have been watching because a mist was rising to cover their escape.

Not escape, Millie reminded herself, because they weren't slaves anymore so no man had the right to them. It was the law, Mr. and Mrs. Benezet and their friends told her that, and the law would protect her.

Maybe so, but the law was far away and the men with guns were just outside.

Another shot peppered the door. "Last chance, wench. Come out or we come in."

"Ain't no man my massa," Millie reminded herself as she closed the back door and turned. "Ain't no man got a right over me."

"*Gal!* Get yer ass out here."

Millie crossed the room slowly, stopping only long enough to pick up the iron poker from its place by the stove before opening the buckshot-riddled door.

There were four of them, four big men sitting on tall black horses. Four big men sitting on tall black horses with squirrel guns across their saddles and flour sacks covering their heads with only the eyeholes cut out. She couldn't tell who they were.

Nightriders is what Mr. Benezet called them.

Haints is what she and the others called them. Ghost men that rode out in the dead of night with flaming torches in their hands yelling like hell's own devils and doing what they pleased just like they were still masters. They'd already paid a visit to the Big House back in the spring, sitting on their tall horses and yelling promises about horse whippings and hangings before they set fire to a tarred cross they planted in the kitchen garden.

Millie had nightmares for a week after that and wouldn't have been able to make the walk to the schoolhouse if Mr. Benezet hadn't been beside her.

"They will not hurt thee, Millie," Mr. Benezet told her each and every morning, even after she was able to walk by herself. "Thou hast the same protection under the law as do I and all free men and women. Thou art free and safe and no man, especially no man who feels the need to hide his face, can take it from thee."

The words had given her strength, but they seemed only a memory now that she was standing all alone in an empty schoolroom looking out at four big men carrying squirrel guns with flour sacks over their heads and sitting on four tall horses.

One of the horses shook its head, the bit and bridle rattling, and Millie jumped.

The Haints laughed.

"Well, lookee there," one of the men, Millie couldn't tell which, said, "we got us a lit'l jumpin' frog."

"An' me without m'gigging pole," another said, and all of them laughed again.

"Now that's too bad...I do so love me some frog legs."

"Think there'll be enough t'go 'round? This one looks a mite skinny."

And they laughed some more.

Millie tightened her grip on the poker. "What'cho want?"

The men stopped laughing.

"Well, now, what *do* we want? How 'bout a song? I do so miss hearin' them songs your kind used t'sing, 'minds us of the good days." One of the men moved his horse forward a few steps. "How many chicks ya got in there, gal?"

Millie pulled the door closed behind her. If the Haints thought the children were still inside the schoolroom, they might not do anything.

"They just babies," she said, lifting the poker so the men could see it. "Ain't done nuthin' to be bothered with."

"Now did we say we was gonna bother 'em?"

One of the Haints spurred his horse closer and Millie raised the poker. The man stopped the horse.

"Looks like we got a fighter, boys."

Millie lifted the poker higher. "Go 'way! This here school b'longs to Mr. Benezet and his friends. This Quaker land!"

The man on the tall horse leaned forward over his saddle. Millie saw bright blue eyes peeping out at her through the holes in the flour sack.

"Wasn't and shouldn't be. Him and his damned Quaker abolitionists ain't any better'n the rest o'them carpetbagger sumabitchs. Now, put that poker down and get over here. You do what you're told and we'll make it easy. Keep sassing us and it'll go hard."

Millie didn't know why she did it or even realized that she had until the poker flew out of her hand and hit the ground a few feet in front of the Haint with enough force to spook his horse.

It twisted its head away from the sound and jerked to one side quick like a cat going after a mouse. The man fell off backward, startling the other horses and sending his own mount hightailing it down the road. It took a moment for the three other Haints to get their horses under control so they weren't looking at the man on the ground, but Millie was and saw his face when he pulled the flour sack off his head.

"Goddamn your worthless—" He looked up at her, looked right up into her face and then there was no mistaking who he was.

"Mr. Leeworth." She'd only whispered the name but the man, the lawyer who had sat at Mr. and Mrs. Benezet's table and broken bread with them, and who had smiled at Millie when he watched her sign her name to the papers he'd drawn up that said she was a free woman, glared up at her from the schoolyard dirt. His face was all red and twisted up like a mad dog's and Millie wished he'd put the flour sack back on over his head.

It would have made it easier for her to forget who he was when he stood up and pulled a tiny derringer from his waistcoat pocket.

"Goddamn you and your kind," he said and pulled the trigger.

It was such a tiny bullet it felt like someone had just thumped her in the middle of her chest. It didn't even hurt; it just made her sleepy and all she wanted to do was close her eyes.

MILLIE
1854(?) – October 18, 1872

PART ONE
IMPOSTERS

OCTOBER 2017
CHAPTER ONE

Arvada, Colorado

The man on the screen quarter turned his chair to study the enlarged headline that had appeared behind him…

THE DEAD RETURN
SUFFRAGETTE COMES BACK IN YOUNG MOTHER'S BODY!

… then cocked his head to one side as he turned back to the camera.

"Obviously," he said, "she's come a long way, baby."

Jess tried to stop himself but couldn't. The laughter, which unfortunately contained more than a few stray bits of rice cake, exploded out of him like a cannon, spraying the coffee table.

"Yes?"

His wife came in from the kitchen just as he wiped the last pieces of his 'heart-healthy snack' onto the plate with a napkin.

"Just something on TV," he said, still smiling until he saw her face. Jess picked up the remote and turned off the television just as the late-night host mentioned something about miracles. "What's wrong?"

She sat down on the couch next to him and took his hand, which would have been a sweet and loving thing to do if the look on her face hadn't continued to look grim. Jess sat up straighter and felt his heart begin to race while at the same time doing a quick mental inventory of possible husbandly transgressions.

He was sure he took out the garbage. He remembered taking out the garbage. Did he take out the garbage?

Jess gave her hand a gentle squeeze. "Come on, Monica, you're starting to scare me."

She blinked.

"What? Oh...oh, no, sorry, I was just being..." She laughed and Jess's heart slowed a bit. "...a mom, I guess."

"My mom never looked like that unless she got a call from the principal about me."

"You used to get into trouble?" She feigned shock. "You?"

Jess batted his eyelashes. "Yes. All the time. What's wrong?"

"Oh." She laughed again and this time it sounded forced. "It's Abigail."

"Abigail?"

That surprised Jess enough to bring him back into a full upright and locked position. Abigail? Of their beautiful twin daughters, Abigail had always been the quieter, the easier of the two. Both of them were smart, well-behaved and respectful, the epitome of what the daughters of a Presbyterian minister should be, but where Abigail was humble and quiet, her older sister by three minutes, his namesake Jessica, was the living equivalent of a category five tornado but never in a mean-spirited or vengeful way. The two were as different as night and day. Where Abigail accepted things, Jessica questioned them. Where Abigail was obedient, Jessica was....

Jess took a deep breath. Jessica was just...Jessica.

Abigail was his little princess, was his pride.

Jessica, the tomboy, was his joy and as close to the son Jess always thought he wanted until they were born.

"Are you sure it was Abigail?"

He thought it was a legitimate question. They were mirror twins after all and even though they seldom, if ever, dressed alike, and Jessica's hair was much shorter, he had called them the other's name more than once.

His wife gave him the same look the late-night host had given the camera, but it wasn't the least bit funny on her. Jess cleared his throat.

"Seriously, Jess?" Jess ducked his head in apology and waited in silence. His wife took pity on him. "A boy asked her out."

Jess's heart picked up speed. "She's only thirteen!"

"I know, our baby's growing up."

"Our baby's only thirteen. Who is this boy?" Jess hadn't been aware that he'd gotten to his feet until he realized he had to look down to meet his wife's eyes. "Do we know him? Where does he want to take her? When? Why aren't you saying anything?"

She smiled. "I was waiting for you to stop talking, *Dad*."

Message received. Jess stopped talking and sat back down.

"And to answer your first question, yes, we know the boy. It's Jacob, Zach and Brie's son, you know, from down the block. He shoveled off the driveway last winter. Jacob and Abigail are in the same English class. You know…Jacob. You like him."

"That was before he asked my daughter for a date." She slapped him lightly on the arm. "So where does he want to take her?"

His wife smiled. "To the new *Star Wars* movie this Saturday…with his parents. And then for pizza afterward…also with his parents."

Jess leaned back, crossing his arms in front of him. "You are a cruel woman, Monica Pathway."

She chuckled but didn't deny it.

"But if it's only a date," he said, "and we know Jacob, why did you look so…stricken when you came in?"

Jess watched the look – not stricken, no, he'd been wrong about that, but it was something he didn't remember ever seeing before – return.

"Because our little girl is growing up and it's hard on a mother, knowing everything she's going to have to go through."

Jess got worried again. "Like what?"

His wife just made a little noise in the back of her throat and shook her head. It was sometimes very hard, even as an ordained minister with a master's in counseling, to be the only man in a household of women. Jess wondered how single fathers managed.

"It's just part of growing up," she said, as if that explained anything. "Abigail asked me to ask you if it was okay."

Jess didn't ask why Abigail hadn't asked him herself because he was grateful she hadn't. God only knew what trauma he might have inadvertently caused if she had.

"Sure. Yes. It's okay." He took a deep breath. "What about Jessica? Jacob has a brother, doesn't he…. Axle, right?"

A different look reshaped his wife's face and this one Jess knew – sorrow. "Axle, yes, but no…he didn't ask Jessica. Besides, she has a softball game Saturday afternoon."

Jess exhaled slowly. Thank you, God.

★   ★   ★

Phoenixville, Pennsylvania
Eva Steinar looked down at her hands, folded peacefully in her lap, and realized with something close to shock that they were her mother's hands. She'd had beautiful hands once, everyone told her so – small and graceful, the fingers long and delicate, the pale skin smooth and soft. But that was a long time ago and now her hands were old and wrinkled, dotted with age spots and crisscrossed with the tiny scars she'd gotten over the years.

Just like her mother's.

She should have been more careful with her hands.

She should have been more careful with everything.

She should have paid more attention.

"But I don't understand," she said, because her husband hadn't said a word since the doctor explained what he thought happened. "Curtis was fine."

"No," the doctor said, "he wasn't, and I don't think this was as sudden as you'd like to believe."

Eva squeezed her fingers together until the work-reddened skin turned an ugly shade of yellow.

"Curtis is my son," she said, looking up to meet the doctor's eyes. "I would have known if he was sick."

The doctor met her eyes. "I spoke with the counselor at your son's school and she said both you and your husband were made aware of Curtis's increasingly bizarre behavior."

Eva shook her head. "The woman has always been against Curtis. She's intimidated by his genius."

"Mrs. Steinar, I am reasonably sure neither's the case. Ms. Gates is a qualified adolescent counselor who is simply concerned about—"

"Keeping her job." Eva couldn't believe the vindictiveness of the woman. "I know Ms. Gates and she's a bitter, angry woman who fabricates problems and manipulates parents into believing them. If she was good enough she would have been a *real* counselor with her own practice. I mean, it's high school for God's sake, why do they feel they need a counselor in the first place? A school nurse was all we got when I was in school."

When the doctor looked like he was about to say something, Eva lifted her right hand to stop him. Her fingers throbbed as the blood rushed back to fill them. "You have his charts so you know Curtis was given the Stanford-Binet intelligence test and scored one hundred and sixty-four. I gave him the test myself."

The doctor lowered his chin. "You did?"

"Yes. I found the test online and printed it out and gave it to Curtis. It didn't take him long to finish. He's gifted, a genius, and geniuses don't think or behave the way – other children do."

She'd almost said 'the way normal children do' but knew the doctor would have jumped on the word for all the wrong reasons. Curtis wasn't normal, Eva knew that. Dear God, why would he be normal? He was above normal; he was a genius.

The doctor sat back, nodding in defeat, Eva thought.

"I see. But geniuses generally don't walk into a school's science lab during lunch hour and kill a half dozen rats and guinea pigs, claiming they're alien invaders."

"What?" her husband said. "Jesus, the school didn't mention that. They just said he'd passed out and was brought here. He…Curtis killed them?"

It was the first time her husband spoke since the doctor asked them to sit down and Eva wished he'd remained silent.

"It was the movie," she said quickly, before he could say anything else. Both the doctor and her husband looked puzzled. "What was?"

"What…they said Curtis did. He watched a movie last night on his computer. What do you call it, streaming? Yes, he was streaming this movie on his computer and I happened to look in when I passed his door." Eva rolled the unexpected shudder out of her shoulders. "It was…very violent and Curtis was just sitting there staring at it. He didn't even hear me when I called."

The doctor made a note on the open file in front of him. "Did you try to get him to turn off the computer?"

Eva clasped her hands over her purse. She'd tried. Once she noticed what he was watching – *how could they show things like that?* – she all but ran to his bed and touched his shoulder. She hadn't yelled or shouted because Curtis was sensitive to loud noises, but she had run and somehow forgot he didn't like sudden movements either. And it scared him, must have scared him because he never would have hit her otherwise. Curtis was a good boy, a genius.

She'd scared him and he just reacted. It was her fault.

Thank God for makeup and a husband who wouldn't have noticed a broken jaw, let alone a slight bruise below her right eye.

"Of course I did," she said, "and he turned it right off."

The doctor wrote something else. "But you think those images stayed with him?"

Eva didn't like the direction the conversation was going. "I suppose, but it's the movie's fault. They shouldn't show things like that to impressionable children."

The doctor took a deep breath and Eva felt another shudder weave its way up her back.

"No, you're right, they shouldn't, but most impressionable children only have nightmares. They don't confuse what they saw in a movie with reality the way Curtis did." He set the pen aside and tapped his fingers against the file. Eva found herself watching his hand. It didn't look like a doctor's hand, although she had no idea what a doctor's hand might look like. The knuckles were too big. "Ms. Gates also mentioned he'd had trouble concentrating in class."

"Geniuses get bored easily," Eva said to the doctor's hand. "The teachers don't know how to keep him stimulated."

"And there have been some anger issues."

"Hormones. He's a teenager."

"With paranoid delusions. Has Curtis been having trouble sleeping?"

"No."

"Yes." Eva stopped looking at the doctor's hand and glared at her husband. "I hear him sometimes at night," he added, "walking back and forth and talking to himself. It's more than just hormones, isn't it?"

"Yes, Mr. Steinar. Once Curtis was stable and coherent, I asked a colleague of mine to speak to him and we both feel Curtis is experiencing sudden-onset adolescent schizophrenia."

"What are you talking about?" Eva demanded, but neither the doctor nor her husband seemed to notice.

"I'm very sorry, but it's not as dire a prognosis as you may think."

"He's not sick!"

"I knew something was wrong," her husband said. "I knew it. What can we do?"

"Did you hear me? He's not sick!"

"I think the first thing we need to do is get Curtis on an antipsychotic drug regimen. There are some wonderful second-generation drugs that have fewer side effects and—"

Eva stopped trying to be heard. Instead she went quiet and listened and nodded, and when her husband asked question after question she kept quiet and listened and nodded again. The doctor was wrong. The doctor's colleague, whoever it was, was wrong. Her husband was wrong. *All* of them were wrong and when she got home she was going to call their lawyer and sue Ms. Gates for starting the whole thing.

There was nothing wrong with her son except that he was too bright, too advanced for any of them to recognize. Curtis was a genius and geniuses were different.

"You'll have to make sure Curtis takes his medication every day, Mrs. Steinar."

Eva nodded again and stood up. "Of course I will. Can I see my son now?"

MARCH 2018

CHAPTER TWO

Los Angeles, California

"Can you open your eyes for me?"

A hand touched her arm. Holding her breath, she lay still, played possum until they'd done what they wanted and let her be. When the hand pressed a little harder she couldn't stop her eyes from squeezing tighter together.

"Shh, it's okay, you're fine." She didn't recognize the voice, but it was soft and gentle, not like the others, not like the Haints. "I know you're probably confused, but I need to see your eyes. Do you think you can open them just a little?"

She opened her eyes and immediately shut them. The sky was too bright, like milk glass held up to the sun.

"Sorry, sorry." The voice whispered something and the sky over her darkened. "I've turned down the light. Can you try again?"

Turned down the light? She didn't hear a lantern hissing, but slowly let go her breath and cracked her eyes just a little, and was prepared to snap them shut again quick-quick if needs be. The face looking down at her smiled. He was a white man, but his smile was real, soft and gentle like Mr. Benezet's and his other Quaker friends.

"Hi," the white man said, "I'm Dr. Ellison, but everyone calls me Barney."

"Doctor?"

"Yes."

She screwed up her eyes again just to see better. The room was cool and shadowy dark, but she could see that the walls and ceiling were white. She was in a bed, that much she knew without having to look, but it wasn't stuffed with corn husks or cattail fluff. It was soft and hard all at the same time and the bedding sheets both under and over her felt softer than the linen tablecloth she got switched for, and when she moved her head on the pillow – a real pillow! – she smelled only clean without a hint of lye. Mr. Benezet must have found her and brought her to the Big House.

"I'm alive."

The doctor named Barney chuckled and nodded. "Yes. Can you tell me your name?"

She licked her lips and felt her nose wrinkle. Her lips felt slimy and tasted like…strawberries mixed with lard and they felt funny, thinner and thicker at the same time. The Haints must have hit her a few times after—

"He shot me."

"What?"

"Tell Mr. Benezet it was Mr. Leeworth shot me. He's one of them Haints and he come ridin' with three others down t'th' school. Did the child'en git away? I sent 'em off through the woods and told 'em to get Mr. Benezet. Tell him Mr. Leeworth was the one shot—"

Her throat closed up on itself and it took a powerful lot of coughing and choking before it opened up again.

"It's okay. Breathe. That's it, deep breaths. Here." The doctor held a little blue cup with a white birch reed sticking out of it up to her lip. "Just take a little sip."

The water tasted like it came from a stagnant well, but it was cool and went down real easy. She kept sucking on the reed until she sucked only air. The doctor took the cup away.

"Better?"

"Yessuh. Will you tell Mr. Benezet? He gotta know the polecat he's been dealin' with."

Doctor Barney nodded. "Can you tell me your name?"

"Millie."

"Hello, Millie."

"'Lo."

"So, if I understand you correctly, the last thing you remember was this polecat named Leeworth shooting you, is that right?"

"Yessuh."

She took a deep breath and wished he'd bring her another cup of water no matter how flat it tasted. She wouldn't ask, though. "Where be Mister and Missus? The Haints didn't get 'em, did they? They safe and the chid'en safe?"

Doctor Barney nodded. "Yes, everyone's safe and you're safe too, Millie. You don't have to worry about the Haints or Leeworth anymore. They're gone and will never hurt you again. I promise. Now, why don't you try to get some sleep and I'll come back and talk to you later. All right?"

Before she could answer the doctor Millie felt her body relax as sleep began pouring into her like warm water. She was safe and the children were safe and Mister and Missus were safe and....

★   ★   ★

Arvada, Colorado

They were calling them 'miracles' and that wasn't right. Miracles were sacred things and the work of God, and it troubled him that so reverent a term was being reduced to sound bites that unscrupulous newsmongers fed like sugar cubes to an unsuspecting public.

Besides, it was ludicrous to think the things they were describing could really happen.

Wasn't it?

"Of course it is," Jess told his congregation, "because miracles, true miracles come from God alone...from *God alone*...and not some prime time news special."

He paused to give them a moment to ponder his words and while they did, Jess looked at his wife and daughters sitting in the front pew. He winked and the girls smiled back. Sitting on either side of their mother, they looked like slightly mismatched bookends. Abigail, on the right, wore a flowing lavender and yellow floral dress and looked taller than her sister because Jessica, in a plain white blouse and tan jumper, had a tendency to slump.

He caught his wife's eyes and she gave him a nod before surreptitiously elbowing Jessica gently in the ribs. Because of the nature of his sermon, as well as his position, Jess had to look away when his namesake's posture immediately improved. It wouldn't be proper if the congregation saw their spiritual leader smile at such an inopportune moment.

One crisis averted. He turned back to the topic at hand.

"From God alone do miracles occur and let me assure you there still are miracles in the world, but they are real miracles...not rumors, not tabloid gossip and certainly not the fabricated videos from some internet site. If you are a true believer you know where miracles come from, and we are true believers. We come together every week to bear witness to the fact that we believe in God and the miracles he alone has fashioned. As is written in Mark 10:27: 'With man this is impossible, but not with God; all things are possible with God.' So is it possible that what we've been hearing on the news and reading about is true? Of course, it's possible, because all things are possible with God, but is it likely? No. Why would God do that? Why would the Lord God, who gave each one of us a soul, suddenly decide to switch things around?"

Jess smiled as the congregation chuckled. He'd learned from experience that the more powerful the message he wanted to get across, the greater the need for laughter in order to cleanse the spiritual palate. Without it, he knew there was a good possibility that even the most faithful could be reduced to glassy-eyed automatons that would *Amen* at all the right places, keep in tune during the hymns and tell him how much they loved the sermon without remembering a single word.

"Between you and me, the simple truth is he wouldn't. But, for the sake of argument, let's just say he did – do you think it would be something as obvious as spontaneous resurrections? Or, instead of prophets, he'd use reporters from the *National Enquirer?*"

Someone near the back of the church started to giggle and then another voice began to guffaw, and soon the entire congregation was trying very hard to stifle themselves.

Jess smiled sheepishly as if he hadn't realized what he'd started.

"Okay, that probably wasn't the best example," he said, and laughter rose to the arched ceiling.

Jess shrugged and looked at his family. Jessica was trying so hard not to laugh she looked like she was about to burst. *Go on,* he mouthed, and his daughter's voice joined the others. Abigail, on the other hand, just looked embarrassed. They were so different, like night and day.

His wife looked at him and shook her head.

When the tide of laughter began to recede, Jess leaned closer to the lectern's microphone and cleared his throat.

"But regardless of my verbal eloquence −" *twitter, twitter* "− your laughter proves these rumors are just what they seem. Rumors. No one would laugh if these were true miracles. Now, I know there are a lot of people out there, and possibly some right inside this church, who might still wonder 'but if this is only a rumor, then why are all the news stations and, oh my gosh, the internet, which we all know is the bastion of fact −'" *giggles, guffaws* "'− saying this is really happening?' Because, my dearest friends, they can. It's as simple as that. They can say anything they want.

"Just the other night I watched a 'Special Report' about a little six-year-old girl in the former Soviet Union who, according to −" Jess raised his hands and made air quotes "− documented reports, froze to death when she wandered into a snowstorm, but who, upon being revived, claimed to be Sofia Kovalevskaya, a famous Russian mathematician who died of influenza in 1891. To prove it, they showed the little girl completing what was supposedly Kovalevskaya's final equation. Did anyone here see the program?"

More than half the congregation raised their hands. Jess took a deep breath.

"And did you believe it? Did you believe this child was the reincarnation of a dead mathematician?"

No one spoke, but the hands went down.

"I didn't believe it, not for a minute, because it's too easy a thing to fake. The child on the video was coached, the reports were falsified, and, unless you're very much into the whole zombie apocalypse thing, the dead do not come back. Let us pray:

"Lord, help us to live our lives in joy and strength. Let us have hearts filled with thankfulness. Let us have eyes that see only your light. Let us have minds open only to your truth. Help us to walk in steadfast obedience to your command. All for your glory do we pray, Lord, amen."

"Amen."

"And may the joy of fellowship fill you today and for all the days to come. Go in peace and love." Jess couldn't help himself. "And please watch out for those spontaneous resurrections!"

Only Jessica was still laughing when he stepped down from the raised lectern dais and joined his family. His wife and Abigail looked mortified.

It was going to be a long morning.

"So..." he said, clapping his hands together as they walked up the center aisle, "...who's up for waffles?"

*   *   *

Phoenixville, Pennsylvania

"Come on, Curtis, how about one more bite?"

"Come on. You can do it. There you— Whoops. No problem, no problem. I got it."

"There, all clean. Do you want some more? One more bite. Come on. Come on, Curtis, open your mouth. Come on. One more bite."

Eva set down the pot she'd been washing for the last ten minutes – which was the exact length of time her husband had been trying to get their son to take 'one more bite' of oatmeal that was undoubtedly cold by now. It'd been warm when he'd started feeding him.

She'd been trying for two hours before that.

Every time she'd managed to coax him to open his mouth, there was a better than even chance he'd forget to close it and the lumpy mush would drool out again. The few times he did remember, he'd swallow without chewing but only if Eva touched his jaw in just the right spot.

And then he only choked twice.

Her husband, having already had his bagel and cream cheese and fresh from the shower, had taken over after she'd thrown the first bowl to the floor in frustration. The mess had been minimal; the oatmeal had coagulated and they hadn't used breakable dinnerware since Curtis was a baby and they discovered how much he liked the sound of breaking glass.

While her husband cleaned up, she'd made up another bowl of instant oatmeal, maple-brown sugar.

Curtis hadn't jumped when she'd thrown the bowl, but he did blink. Once.

It was those damned pills.

The medication had turned her brilliant son into a mindless robot. He could barely move on his own, didn't talk, couldn't dress himself and sometimes couldn't even remember to get out of bed to use the bathroom. Eva'd had to put him in adult diapers.

The pills had turned her genius son into a gangly teenaged baby who wet himself.

Her son was gone and she wanted him back.

Her husband didn't seem to notice.

"That's a good boy, Curtis, one more bite. Yay, team!"

Eva picked up the pot and slammed it against the sink.

"Jesus, Eva, you scared him!"

"Did I?"

Eva turned and looked at their son. He didn't act like she'd scared him. In fact, as far as she could tell he hadn't moved at all. He was still sitting in his chair, the oatmeal-dotted dishtowel bib she'd pinned on him still around his neck, and still staring at the placemat in front of him with half-glazed eyes. His eyes had been so beautiful, bright brown and sparkling with intelligence…now they looked dusty, like marbles someone had thrown in the dirt.

"How can you tell, Allan?"

Her husband set the bowl down on the table and began cleaning Curtis's face. Eva glanced at the kitchen clock above the stove. She'd gotten up at six-thirty to change and wash and dress her son, then help him downstairs to feed, *try* to feed him breakfast. It was a quarter past nine, which meant she'd get to try to feed him again in less than four hours.

Eva turned back to the sink and closed her eyes. "We can't keep doing this to him, Allan."

"It'll get better," her husband's voice said from the darkness. "The doctor told us it would take a little time for his body to adjust."

Eva opened her eyes, but the room still seemed covered in shadows.

"Adjust? Those pills are killing him. He's a genius, Allan, he has an IQ of one hundred and sixty-four, but how would anyone know? He's trapped. Those pills they're giving him trapped his genius inside a body he can't control. He can't get out, Allan, and he's suffering." Eva turned but held on to the counter to keep from falling. "Can't you see that? Look in his eyes! Those pills are killing him!"

Her husband rolled the dishtowel bib over on itself before taking it off their son's neck. It was soaked through.

"The pills are helping him, Eva."

"How can you say that? *Look* at him!"

He did, for a minute. Eva saw the quick glance he gave their son before looking away. It was the same kind of look you'd give a *Lost Dog* sign taped to a telephone pole: Poor thing, but it's not my dog.

"Curtis has a serious illness," her husband said, setting the towel down next to the half-full bowl of oatmeal. "You heard what the doctor said. Curtis is schizophrenic. He'll never be cured and it can get worse as he gets older unless he stays on his meds. I know, it's hard right now, but once they find the right dosage, you'll see how much better he is."

"He was fine before."

"He killed those animals."

Eva walked over to the table and picked up the dishtowel and bowl. "He was confused. The movie…bothered him."

"What if it had been a kid, one of his classmates?"

"But it wasn't. He'd never do something like that. How could you even think that?" She carried the bowl and towel back to the sink and turned on the water. "He's a genius…was a genius."

Eva let the water fill the bowl and run out across her hands. "We can't let him suffer anymore, Allan, we owe it to him to stop. I'm not going to give him any more pills."

He moved so fast she didn't have time to do more than gasp when he grabbed her arm and spun her around. She was still holding the bowl and the miniature wave of diluted oatmeal arced across the room and down the left side of his trousers. He didn't notice and she'd never seen him angry before, not like that. His face was red and his eyes, the same color as their son's, were narrowed and cold.

The bowl slipped from her hand, bouncing twice when it hit the floor, but he didn't notice that either.

"Allan, you're hurting me!" She tried to pull away but he tightened his grip. "Allan!"

"Listen to me, Eva, Curtis is sick and those pills are helping him. His brain isn't wired like ours and if he stops getting those pills he could hurt himself or someone else." He let go of her arm. "I'm sorry, but Curtis is my son too, and I only want what's best for him. I'll call the doctor later and see if he can change the dosage. Okay?"

If she'd been able to draw a full breath she might have laughed in his face. After twenty years of being a near-nonexistent parent he suddenly thought he knew what was best for their son.

"Did you hear me, Eva?"

She nodded. "Yes. Okay."

Her husband took a deep breath and she watched the redness drain from his face.

"I'm sorry I grabbed you. I didn't hurt you, did I?"

Her arm was throbbing. "No. I know you love him, I'm just...."

She sighed and patted his chest. "Why don't you go clean him up and then you can call the doctor."

But he didn't move. "Isn't it time for his morning pill?"

"Okay. Why don't you finish cleaning him up in the downstairs bath...I don't want him to slip." Eva nodded toward the puddles of oatmeal water on the floor. "And try to get him to drink some water first or he'll choke."

Eva forced herself to relax when he pulled her into a quick hug.

"I understand, honey, I really do, but it's for the best. You'll see." He gave her a little pat on the fanny as he turned back toward the table. "Okay, big guy, let's go get you cleaned up."

Eva waited until they were out of the kitchen and halfway down the hall – her husband half carrying, half dragging their son – before walking to the cabinet over the stove where she kept all the medication. Curtis had been too curious as a child and liked *experimenting* with the things he'd find around the house. Eva had never removed the child-safety locks on the sink cabinets where she kept the bleach and other household cleaners.

Sometimes even geniuses had to be protected from themselves.

The plastic prescription vial of Thorazine (25mg) and the smaller glass bottle of orange-flavored baby aspirin sat side by side. Eva took down both, emptied the twenty remaining prescription tablets down the drain and refilled the vial with the same number of aspirin. After closing the childproof cap, Eva put the aspirin bottle back into the cabinet and closed the door.

She set the vial on the counter, and had just about finished mopping up the floor when they came back.

"All clean, Mom," her husband said as he walked Curtis over to her. "Time for his pill."

"Allan...."

His eyes narrowed again. "Give him the pill, Eva."

"All right," she said, defeated, and picked up the prescription vial.

All her husband knew was that the Thorazine pills were orange, not the same shade as baby aspirin, but close enough.

"Open up, Curtis," Eva said, holding the tiny pill between her fingers. "Here comes the choo-choo train."

It was a stupid thing to say and once Curtis came back, he'd probably tell her how much he'd hated her saying it, but, for the baby the Thorazine had created, it worked and he opened his mouth.

"That's my boy. Now swallow, Curtis. That's it. All gone."

She made a production of closing the vial and walking it back to the cabinet. Her husband was smiling when she turned around.

"You're a good mother, Eva, it'll be okay. You'll see."

And Eva smiled. "I'm sure I will."

★ ★ ★

Los Angeles, California
Barney watched the sleeping woman for a moment before walking out of the room. The California driver's license picture, a relatively good one, showed the same woman smiling at the camera. Her name was Rosario Maria Guzman, age thirty-six, single, 5'6", one hundred and thirty-four pounds, blk hair, haz eyes, and showed a home address on Los Feliz. She was an organ donor.

The rest of the file contained the medical records from the ER she'd been brought to and the list of the injuries she sustained when her moped was sideswiped by a car: broken left tibia, road rash, minor concussion, nothing life-threatening. The file also contained a copy of the police report, which showed that Ms. Guzman had been wearing a helmet and that the driver of the car, though neither drunk nor otherwise impaired, had still somehow managed to slam the moped and its driver into the side of a concrete retaining wall.

The report stated that Ms. Guzman had been conscious at the scene and in good enough spirits to joke with both the EMTs in transit and the ER doctors, and had been resting comfortably, waiting for her family to show up, when a piece of marrow broke loose from the fracture, traveled to her lungs and caused a seizure. Only about ten per cent of patients experiencing FES (fat embolism syndrome) die. Unfortunately Ms. Guzman had been one of them.

Hazel-eyed Rosario Maria Guzman was pronounced dead at 07:06. When her family arrived twenty minutes later, a woman with honey-colored eyes named Millie had already told him about the Haints and Mr. Leeworth.

Removing the file from the clipboard, Barney smiled as he reached the nurses' station and handed the file to the RN on duty. She smiled back. He didn't recognize her, but that wasn't as rare an event as it once was, back when it all started and he prided himself on knowing the names of all the hospital personnel. Since then, however, the hospital had become inundated with new faces.

No pun intended.

It bothered him that he had to sneak a peek at the name tag clipped to the collar of her scrubs...but he did it.

"Is the family still here, Lydia?"

"In the waiting room." Her smile flatlined. "Can I ask? Is she...you know...one of them?"

Barney nodded. "She is."

The nurse blew a wisp of brown hair off her forehead. "Wow. I mean...wow."

It'd been seven months since the first four arrived, but they hadn't been the last. There were twenty-seven in the hospital now, the woman named Millie the most recent, and God only knew how many there were in other hospitals.

As the old radio station KFWB used to say: "*And the hits just keep on coming.*"

"Her name's Millie, last name possibly Benset or Beseret?" He shook his head. "I'll try to get more detail when she's rested a bit. Where is her.... Where is the Guzman family?"

Nurse Lydia nodded left toward the private waiting room at the end of the hall. "They've been here since she was brought in. Dr. Stallman was the ER doctor on call, but he thought it might be better if you told them."

He was the expert, after all.

Barney sighed. "Right."

"Dr. Ellison? It really is happening, isn't it? I mean, not just here. I didn't believe it when I saw the news reports, but...they're real, aren't they?"

Barney looked down at the clipboard in his hand. "Yes," he said. "They're real."

"Anyone figure out why?"

"Not yet."

Nurse Lydia nodded and sat down. "Wow."

"Yeah."

Straightening his lab coat, Barney glanced down at the clipboard then touched the knot in his tie, brushed the hair back from his forehead, touched the knot in his tie a second time and said a small prayer as he stepped away from the nurses' station. It wasn't OCD or a ritual, although it felt like one – it was just something he did before telling an unsuspecting family member their lives would never be the same again. Seven going on eight months and explaining that even though their loved one's soul had departed, the body was still alive and kicking and, oh yeah, the person inside is a complete stranger to you. Here's a brochure we had printed up to give you the basics.

God.

A few had cursed him, others thought he was joking, a sick joke, one or two had thrown punches and been escorted out by security. Only a few punches ever connected but Barney never filed charges. It would have been like putting salt on an open wound.

There were still others who tried to sue and Barney had heard of a man in Scotland who stabbed the doctor who told him his dead twelve-year-old daughter's body had awakened as a thirty-seven-year-old factory worker who'd been killed in the Triangle Shirtwaist factory fire.

Barney had started carrying the clipboard with him into the initial meetings. Although he never expected trouble, the clipboard was made of bulletproof laminated Kevlar which could be used as a reasonably good shield if the need arose.

Stopping outside the door of the waiting room, Barney gave the knot another quick touch, and lifted the clipboard to waist height. It held three documents: the first was Rosario Maria Guzman's death certificate; the second was the legal department's exemption clause, now standard practice, designed to protect the hospital, the physician(s) and all other hospital personnel/medical transport/etc. from being held legally responsible. The third piece of paper was a form that would legally relinquish rights and/or guardianship of the patient, heretofore to be known as Millie, last name as yet unknown.

Barney took a deep breath and opened the door. The Guzman family looked up.

"I'm very sorry...."

APRIL 2019

CHAPTER THREE

Arvada, Colorado

What are you going to tell them?

Jessie looked at her sister – cheeks glowing pink, an escaped lock from the French knot she and the other cheerleaders wore curling around her neck, Abigail's red-and-white gym clothes still as clean and immaculate as when she put it on after school while hers showed proof of her masterful slide into third – then leaned back against the hard wooden bench and stared at the principal's closed door across from them.

When she didn't answer, her sister nudged her. *It'll be okay.*

Right.

Because there were still people in the halls – office staff and kids leaving detention – they used their inside voices. They couldn't remember a time when they couldn't talk to each other like that, although it might have started around the time when they were little and their parents were constantly telling them to "Be quiet, girls…use your inside voices."

Abbie's hand reached into her periphery and patted the dirt stain on her left knee. *Okay. But maybe you shouldn't have hit him with your catcher's mask.*

Jessie closed her eyes. *He started it.*

Started what?

I don't want to talk about it.

Come on.

Jessie exhaled. Loudly.

Jessie.

NO!

Jessie felt her sister jump. Most of the time their inside voices were softer than their real voices, at least that's how Abbie's sounded in Jessie's head, but shouting was an option. And it sounded a lot louder.

Jessie opened her eyes and looked at her sister.

I'm sorry.

Abbie stared straight ahead as if she'd never seen the principal's door from that angle. Which she hadn't. Abbie was the *good* twin, everyone said so. Jessie had been there before.

She lean-nudged her sister's shoulder and Abbie moved farther down the bench.

Come on. I said I was sorry.

Abbie's gaze remained fixed as 'Kumbaya' started playing inside Jessie's head.

Oh, come on!

It was hard enough to have any sort of privacy if you were a twin, a million times harder if your twin could sneak inside your head, so they had to set up some rules and boundaries: 1) you couldn't lurk, you had to let the other know you were there; 2) inside voices could *not* be used to cheat on a test – Jessie had tried to veto that without success; 3) if one of them didn't want to talk they *would* be blocked; and 4) if one of them wanted some alone time, see #3.

They blocked each other with songs. Abbie used 'Kumbaya' and Jessie 'This Old Man'…mostly because she knew Abbie hated the song and by the time she got to eleven with her own original verse –

This Old Man, he had eleven
He had eleven up in Heaven,
But he didn't like it, praise be and Amen,
So he came back down to start again!
This Old Man, he had ONE!

– Abbie would give up. This time, however, it only took to the first *kumbaya* before Jessie caved.

UNCLE! UNCLE! I said I was sorry!

Her sister lifted her chin. *…praying, my Lord, kumba—*

"I'm sorry."

The song stopped as Abbie turned toward her. *Just tell me what he did.*

He said I play like a girl!

You are a girl!

He said I play like a gay girl!

But aren't you?

Jessie ran a hand through her short pixie cut and grimaced. Her hair felt greasy with sweat from the catcher's mask. She wiped her hand off on the leg of her track shorts.

She'd known since…forever that she was different than her sister. Her sister was a girl but Jessie didn't feel like a girl. Never had. Jessie felt like a boy under her skin, but when she told her parents they laughed and said she was a *TOM* boy and that it was perfectly normal and that she'd grow out of it. For a while that was okay. She could play ball and climb trees and wear jeans and T-shirts but then, one day, she got her period and it wasn't okay.

Her body was changing; she was becoming a woman…which was the exact opposite of what Jessie wanted to be. She hadn't outgrown anything.

It wasn't until she read a very thin chapter in her middle school *Health and Human Development* textbook and saw the terms *transsexual* and *gender identity* that she understood who and what she was: a boy in a girl's body.

She just hadn't told anyone…well, anyone important except her sister.

I'm trans, Abbie, not gay.

Isn't that the same—

Jessie glared at her.

I guess not. I'm sorry he said that.

Jessie turned back to the door. *Thanks.*

Do you think everyone thinks I am too?

What?

Do you think everyone thinks I'm trans…like you?

Jessie almost laughed. And would have if they weren't sitting where they were. *No.*

But we're twins and people think twins are exactly the same. So if you're gay—

Trans.

Whatever! They'll think I am too.

No, they don't. Besides, everyone knows you're a slut.

Her sister's gasp was lost as the door opened. Mrs. Betancourt's right eyebrow arched when she stepped into the hall and saw them.

"Abigail? What are you doing here?"

"Um...moral support. I saw the...whole thing."

Their principal nodded. "You're a good sister and it's just as well you're here. I was going to send for you after speaking with Jessica. I think it best if you both leave practice early today, don't you?"

"Yes ma'am." They'd answered in perfect unison, something they did without even thinking about it. People thought it was adorable. Mrs. Betancourt smiled.

"Well, why don't you and I have a chat, Jessica, and then I'll call your mother to come pick you both up. How's that? Jessica, will you come in, please?"

Jessie walked into the office and sat down in the chair facing the huge desk as Mrs. Betancourt took a pamphlet from the hanging rack next to the door and carried it back into the hall.

"While I talk to your sister, Abigail, you might find this helpful."

What is it? Jessie asked when Mrs. Betancourt closed the door and began walking back to the desk.

LGBT and Gender Identity Series: Talking to Your Parents.

Not even 'This Old Man' could drown out her sister's silent scream that followed.

★   ★   ★

Phoenixville, Pennsylvania

"Go away!"

The knocking came again, louder than before.

"I'm busy."

Knock, knock, knock. "But Curtis, I just want to—"

He threw the calculus book at the door and the knocking stopped. He waited, wanting to make sure the mother had left before returning his full attention to the computer because she could sometimes be sneaky and just stand there knowing it would distract him and keep him from his work.

He didn't bother wondering why she'd interrupted him; she was always interrupting for stupid reasons like eating or taking a shower or, as she called it, 'being with your family'. Stupid, useless things that didn't matter because nothing was more important than the work *he* was doing.

And the mother knew that, she was just too stupid to understand.

His work was always important, but today it was really important.

Today he was going to prove the great Albert Einstein was wrong.

E did not equal mc^2, it equaled nothing. Zero. Zip. Nada. And he was going to prove it.

Because he was a genius, the only real genius in the world.

That was the only thing the mother got right.

Satisfied that the interruption was truly gone, Curtis turned back to his computer and reread the last line of his premise. The premise was the *most* important part of his research dissertation because it would be the first thing the registration committee at Cambridge University would read before accepting it and him into a master's program.

Albert Einstein couldn't do simple math. I can do simple math. I can do every kind of math. Therefore I am better than Albert Einstein in math. According to Google, Albert Einstein's IQ was never measured, although it is believed to be one hundred and sixty, which was the highest estimated number when he was alive, but since no one knows for sure it is an invalid hypothesis. My IQ is one hundred and sixty-four (please see attached file marked GENIUS IQ) which proves I am a certified genius. Albert Einstein wasn't a genius. I am a genius. Therefore I am better than Albert Einstein.

Curtis nodded and flexed his fingers.

As the above paragraph clearly proves, Albert Einstein was not a genius but I am a genius. Therefore if he was not a genius, like I am, his assumption that E=mc^2 can only be wrong. E=mc^2 cannot possibly be right because he was not a genius, which means E=mc^2 is only a made-up equation. It doesn't mean anything if you replace the two with a zero, which is what I've done to prove that Albert Einstein was wrong. In my equation E=mc^0 I prove nothing exists and Albert Einstein was only guessing because he was not a genius like I am.

He smiled. It was perfect. Cambridge would be lucky to have him.

★　★　★

Arvada, Colorado

"How's it going?"

Jess looked down at his empty coffee cup, the fourth since lunch, and sighed.

"That good, huh?"

"Oh, yeah. Absolutely fantastic."

He could feel Monica's eyes against his back as he walked over to the Keurig and popped in a one hundred per cent Colombian pod. While Jess always suffered a touch of writer's block each time he sat down to write a sermon, it had never been this bad. Every possible premise he'd come up with might have worked as a short – very short – homily, but none of them inspired him.

Jess had even resorted to opening the Bible to a random page, closing his eyes and pointing. He'd done it three times when he hit Matthew 7:7 and realized God was playing with him: *Ask, and it will be given to you. Seek, and you will find. Knock, and the door will be opened to you.*

"Who says God doesn't have a sense of humor?"

"That's your sermon?"

Jess turned around, leaning back against the counter and smiling at his wife as the coffee machine did its thing.

"Think it'll work?"

"Hmmm, maybe not."

Picking up a long-handled spoon, she lifted the lid from a pot and gave the steaming contents a stir. The kitchen instantly filled with the aroma of her famous twelve-hour spaghetti sauce.

Jess's stomach grumbled.

"Oh, I have an idea," she said.

"I'm all ears."

She turned, cupping her hand under the sauce-laden spoon and blowing across the dollop of crimson sauce as she walked toward him. "Taste. Does it need anything?"

He tasted and closed his eyes in bliss. All it needed was to be slathered over angel-hair pasta, dusted with Pecorino Romano and shoveled into his belly.

"Mmm."

"Why don't you talk about the Travelers?"

If there'd been more than a taste on the spoon he would have choked on it. Jess opened his eyes. "What?"

"You know, the Travelers, those poor lost souls everyone's talking ab—"

"I know what you mean. No."

"Why?"

"*Why?*" She'd asked it the same way she would have if he'd ordered fish instead of steak at the Texas Roadhouse.

Jess swallowed both the urge to repeat the question back at her and the layer of sauce coating his tongue. "That isn't possible. A sermon is meant to be uplifting and positive and the things you mentioned are unnatural."

His wife carried the spoon to the sink and turned on the water. "They're people, Jess."

"They're blasphemies."

"They're lost souls and isn't that sort of thing in your line of work, Mr. Preacher Man?" She turned off the faucet. "I met one."

Jess had to turn and grab the counter to keep from...doing something. "What? Where?"

"Well, okay, I didn't actually meet one but I saw one. In the market. I mean, I think it was a Traveler. A woman, about my age. The man with her was pointing out all the different kinds of soups and she was just...she was just.... I guess she could have been a foreigner, but the way she looked when he gave her a can of chicken noodle soup...."

Jess pushed away from the counter and crossed the room. "What market?"

"Jess, she might not have been a—"

"What market was it, Monica?" His voice had gone so cold for a moment he didn't even recognize it.

"Jess—"

He was looming over her, hands ready to grab her arms and hold on until she told him, when her cell phone rang. She smiled up at him and stepped to one side, pulling her phone from the side pocket of her cardigan.

"Excuse me," she mouthed as she swiped her phone. "Hello? Oh, hi.... What? Oh. Okay, not a problem. 'Bye."

Jess expected her to come back and finish their discussion – he had a few things he wanted to say to her – but she continued walking. He heard the jingle of keys a moment later.

"Going to pick up the girls," she called as the front door opened. Jess checked his watch. Both cheer squad and softball practice still had at least another hour.

"Monica?"

"Explain when I get back. Turn the sauce down to simmer and keep an eye on it, okay? Don't put the noodles in until we get back, they cook fast. Okay? Thanks. 'Bye."

The door slammed shut.

Jess stood staring at the spot where he'd last seen her for longer than he probably should have, before walking over to the stove and turning the knob corresponding to the burner under the pot to low/simmer. He rewarded himself with a fresh cuppa Joe. Cup in hand and the heady scent of Italian herbs circling about his head, Jess headed to the office. He had a sermon to write…maybe something about wolves in sheep's clothing.

It should have been an easy enough topic to work with, given the brief – but would be longer – dialog he'd just had with his wife, but he was still thinking about it and staring at the blank screen of his laptop twenty minutes later when his cell phone rang.

"Good evening, this is Reverend Pathway. How can I help you?"

The masculine voice on the other end cleared its throat. "Reverend Jess Pathway?"

"Yes."

"I'm very sorry, Reverend, but your wife's been in an accident."

Jess pushed back from his desk and stood up. "Is she all right? Where is she? What happened?"

"A driver ran a red light and hit your wife's car on the driver's side. Fire and rescue arrived and were able to extricate your wife from the vehicle and stabilize her before transporting her to St. Joseph's Hospital."

Jess was already moving toward the coatrack by the front door when his body stopped moving.

"Only my wife? What about my daughters, are they okay?"

"Your wife was alone in the vehicle, sir."

"Then they're still at school. I have to pick them up." Jess knew he was babbling as he left the house and couldn't remember if he'd locked the door or even closed it as he yanked open the car door and got in. "What hospital did you say?"

"St. Joseph's on Nineteenth. Do you need someone to drive for you?"

"No, no. I have to get my daughters. Tell my wife I'll be right there. Tell her...."

Jess dropped the phone on the passenger seat as he backed the car out of the drive.

Please God, let her be okay. Please let her be okay.

* * *

The spaghetti sauce burned.

* * *

Phoenixville, Pennsylvania
"Curtis?" *Knock, knock, knock.*

"Go away!"

"It's dinnertime."

Curtis pushed back his chair and used the momentum he'd built crossing the room to body slam the door. The hinges creaked and another crack appeared in the frame and the mother yelped on the opposite side.

"I told you to leave me alone!" he yelled. "I'm not hungry! I'm busy! Go away!"

"Curtis, you heard your mother."

It was both of them. The father and the mother. If it had just been the mother (M) Curtis (C) could have made her leave (C>M). The mother was easy, the father (f) wasn't, he could be stubborn (s) and loud (l^2) if Curtis didn't do what he wanted and Curtis didn't like noise.

C>M-f but M+f(sl^2) =>C.

Curtis opened the door.

The father was standing directly opposite the doorway. Curtis poked his head out just far enough to see the mother. She was standing down the hall near the stairs. She was smiling. The father was not.

"It's your favorite, Curtis, Taco Thursday!"

Curtis straightened and looked the father in the eyes. They were almost the same height and he could tell it made the father uncomfortable. The father looked away first.

"Go wash up and then come down to dinner," the father said to a spot slightly to the right of Curtis's face. "And don't keep us waiting."

Curtis watched the father walk away and wondered how many pounds per square inch would be required to push him down the stairs.

★   ★   ★

Arvada, Colorado

Two police officers had been waiting for them in the hospital lobby, but Jess only stopped long enough to get his wife's room number before leading his daughters toward the elevators. The officers didn't try to stop them.

The girls hadn't asked any questions on the ride over and Jess had thanked God for that. Abigail had cried when he told them, but Jessica, his brave girl, had squeezed her lips together and put an arm around her sister's shoulders, pulling her close. And he thanked God for that too.

They weren't children, they were fourteen, which made them old enough to come into their mother's room, but the doctor who'd treated his wife had made it clear without actually saying anything that it might be easier if Jess came by himself. He left them sitting side by side in the otherwise empty ICU waiting room.

"I'll be right back," he told them. "Pray for her."

He could still hear them reciting the Lord's Prayer in harmony as he left the room and followed the doctor to a room halfway down the hall.

"It's bad," the doctor told him, but that was an understatement.

The left side of her face was swaddled in bandages and there was a tube down her throat to help her breathe. IVs dripped fluid and plasma into both her arms. The skin on the right side of her face was discolored by bruises. A small bandage, the kind they used to put on the girls' fingers when they got a boo-boo, covered the point of her chin. The only sounds were from the ventilator and heart monitor; the EEG was silent.

It didn't look like his wife. "Are you sure it's her?"

"Yes. I'm so sorry, Mr. Pathway, but the prognosis isn't very—"

One of the machines started to chime and the doctor pushed Jess aside.

"Get him out of here."

Hands grabbed Jess's arm. "Please come with me, sir."

Jess pulled away. The doctor was pumping the broken woman's chest.

"Code Blue. And get the crash cart in here."

The hands tried to pull him away again, but Jess saw the woman open her eyes and look at him. Jess felt his own heart stop. Just one quick look before:

"Time of death...."

MONICA LEIGH PATHWAY
January 3, 1981 – April 11, 2019

*   *   *

Jess looked at his wife's flower-draped casket and took a deep breath. It had all happened so fast he hadn't had time beyond arranging the funeral and taking care of their daughters to write a sermon. One of the deacons and the lay minister had offered to officiate, but he couldn't let them do it. He needed to be right where he was.

He needed to be there for his wife and daughters and the rest of the congregation.

He needed.

Jess closed his eyes and took a deep breath of the carnations' peppery-sweet scent. He smiled as he opened his eyes.

"Monica loved carnations. She carried a bouquet of white carnations at our wedding and made it clear, when I bought her a dozen long-stemmed red roses for our first anniversary, that she preferred carnations. When I asked her why, since roses were supposed to be *the* flower of choice for special occasions, she told me that was the reason. Everyone got roses because they're flashy and obvious, but carnations were simple and unpretentious, but you always knew they were there. They filled the room with their scent the same way Monica filled a room with her love and joy of life."

He felt his eyes tear up as he looked down at his daughters in the first pew. Jessica was dressed in a dove-gray skirt and pale yellow turtleneck. Abigail's long-sleeved dress was maroon with white lace at the collar and cuffs. He'd asked them not to wear black. Black was for sorrow, he told them, and he didn't want them or anyone to remember their mother that way.

He wore his navy suit with the garish blue-green and orange paisley designer tie his wife had given him the same year he'd given her roses.

They looked so much like their mother. Auburn hair and green eyes. Bright green eyes, bright, sparkling *green* eyes, not blue.

Jess wiped the image and the tears away before nodding.

"Her physical presence may be gone, but she is still with us. She will always be with us in our hearts and memories. Unassuming and gentle as she was, Monica never turned away from things that were important, from things that mattered. Something happened on the night she left us that will stay forever in my mind."

A new sound in the front pew turned his attention back to his daughters. Jessica's reserve finally failed her and she clung to her sister, shoulders trembling with each sob. Seated directly behind them, Laura Wingate, Monica's avowed sister-from-another-mother, reached over the back of the pew and began stroking Jessica's hair, whispering softly. Richard, her husband and Jess's friend as well as one of the church board members, whispered something to their daughter, Carly, who immediately got up and went to sit next to his weeping child.

Jess nodded his thanks.

"I know how much it hurts, Jessica, Abigail, but just know that her last thoughts were undoubtedly of you." Jessica's sobs deepened. "Your mother loved you both so much and would have done anything to protect you...so I feel it's my duty here and now as we celebrate her memory before this congregation to tell you her greatest fear."

Jess watched as his namesake nodded to her sister and sat up, taking the tissue Carly offered and wiping her eyes. She looked so lost. They both did.

"On the night she left us we'd spoken about these so-called Travelers. What are they? Do any of us know? There are guesses, we've all heard them on the news, but the truth is they are profane souls...no, I won't use so holy a term for these *things* that have been cast adrift from the glories of Heaven to prey upon the bodies of the sanctified. We spoke of it...before she left and...the thought of something invading her body when she couldn't defend it...frightened her." *Forgive me.* "She...fell to her knees and begged me that if anything happened to her to make sure her body wasn't stolen by one of these…imposters. It was almost as if she knew what was going to happen."

Jess closed his eyes and let the tears course down his cheeks. He didn't care. This was his penance for the lie he told and the pain he felt because of it. If she were alive, he wouldn't have said it…couldn't have, but he would explain it to her tonight, in prayer, and knew her soul would forgive him.

He took a deep breath and opened his eyes. "Her soul is safe with the Lord and her body…" He reached down and let his hand rest on the casket. It was cold against his palm. "…is safe from the impostors, the imps. And imps is exactly what they are, demons wearing costumes of human flesh. Imps and abominations. But she's safe in our hearts and memories. Thank you all for coming to this celebration of Monica's life. Now, you're all invited to go downstairs where, I've been told, our wonderful ladies have laid out quite a spread. But please, in Monica's memory, no tears. She loved life and she loved all of you too much to want you to be sad on her account."

Jess wiped his eyes and stepped off the dais to accept handshakes and condolences.

"Carly and I will take the girls down," Laura Wingate said as she hugged him. "Would the three of you like to stay with us tonight? You know, just to get out of the house for a bit?"

Jess held her hands as he stepped back. "Monica always said you were one of the good'uns. Thank you, Laura. You can ask the girls if they'd like to spend the night, but I have too much to do."

"Okay. I can come over tomorrow and help pack up Monica's things if you like."

Jess squeezed her hands gently and let go. "I may take you up on that, thanks. See if you can get the girls to eat, especially Jessica. I don't think she's had anything except cornflakes since Thursday."

The woman nodded and walked away. Jess was watching her thread her way back to where Jessica and Abigail were standing with her daughter when a hand closed over his shoulder and turned him around.

It was Richard.

"How you holding up?"

Jess shrugged. "I keep thinking I'll wake up and all of this will just be a bad dream."

"That would be nice, but it's not. None of it is, Jess."

There was something else in the man's voice besides sympathy. "You're not talking about Monica, are you?"

"No, I'm sorry about Monica, but what you said, about Monica being frightened…there's a lot of that going around. What did you call them? Imposters? Imps. Yeah, that's exactly what they are." Reaching into his coat pocket, he took out a small business card and handed it to Jess. "When you're ready, give me a call and I'll introduce you."

Jess looked at the raised black letters on the center of the ivory card: *U.C.U.A.* There was a website address and phone number in the lower right-hand corner but nothing else.

"U.C.U.A?"

"*Unum corpus, una anima*," Richard said. "One Body, One Soul. It's an organization I belong to that shares your feelings about these… Imps. We have monthly meetings. If you'd like to know more give me a call. I think you'll like what you hear." He offered his hand and Jess took it. "All of us are so sorry about Monica, Jess, but like you said, her soul's in Heaven and her body's unspoiled. One body, one soul. Amen."

Jess responded out of habit. "Amen."

★   ★   ★

He knows.

Jessie sat in the chair someone had put her in, holding the plate of food someone else had given her, untouched, and watched the conversation her father was having with Mrs. Betancourt. Or really the conversation her principal was having with her father.

Mrs. Betancourt was doing most of the talking and her father was doing all of the nodding. It'd been going on like that for maybe five minutes. Mrs. Betancourt had cornered him almost the moment he came downstairs and every couple of words her father's gaze would drift away from the woman and settle on her…or, more precisely, on the plate of uneaten food in her lap.

Then his eyes would drift back to her principal and he'd nod.

Because Mrs. Betancourt was probably telling him about his trans twins. Abbie would flip out.

"Eat something."

Jessie continued to watch their dad and principal as her sister sat down next to her.

"I'm not hungry."

"I'm not either," Abbie said but still tooth-picked a cube of cheese into her mouth. *If you don't eat anything every mother in the room will be over here trying to force-feed you.*

Jessie picked up a mini-bagel smeared with strawberry cream cheese but didn't move it anywhere near her mouth. Maybe if the mothers saw her holding it they'd think she was eating.

Her sister nodded her head toward their father. *What do you think they're talking about?*

Three guesses.

It could be about Mom. Their father looked over at them and tried to smile. *No, you're probably right.*

Even though the basement's assembly room was big and filled to capacity, Jessie heard Mrs. Betancourt's words as he shook her hand – "If there's anything I can do to help..." – and turned to walk toward them.

You want me to stay?

Yes.

"How you two doing?" their dad asked and they both shrugged at the same time and said okay. It made him laugh. A little. "Yeah, me too. Abigail, do you mind if I borrow your sister for a minute?"

Abbie!

"Yeah, sure, Dad." *Sorry.*

Jessie put the bagel back on the plate and stood up, following their father through the crowd to one of the small classroom/workshops along the back wall. It was the room where her mother had taught Sunday School, but Jessie wasn't sure if her father knew that.

Or maybe he did and that's why he picked it.

"Sit down, Jessica," he said, touching the chair next to the felt board, her mother's chair.

It felt harder and colder than any chair Jessie had ever sat in.

"You saw me talking to your principal." Jessie nodded. "Is there anything you want to tell me?"

She looked up. "I'm...." Then shook her head.

Her father kneeled down and took the plate from her, setting it on the floor in front of the felt board before cupping both her hands in his.

"It's okay, baby. I know."

Jessie felt something inside her break free. "You do?"

"Yes, Mrs. Betancourt told me about the…altercation you had with that boy." Jessie felt her heart start beating and never noticed it had stopped. That's what they were talking about. "That's why your mom was coming to pick you up, wasn't it?"

The tears started before Jessie could stop them. "Yeah."

"Now, I want you to listen, okay? What happened to your mom was not your fault. It just happened, it wasn't because of anything you did. It was a stupid, senseless accident, and I need you to understand you are not to blame. Please, baby, you have to believe that."

"Bu-but I was. I am."

"No, no, you're not. It…. It was just her time, that's all. Okay? But you have to promise me one more thing. No more fights. I know boys can say stupid things sometimes, but you have to rise above that. You're growing up and that means you need to start acting more mature, even if others don't. I also think you might want to give up softball and find something a bit more…. I don't know. Maybe cheer squad like Abigail?"

Jessie sniffed. Mrs. Betancourt had only told him about the fight; she hadn't been outed.

"Maybe something else," she said. "Chess team or something."

"Or something. So –" he handed the plate of food back to her as she stood up, "– are we good?"

Jessie nodded.

"Okay. I know it's going to be hard, but try to be the woman your mother would want you to be," their father said as he put his hand on her shoulder and led her out of the room, "and her soul will rest easy. Make her proud of you, Jessica. And please try to eat something. Okay?"

"Okay."

What happened? What did he say?

Jessie looked across the room. Abbie was still sitting in the chair where she'd left her.

Jessie?

Jessie picked up the mini-bagel and took a bite. *This Old Man…sure got around…*

FEBRUARY 2021

CHAPTER FOUR

Phoenixville, Pennsylvania

Curtis swallowed as he closed the cabinet and slipped the small pill bottle into his pocket when he heard her come into the kitchen. It was fortunate the cabinet was above the stove, an easy reach for him while she probably had to use a stepstool, so his standing there wouldn't cause suspicion.

"Curtis!"

There was surprise in her voice, as he knew there would be. He seldom left his room; dealing with her and the father taxed his nerves, but since he needed physical verification to prove his hypothesis about her correct he had no choice.

The fact that this thankfully brief encounter would be the final interaction he'd ever need to have with the mother was the only thing that made it tolerable. The father was at work and thus would be no hindrance to his objective.

Which was to make sure his parents suffered the consequences of their actions.

The mother said something.

Sighing, he turned to face her.

She was standing in the doorway and Curtis surmised – given the established evidence that she kept the temperature inside the house at a near-constant 70°F (21.1111°C) during the winter/early spring and was wearing a bright yellow long-sleeved sweater, deep blue fleece leggings and shiny black knee-high boots – that she was going out.

He also surmised that the outfit, which might have worked on a younger woman, looked foolish on the fifty-six-year-old mother and wondered if she even realized that. But, having overheard certain comments about her voiced by his father's colleagues on those rare occasions when the parents invited others into the house, taking into consideration the amount of alcohol (CH^3CH^2OH) consumed, of course, Curtis wondered if anyone had an accurate perception of what the mother actually looked like.

He never attended the gatherings, naturally, but would stand either at the end of the upstairs hallway, if the gathering was indoors, or at his parents' bedroom window that overlooked the expansive back deck if the festivities moved outside, and observe the various male invitees who would inevitably collect there. With the exception of discussions relating to what was being called 'The Traveler Situation', whatever that was – biased news reporting had never held any interest for him – at some point the conversations inevitably turned to the mother's appearance.

She was, according to seventy-three per cent of the overheard discussions, 'still a looker'.

Which seemed overly charitable at best. The mother was an archetypal female specimen of average height (161.8 centimeters), with brown eyes (consistent with fifty-five per cent of the population of the United States) and brown, going gray, hair (eleven per cent of the world population).

The father was a much rarer specimen with blue eyes and red hair (0.17 per cent of the world population).

Curtis had inherited his looks from the mother, which should have created some sort of bond between them, thus offering some measure of affection that would have dissuaded her from her continual attempts to kill him.

And although he'd yet to ascertain positive proof that the father was willfully involved, Curtis had witnessed the father watching while the mother crushed a small orange pill and mixed it into his breakfast juice. A small orange pill from the empty bottle now concealed in the pocket of his slacks. He had taken the remaining sixteen to provide evidence for the coroner during his autopsy.

He was a genius and geniuses left nothing to chance.

The mother was still speaking.

"*What?*"

The mother took a step back. "I just asked what you were doing."

Knowing the probability that he might be discovered in the kitchen was high, Curtis had provided himself with a plausible motivation for his actions. Picking up the can of heat-and-serve split pea with ham soup that he'd opened all by himself, Curtis stepped away from the stove and turned around.

"I was getting something to eat," he said, stating the obvious.

The mother's face shriveled in on itself. It was not a pretty sight. Curtis felt his stomach churn…but that might have just been the poison he'd consumed. Before coming downstairs he'd left a file on his computer labeled *In the Event of my Death* that explained how the mother had been systematically poisoning him over the past…God only knew how long… and implicated the father as her co-conspirator. The police would be sure to check his computer when his body was found and they'd take the mother and father away and put them to death for his murder.

They didn't deserve to have him as a son.

"Oh Curtis." The mother began walking toward him. "Why don't you let me make you lunch?"

"No!" He thrust the open can toward her. The mother backed up another step as if he hadn't already calculated that the distance between them was too great for an accurate hit. Her reaction was as funny as it was predictable and he gave a moment's thought to laughing out loud, before dismissing it. If he laughed, and even though the mother was definitely not a genius, she might guess the reason behind it. "I already told you I made my lunch. Do you think me incapable of doing that, Mother?"

"No, no, of course not." The mother tried to smile and failed. "But, at least let me warm it for—"

"I want it this way!"

The mother nodded. "Well, can I get you a spoon?"

Curtis looked down at the can of semi-coagulated greenness. His stomach churned again. The poison wasn't working fast enough.

Curtis crossed the room and opened the narrow drawer where he knew the mother kept the cutlery and took out a spoon. He wasn't hungry and the poison was making him feel a bit sick, but he dug the spoon into the undiluted soup and shoved it into his mouth.

It was horrible, but he ate another spoonful because she was still watching him.

"Did you want something, Mother," Curtis asked as a gas bubble broke against the back of his throat, "or did you just come in to spy on me?"

The mother licked the red/purple stain on her lips. "I just wanted to remind you that I'm going shopping. Do you need anything?"

Curtis thought a moment. If he hadn't decided to deny them the glory of his intellect and the pleasure of filicide by taking matters into his own hands, he might have given her a list of items that would keep her away for the rest of the afternoon, but he wanted her to find him as soon as possible. Besides the file that would either incarcerate them for life or execute them for his murder, Curtis had left a note taped to his computer monitor with instructions on how to open the file and the phone number for the Harvard Brain Tissue Research Center.

The only disadvantage to his killing himself was that he wouldn't see the looks of adoration and awe on the faces of the doctors when they harvested his brain. But he could imagine it.

"No," he said, pushing the spoon into the can, "but don't take too long, I may want something later."

Holding the can out in front of him like a banner, the spoon handle upright and firm, he left the kitchen without another word. The mother followed him as far as the front hall.

"All right, dear. I'll be home soon. 'Bye."

Curtis watched her exit the house by the garage egress and remained on watch until he heard the sound of the garage door opening a moment after a car engine rumbled to life. One-one thousand, two-one thousand, three-one thous—

The engine sound became lower as the car backed out of the garage, a perfect example of the Doppler Effect that was cut short when the garage door shut.

—and, four-one thousand, five-one thousand.

Curtis only got to twenty-one thousand when a cramp doubled him over. The can fell, splattering the mother's prized oriental hall runner.

If the pain hadn't been so intense, he would have smiled. He didn't know what type of poison the mother had been giving him. The prescription on the bottle indicated it was Thorazine and in his name... which only proved the mother's cunning. She'd somehow convinced Curtis's doctor that he was the one suffering from a mental disorder and, for the briefest of moments, he acknowledged her innate animal cleverness. But it wouldn't save her.

Another cramp, slightly stronger than the one previous, squeezed the contents of his stomach up into his esophagus and required considerable effort to swallow it back where it belonged.

As he straightened, a new and horrible premise asserted itself.

If he continued with the sequence of events as planned, there was a better than average chance (63.4 per cent by quick calculations) that he could pass out and choke to death on his own vomit. The thought horrified Curtis. Besides possibly damaging his magnificent brain from the slow depletion of oxygen, he'd leave behind an undignified corpse.

His genius deserved better!

He'd miscalculated, but there was an easy solution: Given his height (6'¼" or 183.51 cm) and weight (142 lbs) he would only need a drop of some five to seven feet to efficiently and cleanly snap his neck, and the railing that spanned the landing at the top of the stairs would do nicely.

When bitter drool filled his mouth, Curtis found it easier simply to spit it out than swallow it. The sputum was frothy and slightly green, probably from the soup, and when he started up the stairs a wave of vertigo crashed over him. It would have been so easy to give up and just sit down and wait for death.

But it wouldn't be as memorable.

Half crawling, half dragging himself, Curtis entered his bedroom and, after a quick codicil to the file which stated he had to kill himself because of the pain, a quick perusal of the internet showed him how to fashion a noose from two belts – one over the neck, the other around the anchor point.

Apparently death by belt was all the fashion in some circles.

Securing one end of the double belt around the railing before slipping the buckle-noose over his head, Curtis leaned forward and looked over the railing. The house must have gotten taller because the first floor looked so far awa—

*   *   *

Arvada, Colorado
"Hey, Jessie! Wait up!"

Carly's voice echoed through the halls like a song. Jessie could already feel her heart start to race even before she turned around. When she did it only got worse and her heart skipped a couple beats. Abbie said it was so obvious how Jessie felt that Carly had to know, but while her sister had a tendency to look at the world through a rosy haze, Jessie was more of a realist.

She had to be.

"Hey, yourself," was about all Jessie could manage when Carly caught up to her.

The girls' school uniforms, knee-length red plaid skirt, loose white polo shirt under a one-size-fits-most red sweater, seemed to have been designed to conceal rather than accentuate the various underlying shapes, but Carly could have been wearing a black garbage bag and still have taken Jessie's breath away.

Carly was beautiful, maybe the most beautiful girl Jessie had ever seen, and she'd been noticing girls for a while now; but it wasn't just the long ash-blond hair or clear bright hazel eyes or the willowy figure and long ballerina legs, Carly had a great personality too.

And best of all, she was Jessie's best friend.

So maybe she did know.

But Jessie wasn't ready to find out just yet.

"What did you put down for number seven?"

It took Jessie a minute to remember the question, let alone the answer. Carly was wearing perfume that made Jessie think of sunshine and blue skies. It smelled wonderful.

"Battle of Hastings, 1066."

"Oh good!" Carly exhaled and leaned her head against Jessie's shoulder. "At least I got that one right."

The perfume had kicked up Jessie's heart rate to the point where it was pounding inside her head. She would have been happy to stand there for the rest of the day with Carly's head on her shoulder, but the first passing bell had already rung.

"You probably aced it," Jessie said, and shivered when Carly moved her head away. "You know that stuff backward and forward."

"Only because you helped me study. Has anyone asked you to Winter Fest yet?"

Jessie shook her head. Carly, along with every other girl in school it seemed like, had been obsessing about the annual mini-prom since right after winter break. It was just a dance, for Christ's sake, the only difference was that they were both juniors and Carly seemed to think that if she didn't go she'd die.

"Has anyone asked you?" *Please say no. Please say no.*

"No."

Yay! "I'm sorry, but there's still time. Maybe you're just too pretty."

Carly's eyes widened. "What?"

"Um…I mean…. You know how guys are."

"Idiots?"

Jessie laughed. "Yeah. So how 'bout I take you?"

"What?"

Jessie stopped laughing. *What did I say?*

"Um…. I mean, you know, we go together. Stag…or hen or whatever they call it when girls do it…I mean…. You know, if nobody asks us."

Carly bumped Jessie with her hip. "You goof, we'll get asked, but yeah, if we don't let's do it. We'll go by ourselves."

"Together."

"Together," Carly said and turned toward the classrooms across the hall when the second passing bell rang.

"Want to get together tonight?" Jessie called after her. "To study? Or something?"

"Can't," she shouted back over her shoulder, "have pep squad tonight. See you at lunch. Save me a place, okay?"

Jessie waved at the same time a hall officer stepped around a corner and pointed at Carly.

"Hey, no running in the halls."

Jessie smiled as Carly dropped into a fast walk. She was so graceful.

"What are you smiling at?" the hall officer asked. Jessie lost the grin. "Get to your class before I report you."

Jessie saluted and kept to a steady semi-slow walk until she rounded the corner before breaking into a full run.

Fortunately, the meetings never started until everyone had had a chance to vent and grumble. Jessie entered the student counseling office to thunderous applause.

"Thank you," she said, bowing before she sat down, "you're all too kind."

SECOND CHANCES • 53

Hoots and hollers followed. Ms. Samuels cleared her throat loud enough to be heard over the commotion.

"Are we ready to continue?" the school's counselor/life coach asked. "Good, now let's get back to it, people. Jessie, we were applauding Mickey. He came out to his parents last night."

Mickey, small and frail, his blue eyes owl-big behind glasses that could probably cause major forest fires on a sunny day, blushed and ducked his head.

"Yay, Mickey," Jessie said. "How'd it go?"

"Good. I guess they already knew but were just waiting for me to tell them."

"Cool."

"That's usually the case, people," Ms. Samuels said. "We think it's going to be so hard, that the people we love and who have loved us all our lives haven't already guessed. True, there are some families who are gobsmacked when the truth comes out because they never saw it coming, and turn away, but most of the time it's not that hard."

"But they still aren't happy about it."

Ms. Samuels smiled. Jessie didn't know how long Ms. Samuels had been a school counselor, but the principal and her dad thought it might be a good idea if both Jessie and Abbie talked to her after their mom's death. Abbie stopped going after a month.

Jessie stopped the private one-on-one chats a few weeks later and, at Ms. Samuels' suggestion, began coming to the LGBTQ meetings.

Ms. Samuels liked to say she'd never faced a problem too difficult or turned away a soul too broken, and it worked. Even with everything else that had happened, Jessie began to feel better about who and what she was.

But she hadn't told her dad.

He'd had other things on his mind then and still did...they both did.

"Let me think," Ms. Samuels said, "are they happy about it? Yes. No. Maybe. The honest truth is that in the long run it doesn't matter what they feel or think. Except it does, I know. But they don't live in your skin, you have to remember that. I know my own parents weren't pleased, but it was a very different time and place. But what'cha gonna do?" She waited until the laughter died. "The thing is, I'm happy with *who* I am...not *what* I am, because in the end it's only me and pronouns don't count. Okay. Blair, I think you're next in line."

The school's varsity lineman stood up and cleared his throat. "Hi, I'm Blair and I'm gay."

Applause, applause.

"And last night I found out I'm getting a full football scholarship to the University of Tennessee when I graduate."

Cheers competed with the new round of applause. Ms. Samuels got up to hug him and looked like she'd been swallowed by Bigfoot.

"I am so happy for you, Blair! Oh my God, your parents must be over the moon."

He was in full force blush when he sat down. "Yeah. My dad already bought a ton of stuff from their online store."

"Hope he likes orange," Ms. Samuels said. "Jessie?"

Jessie took a deep breath. Up to this point her weekly revelations had been pretty much: Hi, I'm me. I'm trans. I sort of like this person but haven't said anything.

Same old, same old.

But that was all going to change.

"Hi, I'm Jessie and I'm transgender...still haven't told my dad, but today I asked a girl to Winter Fest."

And the room went wild.

CHAPTER FIVE

Phoenixville, Pennsylvania

"But I don't understand," Eva said, "I was only gone a few minutes. It couldn't have been more than a few blocks when I noticed I'd forgotten my phone and I needed it. I always have it with me in case Curtis needs something or…. So I had to go back for it, but I wasn't gone for more than ten minutes, maybe not even that long."

Eva knew she was rambling and repeating the same thing she'd told every police officer and paramedic and doctor who'd come to talk to them since she walked in and found Curtis hanging…strangling… clawing at his neck….

She closed her eyes and took a deep breath. When she opened her eyes again she knew she looked calmer even if she didn't feel it.

"Please, you said Curtis was awake when he arrived."

The doctor, the first who'd seen Curtis in the ER, took a deep breath. Eva thought she looked much too young to be a real doctor, maybe an intern but not a real doctor.

"Mrs. Steinar, Mr. Steinar, as I told you, Curtis was semiconscious and stable when he arrived. There was some difficulty in his breathing from both the neck injury and broken nose."

"It was an accident," Eva said, "or an experiment. He's always experimenting. He's a genius."

The doctor nodded but Eva could tell she was just humoring her. The doctor couldn't care less about Curtis's mind; she was only interested in his poor, broken body.

"After we intubated him and were assessing his injuries, we discovered that his abdomen was rigid."

"What does that mean?"

"Your son was bleeding internally."

"Oh God."

"It was my fault," Eva said. "I should have helped him back onto the stairs but he was choking and I got one of those scalpel things from his room...he dissects things for his experiments...and cut the belt. I tried to hold on to him but...he fell."

Eva felt her husband take her hand and squeeze it.

"It's not your fault, Mrs. Steinar. Your son was strangling and you acted the way any mother would." The doctor looked down at the clipboard in her hand. "Is your son taking any medication?"

"Thorazine," her husband said before she had a chance to answer. "He was diagnosed with schizophrenia a few years ago."

"Thorazine?" the doctor repeated.

"I don't remember the dosage, Eva, do you? Eva puts it in his food. Curtis doesn't like taking pills."

"Mr. and Mrs. Steinar, there was no evidence of Thorazine in your son's system, but we did find acetylsalicylic...aspirin residue when we pumped his stomach, which caused acute hemorrhagic gastritis...." The doctor took a breath. "Curtis was probably already bleeding internally, the fall only exacerbated it. We need to operate immediately to stop it."

Her husband released her hand to take the clipboard the doctor held out to them. Then signed the form and handed it back.

"Will he be all right?"

"We'll do everything we can. Is your son on an aspirin regimen?"

He handed it back. "Not that I know of."

"It was an accident," Eva said, but no one was listening.

* * *

Arvada, Colorado

Jessie leaned back against the wall, smiling and handing out the agenda for the weekly Wednesday night meeting. Although most of the congregation had joined, there were still a few who hadn't seen the light, or the ever-increasing danger, and turned their backs on both the church and the U.C.U.A.

It was her job, besides smiling and handing out schedules, to stand watch in case one of the Imp lovers decided to show up and disrupt the meeting. Not that it had ever happened to them, but during the Christmas meeting her father had shown a video of a man who'd walked into a U.C.U.A. meeting in Bristol, England, carrying a toddler he said was his wife. The baby couldn't have been more than two, but when she opened her mouth....

Jessie shivered at the memory of the woman's voice coming out of the baby's mouth.

But that wasn't going to happen here, not in her father's church, not while she was on watch. Jessie remembered the night her father first told the congregation about U.C.U.A. and why he had decided to join them in their crusade. They were True Borns, he'd told them, men and women whose souls had been placed within their bodies by the one true God and not by some demonic accident. He told them that the U.C.U.A. was fighting for them against the growing tide of laws and support created solely to safeguard the rights of creatures that should never have been allowed to exist in the first place.

It was only when her father had asked them all, as one, to stand and come forward and sign their names to the U.C.U.A. register that a few members stood up and left.

But Jessie remembered who they were and none of them were going to get in if she had anything to do with it.

Jessie.

She turned toward the front of the church and saw her sister draping the U.C.U.A. altar cloth, white lettering on royal purple with gold trim, over the lectern. For some reason Paul Lister was helping even though her sister had never needed help before.

Wazzup, buttercup?

Abbie laughed at something Paul said and didn't so much as glance in Jessie's direction.

Paul just asked me to Winter Fest!

Woo and hoo.

That got her a quick, and dirty, look. *You could be happy for me.*

I'm thrilled beyond words. To prove it Jessie yawned.

Sigh.

"Good evening, Jessica."

Jessie turned and smiled. "Good evening, Mrs. Thompson. One Body, One Soul."

"One Body, One Soul," their old babysitter answered. "Oh, now who is that young man with our Abigail? Is that little Pauly Lister?"

Jessie turned as if she hadn't noticed. "I think it might be."

"They make such a cute couple, don't they? Do you have a young man, Jessica?"

"Not yet," she said, handing the old woman a schedule. "I think there are still a few seats up front, Mrs. Thompson."

"Well, don't worry, dear," Mrs. Thompson said as she toddled away, "I'm sure you'll find someone."

Jessie kept smiling.

"Hey, Jessie!" Carly was suddenly next to her, snaking an arm around her waist. "Do you see who's with your sister? I didn't know they were dating."

"I'm not sure he knows either," Jessie said, and was about to suggest that they both wear U.C.U.A.-purple dresses with white rose corsages to the Winter Fest when her father waved her over. "Gotta go. Be right back. Do you mind handing out the rest of these?"

Jessie handed Carly the stack of paper.

"Sure. Okay, let's meet for cocoa and donuts downstairs after the meeting. And find out if they're going to the dance together."

Jessie gave her a thumbs-up and saw the bemused look on her father's face as she hurried up to him. Abbie and Paul were still 'straightening' the cloth on the lectern.

"I know it's her turn this week," he said, "but Abigail looks a bit busy, so would you mind calling roll tonight?"

"Sure!"

Jessie took the thick purple-and-white book from him and carried it proudly to the lectern. The joy and honor she normally felt was doubled by the look her sister gave her.

It's my turn!

You're busy. Dad said so. Go sit down with Pauly.

His name's Paul. "Good meeting, sister," Abbie said out loud as Jessie took her place at the lectern. *Try not to mumble like you usually do.* "Come on, Paul, you can walk me to my place."

Jessie waited until both of them were seated, Abbie in the first pew, Paul in the third with his family, before smoothing a wrinkle on the altar cloth. Abbie glared then humbly joined the congregation in lowering their heads as their father raised his arms in benediction. Jessie dropped her chin and closed her eyes.

"Welcome, my friends, and may the Lord bless you as you are

now, in one body with the one and only soul he gave you upon birth, and may he keep you thus for all the days of your life here and for your life eternal. *Unum corpus, una anima.* One body, one soul forever. Amen."

"Amen."

Jessie's *Amen* came just a fraction of a second after the others because she wanted to make sure their father heard her. Abbie might have been asked to Winter Fest and even have a boyfriend, but she would never be as committed to U.C.U.A. as Jessie and their father knew it.

He'd even talked about the possibility of Jessie attending U.C.U.A.'s seminary program in Oslo when she graduated. "Your mother would be so proud of you, Jessica."

"And now my daughter will call the roll. If you will, Jessica?"

Jessie opened the book and placed her finger by the first name.

"Ellen Appleyard."

"Present."

"Trey Appleyard."

"Here."

Calling the roll was one of the U.C.U.A.'s most important tenets. A person's name defined who they were as much as their soul did, and it was essential that the organization keep scrupulous records for posterity.

"Riley Tabor."

Jessie counted to five as heads began to turn in the pews before her. "Riley Tabor?"

Taking the pen from its special pocket on the inside of the cover, Jessie made a small *X* next to the name and looked at her father. It was the second *X* by the name. Her father nodded.

"Richard Wingate."

"Here."

"Laura Wingate."

"Here."

"Carlene Wingate."

It was hard keeping a straight face when Carly wrinkled her nose, but Jessie managed. Carly hated her given name.

"Present."

Jessie closed the book, left the lectern and walked to her place in the first pew.

I get to call roll the next two weeks, Abbie thought at her when she sat down.

Only if you're not busy....

"Please stand," their father said, "for the declaration."

Jessie took her sister's hand and closed her eyes, reciting the words of the U.C.U.A. creed the same way she once recited the Lord's Prayer.

"I am as the Lord God made me. I am this body he created for me and imbued with the one soul that he alone fashioned. I am myself, born into the body I wear and animated with my soul that was placed in it by God's hand. I was born whole and complete in mind, body and spirit. I am one with my soul and my soul is mine alone. I am one with my body and my body is mine alone. My body and soul are united by the Lord's handiwork and no other has sway over them. My body and soul are mine and so it will be unto the end of time. 'For we were all baptized by one Spirit so as to form one body.' *Unum corpus, una anima.* One body, one soul forever. Amen."

Jessie let go of her sister's hand as she opened her eyes. "Amen."

"You may be seated," their father said and waited until everyone had settled down before taking his tablet from his suit coat pocket. "It has only been a week since our last meeting, but according to the U.C.U.A. update I received just this afternoon there are now two hundred and fourteen more documented cases of newly arrived *imposters* recorded in Colorado, thirty-six in the Denver metro area alone."

Groans and gasps competed with the whispers that seemed to grow louder as Jessie sat in silence, feeling sick to her stomach. The thought of someone else living in her body always made her want to throw up. Or scream.

"Two hundred and fourteen documented, recognized, acknowledged and *accepted* cases. But have you ever wondered who is accepting these imposters, these abominations unto the Lord? Well, I'll tell you. Those in power accept them, the elected officials of the world's governments, men and women who should know better are the ones who accept them. But not only do they accept these so-called *Travelers* –"

Her father had said the word the same way he would any profanity, as if it left a coating of filth on his tongue. Jessie swallowed.

"– but help them find a place in this world, in our world, by teaching them, training them, showing them how to blend in, how to disappear so no one...*no one* can tell them apart from anyone else. The governments of this world are making it easy for the Imps to pass themselves off as True Borns!"

Without warning, their father slapped the top of the lectern with the flat of his hand, skewing the cloth Abbie and her new boyfriend had taken way too long to drape and making everyone, Jessie included, jump.

"And it has to *stop!* You know that and I know that, but how can we, as individuals, hope to fight against a government that will not see the truth when it is right in front of them?" He smiled and Jessie leaned forward. "By the simplest and most honorable method possible, we exercise our right to vote. Now, in a fair and just world, which obviously this isn't —"

Jessie joined in the laughter.

"— this would be an election year and we could start at the top, but there isn't even a special election coming up. However, there is a woman, a well-known and respected lawyer who not only believes in our cause but who has made it her personal goal to challenge each and every one of these so-called 'Travelers' Rights' laws that have been passed."

Jessie sat up straighter. If she was right, Jessie knew exactly who her father was talking about. The three of them had gone to Washington, D.C., for the National U.C.U.A. True Born Convention the summer before and while they were there had watched a tall gray-haired woman in glasses captivate the audience in the convention center's main assembly hall.

It didn't hurt that she was a Colorado native or that the commercials for her law firm reflected her principles.

"*Are you working in a mandated T-inclusive environment? Are you forced to work with individuals known as Travelers? Do you think you've been terminated so a Traveler could take your job? Do you feel discriminated against because you are True Born? Do you feel that no one cares? Well, I care. I'm Celeste Luthe and I will fight for you and your rights as a True Born. One body. One soul. One law. Our law. God's law. It's time we took it back.*"

Their father's smile grew as the whispering began.

"That's right, I'm talking about our very own Celeste Luthe. As you all know she has been spending her considerable legislative talents and experience resisting the ever-growing crop of new laws supporting these abominations. She's particularly focused on the recent bill that would give them voting rights, something that must be stopped at all costs."

He paused and Jessie leaned forward again, knowing something big was coming. "And, I have it on good authority, she will also be announcing her formation of a campaign team and her candidacy for the office of President of the United States of America in 2024!"

Jessie was among the first on her feet, applauding and *whup-whupping*, much to her sister's embarrassment. Their father laughed and let it go on for a few minutes before motioning everyone to take their seats.

"Well, I'm sure she heard that in Cherry Creek, but hang on, it gets better. Ms. Luthe has personally invited every Colorado U.C.U.A. chapter to attend the rally that will begin —" He paused, building suspense. Jessie grabbed for her sister's hand at the same moment Abbie grabbed for hers. "— at the site of the soon-to-be opened Travelers Center at the University of Colorado campus in Boulder."

No one was whispering now.

"Leave it to the Boulder bleeding-heart liberals."

"What else can you expect from Berkley East?"

"Just what a nuclear-free zone needs, right?"

Jessie watched her father watching those gathered before him.

Think Dad would make a good vice-president?

Abbie looked at her. *You really want to live in Washington, D.C.?*

"Dearest friends." Their father hadn't raised his voice, but the church went quiet again. "It's not the town, it's not even the people, it's the fact that we have been invaded and the governments of the world don't know how to deal with these imposters…the Imps who walk among us concealed in flesh that is not their own. The governments of the world don't know what to do with them, but Celeste Luthe does and she will tell the voters of Colorado this coming Saturday. And to make sure those watching from home know exactly who *we* are, I've ordered two U.C.U.A. banners for the side of the church bus!"

He had to wait until the cheering died down.

"But I think we still may need to carpool, so if anyone with an SUV or similarly large vehicle will come see me after the meeting, we can get things started. One more thing, Ms. Luthe has asked that everyone wear U.C.U.A. certified apparel, so if you'd like to purchase a bright new sweater or scarf or baseball cap for the news cameras, my daughters, Jessica and Abigail, will be in the church store and more than happy to take your money."

Everyone laughed.

"All rise," their father said, and led the congregation in the unofficial U.C.U.A. hymn, 'How Great Thou Art', with special emphasis on the words *"then sings my soul."*

"Go in peace and in the knowledge that you are True Born and beloved of the Creator who made you," their father said when the song ended. "One body. One soul."

"One body. One soul."

Amen.

CHAPTER SIX

Nederland, Colorado

Jessie wrapped her gloved hands tighter around the Styrofoam cup, hoping to leech out every last molecule of warmth from the rapidly cooling hot chocolate. It was working about as well as the folded blanket between her fleece-lined jeans and the bench was keeping her butt warm.

It got really cold at 8,200 feet. After the rally/demonstration, the whole congregation had come up to the Barker Meadow reservoir in Nederland for an impromptu ice skating party to celebrate.

If she had any sense, she'd walk up the hill to the burn barrel most of the adults and a few of her *brighter* peers had gathered around or, like her sister and Paul, wrap up in a blanket and find a car to sit in. Barf. But it was obvious the only sense she still had that wasn't frozen was her sight, and for the moment that was enough because it gave Jessie a chance to stare at Carly without being creepy about it.

Dancing across the ice to the music from the portable speaker her dad had hooked up to his iPhone, Carly spun and jumped and did little cha-cha-cha moves that sent shivers up Jessie's already frozen spine. The music was something country-western (*puke*), but it was a distraction Jessie could easily ignore as she watched Carly move across the ice, an insubstantial being, an angel darting in and out of the beams of light from the car's headlights.

"Aren't you cold?"

Jessie took a sip of the lukewarm cocoa as her father sat down next to her, glad she'd chosen one of the picnic benches off to the side, away from the cars and their headlights. It was too dark for either of them to see each other's faces, but the cold Colorado starlight was just enough for Jessie to see the A VOTE FOR LUTHE/IS A VOTE FOR US campaign button on the front of her father's down jacket.

Every U.C.U.A. member was given one. Jessie put hers on the front of her sweatshirt just above her heart. It sucked that she couldn't vote, but she'd do everything else to help get Celeste Luthe elected.

It was important that True Borns took back their place in the world.

Carly thought so too. After the rally, they'd shared a seat on the bus – Abbie had gotten a ride with Paul and his parents – and talked about volunteering and getting the word out.

It was the best twenty-five-minute road trip Jessie'd ever been on.

"I'm fine."

He made a fatherly sound. "Sure you are. I've only been sitting here for a few minutes and I've lost all feeling below the waist."

Jessie hoped there was enough light for him to see her smile. "That's because the cold affects the elderly faster than the young."

"Ouch. You haven't seen your sister around, have you?"

The last time Jessie looked, the windows had been steamed up pretty good. "Um...."

Abbs?

– – –

Hey Abba-dabba!

Geeze. What?

Dad's looking for you.

– – – Be right there.

"I think I saw her with Paul Lister. Maybe over by the barrel?"

"Still Paul Lister, huh? Okay. Well, I'll...yeah." Jessie watched him push back his left sleeve. A faint bluish-green illuminated the watch face. It was only a little after nine, but the high country got dark fast.

"It's Saturday, Dad," she said before he got a chance.

"And tomorrow's Sunday, daughter, and we have to be up and out by seven. Besides, if we don't leave soon, we'll have to use ice tongs to move you."

"Ho, ho."

Jessie handed her father the cup, stood and wobble-walked across the narrow patch of snow to the edge of the frozen reservoir. The skates were a little large – a local Nederland U.C.U.A. member had graciously opened his winter sports shop and outfitted them all – and she hadn't been on the ice once that year, but the moment the blades hit the ice muscle memory took over and she was gone.

"Hey! What did I just say?"

"I thought you wanted me to move. Just a few minutes, okay? Carly, wait up!"

Jessie knew her father must have said something, she saw the words floating around his face, but the sound was lost when she literally hit the ice running. She wasn't as good as Carly when it came to doing all the fancy Ice Capades stuff – who was? – and no way near as graceful, but if there weren't too many turns involved, she could move at a reasonably good clip and stay on her feet.

Most of the time.

"Hi!" Carly's breath clouded the air between them. Jessie breathed it in.

"I needed to warm up a little," she said and began rubbing her arms through her parka. A little too vigorously as she discovered when her left foot twisted out from under her and she started to go down. Jessie tensed, already feeling the solid impact against her ass, when a hand caught her and pulled her back from the edge.

"Whoa, girl!" Carly held Jessie's arm until she got the skate back under her. "You okay?"

"Yeah. I'm a klutz. Thanks."

"No problem. I think the ice is getting frosty or something, I almost took a header a little while ago."

"Yeah. Frosty."

Jessie probably would have stood there, mentally and physically tongue-tied, if Abbie's voice hadn't suddenly broken the spell.

Dad wants to go. Come on.

Jessie looked back over her shoulder. Backlit by the headlights her father and sister were silhouettes standing a few yards from shore. Only her father and sister; Paul Lister was nowhere in sight. Her father waved. Jessie waved back then grabbed Carly's hand and even though she knew it was impossible since they were both wearing gloves, her hand felt warmer than it had all night.

"One more spin," Jessie shouted at the same time she kicked off against the ice. "Hurry up, before they send out the bloodhounds!"

"You're on!" Carly said, pulling her hand away and swatting Jessie's arm. "And you're it!"

Ice tag! Yes! When Carly took off, blending into the shadows along the left edge of the reservoir, Jessie followed without hesitation and came within a few inches of tagging her back when her friend changed leads and shot off toward the rocky outcrop that dotted the shoreline.

Jessie! Come on! I'm cold!

Go find Paul.

I mean it – let's go! Abbie's voice thundered inside her head and she flinched.

And down she went.

Her legs went one way, her upper body the other and her left side took most of the impact as she skidded across the ice toward a dark shape the size of a Smart car.

This was going to hurt.

A lot.

Jessie braced for impact when Carly came to her rescue again…more or less. They slid across the ice together before going face-deep into a drift of crusted snow. It wasn't as hard as a rock, but it was close.

"*Jessie!*"

Jessie pushed herself out of the snow and opened one eye, the one that wasn't filled with ice crystals.

"Carly? Is that you?"

"Oh my God! Jessie, are you okay? Can you see me?"

Jessie managed to get her other eye open. "It's so blurry. Come closer."

Carly leaned in close enough for Jessie to feel her warmth against her face and Jessie kissed her. It wasn't planned, it just happened.

"Carly, I'm—"

Somewhere in the distance a car horn honked twice, the echoes chasing down the canyon walls.

Jessie, what's going on? Where are you?

"Jessica? Carly? Come on, girls. Time to go!"

"Carly?" Jessie reached up just to brush the snow off her friend's cheek but she pulled back and swatted Jessie's hand away.

"Don't touch me."

"Carly, I didn't mean…. It's not like that."

For a moment Carly was nothing but a silhouette against the darkness.

"Oh, my God."

"Carly, listen…."

"That's why you wanted us to go to the Winter Fest together, isn't it? Oh, God, that's why, isn't it?"

"It's not like that. You're my friend." Jessie reached for her. "I love you."

The starlight glinted off Carly's skates as she stood up. "Stay away. from me. Don't ever talk to me again. I hate you."

The car horn honked again.

Come on, Jessie!

Jessie looked back toward the shore. A line of cars was making its way toward the access road, but her father was still there, backlit in the glow of headlights from the few cars that still remained. He waved as Jessie sank her blades into the ice and stood up.

"Come on, girls! Time to go!"

His voice sounded so close in the frigid air it was almost as if he was standing on the ice next to them. If she could hear him so clear, had he heard them?

Jessie wasn't thinking of anything but catching her friend and trying to explain that it would never happen again. That was all she wanted to do, but Carly saw her, switched leads and began skating so quickly Jessie would have sworn she'd seen blue sparks come off the blades each time they hit the ice.

"Don't come near me!" Carly was moving away; she was a much better skater than Jessie. "Don't touch me! I hate you. I never want to see you again. I'm going to tell everyone about you. *Freak!*"

"Carly! Wait!"

"*Freak!*"

If she'd stayed near the rocks the way they'd come, it might have been okay, the ice was thicker there, but Carly turned and skated straight across the manmade watershed, aiming for a narrow spit of land. Jessie tucked in her shoulders and skated faster.

They were only a yard apart when the ice broke beneath them.

The thundering snap and roar that followed was almost loud enough to cover the sound of Carly's scream as the frigid water covered them.

JESSIE!

CHAPTER SEVEN

Jessie!

★　　★　　★

— — —

★　　★　　★

Boulder, Colorado
"Come on, Jessica. Stay with me. Push another of EPI. Anything?"
　"We're losing her."

★　　★　　★

— — —

★　　★　　★

"Charge to three hundred. Clear."

★　　★　　★

— — —

★　　★　　★

"Come on, Jessica. Come on."

★　　★　　★

          ★   ★   ★

"Charge to three hundred and fifty. Clear!"
  "Anything?"

          ★   ★   ★

          ★   ★   ★

"We lost her."

          ★   ★   ★

"Dammit. Time of death...."
  What? Where am I?

          ★   ★   ★

"Wait!"
  "We have a heartbeat."
  "Attagirl, Jessica."
  "Come on, honey, you can do it."
  "Come back."
  What?

          ★   ★   ★

"We got her."

          ★   ★   ★

I died?

★　　★　　★

"She's back."
Oh God NO!

★　　★　　★

"Jessica?"
"Hmm?"
"Can you open your eyes for me?"
Jessie tried but it felt like someone had glued her eyelids shut.
"That's good, you're doing great. Come on, keep trying."
Come on, Jessie, open your eyes.
Abbs?
Yeah. I'm here, it's okay. Open your eyes.
It took almost all the strength Jessie had, which didn't feel like much, but she finally managed to pry open her right eyelid just enough to see a bright white flash. Jessie jerked back.
Ow. Whazzat?
"It's just the doctor looking in your eye," Abbie said out loud. "It's okay. Really."
"Yeah, it's just me. Hi," another voice said, "and you're doing great, Jessica. Okay, now can you open your other eye for me? That's right, nice and big. Good."
The light flashed in one eye and then the other and left behind a dull yellowy-mauve afterimage that bobbed and weaved across the face of a smiling man Jessie had never seen before.
"Hi Jessica, I'm Dr. Hayes."
Jessie grunted.
"Can you tell me your name?"
"Jess...aaa."
"Throat sore?"
Jessie nodded and even that hurt.
"I'm sorry. We had to intubate you and the tube can cause some irritation. Okay, open your mouth and the nurse will spray your throat with a numbing agent. It doesn't taste very good, sorry again, but afterward you should feel a lot better. Okay?"

The doctor stepped back to give the middle-aged nurse room. Jessie opened her mouth and only twitched a little when the cold spray hit the back of her throat. The doctor was right. It tasted horrible.

"Yuck."

"Warned you," the doctor laughed. "But now we know you can talk. Can you tell me your name?"

Jessie swallowed. "Jessica Pathway."

The doctor reached down and gently squeezed her upper arm. "You gave us one heck of a scare, Miss Jessica Pathway, but it looks like you're going to be okay. Welcome back."

Jessie's body went cold and for a moment she couldn't breathe. It was like being under the ice again, suffocating as the cold water poured into her lungs.

Welcome back. That was what they said when a Traveler arrived. She'd seen it enough times on the confiscated videos U.C.U.A. sent her father.

Oh God. She was one of them. She died and her soul had entered another body.

She was one of them, an Imp.

OhGodohGodohGodohGodohGodohGodohGodohGodohGodoh

Jessie, it's okay. Calm down.

Jessie grabbed the front of the doctor's lab coat. Her skin was pale, much paler than it should have been, and the knuckles of her hand were bluish. But it wasn't her hand. It wasn't her arm.

"Please, I don't want to be like this!"

Jessie, listen. It's okay.

"Like what?"

"Please — *No!*"

The doctor pried her hand free of his coat but held it tight between his own. "Jessica, it's okay. You're okay. You've had a terrible shock, but you're fine. We're going to give you a sedative—"

"*No!*"

"Just a slight one to help you sleep. Your body needs to recover. Just rest and when you wake up your father and sister will be here."

"No, no, please! Don't let them see me like this! Please, don't... don't let them...don't let them see...."

Jessie....

* * *

It was a dream.

It would have been nice if it had been a dream, but when Jessie opened her eyes again and saw their faces she knew it was a nightmare. Their father was trying so hard to smile it looked like he was wearing a mask and Abbie wouldn't even look at her, she was standing at the end of the bed staring at the blanket covering Jessie's feet.

Oh God.

Their father's fake smile widened. "Hey, baby. How do you feel?"

Jessie ignored the question.

I know what happened, Abbie. Why are you both here?

Her sister shook her head but didn't look up as their father took her hand.

She pulled away.

"Jessica, what is it? Are you in pain? What's going on?"

Get him out of here, Abbie.

Abbie's eyes were shining when she finally looked up. *What?*

I died and came back. I'm one of them.

Abbie burst out laughing and crying at the same time. Their father let go of Jessie's hand and reached for Abbie.

"Abigail! What's wrong with you?"

"She thinks...." Her sister took a deep breath. "She must have heard the doctors talking about something else. I bet she thinks she's a...you know."

The smile finally left their father's face as he scooped Jessie off the mattress and pulled her into a hug. "Oh, God, baby, no. No, you're fine, you're still you. Your soul and body are still one."

Jessie took a deep breath, pulling his scent into her. "I am? Really?"

"Here, goofus."

Jessie looked over her father's shoulder. Abbie had taken the small compact out of her purse and was holding it out to her. Their father saw it and shook his head.

"No, not yet. Your face is a little...bruised from the accident."

"Dad, it's cool." Coming around the opposite side of the bed, Abbie handed Jessie the mirror. *Knock yourself out.*

Jessie waited for her father to move out of the way and took a deep breath. The fingers of the body opened the compact and the arm raised it until Jessie could see the face – bruised and battered with enough stitches above the left eyebrow and holding the swollen bottom lip together to make Frankenstein's monster jealous.

Jessie burst out laughing.

Her face was a mess, but it was still her face.

Happy now? Abbie took back her compact and snapped it shut.

You could have told me.

Would you have believed me?

"Thanks, Abigail." *Bitch.*

"Anytime, Jessica." *Wimp.*

Their father looked a little puzzled when they both laughed. "It never dawned on me that you'd think...." He shook his head. "I'm so sorry, you must have been terrified. Can you ever forgive me?"

There were tears in his eyes and Jessie was afraid if he started crying she'd start and never be able to stop.

"Dad, you didn't do anything, I just...." Jessie touched her throat. "Can I have some water, please?"

"Sure, baby, I'll get it." Her father wiped his eyes as he turned toward the water pitcher on the bedside table.

How's Carly?

Abbie put the compact back into her purse and began studying the blanket again.

Abbs, tell me.

Her sister shook her head.

"Dad, how's Carly?"

"Here," her father said, holding the cup and flexible straw close to her lips, "drink some."

Jessie finished the cup and nodded for him to take it away. "Is Carly okay? Can I see her?"

"Not yet, baby."

"Why?"

Their father held the empty cup in his hands, rolling it back and forth. "Carly's still unconscious. She was trapped under the ice longer than you were so it'll just take a bit more time for her to wake up."

Jessica looked at her sister. *Is she dead?*

Abbie shook her head.

Their father was still rolling the cup in his hands when Jessie looked back. "When will she wake up?"

"I don't know, hon. I've talked with Richard and Laura and all I know is that Carly is in a medically induced coma but the doctors are hopeful she'll wake up soon."

"It's my fault."

Their dad set the cup back on the rolling bed tray and took her hands. "No, it's not, baby. Both of you were just skating, no one knew about the thin ice. It was an accident, that's all, just an accident. It wasn't your fault."

It was almost the same thing he'd said about their mother's accident. It hadn't been her fault then either.

Except it was.

Just like now.

Abbie.

Abbie shook her head. *It was an accident.*

But you heard what she said, didn't you?

She didn't answer.

Jessie pulled her hands in, bringing their father's with her. "Dad, I was chasing her."

"You were having fun, Jessica, enjoying yourselves."

"But she said—"

He closed the gap between them and kissed her forehead. "It was an accident, that's all it was."

Jessie nodded.

He knew.

★　★　★

Phoenixville, Pennsylvania

Curtis's face was smooth and calm, the way it always looked when she crept into his room at night to make sure he was still breathing, and the tube in his mouth and the IV in his arm and the pump that was breathing for him didn't make any difference.

He was just asleep and he'd wake up when he wanted to.

She'd told that to the doctors and nurses but could tell they didn't believe her. That was because none of them knew Curtis the way she did. He was her son, after all.

He'd wake up. Of course he'd wake up.

Eva rubbed her arms under the thin robe one of the nurses had brought her and wondered if she should call and ask her husband to bring her a sweater from home.

Then remembered he wasn't speaking to her at the moment.

After the doctor's little revelation about the aspirin, her husband had actually accused her of causing Curtis's attempted...Curtis's accident because she'd stopped giving him the Thorazine.

If the doctor had simply kept out of it, she could have reminded her husband what Curtis had been like on the drug, but that hadn't happened. Not only had the doctor sided with her husband, and the almighty prescription drug industry, but went so far as to suggest the aspirin caused the bleeding in Curtis's stomach and not the fall.

As if baby aspirin could do any harm.

It was *baby* aspirin, for God's sake!

But whatever caused it, Curtis had bled a lot and the *accident* had caused some minor swelling in his brain – "*It's not uncommon in cases of strangulation, Mrs. Steinar.*" – and now he was sleeping peacefully.

Just like a baby.

Eva pulled the robe tighter around her shoulders.

"Oh, my God, Eva, I'm so sorry."

Eva turned as her next-door neighbor, Sue Ramos, rushed into the room. The spry seventy-two-year old had babysat Curtis when he was a toddler, before his genius became evident, and still brought over cookies every time she baked. Eva had called the older woman right after her husband stormed out, taking the car with him. Eva had to go home and pack some of Curtis's things for when he woke up, knowing how much he'd hate the indignity of being in a backless hospital gown.

"This must feel like a nightmare," her neighbor said, wrapping her arms around Eva's shoulders. "Is there anything I can do?"

Eva hugged the woman's arms. "You're doing it. Allan had to leave...work, you know."

"I know, I was married." She gave Eva another quick hug then stood up and walked to the bed. "He looks like he's sleeping."

"That's what I think."

The woman nodded. "How is he?"

"The doctors say he came through the operation just fine –"

"Operation! My God."

"– but we'll have to wait until he wakes up before they can run more tests."

"Of course," her neighbor said and leaned over to brush a damp lock from Curtis's forehead.

"Don't do that."

"What?"

"It's just that he hates being touched."

"Oh. Of course, sorry," she said and moved away from the bed when Eva stood up. "Do they know what happened?"

"An accident," Eva said quickly, and was almost happy when a nurse or intern or doctor, everybody who worked in the hospital wore scrubs and clogs, walked in and asked if he could speak to her for a moment. "Will you excuse me for a minute, Sue?"

Eva saw her neighbor smile in consent and followed the doctor or intern, it had to be one or the other since nurses didn't talk one-to-one with family members, out into the hall.

"Mrs. Steinar, have you and your husband given any thought about donating Curtis's organs?"

It wasn't a doctor or an intern, it was a vulture.

Eva left without answering and returned to the room to find her elderly neighbor leaning over Curtis and pulling down his left eyelid with her thumb.

"Sue! What are you doing?"

The ex-babysitter moved her hand away and stood up. "I had some medical training when I was younger," she said. "I was just checking Curtis's eyes...you know, his visual reflexes. So, are you ready to head out?"

If there had been anyone else she could have called for a ride, Eva would have thrown the old woman out, but given the circumstances, she simply smiled and left the thin robe draped over the chair as she walked back to the bed.

He looked like he was asleep.

"I'm just going home for a moment, Curtis, but don't worry, I'll be right back with your laptop so when you wake up you can finish whatever experiment you were working on. I know geniuses are always working on something.

"Just wake up, Curtis. Do that for me. Just wake up."

CHAPTER EIGHT

Boulder, Colorado

Jessie folded her hands in her lap and listened to the soft voices of the congregation's prayer circle in the corridor outside Carly's room. Abbie'd told her there'd been a similar contingent outside her room when she'd been unconscious, but when she woke up the group said a prayer of thanksgiving and joined those holding vigil outside the ICU.

Hospital regulations wouldn't allow more than five or six in the hall at once, but Abbie said the rest of the congregation stayed in the lobby and took shifts so neither Jessie nor Carly would be alone and without God's words through their ordeals.

After her sister told her that, Jessie had never felt more loved or less deserving of that love.

All of it was her fault. Again.

Jessie took a deep breath and let it out. *Please, God, let her be okay.*

"I know," a voice to her left said, "it's hard, but you have to keep your faith, Jessica. God saved you and we know he'll save Carlene as well."

Jessie nodded without looking up to see who said it. Not that it would have mattered; they'd all been telling her the same thing, more or less, for the last three days.

Only three days, a miracle some of them said, but she still looked like the star of a low-budget horror movie. The stitches had stopped oozing, but they itched, and a few of the bruises that decorated her face had only that morning begun to turn from overripe plum to a gorgeous shade of bilious yellow-green.

If Carly woke up and saw her she'd scream – *Get away from me! Freak!* – so maybe it was okay that she was still unconscious. The only reason she was sitting there like a gargoyle was because, after explaining Carly's injuries – a fractured skull, cracked collarbone, pneumonia – her doctor had thought it might help if Carly heard her best friend's voice.

Jessie had almost told him that wasn't her.

The door opened and Jessie braced herself when her father came out into the hall. "Ready?"

Jessie looked up at her father and decided not to lie. "No."

"I know, it's going to be hard, but if it's any consolation, I'm very proud of you."

"Don't be."

"Can't help it, you're my kid and I'll always be proud of you." He walked around to the back of the wheelchair and Jessie felt it shudder when he gripped the handles. "One. Two."

Jessie remembered the silly game they played when she had to take medicine or get a bandage ripped off. He'd count to two and when she was ready she'd say three.

She took another deep breath. "Can we talk later, just you and me?"

"Of course we can, you know that."

"Okay. Three."

Jessie held her breath as they entered the room. Carly's parents looked up and smiled. They looked a lot older than the last time she'd seen them. Almost as if it'd been three years since the accident instead of three days.

"How are you feeling, Jessica?" Mrs. Wingate asked.

"Sore, but okay."

"Well, you look just…. You look fine, dear."

Jessie nodded. "Thanks."

"Carly?" Mr. Wingate reached over the bedrail and touched his daughter's shoulder. "Jessica's here. Can you open your eyes and say hi?"

Jessie leaned forward in her wheelchair and swallowed the scream that suddenly filled the back of her throat. They'd shaved off Carly's beautiful hair and given her a halo of cold steel that encircled and was screwed into and through the thick gauze turban they'd wrapped around her head. She was sitting up, back propped with pillows to keep the metal brace holding her neck and head together upright.

Carly was lucky she was unconscious; it would have been really hard to sleep in that position.

All things considered, Jessie realized she'd gotten off lucky. When she'd fallen through the ice, just as she was going under, she'd careened off the broken edge – giving herself one hell of a black eye and opening up a few facial gashes. Carly had hit face-first too, but hadn't been as lucky. She'd split her upper lip and probably knocked out a few teeth. Jessie couldn't tell because of the breathing tube they'd taped to her mouth, but it was easy to see that she'd broken her nose by the lavender-yellow-green bruises that covered both her eyes.

Yeah, she wasn't lucky at all.

"Come on, honey," Mr. Wingate repeated, "say hi to Jessica."

"It's okay," Jessie said because Carly couldn't. "She doesn't have to."

Mrs. Wingate stood up and walked over to Jessie to give her a hug. "But she will. You're Carly's best friend, she loves you so much. And she'll tell you the same thing when she wakes up."

Jessie doubted that because she knew exactly what Carly would say.

Get away from me.

I hate you!

Freak.

"Yeah," Jessie said, "I'm sure she will."

Mrs. Wingate stood, walked around to the back of the wheelchair and began pushing Jessie toward the bed. "I think she knows you're here."

Freak!

FREAK!

"Talk to her, Jessica. Go on, it's okay."

No, it's not. She doesn't want me here. "Hi, Carly."

Nothing. *Thank you, God.*

"Um, it's me, um, Jessie...Jessica and, uh, I, um I just woke up so, uh, you can wake up now too. Okay? I know it's hard and your throat's going to hurt, but you can do it. You're the strongest person I know, Carly, so come on and wake up, okay? Just wake up and say hi. Okay? Just wake up and I promise I won't bother you anymore. Just wake up."

When her breath finally gave out, Jessie collapsed against the vinyl backrest and jumped when someone touched her shoulder.

"That was lovely, Jessica," her father said. "Shall we all join hands for the invocation?"

Forming a circle, they clasped hands and closed their eyes.

"Hear me, O Lord," her father said, "for I am as you made me, one with my body and soul, whole and complete, an individual created and blessed with a soul which you have given to me alone. In one body and with one soul I came into this world complete, and with that same body and soul I shall leave it. My eyes see, my ears hear, and my mouth speaks to the glory of the one and only life I was given and to the one true death I will receive when I am set free. I have but one body and one soul that I can call mine and I will shun those that hide behind a stolen face. One body, one soul for this world and for all eternity. Hear our prayers, O Lord, for thy daughter who now lies here broken and in need of your strength. We beseech thee, O Lord, to bring our beloved Carly back to us, alive and whole, her soul safe and protected within the body you gave her. But, if in your wisdom you choose to call her home—"

Carly moaned.

Mrs. Wingate broke free first, racing toward the bed with Jessie right on her heels. Jessie wasn't supposed to walk except to go to the bathroom or with a nurse accompanying her around the ward, but no one said anything.

"Carly?"

Carly's lips twitched around the breathing tube and her eyelids fluttered.

"She's waking up! Carly's waking up!"

From the hall came a chorus of *Thank Gods* and *Hallelujahs* as Jessie's father pulled her away and sat her down in the wheelchair. He was laughing with tears in his eyes.

"It's a miracle," he kept repeating, "a *real* one. God heard us. It's a miracle. She's waking up."

"A miracle," Jessie repeated but grabbed her father's arm when he started to move away. "She really is waking up, isn't she?"

"Yes, she is."

"About that talk...the one, you know, I wanted to have, um, with you."

He nodded and made his face go serious. "Sure, we can do that, but how about we do it later?"

"Yeah, later would be good."

Her father kissed her cheek. "Come on, let's get you back to your room, okay?"

"Okay."

Abbs?

How's Carly? Is she....

She's waking up, Abbs. Carly's waking up.

Oh my God! That's great.
Yeah...it's a miracle.

★   ★   ★

Phoenixville, Pennsylvania

"So, I'm thinking that instead of going directly to Cambridge, you might consider taking a few courses at Penn State to start. I know, I know, but it doesn't have to be the campus closest to us. You're a young man and you want to be out on your own, but would you think about it? It would mean a lot to your father and me, but, of course, we understand if you'd rather not. Still, if you'd think about it, I would appreciate it."

Eva finished massaging the cream into his hands.

"It's the air-conditioning," she told him, "it dries out the skin. Do you like this cream? It's rich in lanolin and vitamin D, and I made sure it was fragrance-free. I know you didn't like the lavender-scented kind I brought last time, it really was too much, but this one is all right, isn't it?"

The tracheotomy tube taped to the center of his throat moved. Eva had told the doctors he could swallow, but they'd insisted on putting in a gastral feeding tube...as if his poor stomach hadn't already been through enough...and, of course, her husband had signed the consent form while she was down in the cafeteria.

"I told your father you'd hate it...and you can tell him the same thing when they remove it. I'll remind you if you forget."

Standing up, Eva swung the rolling bed tray into position in front of Curtis and opened his laptop. When it came on Curtis twitched.

"I know I sound like I'm harping, but would you like to look at the Penn State website? Maybe check out a few of their online courses? I know you must get so bored in here."

Eva watched as his glance rolled across her face to a spot somewhere beyond her. The doctors told her he was unresponsive and tried to tell her that even though his eyes were open he wasn't conscious. They called it a waking coma and Eva almost laughed in their faces.

They had no idea how easily Curtis manipulated them.

He wasn't unresponsive, he was *non*-responsive, but after the first hundred times of trying to explain the difference, Eva had given up. Let them think what they would, she knew the truth.

Besides, Curtis had never been much of a talker to begin with.

Eva tapped the tabletop with her nail until her son's roving eyes found it and fixed on it. If she'd let him, he'd stare at the computer twenty-four hours a day. His ability to concentrate was amazing. Waking coma, indeed.

"Mrs. Steinar?"

Eva turned as two men walked into the room.

"Good morning." Eva put a hand on her son's shoulder. "Say good morning, Curtis."

His shoulder twitched.

"He's thinking about taking a few classes at Penn State."

The men smiled.

"Mrs. Steinar, I'm Dr. Morrow, chief of neurology, and this is Walter Polster, the hospital's chief administrator."

"How do you do."

"Mrs. Steinar," the hospital's chief administrator said, "is your husband here, by any chance?"

"He's at work."

"Well, we'd really like to speak to both of you."

Eva sat down. "He'll be here around six if you'd like to come back."

The two men exchanged glances before the chief of neurology shook his head.

"I don't think that will be necessary, Mrs. Steinar. When Curtis was transferred here from the hospital in Haverford, we ran a battery of tests, both neurological and physical, to determine his overall condition and capabilities to get a baseline. Since then we have tested twice and, given the lack of any obvious improvement, I'm afraid there's nothing more we can do for him."

"What do you mean by that?"

"Curtis is stable, but he can't breathe on his own and needs a gastric feeding tube—"

"He can swallow, you know that."

The man nodded. "But not consistently, there's always the danger of pulmonary aspiration."

"Well, then this is the best place for him, isn't it?"

There was another quick exchange of looks and the chief administrator took over.

"I'm afraid it's not," he said. "While we are one of the area's top rated trauma centers and health-care providers, we feel it's in Curtis's best interest that he be moved to a facility that is specifically designed to care for him and his needs. I'm afraid the hospital simply doesn't have the resources or space to continue palliative support for Curtis."

Eva looked at her son. He was still staring transfixed at the computer screen.

"There are a number of facilities we can recommend," the chief of neurology said, "that can provide long-term rehabilitation and hospice care."

Eva turned, glaring. "Hospice is for the dying, Curtis is alive."

"Yes, he is, but in his present state Curtis is susceptible to a number of medical issues his compromised system will not be able to fight. If you wish for him to remain here we will continue to care for your son to the best of our abilities; however, if you hope to see more progress—"

"We feel," the chief administrator interrupted, "that it would be better if Curtis was transferred to a long-term care and rehabilitation facility."

Eva stood up and walked to the window. Curtis's room faced the parking lot.

"Yes, I definitely think Curtis deserves a better facility, one that will recognize his genius and abilities. I'll speak to my husband tonight."

The men were staring at her when she turned around.

"Have our bill ready, won't you?"

PART TWO
ENDINGS

MAY

CHAPTER NINE

May 18

Arvada, Colorado / 4:34 p.m.
They were still staring at her.

She couldn't walk down a hallway or into a classroom or run track or even find a nice quiet corner of the quad to sit and eat lunch, alone, without feeling their eyes on her.

Not that she ever caught them doing it, they were too clever, too fast, but she knew they stared just like she knew they still whispered about her – because she'd been the girl who fell through the ice but came back like nothing had happened.

Except it did, to her friend, who didn't come back.

And it wasn't just her fellow students. Jessie had caught her teachers doing the quick stare-and-look-away.

It was like being under a microscope.

Or the star of a freak show.

I hate you! Don't touch me! Freak!

Abbie had gotten some of the fallout for being her sister but, in true rah-rah cheer squad fashion, tried to put a positive spin on it.

They're just worried about you, Jessie.

Let them worry about finals and graduation and the stupid senior prom and leave me the hell alone!

If just one person had called her Frankenstein when she showed up at school her first day back or asked her what happened or just stared and didn't look away it might have been easier to pretend everything would get back to normal.

Even though she knew it never would. She was the girl who came back. Alone.

Jessie had finally accepted that on the last Monday in April when Carly's parents brought her home. It was called *locked-in syndrome* and it meant, according to Google that Carly was awake and knew everything that was happening around her but couldn't do anything about it except twitch and mutter and maybe, if she was lucky, open her eyes.

Carly was trapped inside her body and it was all Jessie's fault.

And there was nothing Jessie could do about it.

"How's it going?"

Jessie blinked and the world came back in real time. "What?"

"I'm sorry, I didn't mean to startle you. I was just asking how your studies are going."

Jessie looked up from the language arts textbook she'd brought with her. Finals were a week away so she always made sure to bring a book or worksheet with her when she came by to sit with Carly after school. It was a great cover and as long as she *looked* like she was studying her father was okay with her spending hours at Carly's bedside.

Of course the truth would come out once she got her grades.

"Fine. They're fine."

Mrs. Wingate smiled at her from the doorway. "I'm going to start dinner. You're more than welcome to stay if you like."

Jessie got the same invitation every time she visited, just like she had when she came over to work on a project with Carly. But she knew Mrs. Wingate was just being polite. Jessie was fine and their daughter wasn't…why would they want her there?

"Thanks, but not tonight."

"Well, then can I bring you a snack?"

"No thanks, Mrs. Wingate. I'm okay."

"Are you sure? Carly's always ravenous after school. How about an apple?"

"Yeah, okay. That sounds good."

It didn't, but what was she going to do, tell Carly's mom that she hadn't been hungry, really hungry, since the accident, was living on yogurt and crackers and string cheese and had rediscovered her childhood talent of pushing food around her dinner plate without actually eating any of it?

What a revelation that would have been.

"How about I add a few oatmeal and raisin cookies," Carly's mom asked from the doorway. "They're your favorite, right?"

Jessie smiled. Oatmeal and raisin were Carly's favorites. "Yum."

"Good. I'll be right back."

"Okay."

When Mrs. Wingate left, Jessie closed the book and tipped the rocking chair forward. The rocking chair was Carly's place and she'd sit there, rocking back and forth, talking about one thing or another while Jessie sat on the floor at her feet and gazed upon her beauty.

Jessie still could, gaze upon her beauty and all that, but it was different looking at her from the chair. It was still Carly's chair and after Mrs. Wingate fed Carly paste through her stomach tube and changed her adult diaper Mr. Wingate would put her in the chair so she'd remember what it felt like. But until then Jessie could sit in it.

And pretend.

"Your mom made oatmeal cookies," Jessie said, "with raisins. Mmm. You better wake up or I may eat them all."

It wouldn't have been a reasonable threat even if Carly had been awake. They both knew Jessie hated raisins in cookies. And hated walnuts in brownies. And practically gagged at the thought of anchovies on pizza. Aside from Abbie, Carly was the only other person in the whole world who knew everything about Jessie.

Well, almost everything.

Scooting the rocking chair closer to the bed, Jessie took Carly's hand.

"I know you can hear me, Carly, and I'm so sorry. I didn't mean to scare you, but I do love you. See, I'm...I'm not gay and I would never have, you know. I'm...I don't feel...I've never felt like a girl inside, you know. I'm trans and I love you. So it's not really weird if you think of it that wa—"

Carly's hand twitched.

"Carly?" Jessie squeezed her friend's hand gently. "Do it again, okay? Squeeze my hand."

For a moment nothing happened, then Carly made a sound and her hand twitched.

"Oh my God. Carly.... You moved your hand on purpose, didn't you?"

Twitch.

"Oh God, Carly, I'm sorry." Jessie pressed the hand to her lips and held it there. "I didn't mean to scare you, but this is so great. And what I just said, I wanted you to know because I...."

Still holding Carly's hand, Jessie looked back at the door and held her breath, listening until she heard the soft metallic sounds coming from the kitchen.

"I really love—"

Carly's eyes were open, staring at Jessie.

"Carly?"

Carly's eyes widened for a second then shut and didn't reopen.

"*No!*" Jessie let go of Carly's hand and began shaking her. "Carly, open your eyes again. Come on, open them, okay? Carly, come on, you can do it."

Carly's eyelids fluttered but didn't open.

"Please, just open your eyes one more time. Just open them and I'll go away and never come back. Come on, open your eyes again."

Freak!

Jessie laid her friend's hand on the bed and stood up. The word was so clear, so real it was almost as if Carly had somehow learned to use her own inside voice.

"I'm not a freak, I'm just...different, but I do love you. I've loved you from the first minute I saw you...but I won't do anything, okay? I shouldn't have kissed you and I'm sorry I scared you. I didn't want it to be like that. Can you forgive me?"

Don't touch me. Leave me alone.

Freak.

"I'm not a freak, Carly, and I still want to be your friend. Just your friend, nothing else. I was wrong to...you know, and I shouldn't have done it. I should have told you first and...but I know you could never love me like that and I know you're mad and hate me right now, so if you want me to go, just do something, okay? Open your eyes or yell at me or call me a freak again and I'll go away and never come back. I promise. Just do something and I'll go."

Carly didn't open her eyes or mumble or move...except for the little finger of her right hand.

Twitch.

Jessie picked up her textbook and held it against her chest, wrapping both arms around it for protection.

"Was that it? Did you do that on purpose? If it was, do it again and I'll—"

"Jessie? Did you say something?"

Jessie glanced at Carly's little finger – it didn't move – then turned toward the door.

Mrs. Wingate was holding a plate of cookies and sliced apples in one hand and a glass of milk in the other.

"I was just telling Carly about school. You know, stuff."

"That's nice. You're a good friend, Jessica. Here's your snack."

Mrs. Wingate waited until Jessie sat down in the rocker before handing her the plate and glass. Jessie set the milk and plate on Carly's bedside table, an easy reach from the bed if only Carly would open her eyes.

"There's still a couple dozen left, Carly," Mrs. Wingate said as she walked to the bed and took her daughter's hand, "and I don't want them to go to waste. Do you think I should give them to Jessica to take home? Would you like that, Jessica?"

Shoving a cookie into her mouth, Jessie rocked herself out of the chair and stood up.

"Ah otta oh…." Jessie picked up the glass and drained half of it. The cookie despite the raisins was a bit dry. "I gotta go."

"But, your snack."

"Um, it was really good but I forgot I have…this thing I promised to do with Abbie. Sorry about wasting the milk and stuff."

"Oh, don't worry about that, I'll just put the cookies in a baggie so you can take them home."

"Great."

"Come along, I'll walk you down. Say goodbye to Jessica, Carly. Will we see you tomorrow?"

Jessie looked back at the bed. Carly's little finger twitched.

"No, not tomorrow."

Carly's hand lay still.

★   ★   ★

Denver, Colorado / 7:52 p.m.

The Colorado Council of the U.C.U.A. was very good about keeping its chapter membership records up to date, so all it took was a moment's pause to verify that the name and face on his ID card matched those in the electronic database, and Jess walked through the doors of the Pepsi Center. The invitation had included a section and seat number, so it felt very similar to going to an Avalanche or Nuggets game. The only differences were that Jessica wasn't with him and he doubted there'd be food and beer vendors walking up and down the aisles.

Even the atmosphere inside the giant sports arena felt like a game night: the air crackling with excitement and filled with the sound of cheering voices and stamping feet, as a near-record crowd looked down at the five chairs and speaker's podium on the raised purple-and-white platform that had been erected on the division line. Three cameras – right, left, center – faced the platform while a fourth, hand-held, filmed the crowd.

When Jess's section appeared on the jumbotron they all stood up and hooted.

The sense of being at a sold-out game increased exponentially when the giant screen shifted away from the crowd to follow five people, two men and three women, as they walked out onto the court and made their way to the platform.

The crowd, Jess included, went wild.

He knew the faces of the U.C.U.A. International Executive Council almost as well as he knew the faces of his daughters. If there had been room between the rows of seats, Jess would have fallen to his knees and given thanks, but since there wasn't, he collapsed back into his seat when Lady Cassandra Bellingham-Deighton, a petite gray-haired woman in a deep purple tailored suit and sensible shoes, walked to the podium and raised her hands for silence.

"The members of the U.C.U.A. International Executive Council wish to thank all of you for coming tonight. We have traveled through many countries and countless cities and in each have met the men and women who are at the forefront of our organization...men and women like all of you who are gathered here tonight...and we are humbled by your strength and perseverance. We applaud each and every one of you!"

The remaining four council members stood as a group, turned so that each would be facing a section of the stadium, and applauded.

"*Unum corpus. Una anima,*" Lady Bellingham-Deighton said into the podium's microphone. "One body. One soul."

"One body!" The crowd chanted back. "One soul!"

"And now it is my extreme pleasure to present a man who surely needs no introduction, our own Dr. Kan Ölversson."

Jess watched the giant monitor as the small woman stepped back and a Viking god stepped up to the podium. The man had given up a lucrative career in clinical neuroscience when he witnessed, firsthand, a close personal friend die during an epileptic seizure only to awaken as a complete stranger who spoke Cantonese instead of Icelandic.

He was one of the founding members of U.C.U.A. and had spent the last four years, and his considerable knowledge, in an ongoing and well-promoted search to find a solution to the problem.

Raising his arms, the man smiled down on them from the jumbotron's screen.

"My fellow True Borns, prepare yourselves for a revelation.... I have the answer we have been searching for."

CHAPTER TEN

May 24

Arvada, Colorado / 1:23 a.m.

Jess couldn't get the images out of his head. The video, only fifteen minutes of it, if it was even that long, was simplicity in itself. One step that was so simple a child could accomplish it without effort.

A figure of speech. The Executive Council had made it clear that for insurance, liability and legal purposes no True Born under the age of twenty-one would be allowed to perform the procedure.

It really was so simple and straightforward that Jess was amazed no one had thought of it before. And when he raised his hand to volunteer, he'd felt a sense of illumination and clarity and joy that he hadn't felt since being ordained.

There'd been a number of papers to sign, of course, including the standard release and indemnity forms, verbal oaths to repeat and be recorded and a new photo ID for the DME (durable medical equipment) authorization card, so the meeting had gone on far longer than usual, but Jess left the Pepsi Center feeling as though it was God, by way of the U.C.U.A., who had revealed to him his life's true purpose.

But it was late.

Shutting the passenger's side door as quietly as possible, Jess glanced toward the lighted window on the second floor with a feeling of fatherly concern – *it's after one in the morning and they're still up?* – and excitement – *it's after one in the morning and they're still up!*

What he had to show them could wait until morning, but he just couldn't.

He needed to show them now.

★　　★　　★

Dad's home.

I know.

We better turn off the light.

Why? He already knows we're up.

Studying.

Jessie hunched her shoulders and leaned closer to the French verbs worksheet she'd forgotten to take on her pretense study visit that afternoon. She'd be lucky if she'd be able to conjugate half of them on the final.

Luckier still if she could talk Abbie into breaking their *no cheating* promise.

Which she hadn't been able to.

Yet.

Je parlasse, tu parlasses, il parlât, nous parlassions, vous parlassiez, ils parlassent…. Come on, you know you're better at French than I am.

I'm better at a lot of things.

Jessie sat up and turned toward her sister's side of the room. When they were little, their parents had put their cribs side by side with the headboard against the wall opposite the door, toys to the left and the double desk/bookcase to the right.

It'd been a perfect arrangement until they began middle school and Abbie discovered boys and Jessie figured out she wasn't like other girls. Now Abbie had the right side of the room with the double-wide closet and Jessie had the left with the window and an IKEA wardrobe.

It wasn't ideal, but it worked well enough. So far.

"Come on, Abbs, just this once."

Abbie turned off her desk lamp and stretched. The light from Jessie's lamp turned her sister's shadow into a giant against the far wall.

"No. We made rules, remember? We don't cheat on tests and we don't listen in on each other's conversations like…when…I'm… with…Paul."

Jessie swallowed. She hadn't meant to, and it had only been once… when she was still in the hospital and got bored and…just tuned in. For a minute. Accidentally. Sort of.

She hadn't known they were kissing; she'd thought Abbie was drinking a Slurpee.

"I said I was sorry." Jessie turned around in her chair. "And I promised never to do it again."

The shadow giant glided across the ceiling as her sister stood up and walked to her bed.

"So you say."

Jessie sat up straighter and crossed her heart. "I swear. So will you help?"

Abbie pulled the sheets back and took off her robe. She liked to study in her pjs and robe. Jessie was still in her jeans and sweatshirt.

"No."

"Jesus, Abbie, don't be such a tight-ass."

Her sister feigned shock as she crawled under the covers. "Language! French. Study."

Come on.

Abbie turned on her reading light. The giant disappeared.

On one condition.

Jessie sat up straighter.

Talk to Dad.

Jessie cocked her head to one side. *About what?*

About Carly.

What about Carly?

About her opening her eyes and moving.

Jessie stood up, her shadow more monster than giant as it raced toward her sister. "You just yelled at me for listening to you and you—"

"I didn't mean to, Jessie. I was worried about you and it just happened."

Jessie sat down. *You heard what I said?*

Abbie nodded.

And Jessie glared back. "And you were so high and mighty—"

I'll help you tell Dad if you want.

THIS OLD MAN, HE HAD ONE!

You aren't a freak.

Get out and stay out. I mean it.

Jessie….

"GET OUT!"

"Girls?"

Shit.

"Girls, would you come down for a minute, please?"

Jessie reached the door first, opened it and slammed it shut behind her as her sister reached for it. She kept 'This Old Man' on constant replay inside her head all the way down the hall.

Abbie was only a few steps behind her and coming fast when Jessie pulled to a stop at the second to bottom stair. Their father was standing in the entrance hall, holding a large box.

"We were studying," Abbie said before Jessie got a chance. "I know it's late. We were just going to bed. What's that?"

The box was purple and carried a U.C.U.A. logo in gold letters.

"You won the door prize?" Jessie asked and their father laughed.

"Follow me," he said and headed for the kitchen.

They found him at the breakfast table holding a severed head in his hands.

"Sit down, girls, I have something to show you."

★   ★   ★

Haverford, Pennsylvania / 11:25 p.m.
It was a much nicer room than the one in the hospital and the staff seemed much more invested in Curtis's care and well-being. The facility, on the whole, was far superior and....

Eva gave up trying to think of additional endorsements and shut the laptop. She'd begun keeping an online journal for Curtis to read when he came home, but it was getting harder to find new ways of saying the same thing.

The Transitional Care and Rehabilitation Facility of Haverford, LLC, was much better than the hospital but for the amount of money they charged it should have been.

Of course she wouldn't mention cost to Curtis. He was worth any amount and Eva had made that clear when they admitted him. Her husband still worried about the money; naturally that would be the only thing he'd be concerned about. But what was a few thousand dollars a month compared to their son's future?

Besides, once Curtis healed and reached his full potential, he'd naturally pay his father back. Curtis was a genius and geniuses were always sought after for high-paying positions.

When they weren't saving the world.

Eva looked across the room to where Curtis slept peacefully on a bed that vibrated every few seconds to prevent bedsores and lung infections. A genius probably invented that.

Had she written about the bed?

Eva opened the laptop and began scrolling through her last dozen entries when a nurse walked in carrying a small tray.

"Mrs. Steinar, I thought you might like some juice and cookies."

"How thoughtful. Thank you."

Eva nodded to the window ledge next to the recliner she was sitting in and where she'd slept for the first week Curtis was at the facility. Of course, he probably hated knowing she was there, he was so independent, but she knew how much he hated change.

Although she could tell he felt better about it after she'd brought him some books and his favorite periodic table of the elements blanket.

"Will you be spending the night, Mrs. Steinar?" the nurse asked as she set the tray down.

Eva patted the chair's padded arm. "No, I think I'll just nibble a few of these cookies and head home. I have some of Curtis's washing to do."

"You know we do have a laundry here on-site with forced-air sterilization drying units."

Eva knew exactly what the facility had. Before consigning her son's recuperation to them, she'd done extensive research on both Google and Yelp.

"I know and it sounds lovely, but Curtis likes the way I wash his clothes."

The nurse nodded. "Of course. Well, if there's anything you need you know where the call bell is. And if I don't see you before you leave, good night, Mrs. Steinar."

Eva opened the laptop when the nurse left and scrolled back down until she came to her last entry, adding: *Wonderful service*, and included five asterisks because they were the closest thing that looked like stars.

★　　★　　★

Arvada, Colorado / 1:43 a.m.
They just stood in the doorway and stared at the head. He couldn't blame them. It wasn't the sort of thing he usually brought home from U.C.U.A. meetings.

Molded from soft latex rubber, it had been specifically designed to be gender-neutral and *very* realistic. Under a shaggy hairstyle that looked a great deal like Jessica's pixie cut but would also be appropriate for a man, the face, removed of any genetic or racial identifying markers, was serene, eyes closed as if sleeping. The skin tone was light gray, which accentuated the blue shadows around the eyes, lips and hollows of the cheeks.

It was a perfect depiction of death and, he had to admit, a bit startling until you noticed the U.C.U.A.'s logo and words *For Demonstration Use Only* stamped across the front of the truncated neck.

Jess could tell his daughters were impressed.

"You won a head?" Jessica asked.

Abigail made a face.

Jess had to take a deep breath to keep from laughing. "No. Okay, look, it's late and you both have finals in the morning, why don't you go to bed and I'll tell you all about this when you get home from school."

"You expect us to sleep with a disembodied head on the kitchen table?" Jessica pulled out a chair and sat down. Abigail was still standing in the doorway. "Come on, Dad, give."

"I'm okay to wait," Abigail said, then looked at her sister and took a seat. "Yeah, okay. Show us."

God, he loved them.

Jess turned the head so it faced his daughters.

"It'll just be a quick demonstration. Ready?"

"No," Abigail said, then jumped and rolled her eyes toward her sister. "Yes."

Jess hadn't noticed what Jessica did to make her sister jump. As far as he could tell she'd just been sitting there looking at the head and smiling. Daughters...who knew what went on inside their heads?

"All right."

Jess reached into his jacket pocket and withdrew the other item he'd been given that night. It rested inside a purple case similar in shape and size to the pen and pencil set he'd received from his grandparents when he graduated seminary school.

"*Computers are nice, but a true minister needs to write his sermons.*"

Their gift had been one of the most important things he'd ever been given.

This was a close second.

Abigail gasped when he took out the syringe and Jessica jerked back against her chair.

"It's okay, this one is only to demonstrate with. See?" Jess attached the needle to the syringe base and tapped his finger against it. "It's plastic, no owies."

The girls smiled at the word they once used for shots.

"I'll be getting a shipment of real ones in a few days, so if a box arrives when I'm not here, just put it on my desk, okay?"

When they nodded he reached down and took out an empty sponge-topped vial from the box. Only for show; the real ones, filled and ready, would be shipped along with the syringes.

Jess set the items side by side on the table next to the head and waited for Jessica to reach for them. She'd always been the more curious of the two.

He put his hand over hers.

"Not until you're older."

"But it's empty."

Jessica looked up at him. Normally he would have let her lead him into a full discussion, and that would come later, but it was late and he was too keyed up.

"The real ones won't be."

"What will they be filled with?" Abigail asked.

"Sodium hypochlorite."

"Bleach?"

Jessica looked at her sister as her hand slid out from under his. "Show-off."

Jess smiled and picked up the syringe and vial.

"That's right, just ordinary common bleach. Now watch, it's very simple." Piercing the sponge with the plastic needle, Jess pantomimed filling the syringe. "Dr. Ölversson said it didn't take much, but suggested we always use a full syringe to give the family members a sense of security."

Jess looked at his daughters as he withdrew the needle. Under the warm yellow overhead light, the girls' green eyes deepened into sparkling emeralds.

"We have been given a weapon in our continuing fight against the imposters that seek to corrupt us." The words weren't his; he was repeating the ones he'd heard after the video, but he wanted his daughters to hear them and feel the same sense of power they had inspired in him. "We might not be able to do anything about the imposters that already walk among us, but we can stem the tide. With this."

Putting the vial down, Jess held the syringe up as if it did contain fluid, and cupped the head under the chin the way he'd seen done in the video. His daughters watched, silent.

"Okay. Imagine this is someone who has died...a friend or loved one or the loved one of a friend, or even a stranger whose loved one has asked us to help ensure that the blessed dead be laid to rest whole. One body. One soul."

"One body, one soul," his daughters answered.

"Dr. Ölversson has concluded it takes approximately three minutes for a Traveler to invade the body, if it's going to happen, but in those three minutes the individual is clinically and *legally* dead. So...."

Holding the head steady, Jess inserted the needle into the right ear and depressed the plunger. Abigail gasped, but Jessica remained silent, her eyes following his hand until he withdrew the syringe and laid it on the table.

"The bleach destroys enough of the brain tissue," Jess said as he withdrew the needle and set it on the table, "to render it unusable for subjugation by any malignant entity."

"But what if it..." Maybe it was the overhead light, but Jess thought Abigail looked almost as pale as the latex head. "...a Traveler arrived *before* the three minutes are up?"

"Seriously?" her sister asked. "You just do it. It's not like you're really killing anything. A Traveler already died, we'd just be making sure a True Born's body doesn't get stolen."

"No," Jess said, "if that were to ever happen we'd have to stop."

"Why?"

"Because then it would be murder."

"No, it wouldn't."

"Stop it."

Both of them, father and namesake, watched Abigail push away from the table and leave the room. Jess took a deep breath.

Jess picked up the box and packed away the demonstration tools. "Do you think I should talk to her?"

"No, she'll be okay," Jessica said. "She can't even dissect a frog in biology without worrying about hurting it. She'll come around."

"She doesn't have to and neither do you. This is completely voluntary."

"Okay. Can I try?"

He reached over and patted her hand. "I know it's late and you're probably sleepy, but didn't you hear me say you had to be older? It's a U.C.U.A. directive. You have to be twenty-one. Legal stuff, you know how it works."

"But think how good I'll be in four years if I start practicing now."

Jess shook his head and slid the box across the table. He knew a father shouldn't play favorites, especially a father with twins, but sometimes he just couldn't help himself.

CHAPTER ELEVEN

May 31

Haverford, Pennsylvania

Eva took a sip of iced tea one of the day workers – *Hi, my name is Julie* – brought her and looked out through the solarium's massive picture window to the facility's rose garden and half acre of landscaped walking paths. Beyond the bright and smudge-free window, the roses were still leafing out and the buds just beginning to swell, but at least the warm weather had finally arrived.

And if it continued, she'd have to show Curtis the roses.

He liked roses, or had when he became interested in rose hybridization and tried to cross one of her white Saratoga Floribunda roses with a Blumex Parrot tulip to create the first-ever rainbow rose. Eva could still remember him huddled over his worktable carefully dissecting one rose plant after another and then grafting the pieces back together with glue he'd made from beeswax and honey. It had been a wonderful month. He'd actually come down to dinner excited, so full of words, describing everything he'd done or was going to do and what awards his roses, The Curtis Genius Rose, would win once they bloomed.

When the grafts didn't take and the plants died he'd blamed her for not getting hardier stock and retreated back into silence and his room.

But Eva still had the memories of that one perfect month and it had only cost them a little over six hundred dollars.

Maybe he would like to see the roses.

"I'm sure he would," Eva whispered, making sure her mouth was hidden behind the rim of the plastic tumbler. There were too many long-care (a.k.a. terminal) residents, Alzheimer's mostly, who mumbled and muttered to themselves and she didn't want anyone to think she was one of those poor souls.

Curtis would never forgive her.

Finishing the tea, Eva checked the time on Curtis's Seiko watch. She'd been wearing it since his accident to keep it running because, as he explained to her once, it didn't have batteries but generated its own power by using the kinetic energy created by movement. Or something like that. The only thing Eva knew for certain was that it kept perfect time, which at the moment was unfortunate since it showed it was 11:14. He still had another fifteen minutes of hydrotherapy.

Eva sat back and tapped the empty tumbler against the arm of the lounge chair, smiling and holding it up when the duty nurse looked up.

"Can I get another?"

★   ★   ★

Arvada, Colorado / 9:14 a.m.

"I'm sorry, Jess, but could you go over it again, please?"

Nodding, Jess removed the syringe from Fred's ear – Jessica had decided the rubber head needed a name – and set it down on the table, covering it with his hand because he'd noticed Laura Wingate staring at it during his first two demonstrations.

"Sure, Richard, not a problem."

And it wasn't.

They were friends, more than friends. Richard had not only brought him into the U.C.U.A. but stood by him during the darkest time of his life after Monica died. Jess would stay there all day and night and explain until his voice went if that was needed. He knew what they were both thinking while he demonstrated the procedure and he couldn't imagine the pain it was causing them.

Carly wasn't out of the woods yet.

"Okay, once it has been verified that the individual has passed and is declared legally dead, and remember this has to come from a licensed physician or certified EMT, you insert the needle into the ear canal and inject the solution into the brain."

Jessica had suggested he use the term *solution* instead of *bleach*. She said it made it sound more scientific.

"And that will stop anything from happening?"

"Yes."

"But you have to do it right after the person…dies."

Jess nodded again. Neither Richard nor Laura had been to a U.C.U.A. meeting or attended Sunday service since they brought Carly home from the hospital, which was completely understandable, and even though he felt a bit like a circling vulture – there was still a chance Carly would recover – Jess knew he had to be there to show them their only weapon against the unthinkable.

"And then you just...." Laura nodded at Jess's hand.

"Yes."

"Okay," she said. "Okay."

Jess watched her fold her hands on the big dining room table that had been the center piece for birthday parties – his own surprise *Lordy, Lordy, Jess is forty* – dinner parties and God only knew how many school projects – and nod. "Okay."

"And when it's done, we have assured the loved one's body and soul are joined forever in death. One body, one soul."

"One body, one soul," Richard repeated, but Laura only nodded again. "Okay."

Jess took a deep breath and uncovered the syringe, watching them watch him as he lifted it toward Fred's ear. They were his dearest friends and they seemed on the verge of collapse, but Jess knew that if he gave in to his compassion and left without making sure they knew how to prevent an Imp from stealing another's body, perhaps that of their own daughter, he'd never forgive himself.

They didn't deserve what had happened to them.

None of them did.

Jess stopped moving the syringe forward and reversed direction, holding it out across the table's polished surface.

"Would you like to try, Laura?"

Her eyes widened as she pushed back in her chair.

"I'll do it," Richard said, reaching for the syringe, but Laura stopped him.

"No, it's okay, I'll do it."

Jess handed her the syringe and turned Fred to him as he pushed the head toward her. The first few times were easier if you didn't see the face.

Laura took a deep breath. "What do I do?"

"Cup the chin with your free hand. That's right."

"It's cold."

Jess nodded. "Now, bring the syringe up to the ear. All it takes is a slow and steady pressure. The needle is fine enough that there won't be any resistance. Just keep going until you can't push any farther. Then push the plunger all the way in."

"Seems easy enough," Richard said, but winced visibly when his wife stabbed the needle into Fred's ear. "Yikes!"

Jess stood up and leaned across the table, gently pulling Laura's hand, and the syringe, out of the latex.

"You don't have to stab, Laura. Just nice and easy. Take your time." Together they slowly guided it back in.

"That's it?" She sounded relieved. "That's all it takes?"

"That's all." Jess sat back. "It's very quick and easy."

"Does it hurt?"

"It can't hurt, Laura. The soul is gone and only the dead body remains. This –" he held up the syringe, "– is just to ensure that it remains that way."

Laura nodded and sat back.

"It's not hard at all."

"No," Jess said, "it's not."

"You want to try, Rich?"

His friend shook his head and stood up.

"Maybe later," he said. "I have to get to work. Even a boss has to set a good example."

Jess tried not to show his disappointment as he set the syringe aside and shook Richard's hand.

"Not a problem, Rich, and maybe I'll stop in. I've been thinking about increasing my life insurance."

His friend squeezed Jess's hand lightly and released it. "Sounds good. Okay, then." He bent and gave his wife a quick kiss on the cheek. "I'll be home around six. Talk to you later, Jess."

Jess nodded as he put Fred and the syringe back into the official U.C.U.A. carrying case he'd bought online. Made of molded plastic, the unassuming case – matte black with no identifying marks or logos – had a central cushioned cradle that held Fred secure and side pockets for the veterinary syringes and the boxes of prefilled ampoules Jess had ordered.

Because he'd been one of the first to place an order, he'd get a significant discount on the first reorder and an extra syringe as a thank you gift.

Jess pulled a syringe and ampoule from the case and put it down on the table in front of Laura.

"I'll leave these with you," Jess said as he closed and locked the case. "I'll also be sending an e-form for you and Richard to fill out. If you can get it back to me as soon as possible that would be great."

Taking out his phone, Jess opened the camera app and took Laura's picture, making sure it showed the syringe and ampoule in front of her.

"For our files," he said and put the phone away. "Okay, call me if you have any questions or…anything, okay?"

She nodded.

"As soon as you get the form back to me I'll put you on our standby list, okay? Oh, and tell Richard he can order more prefilled vials on the U.C.U.A. website store under Educational Supplies."

Something twitched the side of Laura's mouth as she stood up. "Educational Supplies, right. Can I help you carry that?"

Jess picked up the case and shook his head. "Thanks, but I'm getting used to schlepping him around."

"Him?"

"The case."

"Oh."

The case got in the way when Jess stepped in to give her a hug at the front door.

"It'll be all right, Laura," he said and believed it with all his heart. "One body. One soul."

She smiled and nodded and closed the door in his face.

JUNE

CHAPTER TWELVE

June 9

Arvada, Colorado

Summer Session wasn't as bad as Jessie thought it would be.

It was worse.

Other than the fact that the school's normally stringent dress code had been relaxed to the point that students only had to be fully clothed and wear shoes – which meant shorts, tees and flip-flops – and the classrooms and indoor quad were air-conditioned, it became very obvious by the amount of work given and its level of difficulty that the teachers didn't want to be there either.

If nothing else, it made Jessie understand the importance of never being put on academic probation again. Her dad had hardly flinched when he saw her report card and the letter that accompanied it, and Mrs. Betancourt had been sympathetic when she called Jessie into her office to 'discuss the ramifications' of her failing four of her six classes.

Which, apparently, was perfectly understandable.

'We know how hard these last few months were for you, dear' had become the excuse on everyone's lips except hers.

Yeah, the last few months of her life sucked, but she'd failed the classes because she hadn't studied and now she could either return in the fall and repeat her junior year or sign up and complete all three summer sessions so, if she passed, she could come back to school a senior.

Gee...decisions, decisions.

Summer School it was!

Of course, the fact that Abbie was at the U.C.U.A. Teen Retreat

Camp (a.k.a. See You At Party Central) in Aspen having the time of her life didn't help.

Especially since she'd been giving Jessie updates at least five times a day.

It's so beautiful up here!

You should see the new swimming pool, it's humongous!

I saw a moose! Really a moose!

Jessie stared at her pop quiz paper, trying to remember what the imperfect subjunctive conjugation of *agrandir* was, when Abbie's voice popped into her head. Again.

Jessie, you'll never believe it! I caught a fish!!!!

Jessie groaned.

"*Avez-vous dit quelque chose*, Mademoiselle Pathway?"

Jessie?

Shh! "Um. *Non, désolé*, Madame Greenbaum."

Jessie looked down at the test paper. *Go away.*

But I caught a fish!

Whoot. Whoot.

You're not being very nice.

I'm taking a test!

Fine. I'll talk to you toni—

Jessie started a chorus of 'This Old Man' and kept it up until the old man had knick-knacked on a door, then guessed and wrote down *agrandisse*.

Je suis tellement foutu.

* * *

Haverford, Pennsylvania

She must have either been engrossed in the novel, or else fallen asleep, because she jumped when her husband plopped down in the chair opposite hers. Eva watched his Adam's apple slide up and down behind the stubble on his neck as he downed the contents of the water bottle he'd brought from home.

He didn't like to ask the staff for anything even though they were paying for it.

Eva closed her book. "Well? How did it go?"

He continued drinking as if he hadn't heard her, but she knew the real reason: he was upset about being there on his day off even though it was his turn to accompany Curtis on his Wednesday PT rounds. And God, didn't he look the part – he hadn't shaved and was wearing old shorts and a faded Hawaiian shirt like he was on some sort of budget cruise.

Eva was about to say something when he finished the water and belched.

"That hit the spot," he said. "The hydrotherapy room was horrible today."

Eva was instantly on alert. "Why? What happened?"

Her husband shrugged as he settled back in his chair. "It was hot, like a sauna."

And as an HVAC contractor he would know about that. He might not know much about anything else, but ask him about the latest innovations in heating or air-conditioning and he sounded almost gifted, almost as bright as his son…if she was being generous. Eva had never given much thought to his job, she couldn't call it a career since it was certainly not something she could brag to friends about, but it was profitable enough to provide for her and pay for Curtis's rehabilitation until he was ready to come home.

It probably wouldn't be enough to pay for even one semester at Cambridge, or even Penn State, but there was no doubt in her mind that Curtis would obtain a full scholarship to any university he chose.

Once he got home.

"It's supposed to be warm," she reminded him. "How did Curtis do?"

"Okay, I guess. Dr. Groundling wants to talk to us."

"Oh God, now what?"

The last thing Eva needed was another face-to-face with the facility's executive administrator. Dr. Groundling was a self-absorbed, emotionless woman, undoubtedly childless, who believed that charts and graphs and cases similar to Curtis's were undeniable, uncontestable facts and had little, if any, room for a mother's intuition.

Eva couldn't wait for the day Curtis decided he'd had enough and walked out.

Then where would her uncontestable facts be?

"I don't know," her husband said. "She just asked if we could stop in and see her before we left."

"I'd rather not." Eva closed the book and checked the time on Curtis's watch as she stood up. She knew his schedule by heart – after hydrotherapy, he would be dried off, given a massage to prolong the increased circulation, then dressed in shorts and put under a full-spectrum light for fifteen to twenty minutes – but looking at the watch made it appear she had appointments to keep that were far more important than listening to whatever Dr. Groundling had to—

"Mr. and Mrs. Steinar, I'm so glad I ran into the both of you."

Dr. Groundling. *Damn.*

Eva looked up as the short, square block of white came barreling toward them: white coat, white hair, white pantsuit and pale gray eyes.

"Do you have time for some coffee in my office?"

"Not really." Eva slipped the book into her purse and began to walk away. "I need to pick up the new issue of *Science News* for Curtis before he gets back to his room."

The square woman blocked her path.

"You have time, Mrs. Steinar. I've ordered another EEG done on Curtis."

"What?" Eva wished she still had the book in her hands so she'd have something to swat the woman with. "We didn't authorize that."

"Let's go to my office, Mrs. Steinar. It'll be much quieter there, don't you think?"

Eva flinched when her husband stood up and took her arm. Except for the three of them and an old woman in robe and slippers happily muttering to herself in front of the large screen TV, the room was empty.

"Quieter than what?" she asked.

The square woman smiled and offered to let Eva and her husband go ahead of her.

* * *

Arvada, Colorado

"So, how's everyone doing?"

Slumped back against her chair, legs outstretched, arms folded across her chest, Jessie looked around the room. There were only four of them from the group and even though counselors and other 'nonessential personnel' were given the summer off, Ms. Samuels came in and opened her office every lunch hour so they, the summer rejects, could, if they felt like it, come in and talk about whatever was bothering them.

None of them had missed a day since the first session started.

Ms. Samuels nodded. "That good, huh?"

Jessie slumped lower in her seat. She hadn't said much those last few months after the hospital and Carly thing, and she had even less to say now, but just being there, with her kind – failures and freaks – helped. It was safe in Ms. Samuels' office; it was where she belonged.

An exaggerated sigh made Jessie turn to her left.

"Hi, Nick, gay, bipolar, need three art units to get my diploma out of hock."

"Hi, Nick," four voices answered.

Nick produced another *my life is over* sigh. "My mother wants me to learn how to make mulgipuder."

"Muddy what?"

"What the hell is that?"

"It's a traditional Estonian casserole –"

"What's Estonian?"

"– made with potatoes and groats with a bacon sauce."

"What are groats?"

"Hang on." Jessie along with everyone else in the room watched and waited while Steff – gay, brilliant and taking summer classes just for fun…definitely a freak – double thumbed his iPhone. "Groats are the hulled kernels of various cereal grains, such as oats, wheat, rye and barley. And…." His fingers tap-tap-tapped. "Estonia is a country in Northern Europe bordered on the north by the Gulf of Finland, with Finland on the east and the Baltic Sea and Sweden on the west. Why does your mom want you to learn that?"

Everyone turned back to Nick. He blushed all the way up to the roots of his white-blond hair.

"Because she said it was her cooking that won my dad and she wants me to be able to find a man just as wonderful with my cooking."

"Awwwww."

"Well, I think that's great, and keeping family traditions alive is keeping history alive. Now...." Ms. Samuels smiled. "How about you, Jessie? How are you doing?"

Heads turned. Pushing herself into a semi-erect sitting position, Jessie studied the tops of her canvas boat shoes. She hated flip-flops, but that wasn't much of a confession.

"Hi. Jessie. Transgender. Still haven't told my dad."

"Hi, Jessie."

"Um."

"How are your classes?"

Jessie shrugged. "Okay."

"And...?" Ms. Samuels usually didn't push, but Jessie definitely felt a shove.

"Uh.... I, um, guess I miss my sister. She's at the U.C.U.A. summer camp up in Aspen and—"

"You're a Onesies?"

Jessie glared at Melissa, their bi anorexic. "We don't like being called that."

"I always thought that sounded like something a baby would wear," Steff said.

"Yeah, baby nutcases," Nick laughed.

"Hey, safe zone, people," Ms. Samuels reminded everyone. And everyone ignored her.

"But you are?" Melissa asked.

Jessie sat up straight and proud. "Yes, my whole family is. And we call ourselves True Borns because we are only born once and only have one body."

"So was I," Melissa said. "We all were."

"Then all of you can join."

Melissa shook her head. "My dad says it's not right."

"What's not right?"

"Hey," Nick said, "I saw that demonstration up in Boulder, you know, on the news."

"Why don't you just leave them alone?" Melissa asked. "They aren't hurting you."

"Were you there?" Steff asked. "At the demonstration?"

"Yeah," Jessie answered Steff and ignored Melissa. "And it was great. And I mean it, *all* of you can join the U.C.U.A. It's really great, besides the camp, we have, you know, lots of activities and my dad's not only a minister, he's the head of the Arvada Chapter and the other night he came home and showed my sister and me a way that can stop the Imps forever."

"Imps?"

Jessie looked at Ms. Samuels and smiled. "Imposters, that's what we call the Travelers, but they're not going to be a problem for long. I can't tell you how, you have to be a member to know that, but if you join—"

"*Stop!*"

Besides never pushing someone to talk, usually Ms. Samuels never raised her voice.

Until that moment.

Jessie felt her neck pop as she jerked her head up and she probably wasn't the only one. The four of them were all staring at Ms. Samuels as she stood up, her arms wrapped around her belly like she was in pain.

"How dare you. This is supposed to be a safe place, a sanctuary without prejudice or preconceived ideas about what a person is. How *dare* you come into this room and presume to know anything about people who found themselves in a situation they had no control over. I thought better of you, Jessie." Ms. Samuels finally stopped staring at Jessie and looked at the others. "Don't you understand, all of us are one thing on the outside but something else underneath…just like a Traveler. They're someone else inside."

Without taking her eyes off the woman who'd gotten her to open up about her feelings and told her it was okay to be different and pretended to care, Jessie grabbed her backpack off the floor and slowly stood up.

"You're one of them, aren't you?"

"Jessie, let me explain."

"You're a Traveler."

The thing she'd known as Ms. Samuels licked her lips as, one by one by one, Melissa, Steff and Nick picked up their backpacks and book bags and stood up. The Imp took a deep breath and nodded.

"Yes. I think the meeting's over."

Jessie watched the three leave but couldn't move. The Imp was standing between her and the door.

"Jessie, please…."

It took a step toward her and Jessie backed up so quickly she almost stumbled over the chair. The Imp walked back to its seat and sat down, hands raised as if she…*it* expected to be attacked. Jessie raced to the door.

"Wait, please." Jessie opened the door, keeping it between her and the Imp. "I'm not a monster."

"Yes, you are, all of you are. You don't belong here."

"Don't you think I know that? Jessie, I don't know why this happened, but it did and I'm…Jessie, I'm just a person."

"You're an imposter!"

The Imp looked down. It was wearing a pale blue, sleeveless dress with a summer-weight sweater draped over its shoulders because Ms. Samuels always complained about the air-conditioning.

Jessie wondered if the real woman who once wore that body had been bothered by the cold or if it liked blue summer dresses.

"You're right, Jessie, I was an imposter, but that was long before –" it lifted its hands and looked at them, "– this happened. My name was George Samuels and I was born in 1907 to a very respectable, very conservative family…and always knew that I'd been born into the wrong body. Just like you."

Jessie gripped the doorknob. "I'm not like you."

"I meant transgender. Back then the concept of gender dysphoria did not exist and was not even hinted at. If you acted or dressed like a member of the opposite sex you weren't just called names. It wasn't a very enlightened time, especially not in the small Nebraska town where my family had lived for generations, so, for the first eighteen years of my life I dressed and acted like the son my parents thought I was."

The doorknob felt very hot against Jessie's palm. "I'm not like you."

"It was only after I graduated and told my family I was taking a bus to Los Angeles to seek my fortune, that I finally became who I always was. George Mason Samuels got on the bus in Barstow, but it was Georgina Mary Samuels who arrived in the City of Angels on a one-way ticket. I didn't need to pretend anymore. I was Georgina and people accepted me as Georgina. I had a life and I had friends. I even found a job as a typist file clerk and started taking night classes in psychology, eventually getting my degree. I knew I wanted to help people like me…even before I knew there were people like me.

"My life was perfect until one night as I was coming home from work, a man grabbed me and pulled me into an alley…and discovered that Georgina didn't exist. As he was beating me to death he called me an imposter, so you can understand why I don't particularly care for that word. The last thing I remember was the look of disgust on his face.

"Georgina woke up in a hospital in Fort Morgan on November 24, 2019 in the body of a woman who'd been beaten to death by her husband. Full circle. I never asked or wanted to come back, Jessie, and I don't know why it happened, but I came back as the person I always knew I was."

"*I'm not like you!*"

"I didn't say you were."

"You did. You said I was like you."

"No, Jessie, I just meant I was transgender and—"

"I'm not like you. You're a freak. Why don't you kill yourself and go back to where you belong!" Jessie swung the door open and stepped out into the hall.

"Jessie, wait. Stop!"

Too many years of childhood-learned obedience stopped Jessie in the doorway, but she didn't turn around.

"I never told anyone about…who I was before, about George, because by that time I was Georgina. The hospital staff only knew that a woman died and came back in a different woman's body and I never corrected them. But I still know the consequences of living with a secret and you don't have to. The world has changed, Jessie, you have the right to be whoever you are."

"I'm not like you, imposter. I'm real."

It didn't say another word as Jessie walked down the hall, out through the main entrance and kept walking all the way home.

CHAPTER THIRTEEN

Haverford, Pennsylvania

Eva let the roll of paper slip from her fingers to the floor, giving the four parallel lines that covered it only the most perfunctory glance. The lines, some squiggly, some straight, didn't look any different than the first EEG printout they'd taken of Curtis in the emergency room –

Gamma: cognitive functions (straight)

Beta: logic and understanding (straight)

Alpha: the bridge between the unconscious and conscious (rolling waves)

Theta: dreams (larger waves)

Delta: a state of consciousness in infants (spikes)

– so Eva saw no reason why Dr. Groundling felt obligated to show her more of the same thing. Or continually repeat herself. Curtis would wake up when he was ready.

"As you can see, Mr. and Mrs. Steinar, there's been no change in Curtis's EEG."

Eva suppressed a yawn as her husband picked up the slippery ribbon of paper and handed it back to the doctor.

"That's not good, is it?"

"No, it's not. I'm so sorry, Mrs. Steinar, Mr. Steinar. Given Curtis's persistent status, it's doubtful that he will ever regain full consciousness. He has lower brain activity, which means he may occasionally appear to wake up or respond to outside stimuli, but he's not deliberately controlling these actions. There is very little more we can do for him in terms of restoration therapy."

Eva felt a grinding pressure on her hand and looked down to discover her husband had grabbed it. It took some effort but she finally managed to pull it free.

"So what are you telling us," she demanded. "Are you kicking him out?"

"No, not at all, Mrs. Steinar." Dr. Groundling folded the roll of graph paper into squares and set it down on her desk, where it unfolded itself. "Of course you may take him home and we'll be happy to provide you with the name of home-care specialists, but if you'd rather he remain with us, we'll move Curtis into our palliative care unit."

"That's a hospice." Eva rubbed her hand. "We've already made ourselves clear on that matter. Curtis is not dying."

The doctor sat up and squared her already square shoulders. "No, Mrs. Steinar, he's not. He is more susceptible to airborne and systemic illnesses in his present condition, but barring contagion he can continue as he is for a number of years. His body can be maintained, Mrs. Steinar, but we have no idea of how much, or even if Curtis is aware of what's going on around him."

"He's always been introverted," Eva said.

Dr. Groundling nodded. "As I was saying…if you decided to take Curtis home, we will provide health-care visits, but if his condition were to suddenly deteriorate he would have a much better chance of recovery if he were still here."

"Then I guess he should stay here. Don't you think so, Eva?"

She hated the thought, but the facility was still the best place for him…until he woke up. Eva nodded and saw Dr. Groundling smile.

"I'll see that he's moved as soon as possible. I understand how helpless you must feel, but we have to face facts and one of those facts is that Curtis will never wake up."

Eva slid the purse strap over her shoulder and stood up, ignoring her husband's questioning look the same way she'd ignored the lines on the EEG.

"Facts are made to be challenged. Do you know who told me that, Doctor? My son, Curtis. Curtis wouldn't accept something just because it was called a fact and neither will I. Can you prove, without a shadow of a doubt, that Curtis won't wake up?"

Dr. Groundling looked nervous. "Well, no, there have been cases…."

"Then don't call it a fact. Now, if you'll excuse me, Curtis should be back in his room by now and I want to explain to him why he's going to be moved. Geniuses require details, you know."

She could feel them both stare at her as she left the office.

*   *   *

Arvada, Colorado

Jess looked at the time on his phone then swiped the screen with his thumb and hit the contact icon. Jessica's quick-dial number was two, Abigail's was three. His wife's had been one and he'd never reassigned it after erasing her last voice mail.

If she were still here, she would have known what to do and what to say, and what message he wanted to convey to their firstborn. It seemed so effortless for her, not so much for him.

Jess closed his eyes and lifted the cell phone to his forehead, rubbing it against the lines that seemed to have grown deeper since he became an only parent. His wife wouldn't have been standing there, mentally running down options and platitudes and....

He lowered the phone and opened his eyes. No, his wife would probably have gotten in the car, found Jessica, picked her up, taken her over to Old Town for ice cream at Scrumptious and then driven over to the Arvada Center so they could wander around the outdoor art exhibits while their ice cream melted, and listened to whatever Jessica wanted to talk about.

That's exactly what she would have done, so why couldn't he? All he had to do was get in the car and—

The front door opened and slammed shut.

"Jessica?"

There was a pause and the sound of a backpack hitting the foyer floor. "Yeah. It's me."

Jess looked up and nodded. *Thank you.*

He found her in the kitchen standing in front of the open refrigerator, downing mouthfuls of orange juice directly from the carton...until she saw him.

"Sorry," she said/choked as she lowered the carton and began screwing the cap back on.

Jess sat down at the kitchen table and pulled out a chair. "Why don't you bring it over and join me."

He watched her close the refrigerator door with her foot then walk over to the sink and grab two glasses from the drying rack.

"None for me, thanks," he said, and she put one glass back before sitting down. Jess waited until she'd poured the juice.

"I got a call from your school."

She picked up the glass and took a long swallow. "Uh-huh."

"You want to tell me what happened?"

"I left and I'm not going back."

"Okay, but I think that was more a statement than an explanation."

She took another swallow.

"Your principal said it had something to do with your counselor, Ms. Samuels?"

Every muscle in her body went rigid. Jess had no idea Jessica was even talking with the school counselor, but it was obvious something had happened.

He reached out for her hand and felt her pull away. That worried him.

"Jessica, look, if this is about your grades last semester, it's okay. You'd been through a lot and—"

"I'm trans."

"You're what?"

She put the glass down and sat back. "I'm trans…transgender. I'm…I feel like…I'm male inside."

"Ah."

This was unexpected, but it wasn't as if he was at a complete loss. There'd been church-sanctioned seminars and study groups that he'd attended which dealt with the subject and how to handle it, so he knew he had to remain calm and be supportive and positive.

As much as possible.

Jess took a deep breath and kept his hand within reach. "No, you're not."

Her eyes widened. "What?"

"You're not transgender, Jessica." He hoped the smile he gave her looked calm and supportive and positive. "But you are probably gay and that's fine."

"Um, no, I'm trans, Dad, and that's not the same thing."

Jess pulled his hand back. "No, you're confused, but you don't have to worry, I love you and always will, no matter what your lifestyle."

"Dad, you're not listening…."

"I am, Jessica, I am listening, but you have to understand, you can't be transgender. One soul, one body…the same as any True Born, and you were born a girl. Being transgender would be like turning your back on the soul God placed inside you. It'd make you a kind of imposter, like...."

"I'm not! She said I was like her because I'm the same way!"

"What way? Who said what?"

"Ms. Samuels."

"The school counselor?"

There were tears streaking down his daughter's face as she nodded. "Yeah, we have this group that meets at lunch and it's supposed to be a safe place for people like me, you know to come and talk but...she said I was like her because I'm trans, but I'm not!"

Every muscle in Jess's body tightened. "Like what? Jessica, I don't understand."

"She was born a guy and got killed because she dressed like a woman, but I don't dress like a boy and—"

"Killed?" Jess found himself on his feet and moving around the table to grab his daughter's arms and pull her to her feet. It was only the sudden fear in her eyes that stopped him from shaking her. "What did you just say, Jessica?"

His daughter looked into his eyes. "She's a Traveler!"

Jess released his grip on his daughter's arms so he could pull her into a hug. "Oh, my God, oh my God. Is she the only one working there?"

"I – I don't know."

She began to cry. Jess could feel the small hitches of her sobs as faint shudders and twitches. She'd cried like that at her mother's funeral, quiet and almost unseen. He stroked her back.

"It's all right, baby, you don't have to worry. I'll find out and when I do.... You and your sister are not going back to that school and I'm going to make sure everyone knows about.... My God, I never even thought to ask. Why would I? What kind of a father am I?"

She hugged him tighter and said something he couldn't make out, but he kissed the top of her head as if he had.

"I'm so, so sorry, Jessica, but I can promise you something like this will *never* happen again. I'm going to expose them. God, look what only one of them has done to you." Jess straightened. "They can't get away with it. They can't be allowed to continue to infect our children like this. That's what it is...an infection...they infect our children into accepting them. Clever monster, but it's not going to work. I'm going to let the U.C.U.A. know and demand that an investigation of the school system, not only here in Colorado but worldwide, to ensure that True Born children are protected from their influence and corruption. You did a brave thing, Jessica, and I'm proud of you."

She lifted her face and tried to smile.

"And I want you to promise me something, okay? I want you to forget everything that creature told you. Your soul and body match just as God intended, and I'm glad you told me you're gay. If you like we can start a LGB group at church, what do you think?"

It took a moment but she finally nodded. "It's LGBTQ."

Jess exhaled slowly. She was back.

"I'm sorry you had to go through that, Jessica. That thing intentionally misdirected you to believe you were like it. It tried to convince you that you were one person on the outside and another on the inside, just like a Traveler. But you're not an imposter, you're a True Born and my beloved daughter and always will be. Now...."

Jess gave her another kiss and pushed her away. "Finish your juice and don't worry about anything. This wasn't your fault, this was a revelation. If you'll excuse your old dad, he has a few calls to make."

He left his daughter standing and in tears, and was inspired by her courage.

One body. One soul.

★　　★　　★

Jessie wiped her face and sat down, pushed the glass of juice away from her when just looking at it made her stomach twist in on itself.

Abbs?

Hey! God, I wish you were here. We're going to have a cook-out tonight and—

Ms. Samuels is a Traveler.

What?

I told Dad and he's going to find out if there are any others at the school. But we won't be going back there anyway.

What? Wait. What? Jessie, what's going on? What happened?

Jessie closed her eyes and hit mental replay.

Wow.

Yeah.

So, what now?

Jessie picked up her glass, carried it to the sink, and poured the last few swallows down the drain.

Nothing.

I mean about you being transgender.

But I'm not. I told you what Dad said. It's all Ms. Samuels' fault.

Jessie.

I'm probably not even gay.

Jessie turned on the faucet and garbage disposal and discovered the combination was better at blocking her sister than any childhood song.

She'd have to remember that.

CHAPTER FOURTEEN

June 22

Haverford, Pennsylvania / 11:30 a.m.
"You know how I hate to complain...but I honestly don't know how much more I can take of this place. I mean, the rehabilitation center wasn't too bad but this.... My God, they're impossible. They refuse to listen to me, can you believe that? Yes, they do a wonderful job with you, but they still don't understand the workings of your mind. I try to tell them how a genius's mind works, but they won't listen. It's maddening."

The one-sided conversation Eva had started when she'd been *allowed* into his room – *I'm sorry, Mrs. Steinar, but you know the rules. It's very important that we monitor Curtis's food intake in a quiet and controlled environment and your presence seems to...disrupt that* – continued as she pushed his wheelchair across the empty lobby.

Eva couldn't remember the last time she saw anyone, other than the nursing staff, sitting on one of the sofas or lounging in a chair or reading a book or playing cards or watching the flat-screen TV that always seemed to be on.

The lobby was beautiful but an obvious indulgence that she and the families of other long-termers were paying for. The patients never used it because most of them were either confined to their beds or dying or both. Curtis was the exception, which made it all the more infuriating that she was required to sign in and sign out and obtain a pass if she wanted to take her son outside.

And why she always pushed him through the lobby instead of taking the shortcut through one of the side doors.

She was paying for the lobby, dammit, and she was going to use it.

Especially today.

"Do you know what that doctor told me? He said you'd run a *slight* temperature last night and thought it would be best if you just rested today and asked me to come back tomorrow. Can you imagine? Well, I told him I *would* be back tomorrow but I was also going to take you outside to see the roses today."

Eva exhaled. "Listen to me babble. I'm sorry, I forgot you heard all that, but it's just that they make me so angry sometimes. They treat you like a child...they treat us *both* like children...as if I don't know what's best for you."

The warm air, already heavy with humidity, engulfed them as Eva pushed the wheelchair through the automatic doors and into the bright summer sunshine.

"All you need is a little fresh air. Ah. Take a deep breath, Curtis, doesn't this feel better than being stuck inside?"

Curtis's head bobbed up and down, agreeing with her – *How can they think he doesn't understand?* – as they continued down the path to the rose garden.

"They don't know what you're capable of, Curtis, that's the problem. And I understand your reluctance to show them, I know how you hate to show off, but if you could just let them know they're dealing with a true genius, it would help. Could you do that for me?"

Curtis bobbed his head yes.

"Thank you. Oh, my, it is warm, isn't it? How about we sit down for a minute?"

Eva pushed the wheelchair into the deep shade next to a stone bench and made sure the brake was set before sitting. She'd fibbed to the doctor; Curtis didn't like the sun or being outside, but she'd be damned if she was going to let *anyone* else decide what her son was or was not going to do.

"Fever," she said, but immediately reached over and placed the back of her hand against her son's forehead. Curtis's skin felt clammy and a bit warm, but it was a hot day and boys perspire. "You don't have a fever. If you had one last night it was because they keep those rooms too warm. I told them you don't like that, but...."

Opening her purse, Eva retrieved his tablet and set it on his lap. "Now, I know you'd much rather be inside with your computers and books, but we can't let them win, Curtis, we just can't. So, just show them one simple equation or something and I'll buy you a new external hard drive or whatever you want, okay?"

Curtis's body suddenly jerked to the left, his head lolling, coming to rest against his shoulder as his eyes searched for her face. Eva laughed and straightened his head. His cheeks were warm but it was summer, after all, and he looked perfectly well. His eyes, when they met hers, were clear and bright, actually sparkling.

"I know it sounds like a bribe, Curtis, but it's an incentive. So, what do you say? Will you show them how bright you are?"

His sparkling eyes drifted away from her.

Eva exhaled. Bright and accomplished and stubborn as a mule if someone, especially her, asked him to do something. He'd been that way since he was little.

"Fine, but I'm only thinking of you, Curtis." Eva swallowed her frustration as she turned on the tablet and swiped the screen. "So, if you'd rather they think you just have a normal IQ, that's your choice."

She saw his right hand curl into a fist.

"Don't get mad at me, young man, I just want them to know how brilliant you are. I can only imagine how bored you must be."

His chin bobbed against his chest in what was obviously a nod. How could they say he'd never get any better? He already was better, a hundred times better than when he first arrived. And a million times better than when she'd walked in and found him, choking, his face turning blue as he dangled from that belt....

"Oh God." Eva closed her eyes until the memory went away.

"I know it was an accident, some experiment gone wrong." She opened her eyes. "But *you* have to tell them that, Curtis, because they don't believe *me*. Please, just tell them it was an accident, show them you're in there. Sorry, sorry."

Eva turned away to hide the tears in her eyes. When Curtis was a child any strong emotion or loud sound terrified him, either turning him into a quivering near-catatonic mess or a one-boy demolition team. The doctors said it was because of the schizophrenia, that he couldn't handle normal stimuli, and she'd almost believed them. It wasn't until she read an article in an online medical journal that suggested that a certain percentage of children who exhibit aberrant behavior and who had been misdiagnosed as schizophrenics had exceptional intelligence and only acted out from the frustration of not being recognized as geniuses.

Geniuses, the article kept repeating, reacted to the world differently than the rest of us.

Curtis had never been sick, he was a genius.

"All right, I'll stop talking about it. You'll show them when you're ready and not before, I accept that. But, we can't let you just sit around like those people inside, you're a genius and geniuses have to keep busy. So...."

Eva scrolled through the list of online college courses she'd downloaded right after Curtis's accident. There were only a few hundred courses and they'd already been through the list three times, but there was still a possibility something would pique his interest.

"Let's see...we're up to the Q's. Ah, quantum cryptography. That sounds fun, doesn't it?"

* * *

Arvada, Colorado / 9:30 a.m.
If looks really could kill, Jessie knew she'd be facedown in the school parking lot, bleeding from a hundred wounds, flayed alive and gutted like a fish.

She took a deep breath and pasted on a smile. "Hey, Abbs! Over here!"

The look intensified. Jessie let go of the smile and leaned back against the sun-heated driver's side door, watching her sister pointedly ignore her as she dug through the pile of duffle bags next to the idling bus.

So, have fun?

Shut up.

Yup, wounded, bleeding, flayed, gutted and possibly beheaded.

It was going to be the longest three-mile drive home in history.

It wasn't my fault.

I. Said. Shut. Up.

Jessie nodded even though no one noticed. It hadn't been her fault, at least not the part where the U.C.U.A. decided to cut camp short so they could attend a two-week 'Identification and Disclosure' course.

All she'd done was expose an Imposter, dammit. True Borns did that all the time!

Jessie was about to think-tell her sister those exact words – she could only glare so long – when a tall, lanky boy with curly brown hair and glasses began helping Abbie plow through the pile. Abbie looked up at him and gave him a look that was the total opposite of a glare. Jessie didn't recognize him, but whoever he was, he wasn't boyfriend Paul. And Abbie didn't seem to mind. She was all giggles and flirty and—

Where's Paul?

Her sister ignored her to say something to the tall unknown and tossed her hair as she pointed to her neon-pink bag. The tall unknown said something back and mimed diving in. Abbie laughed and was still laughing, on the outside, when she glanced across the parking lot.

Jessie shivered despite the morning's already seventy-eight degrees and climbing temperature.

She was still trying to rub some warmth back into her arms when they, Abbie and the tall unknown, headed for the car.

Abbie was still all bubbly and smiley...still only on the outside...so Jessie smiled back.

"Hey, Abbs," she said and nodded to the unknown. "Hi."

"Hello," the unknown said. "I'm Nigel Lebbon."

Jessie nodded. *English. You always did have a thing about British accents.*

Shut. Up.

Yes, Mum.

Abbie's smile twitched. "Nigel, this is my sister Jes—"

"Jessica Faith," he said and lunged for her hand, swallowing it in both of his. "I am honored, you are an inspiration. We heard about what you'd gone through, my God, it must have been so horrible. I can only imagine the betrayal you felt when you found out. I recognized your sister immediately, but I still had no idea that I'd have the honor of meeting you." He chuckled. "Listen to me blather, I am so very pleased to meet you, Jessica Faith."

Jessie could feel the rise in temperature coming from her sister when he leaned over and kissed her hand. She didn't know what to do with it afterward.

"Um. So…. Hi. Thanks?" She turned her hand and shook his. "Yeah. Um. Can we give you a lift?"

"Would you? Oh, that would be wonderful! I was going to ride home with the Pattersons. I'm staying with them for the summer and then—"

"Nigel's going to the University of Denver in the fall," Abbie interrupted, planting her hand against his arm, laying claim, "to study information and communications technology, just like me."

You are? Since when?

Shut. Up.

"Isn't that a coincidence?" He was still beaming at Jessie and it was making her skin crawl.

"Well, Abbie's always been interested in communicating." *Most of the time.*

The glare returned, briefly.

"Outstanding. Might I impose on you to drop me off? Do you know where the Pattersons live?"

"Yes," Abbie said as Jessie nodded.

"Fantastic. Let me just drop my gear off and ask if they wouldn't mind if I ride over with you." Nigel from England turned, took three steps and turned back to them. "Oh, and what do you say in this country? Um, side-by-side!"

They both looked at him.

"You mean shotgun?" Jessie asked.

"Oh, of course. Shotgun!"

Jessie watched him jog away when she heard the driver's side door open.

And slam shut.

I'm driving.

Okay.

Jessie climbed into the back seat and fastened her seat belt.

I'm sure I wasn't the only reason he started talking to—

The unmistakable sound of Abbie's fingers squeezing the steering-wheel cover filled the car. Jessie didn't need any visual image filling her mind; she could feel those same fingers closing around her throat.

English Nigel was running back toward them, sun glinting off his glasses and waving something in his hand.

The something turned out to be three twenty dollar bills.

"The Pattersons said we should go to Steuben's and have breakfast on them," he said as he slid into the shotgun seat, turned toward Jessie and snapped on his seat belt. "Sounds wonderful and I am a bit peckish. Shall we?"

"Sure!"

"Yay!"

Jessie sat back as Abbie started the car and joined the line heading out of the parking lot.

"Now, while I did see the demonstration on the telly – you were brilliant, by the way, Jessica Faith, very regal – I want you to tell me what it was like when you found out your teacher was a Traveler."

"Call me Jessie," she said and tried not to elaborate too much on her role as the whistleblower.

Not that it mattered, he was enthralled, and Abbie kept singing 'Kumbaya' inside Jessie's head all the way to the restaurant.

CHAPTER FIFTEEN

Haverford, Pennsylvania / 12:22 p.m.

Eva managed to turn her head and cover the yawn before Curtis noticed. He hated to see people yawn. He told her once that he'd proven yawning did not mean a lack of oxygen; it meant boredom. If he saw her yawn, he'd assume she was bored with him, which wasn't and never would be true. But she'd discovered early on that it was always better not to argue with him.

Curtis's logic was impeccable.

Sitting up straighter, she feigned a cough into her hand and took a deep breath as she turned toward him. "It's so peaceful out here. And warm. Don't you think it's warm and peaceful, Curtis?"

She'd been cautious for no reason. Curtis wasn't even looking in her direction. His head thrown back, he was staring up at the trees, specks of sunlight dappling his upturned face with gold. He was probably calculating the weight of one sunbeam on a leaf or something equally important, and she wouldn't have disturbed him for the world...if he didn't look so uncomfortable.

Standing up, Eva took his head in her hands and slowly tipped it forward. His throat made a little clicking sound.

"You're welcome. Now, let me see." Eva checked the time. It was almost lunchtime, but Curtis was on a different schedule and wouldn't get his next feeding until two. Apparently the food paste they injected directly into his stomach took longer to digest, and she could wait until then. "I think you've done enough work for the moment, don't you?"

Curtis's gaze flickered on her for an instant and moved on.

"I know, you'd rather keep working, but even Stephen Hawking took a break now and then. And you know what they say about all work and no play."

Picking up the tablet, Eva closed the file and opened the game app.

"You like this one, don't you?" She turned the screen toward him.

"I used to play this when you were a baby, but I was terrible at it. I could never get the blocks to go where I wanted them quick enough. It was frustrating, but I know you're much better at it. I'll just put it on demo mode until you're ready."

Curtis's left leg jerked but his eyes had found the screen and stayed there.

How could *they* say he wasn't better?

★   ★   ★

Arvada, Colorado / 10:22 a.m.

One of the things Jessie loved about Steuben's restaurant was the service.

It felt like they hadn't been sitting for more than just a few seconds before their orders were taken: Huevos Rancheros for Nigel ("I'm going to be here for a while so I'd better start eating cowboy food." Abbie: "Tee-hee, tee-hee." Jessie: <gag>) and Avocado Goddess Toast for Abbie. Jessie had selected the humongous Smothered Breakfast Burrito in the hopes that it would provide enough distraction to ward off Nigel's seemingly unlimited questions.

Not that he should have had any more since the game of 'Twenty Thousand Questions for Jessica Faith, the Brave' they...he'd played on the ride over.

But that became a moot point when Abbie, out of kindness or self-interest, dominated the pre, during and après-conversation with her own questions about the U.C.U.A. in England and what he liked to do in his spare time and if he'd like to go hiking in the high country because she just loved hiking in the high country... etc., etc., etc.

While filling Jessie's head with the lilting strains of 'Kumbaya'.

The girl had talent.

Jessie was reaching for her cup of coffee when Nigel did his own reaching across the table and took her hand.

"So, Jessica Faith." He gave her a little wink. "How do you feel about hiking?"

The sudden silence inside her head was almost painful. Jessie pulled her hand away and smiled.

"I hate hiking," she said, "and I like girls. Could you pass the cream, please?"

Abbie choked on a crumb of avocado toast as he handed Jessie the creamer.

"Thanks."

And turned his attention to Abbie.

"So, Abigail, where will our first hike be?"

Abbie glanced at Jessie as she wiped the crumbs from her mouth.

Jessie, I....

I lied.

What?

I really like hiking...and you're welcome.

They ignored her for the remainder of their meal.

It was heaven.

★　★　★

Haverford, Pennsylvania / 1:43 p.m.

"Help me! Please! My son!"

Eva could feel her heart pounding against her rib cage and prayed it wouldn't give out until she got him inside. Her legs had twisted out from under her once as she pushed the wheelchair up the deceptively steep incline. If she hadn't been holding on to the chair handles she would have done worse than scrape the skin off her right knee.

The wound felt like a hundred wasps were stinging her, but it didn't matter. Nothing mattered but Curtis.

"Help me!"

Two male nurses or interns or whatever appeared out of nowhere – *thank you, God, thank you* – one grabbing her, the other trying to wrestle the wheelchair from her. Curtis didn't move, hadn't moved since she woke up.

"Please, help me."

"I'm trying to, ma'am," the man standing beside her said, "but you have to let go. I have him, it's okay."

"He won't wake up. I must have fallen asleep, but it couldn't have been more than a few minutes. And we were in the shade. I made sure of that but when I woke up...the shade...his face was so red and he was shaking. That's what woke me up, I heard the wheelchair shaking. I thought he was just asleep, but he wouldn't wake up. Why isn't he waking up? Curtis? *Curtis!*"

The man holding her pulled her away from the chair. "He'll be okay, just let Jeff take him."

Eva let go of the handles and watched the man disappear with her son into the building.

"I just closed my eyes for a few minutes." She clung to the man's arm as they continued slowly up the walk. "It couldn't have been longer than that. Curtis hates the sun. You saw how red he is, that's because he burns so easily. I didn't think to bring any sunblock. Why didn't I bring sunblock?"

"It's okay. Let's just get you inside, okay? Jeff will see that Curtis is taken care of, I promise."

Eva looked at the man and nodded. "It was so warm and.... We both must have fallen asleep, but he won't wake up."

"Yes, ma'am." The man's voice was very soft and gentle, a contrast to the strength she felt as he helped her walk. Her knee was really beginning to hurt; she couldn't stop limping. "Are you okay?"

"I slipped," she said and for some reason that made her laugh. "I'm clumsy." Eva stopped laughing. "Why did I fall asleep?"

"You were probably tired."

Eva nodded; she still felt tired, almost too tired to walk, but she did – one foot after the other until they entered the building. The lobby was cold and so dark after the almost blinding sunlight she couldn't see for a moment. But when she was finally able to, he wasn't there.

"Where's my son? Where's Curtis?"

"I'll go check, ma'am," the man said and waved to the nurse at the reception desk. "Can we get a wheelchair over here?"

"Curtis already has a wheelchair," Eva told him.

"This one's for you," he said, taking the one the reception nurse brought and helping Eva into it. "We need to take a look at your knee."

"It's only a scrape." Eva would have stood up and demanded they take her immediately to her son, if her legs hadn't started to tremble. "Please, I need to see my son."

"I know, and I promise we'll go find him as soon as we get you taken care of. You've got a pretty good sunburn too."

"I do?" Eva lifted her arms and noticed how pink they were. Pink, not red. "Oh, I guess I do. It doesn't hurt."

"But it still needs treatment," the man said. "Let's fix you up and then I'll go check on your son."

"Curtis. My son's name is Curtis Allan Steinar and he's a genius."

"Yes, ma'am." The man nodded and pushed her toward the nurses' station, where he left her with a promise to come back and get her once he found out about Curtis.

But he didn't.

Dr. Groundling came to talk to her after a nurse had cleaned and bandaged Eva's knee and applied a cream that smelled like coconut to her face and arms.

"How are you doing, Mrs. Steinar?"

"Where's Curtis? Is he back in his room? Take me to him."

The doctor glanced at the nurse over Eva's shoulder and nodded. The nurse moved away.

"He's resting, Mrs. Steinar. His fever's back and it's rather high."

"It's just the sunburn. I should have brought sunscreen. I need to see him, please take me to him."

"Before we do that, can I ask if your husband's here?"

Eva sat up straighter and clutched her purse. Something crunched inside, probably the tablet. The screen had cracked almost in half when it fell to the ground. She didn't think it could be repaired, but she couldn't just throw it away. It belonged to Curtis.

"No," she said, "he's at work."

"I think it might be best if you called him and asked him to come."

"Why? What's wrong? Where's Curtis? Why won't you take me to him?" *Oh God.* "He's dead, isn't he?"

"No, Mrs. Steinar, he's not, but he is in the ICU and I think your husband needs to be here as soon as possible."

He wasn't dead. Curtis wasn't dead. That's all that mattered.

"All right."

The call didn't take long. It was almost as if he'd been expecting it.

Eva turned off the phone and put it back in her purse. "He'll be here as soon as he can. Can I see Curtis now?"

Dr. Groundling licked her lips. "It might be best if we waited for your husband."

"Now. Please."

"I want you to prepare yourself first."

"I'll be fine."

"Mrs. Steinar, if you would just give me a moment to explain."

Eva looked into the doctor's eyes. "Does he have a moment?"

Dr. Groundling didn't answer.

She didn't have to.

CHAPTER SIXTEEN

Haverford, Pennsylvania / 7:10 p.m.
They wanted him to die.

No one had said it out loud, of course, since that way lay lawsuits, but Eva knew that's what they hoped would happen the moment she'd walked into the narrow, eight by ten white room. If they didn't want him to die, they would have put him back in his own room, the one she and her husband were paying a premium for because it faced west and had a lovely view.

Dr. Groundling had said it was because of the severity of Curtis's sunburn and his body's inability to regulate his internal temperature. The sunburn had caused him to spike a fever of 103.8 degrees and they needed to put him into a sterile and controlled environment.

Blah, blah, blah.

It was just medical gobbledygook for wanting to pad his bill before they let him die.

They were just waiting it out. Vultures.

The only decent thing they'd done was to leave her alone with him. Her husband had walked over to the cafeteria on the rehabilitation side of the facility for coffee, or something. God only knew why he'd bothered to come in the first place since he hadn't spent more than ten minutes with Curtis since he arrived.

It was too hard, he told her, to watch him die.

After carefully folding the gooey tissue in half, Eva dropped it with the others on the top of the rolling tray table and pulled a new one from the box. They'd covered Curtis's face and arms in a thick layer of hydrocortisone cream, with aloe, for his sunburn, and tucked packs of cooling gel around his torso to bring his temperature down.

When she first walked in she'd tried to tell them that Curtis hated creams and lotions and tried to wipe it off. They stopped her that time, but they were gone now.

Eva carefully wiped the cream from under his left eye.

"You need to wake up now, Curtis," Eva said, dropping the saturated tissue and getting another. It didn't matter how hard she rubbed, she couldn't get it all. His forehead was greasy when she pressed the back of her fingers to it, but it was cooler. The fever was going down. "Do you hear me? You have to wake up. I need you to wake up."

"Hon?"

Eva looked up as her husband walked into the room. His collar was unbuttoned and his tie was loose and he wasn't holding a cup of coffee. Dr. Groundling walked in behind him.

"Hon," he said, "we have to talk."

★   ★   ★

Arvada, Colorado / 5:10 p.m.

Hell.

This was Hell and she wasn't alone.

You don't have to sit here.

Yes, I do.

Jessie stopped rocking when her sister got up from the desk and came around to the opposite side of the bed. Their father was downstairs with Carly's parents. They'd called him just after lunch and asked him to come over.

He called them on the house line three hours later. Abbie had grabbed the phone, probably thinking it was English Nigel or someone, while Jessie....

She couldn't remember what she'd been doing when Abbie walked in and told her, out loud, that they needed to get over to the Wingates' as soon as they could. She'd drive.

Jessie remembered Abbie pulling the Kia Soul they shared in next to their father's Escape and hearing Mrs. Wingate crying even before they were halfway up the front walk. She remembered feeling scared and helpless and hopeless so it was weird that she couldn't remember what she was doing when the call came.

Jessie leaned back and started rocking.

In the two hours she'd been there, Carly's breathing pattern had changed. No one seemed to notice, or, if they did, they didn't mention it or what it meant. But they didn't have to. Jessie had sat there and listened as each breath grew more shallow and the pauses between grew longer and longer. No one said Carly was dying, but that's what was happening.

And they were there to say goodbye.

Abbie had starting crying the moment they stepped into the house, but Jessie just walked up the stairs to Carly's room and sat down in the rocking chair like she'd done so many times since the accident. Crying wouldn't help.

She heard Abbie sniff from the doorway. "Why don't you come downstairs, just for a little while?"

Jessie shook her head. They weren't using their inside voices. It didn't seem right to keep anything inside.

"Do you know why they call it a deathwatch, Abbs?"

"Geeze, Jessie...."

"It's a vigil to protect the body from evil spirits." Jessie looked up at her sister. "Why don't you go down? We'll be okay."

Her sister left without saying another word.

Jessie continued rocking – *thump, bump...thump, bump* – until she realized how much it sounded like a heartbeat and stopped.

"Abbie's seeing this new guy. English. Seems nice, I guess. Maybe a little nerdy, but that's not a deal breaker. You wanna laugh? He was making a play for me, can you believe it? Abbs was so pissed off." Jessie laughed. "You should have seen his face when I told him I liked girls. A complete stranger. It was easy...just as easy as telling my dad. See, no more secrets."

Jessie looked at her friend's face and wondered if Carly knew she was lying.

"I should have told you first and I'm sorry I didn't. You were...*are* my best friend so I should have told you first. And shouldn't have, you know, kissed you like that. I didn't mean to scare you. I just thought...I don't know, maybe I thought you already knew. Dumb, huh?"

Jessie watched her friend's face. Carly hadn't opened her eyes or moved since they walked into her room, but maybe she knew Jessie was there and knew she wasn't alone.

God, she hoped Carly knew that.

Dying was hard enough without doing it alone.

Jessie pushed herself out of the chair and took her friend's hand. Carly's skin was warm and soft.

Freak! Don't touch me! Leave me alone!

Jessie took a deep breath but didn't let go.

"I was wrong to do that, Carly, I was wrong about a lot of things except one. I love you. I still love you. Good—"

Carly opened her eyes and stared at Jessie.

"Carly? Oh my God, hi. I was just…. Carly?"

Carly's eyes got bigger and bigger then rolled back into her head as her body jackknifed, went rigid, and collapsed back onto the mattress.

"Carly? *Carly!*"

Carly was staring at the ceiling. She wasn't breathing. No. *No.*

"*Dad!*"

★ ★ ★

Haverford, Pennsylvania / 7:15 p.m.

"No."

Her husband tried to take her hand but the sunburn cream they put on her made it slippery and he couldn't hold on. She pulled away easily.

"Eva, please. Think of Curtis."

It was the first time since Dr. Groundling told them that Eva looked at her husband and actually saw him. Up until that moment he'd been a blur.

"Curtis is the only person I have been thinking of. You're one to talk. I've been here every day and night. How dare you say something like that to me?"

"Eva, I only meant—"

"I know what you meant and I said no."

He tried to take her hand again. "It's time."

He'd blocked her into the corner next to the bed so she couldn't move without shoving past him. It was only the thought of touching him that stopped her.

"And what time is that, Allan?"

"You heard what Dr. Groundling told us. He's gone."

Eva glanced toward the doctor, Curtis's executioner, who'd had the sense to stay near the door. "No."

"Mrs. Steinar, I understand how upset you are—"

"You don't understand anything. Either of you. I said no. Get out and leave us alone."

Dr. Groundling walked to the opposite side of the bed and Eva tried to grab the bed's handrail but couldn't hold on. Damn cream.

"Mrs. Steinar, I'm so very sorry. We did everything we could for Curtis, but the fever caused a cascade effect. There's no brain function, Mrs. Steinar. The ventilator is only keeping his body alive; Curtis is gone."

Eva looked at the monitors on the wall behind the bed. "His heart's still beating."

"It is and might continue for a few minutes once we disconnect the ventilator, but it won't last."

"Then don't turn it off."

"Mr. Steinar signed the release."

Eva turned toward her husband, a broken man in a rumpled business suit with his tie hanging around his neck like a noose, and slapped him across the face. He finally backed up.

"Mrs. Steinar!"

"I don't care what he signed. You're not going to kill my son! He's a genius."

"He's dead, Eva!"

Eva pressed her hand against her son's beating heart. "Wake up, Curtis. You need to wake up now."

"Eva, stop it."

"Mrs. Steinar, please."

"Eva...."

Eva grabbed the front of Curtis's hospital gown with both hands. "*Curtis, wake up!*"

A pair of hands grabbed her arms and began to pull her away. It was the same orderly who'd helped her into the lobby.

"Will you take Mrs. Steinar to the family room, please?"

"*No!*" Eva tightened her grip.

"Let go, Mrs. Steinar, please."

"Curtis, wake up!"

"Eva, for God's sake, let him go."

"Curtis, listen to me. You have to open your eyes. Open your eyes.

If you don't they're going to turn off the machine that's helping you breathe. Curtis, they're trying to kill you! Open your eyes!"

"Please, Mrs. Steinar, this isn't helping."

"Eva!"

"*Open your eyes!*"

"Mrs. Steinar! Stop it!"

The orderly pulled and Curtis's gown slipped through her fingers. "*No! Let me go!*"

"I'm so sorry, Mrs. Steinar. I'm so sorry."

"He's just being stubborn!" Eva screamed as she was pulled backward toward the door. "Can't you see he's just being stubborn? He's a genius and geniuses do things on their own time. Curtis, open your eyes! Curtis, listen to me. *Open your eyes!*"

Eva felt the air leave her own lungs when Dr. Groundling nodded and the nurse turned off the machine.

★   ★   ★

Arvada, Colorado / 5:15 p.m.

Jess had tried to get his daughter to go downstairs with her sister to comfort Carly's mother, but didn't have the heart to demand it. Abigail had gotten hysterical, taking comfort instead of giving it, while Jessica's eyes stayed dry, her resolve firm.

"I have to stay here," she'd told him. "I have to be here for her."

Her words had humbled and strengthened him. Up until Richard had called him, everything had been only a proposal, an option, ethereal and abstract. Now it was real and he held it in his hand.

Keeping it low and out of sight, Jess watched his friend from across the room. He'd purposely chosen a spot farthest from the bed, waiting in the shadows until he was needed.

Carly's body twitched and took a rattling breath. Jessica stopped rocking and leaned forward. Richard reached down and took his daughter's hand.

"It won't be long now, will it, Jess?"

"No. Did you call Don?"

Richard nodded. Don Chase was an EMT and member of both Jess's congregation and U.C.U.A. chapter. The three of them, Jess,

Richard and Don, had discussed what would happen if Richard called. Don would get the call on his private number and make sure he didn't arrive too soon. Afterward he would verify time of death and fill out all the paperwork before transporting Carly's body directly to a U.C.U.A.-owned funeral home. The coroner, another member of the congregation, would meet them there and sign the death certificate.

It would all be very cut and dried, step by step.

Once she died and Jess administered the preventative.

Jess straightened his shoulders and watched his friend lean over to kiss his daughter's forehead.

"It's okay, Carly, we're ready," Richard whispered. "You can go. We'll be okay."

Carly took another ragged breath and stopped breathing. Jess stepped out of the shadows just as she gasped but kept walking until he reached the bed.

"Do you have the release?"

Richard looked at him and frowned. "What? Oh, yeah, it's down in the family room. I guess I should get it, shouldn't I?"

"I'll go with you and witness the signatures. Jessica, Mr. Wingate and I are going downstairs for a moment."

His daughter stopped rocking and nodded. "Okay."

He smiled at her and followed his friend out of the room.

"It's going to be all right, Jessica."

"I know."

★ ★ ★

But it wasn't.

When her father and Mr. Wingate left the room Jessie stood up and took Carly's hand. It felt cold. She stopped breathing twice while Jessie watched and when her breath finally came again it rattled.

"I wish we could trade places. I'm sorry." She kissed Carly's hand the same way Nigel had kissed hers. Carly stopped breathing... gasped....and started breathing again.

"Can you hear me, Carly? If you can, it's okay, like your dad said. You can go. I love you...we all love you, but you can go now."

Carly stopped breathing and didn't start again. It was so quiet

Jessie could hear her own heart pounding in her ears as she folded Carly's hands over her chest like Sleeping Beauty. Jessie closed her eyes.

"Dear God...the one who dwelled within this body is gone, and has taken with her a soul that was hers and hers alone. We who are left behind ask that her soul be kept only unto this body and not return. As it was and always shall be, one body, one soul for now and all eternity. Amen. I love you, Carly, and I always will."

Leaning forward, Jessie opened her eyes so she could memorize her beloved's face before she kissed it goodbye.

★   ★   ★

Haverford, Pennsylvania / 7:23 p.m.
...beep...beep......beep.........

They were even crueler than Eva could have ever imagined. After the respirator was turned off, Dr. Groundling had told the orderly to let her go so she could be there to watch her son die.

"I'm so very sorry, Mrs. Steinar."

"Please, Curtis."

............beep............beep..............beep..............

"Open your eyes!"

... ... b e e p ... ...
beep..

★   ★   ★

Arvada, Colorado / 5:26 p.m.
The lips that pressed against Jessie's suddenly parted in a scream as a pair of blue-gray eyes stared up at her. There was another scream from the doorway and her father's voice in her ear when he pulled her away.

"Jessica, what are you doing?"

Jessie could barely hear her father over Carly's screams...except it wasn't Carly's voice. The voice was strange, a child's voice.

"*Mama! Maaaaaam!*"

A Traveler's voice.

Jessie turned and grabbed the front of her father's shirt. "Kill it."

His eyes moved, darting to her then back to the thing on the bed. "What?"

"The imposter. Kill it. It took Carly's body."

He stepped back, taking her with him, and shook his head.

"*Mam! Mama!*"

"It's too late."

"No, it's not. We won't tell anyone. Kill it."

"No!"

Jessie turned and saw Carly's mother holding the imposter and cuddling it...comforting it.

"That's not Carly!" Jessie shouted, but when she tried to get back to the bed to show them her father grabbed her arm and pulled her toward the door. "No! Dad, that's not Carly, you have to kill it. They signed the paper, you have to."

Her father tightened his grip until she gasped in pain. "It's too late, Jessica. It would be murder."

Jessie blinked the tears away. "But it's an imposter."

"Don't cry," Mrs. Wingate said to the thing in her arms as she rocked it slowly back and forth. "Shh, shh, it's okay. You're okay. Shh."

Jessie turned back to her father. "Dad, please!"

But he didn't answer until he'd pulled her out of the room and into the hallway. "Why didn't you call me?"

"I...I was going to but I—"

"Don't. I saw what you were doing." He shoved her away from him then held up the filled syringe, pointing it toward the bedroom. "You did this. You could have stopped it. You should have called me the moment you knew Carly was dead. You let that thing steal Carly's body while you.... God forgive you, Jessica."

Jessie couldn't move.

"I could have prevented this. I could have sent her to paradise with body and soul as one, but you...." He lowered his arm. "Go home, Jessica, you've done enough damage."

"I heard...." Jessie turned and watched her sister creep toward them like a cat that knows a storm is coming. "Is it over?"

"Yes, Carly's dead." Their father looked at the syringe in his hand then threw it against the wall. The sudden stench of bleach made Jessie's eyes water.

What happened? Jessie, what's going on?

"Your sister's going home, Abigail. Give her your car keys."

"They're in my purse. Downstairs."

"Get the keys and go home, Jessica. Abigail, go back downstairs, I'll explain in a moment."

Jessie?

Go.

Jessie stared at their father as Abbie hurried away.

"Dad...please, I didn't do anything."

"That's right, you didn't do anything and now neither can I. May God forgive you because right now, I can't."

"Dad!"

He turned and walked away. "One body, one soul, Jessica. Go home."

Her sister was standing at the bottom of the stairs, holding her car keys.

Jessie, what happened?

Carly died.

Then why didn't Dad.... Oh, God, Jessie, no.

When her sister tried to hug her, Jessie pushed her away and grabbed the car keys.

Jessie, talk to me.

There's nothing to talk about, Carly died and a Traveler took her body and it's my fault! I could have stopped it, but I...I just wanted to say goodbye.

Her sister started to say something else as Jessie ran out of the house. This time she didn't have the energy to sing, this time she just screamed.

STAY OUT OF MY HEAD!

There were only a few cars on the street when Jessie backed the Kia down the driveway – cars filled with people coming home from work or the store or whatever who didn't know what had just happened in the Wingate house.

People who didn't know a new Traveler had been born.

And she'd been the midwife.

There was more traffic when Jessie turned right instead of left onto Wadsworth, heading north instead of home, and kept just under the speed limit until she turned onto Route 128 toward the

Rocky Mountain Metropolitan Airport. The *bing bing bing* of the fasten seat belt reminder kept her company as she accelerated into the unincorporated area.

There were few houses and even fewer streetlights along the stretch of road, but enough line-of-sight visibility for Jessie to see that there were no cops in the immediate vicinity. Yet. Every now and then, as Jessie blew through a traffic light or four-way-stop without so much as tapping the brake pedal, she'd see a bottle rocket or homemade firework go off in someone's yard.

It wasn't really dark enough yet for fireworks, the sky was still bright above the Front Range even if the ground was starting to get a little harder to see, but it was the same in her neighborhood. The Fourth of July was only a week and a half away, after all.

She was going to miss fireworks and hot dogs and Carly and going to a new U.C.U.A.-approved school in the fall and

Jessie?

— —

Jessie, please, talk to me.

— —

What happened? What's going on? Why is Dad so pissed?

Jessie concentrated on the road ahead.

The Foothill Highway was less than a mile ahead when she swerved the Kia onto an access road, kicking a rooster tail of dirt and gravel as the headlights sliced through the deepening shadows in front of her... only illuminating the giant cottonwood for a moment before Jessie slammed into it.

JESSICA FAITH PATHWAY
December 22, 2003 – June 22, 2021

★   ★   ★

Haverford, Pennsylvania / 7:36 p.m.

… … … … … … … … … … … … … … … … … … … …
beep……………………………………………………………………
…………………………beep…………………………………………
…………………………………………………………

....
....

The orderly stepped back as her husband put his arm around her.
"He's gone, Eva, he's at peace."
"Time of death, 19:36."

CURTIS ALLAN STEINAR
September 14, 2001 – June 22, 2021

★   ★   ★

"*No!* Open your eyes. *Open your eyes!*"
Jessie opened her eyes.
Oh God, not again.

PART THREE
BEGINNINGS

JUNE
CHAPTER SEVENTEEN

Haverford, Pennsylvania / 7:37 p.m.

"Dr. Groundling!"

"Jesus...."

"Someone get them out of here!"

Eva couldn't seem to catch her breath as someone, her husband or the orderly, tried to pull her out of the room.

"Mrs. Steinar, Mr. Steinar, please come with me."

"Turn the ventilator back on! Turn everything back!"

"What are his vitals?"

Eva jerked free and walked toward the bed. "Mrs. Steinar—"

"Leave her alone."

"Body temp...98.3."

"Remove the cooling packs and get a warming blanket in here *stat!*"

"Heart rate?"

"65. 83. 98...102. Holding steady at 102 b.p.m."

"Okay. Call Code Blue, let's make sure it stays that way. Curtis? Curtis...can you hear me? Open your eyes. Come on, that's it. Open your eyes. That's right, open...."

The voices stopped and suddenly only the sounds of rhythmic, measured breaths from the respirator and mechanical beeps filled the narrow white room. Eva stopped walking when she reached the bed.

"Cancel Code Blue. Call T Code."

A different voice echoed down the hall outside the room. "Terminate Code Blue. Code T to room 213. Repeat. Code T to room 213."

Dr. Groundling looked up at Eva and took a deep breath. "Mrs. Steinar...."

Eva shook her head. "I told you he'd wake up, didn't I?"

"Mrs. Steinar, listen to me, this isn't your son."

Eva brushed a damp lock away from Curtis's forehead and smiled. "Of course it is."

★ ★ ★

7:43 p.m.

It was so cold Jessie thought she was back under the ice and everything that had happened...everything that she had said and done...including the tree she ran into...were just parts of some horrible near-death nightmare and when she woke up everything would be back to normal and Carly would be okay and alive and—

"*It's too late.*"

"*No, it's not. We won't tell anyone. Kill it.*"

"*No!*"

"*You did this, it's your fault. You let that thing steal Carly's body while you defiled it.*"

"Heart rate's climbing, doctor."

"Push 6mg of...."

Jessie fell asleep.

★ ★ ★

10:06 p.m.

"Can you open your eyes?"

Jessie remembered the last time and only opened her eyes a crack. The voice beyond the glare chuckled and the light went away.

"I know," the voice said, "but I have to check your eyes. I promise I'll be quick. Open wide, please?"

Jessie cranked her eyelids up and tried not to squint as the beam of light blinded first one eye and then the other.

"Both pupils reactive to light." The light blinked off and Jessie watched the purple/yellow blobs bob and weave in front of a woman's face. Just like the last time. "I'm Dr. Groundling and I've been taking care of you. Do you know where you are?"

Jessie raised an eyebrow.

"Right, I just told you I was your doctor, so, silly question. Pretty obvious you're in a hospital, huh?"

Jessie raised the other eyebrow.

"Okay. Do you remember anything?"

She remembered everything: the sound like a bomb when the car hit the tree, the feel of the windshield shattering around her as she went through it, the pain, the taste of blood in her mouth, the cold swallowing her, the last words her father said to her.

Everything…she remembered everything.

Jessie licked her lips and nodded.

"That's good," the doctor said. "Now can you follow my finger with your eyes without moving your head?"

Jessie followed the finger from left to right and back again. The doctor smiled.

"You are doing great."

Where's my dad and sister? she asked, tried to ask, would have asked if she'd been able to a make a sound.

What the hell?

It took a few seconds for Jessie to work up enough saliva to swallow – God, her mouth was dry – and when she did it hurt like hell! Something was wrong, even getting up close and overly familiar with supposed safety glass shouldn't have made her throat hurt like that.

Trying to clear her throat, she discovered almost instantly, was a *bad* idea. It felt like there was something stuck in it, but when Jessie tried to raise her hand to find out what it was, the doctor took her hand and held it.

"Listen to me and stay calm. You were having trouble breathing so we had to perform a tracheotomy."

The cold Jessie felt earlier came back.

"You're still connected to a respirator, but now that you're awake why don't we see if you can breathe on your own? Do you want to try?"

Jessie's eyes went wide all by themselves. The doctor patted her hand.

"I know, it sounds scary, but I'll be right here monitoring you and if there's a problem I'll reconnect you. So, thumbs up or down?"

Jessie nodded, forgetting about the tube in her throat until she felt it scrape against her skin. Her stomach quivered. *Oh God. I'm going to puke through a hole in my neck.*

"Are you okay?"

Jessie put up her thumb.

"Okay, I'll disconnect you now."

Jessie looked around the room, searching for her father. She knew he would never forgive her for what she'd done, but he wouldn't just abandon her.

"May God forgive you because right now, I can't."

Would he?

No. He was probably out in the hall with Abbie, waiting until the doctor disconnected her.

"Ready?"

Jessie lifted her thumb higher and closed her eyes as the doctor reached for the tube.

"Now, this might feel a little funny."

The tube wiggled – *don't puke, don't puke* – and Jessie heard a soft *hiss* and opened her eyes.

"Okay, can you take a deep breath?"

Jessie did and felt the air come in through her neck. Oh God.

"Good, that's great," the doctor said and wiggled the tube again. *Please stop it, please stop it, please stop it.* "Fantastic, considering all that body's been through. How do you feel? Light-headed?" No. "Nauseous?" Jessie raised her thumb. "We'll get you something to settle your stomach. It's been through a bit too. Let's see how you do and if there aren't any problems, I'll schedule decannulation surgery to remove the tracheotomy tube and close the incision. It may take a few weeks to heal and your throat will still be a bit sore, but that will go away. Can I ask you a few questions?"

Jessie had a few of her own, like if her dad and sister were there, but when she opened her mouth nothing came out.

"Hold that thought," Dr. Groundhog – no, it wasn't Groundhog… it was Groundling – said and Jessie watched her pick up a folded gauze pad from the tray next to the bed.

"On the count of three I want you to take a deep breath, I mean really deep and hold it while I place this against the end of the tracheotomy tube. Then when I tell you to, I want you to exhale as hard as you can, okay? One. Two. Three. Big breath."

Jessie pulled air into her lungs via her neck. *Don't think about it. Don't think about it. Don't think about it.*

"And exhale."

Jessie grabbed the thin hospital blanket and felt the air whoosh out of her mouth. She would never take breathing for granted again.

"See how easy that was? Now, can you tell me your name?"

"Jezzzzz." *Oh God that hurts!*

"That bad, huh?"

Jessie nodded.

"Nurse, can I have the numbing spray, please? Thank you. Okay, open up. This might not taste very good, and your tongue might be a little sluggish, but it will help with the pain. Ready?"

Jessie opened her mouth and almost gagged as the fine mist coated the back of her throat. It didn't taste any better than it had after her *other* accident.

"Now swallow."

She did and the doctor was right. Her tongue felt like it belonged to someone else.

"Better?"

Jessie shrugged and both the doctor and nurse laughed.

"Okay, can you tell me your name?"

"Dezzika." The tracheotomy must have really done a job on her vocal cords, her voice sounded low and scratchy. "Gzz…Jzzzaaaka."

Dr. Groundling's smile tightened.

"Jessica?" the doctor repeated and Jessie nodded. "Jessica what?"

Jessie took a deep breath – God, she loved breathing – and concentrated. "D…Jah…Jezzzeeka fah…faytha pat…way. Jezz-i-ca Fffat-tha Paff…Pa-tha-way. Pathway." Whew.

"Jessica Faith Pathway, is that right?" Jessie nodded. "Did you get that, nurse?"

"Yes."

"Mmm my f-fader n sssder?"

The doctor turned back to Jessie. "What?"

"Mmmeye fadder n sssser."

"Your father and sister? You want your father and sister?"

Jessie took another deep breath and nodded.

The doctor's smile flattened a bit, but she nodded as she took something else off the tray.

"I'll have someone find out, but right now I think you need to rest." It was a syringe, much smaller than the one her father had smashed against the wall. "We'll talk later, okay...Jessica?"

Jessie raised her thumb as the rest of her body went weightless and began to float away.

★   ★   ★

Broomfield, Colorado / 8:06 p.m.

"Are you ready, Mr. Pathway?"

It was so ingrained in his own image of himself that Jess almost corrected the woman, not Mr., *Reverend* Pathway. He was standing in a hospital room about to look at his daughter's mangled body and some part of his brain was concerned about titles.

Dear God, what did that say about him?

"Mr. Pathway?"

Jess nodded and took a deep breath that he tried to hold as the doctor pulled back the sheet covering her face. It was no use, it escaped in a sound he'd never heard before, let alone made. The only thing he recognized on her was her hair. They must have washed it because there wasn't any blood in it.

She looked like a broken doll with some of the pieces missing.

"Oh, my God."

His legs buckled and if the doctor hadn't caught him he would have fallen on top of her.

"I'm so sorry, Mr. Pathway," the doctor said and put the sheet back over her. "I'm so very sorry."

Jess got his feet back under him and stepped away from the gurney. It wasn't as if he hadn't known what to expect; he'd already spoken with the police officers who'd been first on the scene.

"Do you know if your daughter had taken anything? Was she depressed about something?"

"Yes, she was depressed, her friend had just died and I...I...."

I blamed her.

The police estimated Jessica had been going close to 80 mph when she hit the tree. There was nothing left of the car. They were very sorry, so very sorry.

"If it's any consolation, Mr. Pathway, it's more than likely that she died instantly upon impact. There wouldn't have been any pain."

"Thank you. Her body...." Jess realized he was staring at the floor at his feet and not the gurney. "Is there any chance.... My daughter was a True Born."

"You don't have to worry, Mr. Pathway, the damage was too severe."

Jess closed his eyes and wept in relief.

"I'll leave you alone with her."

"Thank you. Could you.... Her sister's in the lobby. And I...."

"I'll sit with her," the doctor said, walking to the door. "One body, one soul."

"One body, one soul. Thank you."

Jess waited until he heard the door close before opening his eyes. When he did all he saw was a shape beneath a pure white sheet. It could have been anyone under there and that made it easier to do what had to be done.

The doctor had said there'd been too much damage, and maybe there was, but he couldn't take the chance, not after their last conversation.

As Jess walked back to the gurney, he reached into his coat pocket and took out the syringe. It was lucky he always carried extras in the car. He left the sheet in place as he turned the head to one side, only pulling it back enough to expose her still perfect, undamaged ear.

"I'm so sorry, baby. I shouldn't have spoken to you like that and I didn't mean it. I love you, sweetheart."

Jess inserted the needle and slowly injected the bleach into his daughter's brain.

"The one who dwelled within this body is gone and has taken with her a soul that was hers and hers alone. We who are left behind ask that her soul be kept only unto this body and not return. As it was and always shall be, one body, one soul for now and all eternity. One body." Taking a deep breath, he withdrew the needle and covered her. "One soul. Now and forever. Amen."

CHAPTER EIGHTEEN
June 23

Haverford, Pennsylvania / 4:32 a.m.

"Where's my dad?" Her voice sounded so low and grumbly she could barely recognize it.

The face looking down at her was young and male, just Abbie's type.

"I don't know, but we can find out. Hi, I'm Dr. Leader and I'll be your anesthesiologist."

The anesthesiologist reached over and touched the tube that was still sticking out of Jessie's throat. They'd capped the end so she could talk – and breathe normally through her nose, thank God – but decided to leave it in. Just in case. It still turned Jessie's stomach whenever she accidentally brushed against it.

"They'll be taking you down to surgery in a few minutes to remove your trach tube, so the next time you see me will be in the OR."

Jessie nodded as carefully as she could and tried to sit up.

"Hey, whoa, pardner, you've already been prepped, so don't be pulling out your IVs, okay? Besides, you have nothing to worry about, it's a very minor procedure and I'll be right there monitoring every breath you take and making sure you have a pleasant sleep. Unless you'd like to stay awake and watch."

Jessie shook her head. "Sleep."

"Sounds like a good plan. Okay. Remember the next time you see me I'll be in a mask. A little nervous?"

Jessie nodded again.

"Well, you're allowed to be, but only a little. Now, I'm just going to give you a little something to take the edge off. Ready?"

Jessie felt something warm race up her arm and the world got fuzzy and comfortable.

* * *

4:43 a.m.
"Hey there."

Jessie pried her eyelids apart.

"See...I told you I'd be the one in the mask. Didn't I tell you that would take the edge off? And if you thought that was good, you'll love this." Jessie felt a slight tug on the inside of her left elbow, "Now, count backward for me from one hundred."

"100...99...98...9—"

* * *

5:32 a.m.
"And...you're back. Can you open your eyes?"

Jessie was getting really sick of people asking her that.

She opened her eyes. The face looking down at her now was female and not so young, but nice. She was wearing a green scrub cap.

"How do you feel? It's okay, try and say something."

Jessie swallowed. "Hurts."

"Good! I mean, it's not good that it hurts, but just trust me, it's all good. Okay, you can go back to sleep now."

"Okay."

* * *

6:04 a.m.
"Jessica. Jessica, can you open your eyes for me, please?"

Jessie groaned and gave them one eye, but it seemed enough.

"Sleepy."

"I'm sure you are, but I need to know how you feel. Remember what I told you about the numbers?"

Jessie frowned. Numbers?

"Okay, I guess you were still a little out of it. Pain scale, one for no pain, ten for a lot. Are you in any pain and if so how bad is it?"

Jessie held up three fingers.

"Good. Now, do you think you could swallow for me?"

Jessie swallowed and flashed all five fingers three times.

The nurse laughed. "Well, your reflexes are good. You'll still be a little raw for the next few days, but once the incision heals you won't even notice the scar and…."

* * *

6:14 a.m.

"Hi. How're you feeling?"

It was a completely different face: male, about her dad's age, with a beard.

Jessie blinked awake and held up two fingers.

"Great. Okay. Go back to sleep."

Jessie closed her eyes.

* * *

6:26 a.m.

Jessie opened her eyes and jumped. The new nurse had ash-blond hair and hazel eyes and looked like Carly. And for a moment Jessie's heart skipped a beat until she remembered that Carly was dead and her body stolen because Jessie had kissed her instead of calling her dad.

She should have called him, but he should have killed it.

It wasn't as if it was a real person.

Jessie tried to sit up and felt something tighten around her arms.

"Hey, hey, what's wrong? It's okay, calm down. You're fine, just try to relax. Sometimes patients have a reaction to the anesthetic. It gives them nightmares."

Jessie blinked. It wasn't a nightmare. It was her fault, all her fault.

And she couldn't even manage to kill herself.

"Where's my dad?"

The nurse shook her head. "I don't know, but how do you feel?"

Jessie lifted two fingers then touched them to her throat. All she could feel was a thick bandage.

"All gone and in a few months you won't even notice the scar. Do you think you feel up for a visitor?"

A little of the fear she'd felt earlier came back. "My dad?"

"No. It's a very nice lady who works with some of our special patients. She's not here but she will be soon and she'd like to talk to you, if that's okay."

Jessie shrugged and the nurse smiled.

"You'll like her and she'll help you figure things out about... you know."

Jessie nodded. Oh, she knew all right...she knew that the very nice lady who worked with the 'special patients' had to be a shrink who wanted to talk about why Jessie'd tried to kill herself. Maybe her father wasn't there because he was busy signing papers to have her committed to a loony bin. Jessie tried to swallow.

"Can I have some water?"

"Might be a little too soon. Anesthetic can also give you the tummy wobbles. I can get you some ice chips or would you rather have a Popsicle?"

"Popsicle."

"Kid after my own heart. Any preference on flavor?"

"Cherry."

"Okay." The nurse walked to the end of the bed and stopped. "Is it okay if the lady talks to you?"

Jessie nodded.

"Great. Okay, hang on and I'll be right back with your cherry Popsicle."

The nurse left through a curtain that fluttered open just enough for Jessie to see her reflection in the room's sliding glass door.

She screamed, inside and out.

ABBIE!

★　　★　　★

Arvada, Colorado / 4:26 a.m.

JESSIE!

The scream followed Jess into consciousness and for a moment all he could do was sit up and try to remind himself it was only a nightmare and that he was awake – sitting bolt upright on the couch, disoriented, heart pounding and staring bug-eyed into the semidarkness, but awake.

Jess took a deep breath.

He didn't know how long he'd been asleep, or even remember falling asleep; all he remembered was helping Abigail to bed and then standing in the hall and not being able to move until her sobs ended and she fell asleep. He would have stayed like that all night, guarding her, his only child now, if there hadn't been so much to do, so he went downstairs and started making phone calls.

Not to his parents or his wife's; he'd tell them in person later that morning, but he'd left messages for the church secretary and at the funeral home that had handled his wife's service, and told those friends he thought needed to know.

But not the Wingates.

Jessica was dead because of them.

Jess rubbed his eyes as the room brightened and glanced down at the small flashing light on his cell phone. Someone had returned his call. Was that what he thought he heard? The phone's ring getting scrambled in his head to sound like a—

"*Jessie!*"

It wasn't a nightmare, it was Abigail.

Jess barked his shin against the side of the coffee table as he ran from the living room and took the stairs two at a time, not feeling the pain until he was standing in the doorway of his daughters' room.

His daughter's room.

Abigail was standing next to her bed, hair disheveled, wild-eyed, reaching for him. Jessica's bed was empty.

"*Dad!* Dad, it's Jessie!"

Jess's leg throbbed and almost buckled under him when his daughter ran to him, sobbing against his chest.

"It's Jessie."

Jess pulled her closer, stroked her hair. "I know, baby, I know."

"I heard her. She's screaming, Dad."

God, help us. "She's not in pain anymore, baby, Jessica's dead."

She looked up at him. "No, she's not. I can still hear her screaming. Jessie's not dead, she's alive!"

CHAPTER NINETEEN

Haverford, Pennsylvania / 8:35 a.m.
Millie said a small prayer and smoothed down the front of her blouse before opening the door. It was only three flights, hardly enough to put a hitch in her breathing, let alone mess her up any, but she'd seen the looks folks gave her every time she walked out of a stairwell, be it one flight or ten, instead of taking the elevator. The new time might be filled with marvels she'd never have imagined in the before time, but stepping inside a metal box that carried folks up and down like a monkey on a stick just to save a little shoe leather seemed like pure foolishness.

Of course, she might have thought different if she'd taken to the gaudy, narrow, pinch-toed shoes modern fashion claimed every woman couldn't live without. One flight of stairs in shoes like that and her feet would have been as bloody as if she'd walked across a field of cotton barefoot.

Millie was perfectly happy with her comfortable lace-up shoes, thank you very much. They might not be as pretty as some, but their style was familiar and the leather so soft it made her feel like she was walking on clouds.

The metal door closed behind Millie with a thud that was just loud enough to catch the attention of the nurse sitting at the desk.

"Ms. B.!"

"Hey, Mrs. Huff."

Visiting hours wouldn't start for another half hour or so but visiting hours and time on a clock didn't mean a hill of beans. Whenever they needed her Millie came a'calling. It'd taken two years of hard work and a whole lot of getting her head to rethink everything she'd thought of as gospel in the old times, but all the troubles and tribulations had been worth it the first time she helped a Newcomer step out of the old time and into the new. Getting certified as a Transitional Therapy

Counselor had been the second most proud moment of her life right after becoming a teacher in the before time.

The first time was a little boy, drowned when he got swept into a storm drain, and a soldier who died in a field called Flanders screaming for his mama. That had been so hard Millie'd almost turned around and ran from the room, but she didn't.

The little boy's family had been more than willing to take in the young soldier. They still sent Millie emails about how well he was doing, with attached pictures. He was growing up to be a fine young man, they said, but he still had nightmares sometimes.

But they all did, all the Newcomers, Millie included. Sometimes the before times just wouldn't stay where it belonged.

The morning nurse, Mrs. Huff, closed the book she was reading and gave her a sad look. Millie could understand that. One of her own greatest joys was to crawl beneath the sheets at night or find a nice quiet spot during the day and lose herself in a good story. It always made her a little sad when she had to stop.

"Oh, Ms. B., when are you going to get a cell phone?"

Millie shrugged and shook her head. It wasn't a new query, seemed like everybody asked her the same thing, and she could have told them the truth, which was never, but a shrug and head shake seemed to work just as good. Truth was that while she'd gotten real good at things like television and computers and driving automobiles – and she loved driving almost as much as reading – and even though the wonder of talking to folks miles and miles away would probably never get old, Millie liked having time to herself when no one could get hold of her. She'd come from a before time that hadn't allowed her any privacy and she wasn't about to give up an ounce of it now.

"It would make things easier," the nurse said, "especially for you. I called the school to tell them we had to reschedule your appointment."

Millie felt the cool hospital air settle down over her shoulders. "Did something happen to the Newcomer? Did something happen during the operation?"

It would have also made things easier on her if the hospital could do more than just get the Newcomer's name, but protocol only required them to notify every Transition Counselor within a twenty-mile radius after a confirmed arrival and provide copies of whatever medical records they had on the donor body. Since Millie had worked with the hospital before, they always called her directly.

"No," the nurse said, "the decannulation was picture-perfect and there's no sign of post-op infection...."

Millie took a deep breath. "But?"

"The Traveler...."

Millie and the others preferred the name Newcomer, and she'd mentioned that to nearly every medical man and woman she met, but they never seemed to remember, just like they never seemed to remember to use the Newcomer's name. Maybe that was because a name made them too real.

It was a hard thing for some people to learn, almost as hard as learning to use a computer, but if she could do it, dammit, so could they.

"Jessica, right?"

The nurse caught on and nodded. "Jessica accidentally saw a reflection and became agitated to the point that one of the sutures ripped out. The Trave— We had to sedate Jessica and I'm afraid... she's still asleep. Did anyone tell you anything about...her?"

There was something in the way the nurse paused that tickled the hairs at the back of Millie's neck.

All they'd told her was the name and the time of awakening, and Millie preferred it that way. She'd learn more about the donor if she needed to, but for right now her main concern was for the Newcomer.

Reaching into the large toting sack that never left her side, Millie took out the notebook she'd used for scribbling notes.

"Only that her name is Jessica Faith Pathway...isn't that just lovely?...and she seems young and responded well to verbal commands. Her vision and hearing tested at one hundred per cent, but she was having some trouble speaking because of a problem with the donor?"

The nurse nodded. "There was an injury to the neck."

Millie took a pen from the cup on the desk and wrote that down. "Was that the cause of death?"

"It helped."

"Poor thing. We couldn't find a death record for Miss Jessica Faith Pathway in any of the CTPS database records, but we'll keep looking. Did she give you any idea of when she passed?"

"No, and we're not supposed to ask," the nurse said. "That's your job."

"That it is," Millie said and took a pen from the holder on the desk and held the tip above the page. "So when do you think I can come back?"

The nurse glanced at the notebook. "And they didn't say anything about the donor?"

"No. What aren't you telling me, Mrs. Huff?"

The nurse looked up and sighed. "How much time do you have, Ms. B.?"

"As much as the good Lord'll give me."

"Well, I don't want your trip to be a total waste and this way you won't be surprised when Jessica wakes up and you come back." Pushing back from the desk, the nurse stood up and pulled a medical chart from the holder. "The donor's file. You need to read it. I think Conference Room A is empty."

Millie closed her notebook and slipped it back into her tote before taking the chart. It was thicker than most and heavier, even with the nurse still hanging on to it. Millie cocked her head to one side.

"Look at the name, Ms. B.," the nurse said, and let go.

Millie opened the chart cover and only needed to read the patient's name. She closed it, cradled the chart against her chest and nodded.

"Now there's a fly, isn't it?"

"Has this…ever happened before?"

"Stands to reason it must have." Somewhere. Keeping a tight grip on the file, Millie put the pen back into its holder and backed away from the desk. "Thank you, Mrs. Huff. Conference Room A, you said."

The nurse nodded and sat down. "And think about getting a cell phone."

"Oh, I will think about it, Mrs. Huff," Millie said as she turned and began walking away. "I surely will."

Millie passed another set of doctors and two nurses, all of whom smiled and nodded as she walked down the hall to the conference room. Room A was small and cozy, the walls painted a soft yellow and decorated with pictures of summer fields and flowers. The white table might have been a bit too large for the room, but the chairs looked comfortable enough to keep a person's backside content no matter how long a meeting lasted.

After closing the door behind her, Millie took the chair farthest from the door and opened the chart. She hadn't even gotten through the first page when there was a knock and the door opened. A young woman wearing a bright green apron over a pink top and white slacks walked in holding a tray.

"Ms. B.? Nurse Huff thought you might like these." The girl smiled and put down a tall green-and-white cup of steaming black coffee and a plate the size of a serving platter piled with two enormous cinnamon rolls, dripping icing. "To keep up your strength."

"Thank you." Millie smiled back at the girl. "And thank Mrs. Huff for me."

"I will. Enjoy!"

Millie leaned back and looked at the bounty before her.

She had a feeling it wasn't going to be enough.

★   ★   ★

Eva folded her hands across the purse in her lap and made every effort to appear she was hanging on each and every word Mr. Dahms, the authorized representative of the Coalition for Traveler Protective Services (CTPS), was saying.

If she didn't listen and nod at the appropriate times, she knew she'd never be able to bring her son home.

Everything up to this point, after introductions had been made and Dr. Groundling excused herself from the proceedings, had focused on the list of requirements, obligations, care and rights that were guaranteed to each *Traveler*, regardless of race, gender, creed or past servitude, under the law.

Nothing was said about her rights as the *potential caregiver*.

At least she appeared to be paying attention to what the representative was saying; her husband wasn't even trying. He'd been in the same position since taking the chair next to hers: slumped forward, elbows resting on his knees, hands clasped between them, and staring at the floor in what he must have thought conveyed the perfect picture of a mourning father.

When Mr. Dahms asked them if they thought they were strong enough, emotionally, to handle the situation, Eva'd had to nudge a response out of her husband.

"What? Oh, yeah. Yeah."

"We can do this," Eva said. "It will be a blessing."

She wondered if that had been a bit too much when Mr. Dahms frowned.

"I won't lie to you, Mr. and Mrs. Steinar," he said, "it will be hard living with and caring for a stranger...a complete stranger who only looks like your son."

"I understand," Eva said. "Curtis is.... Curtis was a genius, Mr. Dahms, and I know this subject fascinated him."

This seemed to be exactly what the representative wanted to hear, even though it was a complete and utter lie. She didn't know how Curtis had felt about the Travelers or even if he knew they existed. He was a genius and people, even people who came back from the dead, probably wouldn't have interested him.

Curtis was dead.

Her son was dead, but if the Traveler inside his body came back then it stood to reason Curtis could too. He was a genius – not only could he come back, but he'd figure out a way to come back to his own body.

All she had to do was keep his body safe until he returned.

"There is nothing harder than losing a loved one, especially a child. You have my deepest condolences." Mr. Dahms opened the file that he'd set down on the desk when the meeting started and took out a folded pamphlet, holding it out toward them. Eva nudged her husband until he sat up and took the pamphlet, then handed it to her.

The cover showed a beach at sunset with a lone figure, silhouetted by the setting sun, staring out to sea, an upturned sand pail at its feet. Eva couldn't tell if the figure was male or female, but perhaps that was intentional. The initials CTPS were written in script in the lower right-hand corner.

"This will give you a brief listing of the options and services available both to you and the Traveler, including a twenty-four-hour help line. Many of our Homecare Families find it extremely helpful to be able to talk to an advisor during those first few critical days of adjustment. Has the hospital talked to you about grief counseling?"

"Yes," Eva said. Her husband nodded.

"Please consider taking advantage of that service, it will help. May I ask how old your son was, Mrs. Steinar?"

"Nineteen. He'll be twenty in August."

Maybe he'd come back then; he always loved his birthday parties.

Mr. Dahms was nodding.

"Did you say something?"

"Yes, I said that since eighteen is considered the age of majority," he said, "Curtis is an adult in the eyes of the law. We don't have the chronological age of the Traveler yet, but your son's age *can* be taken into consideration if you chose, at any time, to relinquish your responsibilities as stipulated under the Travelers Act of 2019, Section 5-C, which would immediately give full control back to the Traveler. Do you understand?"

They both nodded.

"Good. Now, I want to make this last point clear and assure you that even if you agree and sign the documents, we take the emotional well-being and need of the bereaved into just as much consideration as we do the welfare of the Traveler."

Her husband wiped his eyes with a tissue. "I don't understand."

"It means we can bring him back," Eva said. "Isn't that right, Mr. Dahms?"

"Exactly."

Her husband shifted in his chair. "Where would he go?"

The man handed her husband another full-color pamphlet. This one showed a bird's-eye view of a sprawling campus set among rolling autumn hills. It reminded Eva of the college brochures she'd ordered every year for Curtis.

"This is Initium Novum just outside New Hope," Mr. Dahms said. "*Initium Novum* means New Beginnings and is a residential, fully accredited institution of learning that provides the *adult* Traveler with the skills he or she will need in order to fully adjust to their new environment."

"What if they're just kids...inside, I mean?"

"We integrate them into a general school population. Children are resilient."

Eva nodded. But not geniuses.

Her husband was studying the pamphlet. "How big a place is it? It looks huge."

"Initium Novum has fifty-three resident units, each capable of accommodating between one hundred and two hundred occupants, a staff of 2,240 and a number of day students, but I'm afraid I don't have the current number. The original building and land was bequeathed to us by a patron."

"A Traveler?" Eva asked.

"Her family, yes."

"Of course."

"And they…the Travelers live there?" her husband asked.

"Yes."

"For how long?"

"There is no time limit, Mr. Steinar. They can stay as long as they need to, although we've had quite a few leave us after completing a degree. We also have a network of off-campus residential facilities throughout Bucks and Berks Counties should a Traveler desire to leave the campus but remain apart from society."

Her husband handed her the pamphlet.

"Looks nice," he said. "Doesn't it, Eva?"

"Yes, but we'll be taking him home."

"But this might be something to consider."

Eva handed the pamphlet back to the representative. "He's coming home."

"But he's not Curtis, Eva."

Eva turned to her husband with tears in her eyes. Curtis would have known she wasn't really crying, that the sobs catching in her throat weren't real, but he was a genius and could see through obvious manipulation. He hadn't taken after his father.

She let a tear fall. "I know, but it's someone's son."

Mr. Dahms stood up. "Perhaps I should leave you two alone for a moment."

"No, no…Eva's right, it's…he's somebody's son and he's alone, but—" Her husband had to clear his throat twice. Eva sniffed. "Curtis suffered from schizophrenia and, um, was on medication. What are the chances he, the Traveler, will be the same way? Not that we wouldn't take him, I mean, but…."

Mr. Dahms sat down. "I'm afraid I don't know. You'll have to ask Dr. Groundling about that. I'm sorry."

"Of course."

Eva took her husband's hand. "But we can take him home, can't we?"

Mr. Dahms smiled. She was making his job easy. "Yes, once Dr. Groundling releases him."

She returned the smile. "Can we see him?"

"Soon, Mrs. Steinar. Very soon," Mr. Dahms said and stopped smiling. "There is one other thing I should mention about *him*...."

★   ★   ★

9:42 a.m.

Jessie stared at the ceiling square directly over her head without blinking. She'd been staring at it or the one next to it or the one on the other side of it since she woke up, because that's all she was able to do.

Stare.

She couldn't move because they'd strapped her to the bed to keep her from pulling out her IVs. They said. All she could do was stare at the ceiling tiles and keep quiet, because if she opened its mouth she would start screaming and they'd knock her out again.

But she'd see it...the reflection in the glass of a boy about her age, thin, almost bony, his face all red and greasy, with brown hair slicked back and green eyes.

Her eyes staring back at her from someone else's face.

Her eyes, but not her body.

Oh God.

Jessie squeezed her eyes shut until all she could see were reverse-color ceiling tiles, white dots on a dark gray background melting beneath flashes of yellow and purple.

Someone came in and stopped next to the bed. She could feel them watching her. Jessie kept her eyes closed and pretended to be asleep until they left. They kept coming in to make sure she hadn't somehow clawed apart the restraints and gotten away.

Or killed herself.

Again.

Jessie opened her eyes and made the mistake of licking her lips before she remembered they weren't hers. She had to swallow hard to keep from puking whatever the body had eaten last. Not, if the reflection was accurate, that its original owner had been much of an eater.

God, I really am one of them.

It took two more swallows before Jessie felt safe to lift the head until she had a more or less unobstructed view of the body.

Not that there was much to see.

A blanket covered the body from the broad, flat plain of the chest – she never thought she'd feel sorry about losing the 32Bs – to the twin mountain peaks – God, are those the feet? – at the far end of the bed. The body was skinny and long...very long. Jessie couldn't tell what that might mean in height but she knew it was taller than she was.

Had been.

She'd always wanted to be tall, but not like this.

Turning the head, Jessie lifted the right arm as far as the padded restraint would allow. Big hand, long fingers, long, thin, hairy arm, burned to the color of rare meat and glistening under some kind of sunburn cream. Jessie recognized the smell.

The neck was beginning to complain, but Jessie ignored it and curled the fingers of the hand into a fist. She could feel the short, smooth nails dig into the skin of the palm as she tightened it.

Not her skin.

Not her nails.

Not her hand.

But would it be her blood if the nails broke the skin?

"Oh, you're awake."

The head hit the pillow as a nurse in blue scrubs walked over to the bed and smiled.

"How do you feel?"

"I came back." The voice almost sounded like hers but not really. Not her voice. Not her body. Not her life.

The nurse's smile went straight. "Did someone talk to you?"

Jessie raised the hand closest to the nurse. "Help me?"

Reaching over the bedrails, she took the hand.

"What do you need?" the nurse said, then gasped when Jessie closed the hand and squeezed. "Stop it. You're hurting me."

"One body. One soul."

"What?"

Jessie made the hand squeeze harder. "Kill me."

"Ow! Stop, you're hurting me! Code Gray! Code Gray!"

A man in green scrubs came in and grabbed the hand, prying the fingers back, gently but firmly. One of the knuckles cracked and Jessie yelped more at the sound than the sensation. It didn't hurt, but she felt it.

The man pressed the hand back to the mattress and held it there. "Stop it. Come on, just relax."

Jessie filled the lungs and let go. "Kill me! *Kill me!* Please. I don't want this! I'm supposed to be dead." Jessie looked at the nurse. She was cradling her injured hand against her chest. "Please, kill me."

The orderly or doctor or whatever he was put most of his weight against the hand as he reached over Jessie's head and pressed a button on the wall. "Code Gray, Room 213."

A moment later other faces rushed toward the bed and the room filled with voices layered one on top of the other.

"1.5mg bentazepam. *Stat.*"

"Do you have him?"

"Her."

"Kill me!"

"Calm down. It's okay."

"Somebody talked to him."

"One body."

"Her name's Jessica."

"One soul!"

"Jessica, it's okay, you're going to be okay."

A familiar warmth raced up Jessie's arm and the room began to fade. "Please...." *Kill me.*

⋆   ⋆   ⋆

Millie set the empty plate down on the station's raised counter and handed back the chart. She'd finished off the coffee when she was only halfway through.

The nurse took the chart and put it back in its holder.

"Well?"

Millie nodded. "Well. Is Jessica Faith awake yet?"

The nurse took a little too long to answer. "I think it might be best if you came back later."

172 • P.D. CACEK

A part of Millie wanted to plant herself in front of the desk and not budge until she got to speak to the Newcomer, but the other part was more than a little relieved. This Newcomer wasn't like any of the others she'd met and Lord knows she wasn't ashamed to admit that she was worried. She was more than worried about what she was going to say to Miss Jessica Faith and how she was going to say it. A wrong word or sideways glance and she could cause more harm than help. Being given more time to think about it was a blessing.

Millie smiled at the nurse.

"That'll be fine, but do you think I could make a call before I left, Mrs. Huff? I'm afraid it's to California."

The nurse didn't so much as raise an eyebrow as she punched a button on the desk phone/intercom and handed Millie the receiver.

"That won't be a problem," she said and stood up. "Take your time. I have to check on the patients."

Millie punched in the eleven-digit cipher without thinking about it. Memorizing numbers had come almost as easy as learning to drive.

"Millie!" The voice on the other end of the telephone line yawned, but otherwise sounded honestly happy.

"Oh, Lord, I forgot about the time. I'm sorry I woke you."

"Not a problem, not a —" yawn "— problem. I need to get up in a few minutes anyway." Millie suddenly heard the sound of an alarm going off in the background. "See, what did I tell you? I'm up. What's up, kid?"

"It's my newest case, Dr. Ellison. I think I might need your help."

CHAPTER TWENTY

June 24

Phoenixville, Pennsylvania

"What are you *doing*, Eva?"

Eva pressed her hands against the small of her back as she stood up and ignored the snap-crackle-pop sounds her spine made as it realigned itself. She wasn't sure a fifty-eight-year-old spine should sound like breakfast cereal, but she had worked it a bit more than it was normally used to.

Glancing at the atomic clock on Curtis's desk, she laughed out loud. It was after five and she'd started on the room right after lunch. No wonder her spine had snapped, crackled and popped.

"Eva, I asked you a question."

Eva let her hands fall to her side and turned. "Brain surgery, Allan, I'm performing brain surgery. What does it look like I'm doing?"

Her husband filled the doorway as he surveyed the room. He must have just gotten home from work because he was still wearing a grimy company polo shirt. God, how could he ever have helped produce a genius like Curtis?

"I thought we decided to get new things."

"Why would we do that? These are perfectly good."

"But they look just like…. I thought we decided it was just going to be a guest room."

"And it is," Eva said, "but our guest is a young man who might like to have young men's things around him. And you know Curtis was always tinkering with one thing or another."

Her husband walked into the room slowly, looking at everything as if he expected something to jump out at him.

"But it's not…. Eva, you heard what Mr. Dahms said. This…the Traveler isn't a boy…inside. It's…. *Her* name's Jessica."

Eva walked over to the desk and sat down, suddenly exhausted. "Well, we'll deal with that when the time comes, but regardless I'm sure *our guest* will love this room as much as Curtis did. Of course I had to buy a *few* new things, mattress, bedding, towels, that sort of thing, oh, and new underwear, of course."

She'd put all of Curtis's undershirts and briefs into a plastic bin and hidden it in the back of her craft closet. She'd bring them out when Curtis came back; she couldn't stand the idea of someone...*something* else wearing them.

"But that's all. We know everything else will fit."

Her husband stopped just short of the middle of the room. "I'm having second thoughts, Eva. I don't know if I can handle it."

"Well, you'll have to."

"Why?"

"Because if you don't I'll kill myself."

He stared at her for a moment, then turned and walked out of the room.

Good.

Standing, Eva walked to the bed and smoothed down the dark blue spread. She'd bought it to replace the one Curtis had stained with some kind of chemical, but knew her husband hadn't noticed.

Just like he hadn't noticed Curtis's genius.

"There," she said, swatting out a stray wrinkle, "good as new."

Eva walked to the middle of the room and began turning in a slow circle, surveying the room. It was perfect, just the same. Curtis would be upset if anything was out of—

She looked at the clock again. 5:42.

"Shoot!"

Eva rushed out the door and reached their bedroom just as her husband was in the process of peeling off his sweat-damp undershirt.

"Hurry up and take a shower," she said. "We can have dinner out."

He turned to look at her, frowning. "I'd rather not."

"Well, I just thought it'd be easier since the caregivers' seminar starts at seven and Doylestown's almost an hour's drive."

Her husband sat down on the bed hard enough to make the box spring creak. "Oh, hell, is that tonight?"

"Why would I say it if it wasn't tonight? Get in the shower and wear something nice…one of your *good* shirts and slacks. I'll use the hall bath."

She'd already picked out her outfit, the midi wrap dress, green with white polka dots, that Curtis once told her he liked.

"Oh, and I don't think you need to wear a tie. It's supposed to be casual."

★　　★　　★

Haverford, Pennsylvania

Jessie?

Jessie stopped counting and closed her eyes. They'd moved her while she'd been asleep. She knew that even though the room looked the same. Except for the ceiling. The squares were bigger and the holes were smaller. She hadn't been asleep for seven hundred and sixty-eight holes.

Jessie, please?

Jessie opened her eyes.

I heard you, Jessie. I heard you scream.

Jessie focused on the tiny space between two holes directly above her. She wasn't there. She was somewhere else. She was in a white field, under a white sky, surrounded by nothing, thinking of nothing, being nothing.

Nothing filled her and the voice inside her head got smaller.

Jessie.

And smaller

Jessie.

And smaller

Jessie.

Until it disappeared.

…

She closed her eyes.

★　　★　　★

Arvada, Colorado

He didn't know what to do with his hands.

All morning and well into the afternoon Jess made sure they were filled and useful, kept busy. They first moved Abigail's bedroom furniture and assorted knick-knacks and boxes of books across the hall to what had been the guest room, then, with the help of a few of the congregation, they had packed up and carried Jessica's things to the rented U-Haul van in the driveway. The last thing his hands had done was close the van's door on his daughter's life.

Now they were empty. He tried folding them under his arms but that made him look unapproachable, which was the wrong image for a minister of God, even a grieving minister, to convey, and slipping them into his pockets would have made him look untouched by the morning's events...and what had precipitated them.

So they hung at his sides, cold and useless, as he walked down the hall.

Abigail was curled up on the window seat, staring out into the backyard, the bay window surrounding her with sunlight. The room was the smallest of the three upstairs bedrooms and even though it was supposed to have been a guest room, it had never seen a guest. They'd never needed one since both of their parents lived within driving distance and they never entertained out-of-town friends. His wife had claimed the room after the girls were born for crafts and hiding Christmas presents, but there hadn't been that much to haul away after her funeral. It'd been empty ever since.

And it still felt empty even though it was filled with Abigail's things.

Jess couldn't remember if it'd been her idea or his for her to change rooms, but it made sense. She needed a space without her sister's ghost watching from the shadows.

Jess cleared his throat and brought his hands together, rubbing them as if he'd just come in from the cold. Abigail turned and when he saw what she was holding his hands stopped moving. It was a small, frayed and tattered stuffed bear, its once bright yellow fur faded to the color of old cream. *Baby's First Bear.* He'd bought two of them in the hospital gift shop the night they were born. Abigail's bear was green, Jessica's was yellow.

"I found it in the closet," she said, brushing the few remaining wisps of nylon fur away from its scuffed black button eyes. "I didn't know she still had it. I haven't seen mine since I was little. I don't even know if it's around anymore...but she kept hers. She never told me. I guess she thought I'd make fun of her about it."

It could have been Jessica sitting there, holding her own toy. They looked so much alike.

"But you wouldn't have," he said, "made fun of her."

She looked at him and smiled. "Yes, I would. And she would have made fun of me if she'd found Greenie. That was my bear's name."

"I remember," Jess said, "and that's Yellow Bear."

She nodded and a tear he hadn't noticed slid down her cheek. "We weren't very creative back then, were we?"

"You were just babies."

"Yeah, she really loved it." Another tear fell as she held the bear out to him. "I think we should put it in her...with her. I think she'd like that."

Jess wasn't sure how he managed to walk across the room and take the toy from her, but he did and his hands finally had something to do.

"I think she would too," he said.

★   ★   ★

Haverford, Pennsylvania

Millie had called before driving back to the hospital and made double sure the Newcomer was up to seeing her.

Yes, of course she could talk to Jessica Faith. Fine, no problem. They'd be waiting for her. Drive safe. Jessica Faith would be waiting for her.

Except Jessica Faith wasn't waiting for her; another nurse – it was Mrs. Huff's day off – asked if she'd mind waiting just a bit. They'd thought it best to keep *Jessica Faith* moderately sedated throughout the night and just wanted to make sure *Jessica Faith* was fully awake.

The nurse had lowered her voice every time she'd said the name Jessica Faith, as if they were curse words. Would she mind waiting?

Millie said she'd be glad to and even managed to smile before excusing herself to head for the nearest privy. She was madder than a wet hornet, but it wouldn't do Jessica Faith or her or the other Newcomers who woke up in the hospital any good if she'd had a hissy fit right in front of God and everybody. What in blue blazes had they done that they needed to keep that poor child asleep?

"They probably wouldn't have had to if they'd let me see Jessica Faith yesterday," she told the woman in the privy's massive mirror. The woman shook her head as Millie stared into the eyes that were still hers.

Or maybe not, the woman said in Millie's voice. Didn't matter what the outside looked like, inside she was still the same and that's what she wanted the Newcomers to remember.

Inside they were still the same.

Lord knows, it was hard enough waking up to find that everybody and everything you knew and loved, including your own self, was gone, harder still to see the face of a stranger staring back at you from a mirror glass, but Millie couldn't imagine what kind of hard it was to die one kind of person and wake up as the opposite.

The woman in the glass exhaled.

It wasn't as if she'd been a chirpy bundle of joy herself when she'd first come to the now times and Dr. Ellison told her what happened. Sweet Jesus, but didn't it take her some time to get used to the whole idea. Still, there was no denying the miracle of it all.

Or the joy.

Once a body accepted it, of course.

And that was why she was there, to help get the Newcomer to accept her...his new life and all the joy and whatever else came with it.

Oh Lord.

"What am I gonna say to you, little girl?" Millie asked the woman in the glass. "What in all that's good and right in the world am I gonna say to you?"

The woman shook her head as Millie ran her fingers through the thick fall of blue-black hair and straightened the collar of her favorite summery dress: red and white stripes like one of the sticks of peppermint candy she had in her toting sack.

Old or young, angry or scared or frightened beyond words, there was something about sucking on a stick of peppermint candy that gave a Newcomer a sweet point in time to anchor to.

And she knew that from personal experience, sucking down four whole sticks while Dr. Ellison told her how she came to be the beautiful lady in the mirror glass. If her mouth hadn't been filled with the first candy she'd ever had that didn't taste of molasses or honey she might have screamed for all of eternity.

Which was the other reason she always carried a peck of peppermint sticks in her toting sack…not that they always worked.

The woman in the mirror glass nodded as Millie slipped the straps of her toting sack over her arm and left the privy.

The new nurse had the chart out and waiting for her when she reached the station, but Millie couldn't help raising an eyebrow in feigned surprise.

"You mean I can see Jessica Faith now?" Millie asked.

"Yeah, sorry about the wait, but they wanted to make sure he… she…. I suppose this happens all the time, but this is the first time we've seen a…gender swap."

Nodding, Mille took the chart. "I'll find out how the Newcomer wants to be called and let you know."

"Thanks. They had to put on restraints. The patient presented as suicidal."

"Well, that does happen from time to time." Millie pulled a cellophane-wrapped stick of peppermint out of her tote and handed it to the nurse. "Suck on it slow and enjoy the flavor."

The nurse smiled as she unwrapped the candy. "Thanks. Good luck."

Millie didn't believe too much in luck, so she looked toward Heaven and said a small prayer as she left the nurses' station.

The room was exactly twenty-seven steps away and Millie counted each and every one of them.

"Knock, knock?" Millie poked her head around the curtain. "May I come in?"

The Newcomer didn't say no, so Millie took that as permission. The young man that Jessica Faith woke up as was a tall drink of water and thin as a rail spike. The report mentioned the sunburn, but Lordy, didn't it half look painful? Millie couldn't get a real sense of his looks with his skin all red and puffed up like it was, but he was passable and my, oh, my, but how those green eyes did sparkle.

Almost as bright as a knife blade.

"Hello, Jessica Faith, my name's Millie Benezet-Guzman, but you can call me Ms. B."

The Newcomer continued to stare at the ceiling. Well, she didn't expect it to be easy. Very few of them were.

Reaching behind the privacy curtain, Millie pulled the visitor's chair up next to the bed and sat down. When the curtain fluffed back into place, the Newcomer's bright green eyes darted toward it like a cottonmouth ready to strike.

This one's as flighty as a new colt. Millie laid the toting sack on her lap and folded her hands over it.

"Used to be Millie Tanner," she said, "but that was the old Master and Missus' names and after we were freed I met up with a Mr. and Mrs. Benezet, who were the best people I ever knew. They were Quaker and I took their name."

Nothing, but then some folks didn't like history.

"My other name, Guzman, belonged to the woman I look like."

The Newcomer's snake eyes landed on her and hardened.

"That's right, I'm a Traveler, just like you."

The bright snake eyes flashed. "Get out! Get out! Get o—"

The low, gruff voice broke into a coughing fit. The toting sack fell to the floor when Millie stood up and pressed her hand against the thin chest. Dear God. She could feel all the ribs.

"Hush, now. Hush, just calm yourself. It's all right." Millie patted the chest as softly as she could, afraid that anything harder might crack one of those ribs. "Just breathe nice and slow, that's right. You've been in…this body's been in a hospital for a long time and it needs to heal up, so just try to breathe easy. That's it, nice and slow. Good. Can I get you some water?"

When the Newcomer nodded, Millie filled the cup on the bedside table and angled the flexible straw downward.

"Not too much," she warned, but the Newcomer latched onto it like a hungry pup. It wasn't more than a second or two before he… she…Jessica Faith had it drained dry. "Better?"

The Newcomer's eyes followed her as she set the cup back on the table and sat down.

"I know this all must seem strange to you and I'm sorry I wasn't here when you first woke up."

The Newcomer's eyes shut tight, like a window slamming. Millie watched a tear get caught in the thick lashes.

"I know, baby, I know. It's hard, but it happened."

The eyes opened, flashing green fire. "I told you to get out, I don't want you here!"

"I know you're scared, Jessica Faith, but that's why I'm here, so I can help you get easy with your new life."

Millie reached out but the Newcomer jerked as if she'd been holding a knife.

"I told you don't touch me! Abomination! *Imposter!*"

Millie's hand started shaking as she moved it away. She'd heard the words before, too many times before, but never coming from a Newcomer. The name-calling, along with the organization it came from, had only started a few years ago and Traveler protocol prohibited that they be exposed to the world they'd woken up in until after she or someone like her had talked to them.

Which meant Jessica Faith Pathway had died and come back sooner than any other Newcomer Millie knew about.

"All right, I won't touch. I'm just going to sit down now, see?" Millie kept her eyes locked on the Newcomer's as she reached down and picked up her toting sack and slipped her hand inside.

"You want a peppermint stick?"

She held one up and the green eyes widened before looking away. "Just go."

"I can't do that, Jessica."

"Don't!" The Newcomer winced in pain. "Don't call me that."

"But you told the doctors that was your name. Isn't it?"

The thin lips quivered. "Not anymore."

Poor baby, poor sweet, lost baby. "Well, I have to call you something. Jess?"

"*No!* My name's Jessie."

Millie nodded. "That's a good name. I knew a man named Jessie once, he was a big, powerful—"

"Kill me."

It wasn't the first time Millie had heard that plea, but it was the first time it hadn't come with tears or terror or pain or even anger. It was just a request, like asking to go outside.

"You know we can't do that. If you'll just let me explain—"

The Newcomer yanked on the wrist restraints and sat up, ropy arm muscles straining. It surprised Millie enough to flatten her back against the chair.

"You don't have to explain anything. I know what happened! I killed myself because I...didn't stop an Imposter from taking my friend's body. I should have stopped it. One body, one soul!"

Millie felt the breath catch in her lungs. Dear God, it wasn't possible. "You're a True Born."

"Yes! And so was Carly. She would have saved me even if she hated me...but I didn't save her. My dad said it was supposed to take three minutes but it was faster. And after he wouldn't do it, he said it was murder. It was my fault." The Newcomer fell back against the bed. "Oh God, that's why, isn't it? This is my punishment for not saving her body. I'm an Imposter."

"We like Newcomer better." Millie lowered her hand but didn't put the candy away. She'd had her own dealings with True Borns and, except for the absence of white hoods, most of them were no different than the men who'd killed her. They hated Newcomers for what they were, but she'd never sat down and talked to one, up close, until now.

And God knows she'd never had one come back. It was too soon.

Millie set the candy aside and took the copy she'd made of Jessie's file out of the sack. While the rest was hospital charts and doctors' comments, the first page was one she'd made up. Divided into two columns right down the middle, it had the donor's name on the top of the left column and Jessica Faith's on the right. She'd filled in the left side the night before using name, age, address, gender, date of birth, date of death – the right was still blank except for the name. The rest they'd fill in together, even though it would have been easier to search for Miss Jessica Faith Pathway in the Newcomer database. But sometimes the old-fashioned way of doing things was better. Written down words and histories only told who they'd been; looking into a Newcomer's eyes and talking to them told Millie who they still were.

Millie set the wrapped candy down on the side of the mattress then reached into her tote and took out a pencil. She scratched out Jessica Faith and wrote the name Jessie in its place.

"I need to ask you a few questions."

"Go away."

"I will as soon as you answer my questions. Will you do that?"

Jessie, the True Born/Newcomer took a deep breath.

Millie slapped the pencil down against the page. "Then I'll just have to sit and stare at you, one imposter to another."

"I'm too tired."

"Then shut your eyes and get some sleep. I'll be right here when you wake up."

Millie made her face go all soft and innocent against the green-eyed glare. "You're not very nice."

"I'm very nice, but I can outwait a mule if I need to." Millie picked up the candy with her free hand. "It'll help, sure you don't want it?"

Jessie raised the hand closest to Millie and shook the restraint. Millie nodded.

"Ah. Well, I can feed it to you, if you like. It really is good."

"Fine." Green eyes rolled, but the mouth opened.

Millie unwrapped the candy, broke off a small piece and carefully placed it into Jessie's mouth. "How's that?" Jessie shrugged one shoulder but didn't spit it out. Millie picked up her pencil.

"How old are you, Jessie?"

"Seventeen."

Millie wrote it down and took a deep breath. The air smelled of peppermint.

"I'm not sure how to ask this next question, but I need to fill in the space. Jessie, are you a boy or girl?"

The silence that settled down between them was as thick as cooling molasses.

"I mean, I know your name is Jessica Faith and that would mean you were a young lady, but now…." Millie reached into the sack and helped herself to a peppermint stick. It didn't much help, but it eased the sudden dryness in her mouth. "I just need to know if…."

"I'm still a girl?"

Millie felt her cheeks flush as the Newcomer's jaw closed around the candy and crushed it.

"Yes, I suppose that's what I'm asking."

One of the shoulders shrugged. "I don't know."

"I don't understand, Jessie."

"I'm trans. I mean, I was trans."

Trans. Millie felt her brow furrow. *I know that word. Why do I know that word?* "Uh...."

The beautiful green eyes shifted toward her. "Transgender. I always felt like a boy inside. Is that why I'm..." Jessie's hand lifted as far as the cuffs would allow, "...like this?"

Millie exhaled before she could stop herself. "Well, that would explain it. You got a body that is a better fit to who you are, that's all."

The green eyes closed. "Like *Ms.* Samuels."

"Who? Jessie, how do you.... Do you know another Newcomer who's—"

"Yeah. She said I was like her...a freak."

"Don't you dare say that! You aren't a freak, Jessie, and I won't allow you to say it. You're a Traveler, just like me and a hundred others. Can you tell me a bit more about this Ms. Samuels? What's her first name?"

Jessie's glare deepened so much that Millie felt it push against her. "George."

"George?"

The weight pushing against her faded as Jessie looked at the ceiling. "*Georgina.* She.... It changed its name even before it.... Ms. Samuels is the school counselor. None of us knew she was an Imposter."

Millie wrote down the name in the margin and underlined it. If Georgina Samuels was a Newcomer, she'd be in the files and maybe, if she was still alive, they could talk to her and find out how Jessie knew about things like *Imposter* and the *True Borns.*

When did you pass, Jessie Pathway? Maybe Ms. Georgina Samuels would know that too.

Millie cleared her throat and moved the pencil over the box marked *M.*

"So, shall I mark *M* for male?"

Jessie nodded and Millie checked the box.

"Now about this other Newcomer you mentioned, Ms. Samuels...?"

"I'm tired."

Millie sat back in her chair and drew another line under *Ms. Samuels.* It was likely Jessie had said all he was going to about Ms. Samuels for the moment, but there might be something in the database about when Jessie would have met her.

"I know, Jessie, but just answer a few more questions and then I'll leave you alone, promise."

The eyes remained closed, but he didn't say no.

"All right. When's your birthday?"

"December 22, 2003."

"And what was the last date you remember?"

"You mean the day I killed myself?"

Millie hadn't expected the sharp twinge near her heart. After so many years of hearing one tragic story after another she thought she'd be immune by now. "Yes."

"It was the same day Carly died, June 22, 2021. How long have I been gone?"

Millie wrote down the date and took a deep breath.

Curtis Allan Steinar
June 22, 2021

~~Jessica Faith~~ *Jessie*
June 22, 2021

The DOD of donor and Newcomer were identical.

"Hey!"

Millie closed the chart and looked up. Jessie's eyes were open and boring holes into her soul.

"Did you hear me," Jessie asked. "How long was I gone?"

"You weren't."

"What?"

"You were never gone, Jessie, not like the rest of us. You just closed your eyes in one place and woke up in another. You came back the same day you died."

CHAPTER TWENTY-ONE

Simi Valley, California

After the call ended, Barney continued to hold the cell phone against his ear for a moment before setting it down on the table.

Four years ago he would have added the information to the growing data he had on the Travelers and not given it a second thought. The phenomenon was still too incredible to do more than take notes and wonder what the hell was going on. They still didn't know, but there was a set of parameters that each Traveler emergence followed: (1) an individual died, (2) the soul of another individual entered and reanimated the body, and (3) usually the gender of the deceased and the Traveler remained the same.

But not always.

Barney knew of fifty-seven recorded cases of gender change.

Millie's Traveler was number fifty-eight.

That was a very low number given the number of Travelers who were emerging around the world on a daily basis, but it happened. What had never happened before, as far as Barney knew, was a Traveler dying and coming back almost instantaneously. No wonder Millie called again.

Barney took a deep breath.

He had a full week of meetings and consultations ahead of him, but he also had a first-rate assistant who was a crack at rescheduling or who could, if needed, take his place...and probably do a better job of it. That was the first call he made after retrieving his phone from the table. The second wasn't so much a call as a quick swipe to the Southwest Airlines site to book their next earliest flight to Philadelphia.

The trip wouldn't cause too much turmoil as long as he was back for the surprise birthday party on Sunday that Amandine had been planning for months and that he wasn't supposed to know anything about.

One tap and he confirmed the Thursday, 5:20 a.m. nonstop from LAX to PHL, after which he called the New Beginnings toll-free 1-800 number and left a message for Millie with his flight information and ETA.

He really needed to get her to change her mind about getting a cell phone.

"Ahem."

He'd just finished typing *Georgina Samuels/high school counselor* into the Notes app when the door of his office, his *homme des cavems*, *cavemen* being the closest Amandine could come to *man cave*, opened. She smiled and the room brightened. She was like Miranda in a number of ways, not all of them, of course, and it was the differences that made it easier to love them both.

"*Bonjour*," she said, "I am making breakfast. How do you want your *oeufs*?"

He smiled and saved the file before slipping the phone into the pocket of his robe.

"I would like my *oeufs* scrambled, *merci*."

★   ★   ★

Arvada, Colorado

Jess found that if he looked at the faces of the congregation or at the sun-bright colors in the stained-glass window set high above the entrance arch, and not at the spray of pink and white miniature roses that draped the white casket in front of the altar, he could focus on the liturgy printed in the memorial program in his hands and almost believe it was just another funeral he was officiating.

"A time of grief," Jess said to the microphone that carried his voice to those who filled the pews and others who were standing along the sidewalls. So many people loved her. "A time of letting go, but also a time of remembering as well."

Abigail sat alone in the front pew, her head bowed, a single pink rose in her hands.

"And we need that, we need to remember Jessica, cherished daughter and sister, beloved friend, but not in pain or grief, for that only darkens our memories of her. We must remember Jessica with love and joy and keep the memory of her smiling face ever before us. Her heart was too ki—" Jess cleared his throat. "Her heart was too kind to want us to suffer because of her. She would want us to go on with our lives and our cause, for she was, as we are, True Born. We should not weep for her loss, but rejoice in the knowledge that as her soul is safe with our Lord God, her body will be safe within its grave, a hollow vessel pure and uncorrupted. One body, one soul."

"One body," the congregation answered softly, "one soul."

Jess closed his eyes and lifted his face toward the arched dome above him.

"Blessed child, my beautiful daughter Jessica, you are safe and we who are left, who have gathered here today, come not to mourn your passing but to remember and be glad of the time we had with you." Jess took a deep breath and felt the tightness that had constricted his chest since Jessica's death start to loosen. "She is at peace. Our Jessica is at peace and bathed in the glory of the Everlasting Light. What we bury here today is not my daughter, it is only the earthly shell that housed her soul and only her soul."

Jess opened his eyes and finally allowed himself to look down at her coffin. It looked so small.

"Jessica was a child of light and brightness and also a child of this church and of the one truth. So let us remember her at peace and whole. I now ask anyone who would like to share their memories of Jessica to raise their hand. Who would like to start?"

Jess smiled at the number of hands that rose. Jessica had been so loved. He wished she had known that, had known how many cared for her. Maybe if she had she wouldn't have been so confused.

Jess chose the first speaker, Mrs. Betancourt, who'd wept bitterly when he told her about Jessica's accident. Jess stepped down from the dais, walked down the center aisle and offered the woman his arm. She leaned heavily on it as they walked back.

As the woman began to enumerate Jessica's virtues and abilities, Jess sat down next to Abigail and took her hand.

All these people, all this love…Jessica would have been so happy.

*   *   *

Haverford, Pennsylvania

After the Imp...the woman named Millie left, and just as Jessie was drifting off, a doctor came in and started asking more questions, mostly about how Jessie felt about being a *he* and if *he* had any questions or if *he* would try to hurt *himself* if they removed the restraints.

No, Jessie had said, *he* wouldn't.

And didn't even after the doctor removed the padded cuffs and walked out of the room.

The woman had said something that Jessie hadn't thought of and it had made every inch of skin on the body crawl.

"Thank you, Jessie. Now, is there anything else I can do before I leave you in peace?"

Jessie remembered puffing up the flat plane of the chest and meeting the Imposter's gaze full on.

"Yeah, tell them to kill me. They can say it was a reaction to medication or something. It happens all the time."

The woman hadn't batted an eye. *"It does in movies. This is the now times, but I can ask them."*

"You will?"

"Sure, you wanna die, I can't make you stay, but you might want to think about something first...what if you die by accident or kill yourself and wake up in another body? You might not like it; fact is, I think you were taught not to like it, but you came back for a reason, Jessie, we all did. I can't tell you what that is and you might never find out, but you came back when others don't so it appears to me that you're supposed to be here.

"But don't let any of us stop you if you wanna try again. Maybe after you come back a few dozen times you'll see reason. Here, have another peppermint. I'll see you later...if you're still here."

And it'd just be his luck....

His.

It was funny how quickly the pronoun changed.

Jessie unwound the multi-control cord from the bedrail and punched the *Nurse Call* button.

A male nurse walked through the curtains and smiled. A male nurse for a male patient, how gender-specific.

"How are you doing?"

"Okay."

"So what can I do for you?"

Jessie took a deep breath and nodded to the privacy curtains surrounding the bed. "Can you pull them out of the way?"

The nurse's smile grew as he grabbed the edge of the curtain and pulled it open. "Yeah, I bet the scenery was a bit boring. How's that?"

Jessie looked at the reflection staring back at him from the glass wall. The ghost boy's face looked pale despite the sunburn.

"Fine."

"Is there anything else?"

The ghost boy shook his head.

"You missed breakfast and a few other meals, so how about food?"

The ghost boy shook his head but the stomach growled loud enough that the nurse laughed.

"Good, I'll go grab you a menu."

Jessie watched the ghost boy momentarily fade when the nurse walked past the glass – if only it was that easy – then sat back and studied the face. It wasn't bad, as faces went, although the nose looked a little out of proportion or maybe it was just the peeling sunburn that made it look bigger. An itch prickled the skin on the left cheek; it was peeling too. In the glass, it looked like the ghost boy scratched his right cheek. Reverse image.

Mirror images. Mirror twins, like Jessie and Abbie.

Once upon a time.

The ghost boy disappeared again when the nurse came back into the room.

"Hey, have you been scratching your face? Don't. I'll get you more cream in a minute. Here." The nurse handed Jessie a printed menu and a kid's blue crayon – you couldn't hurt yourself with a crayon. "I checked with the doc and you can pretty much eat anything you want, but I'd stay away from things like the grilled cheese and tacos until your throat's a little less raw."

"I can have tacos?" But the thought reminded Jessie how sore the throat still was. "Yeah, maybe not. I can have burgers? And sushi? Really? What's water ice?"

The nurse cocked his head. "You don't know what water ice is?"
Jessie shook the head.

"Mark it down. You'll love it and it'll soothe your throat."

Jessie could only guess, but checked off baked macaroni and cheese
with green beans and a roll and chocolate milk. The body looked too
skinny and it was hungry. The nurse took the menu and nodded at
the choices.

"Okay, let me drop this off and then I'll come back for our walkies."

"I'm tired."

"And I'm good-looking, but you still need to get up and move.
You haven't done a lot of that either."

"You mean this body hasn't."

Jessie had hoped for shock but got a laugh instead.

"Not walking, no, but it has had a lot of PT, so you lucked out.
We just have to get the muscles used to moving on their own again.
That's where you come in."

The nurse turned and left, but was back in under a minute.

He snagged the robe off the foot of the bed and handed it to Jessie.
"Slip this on unless you want everyone to see your bare butt."

Jessie slipped on the robe while the nurse walked over to the
closet and pulled out a wheeled upright walker, snapping it open as he
pushed it toward the bed.

"Okay," he said as he released the bedrail on that side and picked
up the controller. "Let's roll. And please make sure your seat backs are
up and tray tables put away."

Jessie felt the bed lower and jerked away as the nurse reached out.
"I can do it myself."

The nurse straightened. "That I seriously doubt. Besides, if you fall
and crack your skull open it'll cost me my job, and I like my job. Now
come on, play nice."

He reached for Jessie again.

"Are you one of them?"

The hand paused. "Them?" Jessie looked up but didn't have to
say anything. "Oh. No. I've always been this handsome. Now, quit
stalling. Up and at 'em."

The room hardly spun at all once Jessie got the stockinged feet
under him and pulled the body into a semi-upright position. It

was weird. The body was tall and long and felt as substantial as overcooked spaghetti. Straightening the arms, Jessie stretched out the spine and was almost standing eyeball to eyeball with the nurse.

Abbie would have to look up.

The thought brought a different kind of dizziness. Jessie leaned forward and took a deep breath. The nurse grabbed the body, steadying it.

"You okay?"

"Yeah."

"Dizzy?"

"A little." Jessie stood up. "It's better."

"You sure? As much as we need you walking, we can take this as slow as you like."

"I'm okay."

The nurse nodded, but didn't move his hand away until he walked around to Jessie's left.

"Take a couple more deep breaths," the nurse told him, "and for what it's worth, you're doing great. Like I said, there's no rush, just take your time."

Jessie took another deep breath and, gripping the walker's handles tighter, looked down as the right foot slid forward across the polished floor. Decked out in its bright yellow terrycloth hospital sock with rubberized soles, the foot looked even bigger than it had when Jessie first saw it tented under a blanket.

"What size are they?" Jessie asked as the left eased up and out, taking the lead. The wheels rumbled softly as the walker moved forward.

The nurse moved his hand to the small of the back and looked down. "Not sure offhand, but they seem to be working just fine. Think they can make it all the way around the floor and back?"

The feet didn't seem to have a problem with that, nor did the hands, which, after Jessie wiped the palms dry against the robe, seemed perfectly at ease gripping the walker's rubber handles. The body might have gotten great PT and was healing nicely, but the jellyfish inside was doing good just keeping it upright and moving forward.

Jessie felt sweat coating the forehead before they were halfway down the first corridor.

"You're doing great. Getting tired?"

A bead of sweat rolled down the right temple. "Yeah. A. Little."

"Okay, why don't we pull in here for a pit stop?"

Jessie should have known there'd be an ambush.

They were waiting for him: the Traveler named Millie and some old guy in a rumpled business suit and tie. The suit didn't fool Jessie; the man had *doctor* written all over him. They both stood up as Jessie push-shuffled into the room.

"Here, let me help you." The man reached for the walker but the nurse stopped him.

"He can do it," the nurse said and stayed at Jessie's back as the body push-shuffled to a chair at the opposite side of the room. Millie, the Traveler, applauded when Jessie sat down.

"That was fine, Jessie, just fine. You won't be needing that walker for long."

"No, he won't." The nurse put the walker next to Jessie's chair and winked. "You did great, kid, I'll come pick you up in a bit."

Jessie watched the nurse leave as the woman and the doctor sat down.

"How are you feeling?" the doctor asked.

Why did doctors always ask that same question? Jessie leaned back in the chair and folded the hands.

"Well, um, Jessie, my name's Barney Ellison and I'm a—"

The hands tightened into claws. "I know who you are."

"You do?"

Jessie made the mouth smile and hoped it felt as menacing on the outside as it did on the inside.

"Every True Born knows who you are. You could have stopped them when they first showed up, but you didn't. You let all this happen."

"No, I didn't, Jess—"

"Jessie!" The hands grabbed the chair arms, nails that were too short clawing at the upholstery. "My name's Jessie! Jess is my...."

"Your father?"

Jessie tried to make the hands push the body up, but they didn't have enough strength yet and the body fell back. Millie was out of her chair and two steps toward him when the doctor stopped her.

"I'm sorry, Jessie, we don't have to talk about it now, but I will need to ask you some questions later." He nodded and Millie sat down. "And despite whatever it is that you've been told about me, I didn't do anything. I was and still am just a witness."

"But you could have stopped it."

"How?"

"You could have sent them back."

The doctor leaned back as Millie looked away.

"You mean kill them."

"They were already dead."

"And you think that makes it right?"

Jessie dragged the too-short nails across the arms of the chair. "Yes."

"Because they were dead."

"Yes."

"Like you were?"

Jessie let the hands go slack. "Yes."

"Do you still wish you were dead?"

Jessie turned and looked at Millie. She didn't look up. "I don't belong here."

"Answer my question, Jessie."

"Yes, I wish I was dead, but I'm not going to do anything, okay?" Jessie watched Millie take a deep breath before turning back to the doctor. "I might come back again."

"Well, whatever the reason, I'm glad because you are a pretty special case, Jessie Pathway, and I need you to understand that, okay? We've never had a Traveler...." The doctor looked at Millie and bobbed his head. "Newcomer, sorry. We've never had a Newcomer come back as quickly as you did."

Jessie sighed and folded the arms across the flat chest. It felt different without the breasts, but the gesture wasn't lost.

"Did she tell you about *Ms.* Samuels?"

The doctor nodded and pulled an envelope out of his coat pocket. Opening it, he took out two folded pieces of printer paper and handed Jessie the one on top.

Jessie opened it and felt the body's stomach clench. It was a printout of Jessica Faith Pathway's obituary notice from the online edition of *The Denver Post*. Fingers that were too long and too thin traced the school photo.

Dr. Ellison cleared his throat. "You were a very pretty girl, Jessie."

"My sister still is."

"The announcement said you were twins."

Jessie nodded. "Yeah, were."

"Would you like to see your sister and father?"

"*No!* You said you read it, didn't you? I'm dead, they buried me." Jessie flapped the paper in Dr. Ellison's face then watched the long, thin fingers tear it into confetti. "They can't find out. Okay? Please?"

The last thing Jessie wanted to do was cry, but the body didn't co-operate. It sat there and sobbed for what felt like hours and Jessie couldn't stop it. The only thing that helped was that Millie and Dr. Ellison didn't move, didn't try to touch or offer comfort. They just sat there and waited until the tears stopped.

And Jessie was grateful for that, at least.

"We won't tell them, Jessie," Dr. Ellison said. "It's not up to us to do that. Are you okay?"

The head nodded but Jessie wasn't so sure. "Can I go back to my room now? I'm tired."

"I know you are, Jessie, but can you just give me a few more minutes?" Dr. Ellison stood, walked across the room and sat down in the chair to Jessie's right. "Millie, will you excuse us, please?"

Jessie jumped when Millie touched the bony shoulder as she walked out of the room.

The doctor, the monster, the man Jessie had been taught to hate, took a deep breath.

"Look, I don't know how you feel, but—"

"Do you want to know how I feel?" Jessie asked. "Damned for all eternity, unclean. I'm an imposter, an abomination in the eyes of the Lord."

"According to the teachings of the U.C.U.A." He smiled. "What, you think I haven't heard enough of that rant? Or don't know what they call me? But they're wrong, Jessie...you're wrong; if you and the others are anything, you're miracles, pure and simple. I was just lucky enough to be there at the start."

Jessie huffed.

"Yes, lucky. Of course that also meant that I was given the honor of becoming one of the supposed experts, which I'm not, but I'm still supposed to be the head honcho, the top dog, the big kahuna, the enchilada grande. What do you kids call the person in charge nowadays?"

Jessie huffed again. "The person in charge."

"Ah. Well, yeah, that's me, but the truth of the matter is I'm only in charge of the Traveler Center in Simi Valley for Ventura and Los Angeles Counties and...what?"

Jessie shook the head. "You know that's a really stupid name. Traveler Center? Sounds like a truck stop."

"We had to call it something." Dr. Ellison sat back, crossed one leg over the other. "What would you call it?"

"Purgatory?"

He smiled. "That's already been used, I'm afraid."

Jessie scratched an itch next to the nose and pulled off a long flake of skin.

"Oh, please, don't do that. It turns my stomach."

"It does?" Jessie dropped the skin on the floor and held up the hand. "But this doesn't?"

"That's different."

"Not from this side." Jessie let the hand drop. "Can I go now?"

Dr. Ellison looked down at the second folded piece of paper. "You told Millie you're...you were transgender, which might be the reason you woke up in a young male body."

"Yeah, instant gender reassignment. So now my body's a better fit for who I am inside?"

"Yes, that's exactly what I think happened, Jessie, and while I know there are others, many, many others, you are the first gender switch I've met."

"Then you need to see Ms. Samuels."

Jessie watched him glance toward the folded paper in his hand. "Ms. Georgina Samuels."

"Then talk to her, I'm tired. Okay?"

"Okay." Jessie watched him put the folded paper back into the envelope. "Last question."

Jessie groaned.

"Why did you kill yourself?"

Jessie leaned forward and stared into the man's eyes. "Because I watched my friend die and didn't even try to kill the Traveler that took over her body. I should have done it even if my dad wouldn't. I owed her that much."

Grabbing the walker, Jessie pulled the body to its feet and glared down at the man who'd been there from the very beginning and could have stopped it.

"Maybe this is my punishment for not saving Carly's body from—"

Music filled Jessie's head and the lungs gasped for breath.

"Jessie?" Dr. Ellison stood up. "What is it? What's the matter?"

"Shh!"

"What? What do you hear?"

"*Shh!*"

A single piano began playing, the music soft and familiar. Jessie recognized it and tears filled his eyes.

"Jessie, what's wrong?"

The piano was joined by a single voice. Ellison pushed Jessie back into the chair and moved the walker away.

"Jessie, you're starting to scare me. What's going on?"

"Shh. Listen. Isn't it beautiful?"

"I don't hear anything. What do you hear?"

Jessie took a deep breath. "Abbie singing. It's 'Bring Him Home' from *Les Misérables*. Have you seen it?"

"Yes. I took my wife to see the movie. She wasn't impressed."

"The stage musical's better." Abbie's voice rose pure and steady and when the song ended Jessie heard their father's voice.

The one who dwelled within this body is gone and has taken with her a soul that was hers and hers alone. We who are left behind ask that her soul be kept only unto this body and not return. As it was and always shall be, one body, one soul for now and all eternity. One body. One soul. Now and forever. Amen.

"Jessie, what do you hear?"

"My funeral."

★　　★　　★

Barney put the envelope back into his coat pocket as he watched the boy walk away, pointedly ignoring the giant dressed in nursing scrubs who hovered at his side.

It was a slow walk, small sliding steps between the wheeled guardrails of the walker. It was an old man's walk, but that would change once the muscles in the legs regained their strength.

Barney heard Millie's quick steps a full minute before she reached his side.

"Where's Jessie headed? I brought a few books." He turned to watch her pull three paperbacks out of her ever-present bag. "Not sure what Jessie likes, but I thought these might do."

Barney took the books and smiled. They were all H.G. Wells reprints. Millie's tastes ran to the classics.

"I think he will," he said and handed them back and watched them disappear back into the bag.

"Well?"

"Well," Barney repeated. "I think Jessie was having a hard enough time even before this happened. I'll ask that a psychological evaluation be done."

"You're not going to do it?"

"No, I'd rather it be done by the hospital. He has a certain, shall we say, well-learned prejudice against me. If I tested him and felt there was sufficient evidence of schizophrenia similar to that of the donor, my diagnosis might come under suspicion."

"You think there might be?"

Barney thought about what had just happened. There might be other answers to what he just saw besides schizophrenia, but none came immediately to mind.

"I don't know and that's why I want him evaluated. Schizophrenia is all about brain chemistry, Millie, and we have no idea whether the physical brain changes when a Traveler wakes or if it simply adapts and accommodates the new memories. But I saw him phase out and experience what might have been auditory hallucinations."

"That poor, poor child."

"I know, Millie, but let's not jump the gun. First he has to be tested and then, even if he's diagnosed, there are antipsychotics that can and will help. Besides, the donor's parents have agreed to take Jessie in and they already know what to do."

Millie didn't look happy, but did look a bit more relieved. "Well, thank God for that. Did you tell him about Ms. Samuels?"

Barney pressed his hand against the front of his coat and shook his head. It was a copy of Georgina Samuels' obituary, dated a few days after Jessie's, and listed her death as the result of carbon monoxide poisoning.

It wouldn't do Jessie any good to see it.

Not now, not ever.

JULY

CHAPTER TWENTY-TWO

Haverford, Pennsylvania

"I don't understand what the problem is. He's been awake for almost a month now. He's eating and walking by himself and Dr. Groundling said he's strong enough to leave. So why are we still talking about this?"

"It's just that I think it might be in Jessie's best interest if—"

Mrs. Steinar, the donor's bereaved mother, stopped Barney with a wave of her hand.

"I really don't care what you think, Dr. Ellison. We signed all the release papers and took all the caregiving classes, which I want to tell you was insulting. I've had a child, Dr. Ellison, I know what to do."

Barney nodded. He'd been warned about Mrs. Steinar, but Mr. Steinar had yet to open his mouth or meet Barney's eyes since they'd walked into the conference room. Despite what their file stated about their willingness to bring Jessie into their home, it didn't take any of Barney's medical skill and knowledge to know Mr. Steinar wasn't as happy with the new direction their lives were about to take as his wife seemed to be.

"I have no doubt you do, Mrs. Steinar—"

"So why did you just say he can't come home with us?"

"I didn't say that. All I said was that I don't think now is the right time for Jessie to move into a less structured setting. He's doing very well as an in-house out-patient here—"

"It's a home," Mrs. Steinar interrupted, "not a setting. Jessie is only seventeen...in here." She tapped her sternum. "Do you honestly think a hospital is better for him than a warm and loving home?"

Barney looked at the team of doctors who had worked both with the Steinars' son and Jessie and saw them look back without offering so much as a shrug. They didn't care if Jessie stayed or left; they had other patients, both True Borns as Jessie called them and Travelers, to care for.

He couldn't fault them. He'd flown back and forth from LAX to PHL so many times over the previous thirteen days (and nights) that the next trip he took with Amandine would be free.

Round trip.

"You're right, Mrs. Steinar, a home environment would be the best thing for Jessie —" He tried to ignore the woman's smug look. "– but I have some concerns."

The woman sat up. "And they are?"

"About Jessie's medication." Barney saw the husband finally look up. "It was noted in Curtis's file that when he was brought in—"

"That won't happen again." Mr. Steinar was staring at his wife. "I can promise you that."

Ah. "I'm glad to hear it because it does appear that Jessie is suffering the same disorder, but seems to be responding with a much lower dose than your son was prescribed. That's one of the reasons I'd like him to stay here, just for a few more weeks, until we're sure the dosage is correct."

"My husband is right, Dr. Ellison," Mrs. Steinar said as her husband took her hand, "what happened with Curtis's medication will not happen again. I'll be keeping the medication in a safer place so there will never be a mix-up like that again. Jessie will get the medication he needs and I will bring him back here for tests as often as you want. Just let us take him home."

Barney leaned back in his chair. There'd been no mix-up. For some reason, and he wasn't about to ask what that reason was at the moment, Mrs. Steinar had purposely stopped giving her son his antipsychotic drug, which had undoubtedly contributed to his attempted suicide. He had no idea why she'd do something like that, but he doubted she'd try it again, especially with Mr. Steinar watching her.

He hoped.

"All right. But there will be weekly mental health checks and if there's evidence that Jessie's condition has gotten worse—"

"It won't," Mrs. Steinar said. "I promise it won't."

Barney rapped his knuckles against Jessie's file and nodded to the doctors. They nodded back, looking relieved.

"Fine. We'll get Jessie signed out and you can take him home."

Mrs. Steinar was all smiles as she stood up. Mr. Steinar just stood up and walked to the door.

"I'll go get the car."

The room emptied out quickly as the doctors followed Mr. Steinar out. Barney and Mrs. Steinar stood up together, but neither of them moved away from the conference table.

"You do understand that Jessie, like your son, will never be cured."

She nodded. "Can I ask you something, Dr. Ellison? My son was a genius, and sometimes genius goes with madness, doesn't it?"

"I've read some reports to that effect, yes."

"So, do you think Jessie's a genius too?"

"I don't know, Mrs. Steinar. We'll just have to wait and see."

★　★　★

Jessie held on to the sink with both hands as he leaned closer to the mirror. When he turned left, it turned right. When he turned right, it turned left.

Shifting the weight to his left leg as a counterbalance – the pills really did a number on his equilibrium, but at least they got the dose right...the first time he'd passed out – Jessie lifted his right hand and waved.

The boy in the mirror waved back with his left.

It reminded him of the 'mirror game' a girl named Jessie once played with her sister, Abbie. They used to play for hours, especially on snow days. They would sit cross-legged, directly opposite each other, and mirror each other's moves. They'd gotten so good that Abbie once suggested they do a 'Me and My Shadow' routine for their middle school talent show, with her as the lead and Jessie as the shadow, but just the thought of getting up in front of people had made Jessie vomit.

But that was then and this is now and times, they did change.

Along with other things.

The boy in the mirror was still too thin, despite all the water ices he sucked down, but at least his face had lost the sunburned and peeling patchwork-quilt look. He needed a haircut and shave...a process, thank God, that only needed to be performed a few times a week –

so far – and seemed more arduous than when he...then she...had to contend with daily leg shaving.

But it wasn't a bad face. The boy's mouth was too wide and he had a slight overbite, but his eyebrows were dark and didn't meet in the middle and matched the color of the thick lashes that framed Jessie's green eyes.

Once upon a time Jessie would have died to have lashes like that.

Who knew that had been a real option?

The boy stuck out his tongue.

Jessie turned away and got three, maybe four steps before *it* woke up.

There were some things about being transgender that hadn't been covered in any of the LGBTQ literature or PBS specials and one thing in particular.

IT.

All Jessie had to do was move wrong or get dressed or wash in the shower or just wake up in the morning and there IT would be, standing at full attention. Jessie had taken Sex Ed (a.k.a. Our Changing Bodies in middle school and Human Reproduction as a freshman) classes and, coming to terms with her own sexual identity early on, knew how and why IT worked. Then, of course, it had been mostly theoretical; now it was a fact.

A hard reality of life was the way Lurch, his 6'7" nurse and personal guide to all things masculine, put it after coming in one day to ask if Jessie needed any more help 'figuring things out'.

This had come right after the man had told Jessie how to pee standing up.

The process had been described – not shown – with as much delicacy, thought, attention to detail and consideration of the circumstances as was possible. It was simple, once he got the hang of it...hah, hah...and Jessie knew it would be. Once he decided to do it. Until then he peed sitting down.

Jessie closed his eyes and counted to ten, waiting for the morning meds to do more than just make him look like a staggering drunk. When they did, IT would give up and curl up inside its tighty-whitey cave like a slumbering naked mole rat.

Divine retribution was not over yet.

Bracing himself in the bathroom doorway, Jessie leaned forward and glared down at the crotch of his pajama bottoms.

Dr. Ellison didn't know what he was talking about. This was purgatory.

*　　*　　*

Arvada, Colorado

It was as if he'd lost both his daughters.

Since Jessica's funeral Abigail had been in a constant daze, barely speaking, her eyes never quite focusing on those rare occasions when they actually met his.

Jess didn't know what to do.

He'd helped so many others he should have been able to help his own child. The words of comfort and succor and platitudes were waiting on his lips. He could repeat them without thought, could tell her he understood what she was going through and remind her that although her sister was gone, Jessica's soul was in paradise and her body safe and peaceful in its grave.

But she seemed beyond his words and it frightened him.

That's why, when Jess first came out of his office and heard music coming from upstairs, he thanked God. The house had been too quiet since the funeral and it'd seemed unnatural. There'd been silence only once before, after their mother's passing, and it made it worse, made the loss all the more real.

Hearing the music gave him such hope that he tiptoed up the stairs as quietly as he could, afraid to break the spell. At first he thought she was praying, her sweet voice whispering along the hall, until he reached her door and looked in.

And even then, for a moment, he could lie to himself. She was sitting on the unmade bed in her new room, eyes closed, hands clasped, still in her nightgown, the morning sun washing over her. If she'd opened her eyes she would have seen him standing there, listening.

Abigail wasn't praying.

"Jessie? Jessie, please. Jessie? Please, Jessie. I know you can hear me. Please, Jessie. Answer me. I know what happened. I know and it's okay. Please, Jessie, just talk to me."

He backed away, intending to leave without her knowing he'd been there, but his foot stepped down onto a loose board and she turned at the creak, blinking as if she'd just woken up. Jess felt his heart shudder.

The corners of her mouth twitched. "Oh, hi Dad."

"Hi. How are you doing, Abigail?"

"Okay. You okay?"

He nodded. "What are you doing?"

"Nothing."

"Slept in."

She looked down at her clasped hands. "Yeah."

"I took my shower early, so there's plenty of hot water."

"Okay."

"I thought I…. How about I make us some breakfast or brunch? I know, how about French toast with peanut butter. That was always your favorite, right?"

Her eyes blinked. "No, I like Nutella."

Peanut butter on French toast was Jessica's favorite. "Okay, Nutella it is. Why don't you grab a shower and get dressed and I'll get things started?"

"Okay."

Jess started to walk away again, and stopped.

"Is there anything I can do?"

"No. Thanks."

"We can talk, if you like."

"I know."

"Please, let me help."

"It's okay, Dad. I'm fine."

Jess heard the bathroom door close when he was halfway down the stairs, but didn't let himself cry until he heard the water running through the pipes.

"Please God, how can I help her?"

CHAPTER TWENTY-THREE

Haverford, Pennsylvania
Jessie sat on the narrow window ledge and looked down into the courtyard. Two nurses in maroon scrubs were sitting at one of the round patio tables near the edge of the walking path drinking coffee and talking. Jessie had 'done the walk' twice a day since 'graduating' from the walker. At first it had been a slow geriatric shuffle but it'd only taken him a couple of days to get used to the longer stride length and bigger feet (size 12 M).

The first time he'd completed the walk unassisted, with Lurch keeping a respectable five feet behind, Jessie came back to find the patio filled with cheering doctors and nurses.

Yay, Jessie!

It was a little more difficult now, with the medication they gave him, but they said he was still making progress and the medication did help.

It helped him not care that he'd died and come back as an Imposter living inside an animated corpse.

No, not true. He cared – really, really, really – but the little orange pills, twice a day with food, helped. A lot. Besides keeping the *IT from the Tighty-Whities* under control, it made his head feel like it was filled with a soft, thick cloud that made everything soft and smooth and took away all the sharp edges. If it weren't for those pills he would have probably ended up straitjacketed in a psych ward somewhere instead of going to live with his body's parents.

Ain't modern medicine wonderful?

"You rang?"

He hadn't, but that was just part of the shtick. Lurch's real name was Jonas, but, he'd told Jessie, when you were the tallest kid in your class since kindergarten and taller than most of your teachers since fourth grade what else would they call you?

"It was either Lurch or Herman, as in Munster." He'd laughed when he said it. "Kids can be mean, but they're only kids. Right?"

Yeah, kids could be mean.

"So what's the story, morning glory?"

Without thinking Jessie scratched the stubble he'd missed on his right cheek. "You came in, you tell me."

The big man rattled the small white paper cup in his hand. "Medication time, gentlemen, medication time."

Jessie still didn't understand the joke, but Lurch always laughed when he said it. Jessie liked the man's laugh; it was big and booming and echoed off the walls. And it made him a little jealous too. He'd never be able to laugh like that. When the body's original owner had tried to off himself, he'd messed up his neck and vocal cords, or something; Jessie forgot all the gory details, but it also meant he'd never hear his real voice again, the one he remembered.

But maybe that was okay. If he opened his mouth and Jessica Faith's voice came out then everyone would know what he was.

Oh God.

The panic attack hit Jessie like a tidal wave, racing upward from the pit of his stomach. If it reached his throat, ruined or not, he would scream and keep screaming because this wasn't right...this wasn't supposed to have happened. He'd died. He was supposed to be dead and buried under a headstone that read *Jessica Faith, one body, one soul,* but he was still alive...*she* was still alive and trapped and....

"Hey, you okay?"

Jessie blinked at the huge hands in front of him, one delicately holding the small pill cup, the other holding a slightly larger disposable cup from the bathroom.

"What? No. No, I'm not okay. Can't you see that?"

The small white cup suddenly got closer. "Okay, okay, just breathe. You've got this, okay? Just relax. Here, take this. They'll help. Come on, it's just panic, nothing's wrong, you're okay. Here, let me help you hold the cups, okay? You're a little shaky, but that'll pass. You're okay."

Jessie swallowed the pill and managed to get most of the water into his mouth.

Lurch took the cups and crushed them together in one palm as he kneeled in front of Jessie and began counting. "One, two, three, breathe, Jessie, nice and slow, that's it, four, five...."

The pills started working when he reached fifteen. Lurch was a good guy.

"Better?"

Jessie took another deep breath and nodded. "Yeah. Sorry."

Lurch elbowed Jessie as he stood up. Then he walked back into the bathroom to toss the cups. By the time he came back the cloud behind Jessie's eyes had gotten thicker and the panic was gone.

He yawned.

"Hey, try to take the excitement down a notch, okay?"

Jessie gave him a thumbs-up.

"So, you ready to blow this Popsicle stand?"

Jessie thought about saying something snarky like "*I have a choice?*" but it suddenly seemed like too much effort, so he just nodded.

"Well, why don't you just sit there and watch me work?"

Jessie did just that; he sat and watched the big man lift the green suitcase that had arrived that morning onto the bed and open it.

"Nice duds," he said, taking out a pale blue polo shirt and tan chinos and laying them on the bed. "You'll be the beau of the ball."

"*Merci.*"

Lurch cocked his head. "You speak French?"

"No. And I suck at conjugating."

"Well, you're still young enough to learn if you want."

"Yeah. Right."

The big man tossed a sparkling white pair of jockey briefs and added matching white tube socks. "I ever tell you about my niece?"

Jessie couldn't remember, sometimes the cloud in his head made things fuzzy, so he shook his head.

"Bonnie was seven when she choked to death on a piece of hot dog at a backyard barbecue, but no one noticed. She was sitting in her playhouse, out of sight, but hey, she was seven, not a baby, so we thought...you know. She wasn't breathing when we found her. I did CPR. I'm trained to help people, but it was too late.

"When the ambulance showed up and they got a pulse, man, we thought it was a miracle. And in a way it is. The Traveler's name is Asoka, she's fourteen years old and from Ajmer-Merwara in India.

As far as anyone can tell, she died in the eighteenth century when she threw herself on her husband's funeral pyre. He was forty-six. Okay, then—"

Lurch clapped his hands and it sounded like a cherry bomb had gone off.

"Can you handle getting dressed by yourself or do you need some help?"

Jessie stood up.

"I'll take that as a 'thanks, Lurch, but I can handle it myself'. Okay, I'll be back in fifteen with your transportation. I know, you can walk, but it's hospital policy." The big man started toward the door, snapped his fingers then walked back to the closet where he pulled out a pair of the nerdiest brown loafers Jessie had ever seen. "Tress chick, kiddo."

Jessie gave him back his own Lurchy growl.

"Nice one," he said and set the shoes down next to the bed before pulling the privacy curtain closed behind him. "Ah'll be bach."

"That's the Terminator," Jessie said and heard a deep, gravely sigh.

"Everyone's a critic. Get dressed."

★   ★   ★

"Allan, will you please sit down? And for God's sake stop drinking that coffee."

He looked at her over the rim of the paper cup as he took another long swallow. Eva sighed and went back to thumbing through a magazine she remembered her mother getting for the recipes and 'helpful life hints'. So far she hadn't found anything helpful in it, but at least she appeared to be doing something useful. Unlike her husband.

From the moment they'd been escorted into the private waiting room, he'd done nothing but pace back and forth, pausing only long enough to refill his cup from the carafe on the hospitality table.

Eva looked up again when he stopped for another refill. *Dear God, he'll be up all night.*

"Seriously, Allan?"

"I don't know how you can just sit there reading." He finished pouring and put down the carafe. "Aren't you the least bit nervous?"

Eva closed the magazine. "Why would I be nervous?"

"Why?" His eyes bulged slightly when he looked at her. Definitely too much caffeine. "We're bringing a complete stranger into our home."

"Jessie's not a stranger, how can you say that?"

Her husband said something under his breath and began pacing again. It had to be the caffeine. They'd met with Jessie, supervised, of course, a dozen times during their Caregiver Orientation course, spoken with him and told him about themselves but, as instructed, refrained from asking personal information of him. He'd tell them about his past life when and if he felt like it and that suited Eva. It wouldn't matter once Curtis came back.

Jessie was just a placeholder, a significant zero in the decimal representation of a number.

She remembered the first time Curtis called her that. He'd just turned seven. Genius.

Opening the magazine, Eva found an article on 'What Pets Really Think' and wished her husband would stop pacing. It was really getting on her nerves.

*　　*　　*

Arvada, Colorado

Jess's knees were aching and he could feel the muscles in his back and shoulders begin to tremble under the strain, but he clenched his clasped hands tighter together and pulled them into his stomach. Prayer was not supposed to be an easy thing and he knew his pain only served to strengthen the appeal.

He'd been kneeling on the hard marble slab in front of the altar for two hours, praying for strength and forgiveness the same way he had every day since Jessica's funeral. It was where her coffin had lain and the memory added to the pain.

But his pain meant nothing. He deserved it.

"What can I do? Dear God, please help me find a way. Abigail is all I have left but she's so lost I can't find her. Please, she is your child as much as she is mine and she needs your help. In your glory, you created them and we were blessed and blessed again when you called Jessica home. Amen. And we know she is safe within your love and at peace, the one soul you gave her safe within your eternal care. I know

Jessica is at peace, but I'm worried about Abigail. She's never been alone before, not truly alone, but now she is and Jessica's death has… confused her."

The image of Abigail sitting on her bed begging her sister to talk to her flashed through his mind. Jess squeezed his eyes tighter together and the image faded.

"Please…show me the way to help her understand the path you've chosen for us to walk. I can't do it alone. Please, how can I help her?"

"Jess? Can we talk?"

★   ★   ★

Jessie was sitting in the recliner when he heard the sound of the curtain being pulled back, followed by the soft whirr-rattle of a wheelchair. The cloud inside his head parted long enough for him to meet the big man's eyes.

"Hey! Lookin' spiffy, Mr. McStif— Um." Lurch cleared his throat. "You look good, Jessie."

Jessie glanced down, but the outfit hadn't changed since he put it on. "For a nerd."

"You can always get new stuff once you're settled." The big man snatched the suitcase off the bed where Jessie had left it as he one-handed the chair toward him. "Okay, climb aboard your sturdy chariot."

The cloud whooshed a little to one side as Jessie sat down and took the suitcase.

"Did you remember your souvenirs?" Lurch asked as he spun Jessie around. *Whee!* "I mean, you never know when you'll want to show off a turquoise puke pan and matching portable urinal, right?"

"Right. Hey, Lurch?"

"Yesssssssss?"

"Thanks."

"Anytime, kiddo, and I mean that, anytime you have a question or just want to shoot the shit, call and if I'm not here, they'll find me. I mean it, okay?"

"Okay."

"Good. Hang on, here we go."

The cloud settled down behind Jessie's eyes so it was easier just to watch the floor directly in front of the wheelchair: seamless white to elevator blue to shining marble-gray blocks that made the wheels click when they went over them. A shadow moved across the blocks toward him.

"Hi, Jessie, big day, huh?"

Jessie looked up and the cloud parted. A little. "Hi, Dr. Ellison. Yeah."

"Excited to be getting out of here?"

"Yeah."

"Are you doing okay, Jessie?"

But before Jessie could add another *yeah* to his repertoire, Millie walked up and handed him a white paper bag tied with a red ribbon.

"A little going-away gift," she said as Jessie opened it. It was filled with peppermint sticks. And one of her business cards, the phone number circled with red ink.

Jessie nodded and closed the bag.

"Thanks."

A weight suddenly descended on Jessie's shoulder. "Okay, pard, this is where I head out. It's been a pleasure, Jessie, really. You be good and take care of yourself, okay? I'll see ya later, sweet p'tater."

"See you soon, you big baboon."

"Ooo...good one."

The hand squeezed and then the big man was gone.

"Looks like you made a friend," Millie said.

"Yeah. He's cool."

"Jessie, Mr. and Mrs. Steinar are here. Are you ready?"

Jessie waited until the cloud had filled in a little more before nodding. "Yeah."

Millie started to walk around to the back of the wheelchair when Dr. Ellison stopped her.

"Can you give me a minute with Jessie?"

"Man talk," she said, and Jessie felt the chair shiver as she let go of the handles. "I'll just go keep the Steinars company for a bit."

Jessie watched her walk away as Dr. Ellison squatted down in front of the wheelchair.

"You know if you don't feel that you're ready to leave, you can stay a while longer, Jessie. Do you want to?"

Dr. Ellison stared into Jessie's eyes and if it hadn't been for the medicine making things all soft and cozy Jessie might have been the first to look away.

"Stay here?"

"No, it'd be something more like a residential facility."

"I'm tired of being a lab rat."

"It wouldn't be that kind of hospital, Jessie."

The brain-cloud parted just enough for one tiny ray of sunlight to break through.

"A nut house?"

"They haven't been called that for a long time, Jessie. No, they're more like live-in spas designed to help people deal with perceptual or emotional problems."

Jessie nodded. "A nut house. You think I'm crazy?"

"No, no, of course not." But the look in his eyes said differently.

Jessie leaned forward and stared straight into those eyes. "I'm not crazy."

And Dr. Ellison stared right back. "Do you still hear things?"

Whoops. Jessie sat back and finally understood what the brain-cloud pills were for. He'd forgotten their secret, his and Abigail's, the day of the funeral. No wonder they thought he was crazy.

"Jessie?"

"No, I don't. Not anymore."

Dr. Ellison reached up and patted Jessie's hand on the suitcase. "Good, it means we got the right dose. There are new medications being developed every day and with time there might even be a cure. If you were a resident at one of these facilities, you'd be at the forefront of any new drug therapy program instigated. Would you consider it?"

"What do you want him to consider, Dr. Ellison?"

As Dr. Ellison stood up, using the arm of the wheelchair as a lever, Jessie saw Mrs. Steinar marching toward them, leaving Millie and Mr. Steinar in her wake.

"Just other potential living situations if Jessie would rather not be a burden to—"

Mrs. Steinar never stopped moving until she'd walked around to the back of the wheelchair and touched Jessie's shoulder. "You'll never be a burden to us, Jessie. You're a blessing. I hope you understand that."

Jessie wanted to open the suitcase and take out the puke tray.

"Now, if you'll excuse us."

Without another word, Mrs. Steinar began pushing Jessie across the lobby toward the entrance doors with Dr. Ellison trotting to keep up. Millie and Mr. Steinar changed directions and fell in line behind them. Jessie had to grip the suitcase tighter to keep it from falling.

The late afternoon heat swirled around Jessie the moment they left the building, thickening the cloud behind his eyes as Mrs. Steinar pushed the wheelchair across the concrete walk to the burgundy Nissan sedan parked along the white-painted curb.

"I'll be calling from time to time to see how Jessie's doing," Dr. Ellison said. The wheelchair shuddered when she set the brakes.

"That's fine," Mrs. Steinar said. She took the suitcase off Jessie's lap and opened the rear passenger-side door.

"And Ms. Benezet-Guzman will be dropping in periodically."

"Of course she will." After sliding the suitcase to the opposite side, Mrs. Steinar turned and helped Jessie out of the wheelchair and into the car. "Mind your head."

Now that Jessie knew what those little orange pills were for, the cloud turned dark and mean and made it all the more difficult to cram his new dimensions into the narrow back seat. He hoped they lived nearby.

The door closed with a hollow thump while Dr. Ellison was saying goodbye. He knocked on the window and Jessie lowered it as Mrs. Steinar got in.

"If there's anything you need, Jessie." He handed Jessie a small white business card. "Or if you just want to talk."

Jessie took the card and folded it in half. "Okay."

Mrs. Steinar turned around in her seat.

"Jessie, close the window, the air-conditioning's on."

Jessie thumbed the window lever when Dr. Ellison backed away.

"Some people just don't know when to quit," Mrs. Steinar said, turning back to the front of the car. "All right, Allan, let's go home."

Jessie shoved the folded card into the front pocket of the chinos and fell asleep.

* * *

Barney watched the car until it turned onto the access road and disappeared behind a landscaped wall of trees. Millie came into his periphery, rubbing her bare arms as if she was cold while her bright summer dress fluttered in the sultry wind.

"Don't you have a plane to catch?" she asked and he nodded. "I think he'll be okay."

"I hope so."

"Well, I'll keep a good eye on him and let you know how things are going."

"Thanks."

"You don't need to thank me, Dr. Ellison. That poor child. Think he'll ever go see his family? I mean, I understand why he doesn't think he can, but, Lord a'mighty." She stopped rubbing her arms. "I'll be praying for Jessie every night."

"Amen," Barney whispered.

CHAPTER TWENTY-FOUR

Arvada, Colorado
Jess didn't feel the pain in either his body or soul as he stood up and turned around. Shock was known to deaden the senses.

The three of them stood at the end of the main aisle, Richard standing slightly in front as if to protect the two who were huddled together behind him. Laura had her arm around....

Jess took a step forward and heard, but didn't feel, his right knee pop. "Get out."

"Please, Jess, I understand," Richard said, but then proved he didn't by starting to walk up the aisle. "I need to talk to you."

"We have nothing to talk about. I told you to get out. You're not welcome here anymore." Jess looked over the man's shoulder. "Not with that thing."

The imposter turned and buried its face, Carly's face, against Laura's neck. Jess felt his stomach turn. "The Scriptures clearly say that in late times some will abandon the faith and follow deceiving spirits and things taught by demons."

Richard shook his head but continued walking. "It's not like that, Jess. She's just a child, a little girl."

"It's an imposter." Jess pointed to the words written on the arch above the altar. "The Way. The Truth. The *One* Life. That is what we believe in, what you believed in. *You* were the one who brought me in, who gave me the truth." He dropped his arm. "My God, Richard, how could you and Laura dishonor your daughter's memory like that?"

Richard stopped moving. "How can you say something like that?"

"How? Turn around and look at the thing wearing your daughter's flesh! Carly will never forgive you."

"Carly's dead," Richard said and resumed his slow steady march toward the altar. "She's beyond forgiving anyone."

Jess forced himself to stand still although a part of him wished his ministry believed in the practice of making the sign of the cross. If there was ever a time for an archaic ritual it was now.

"I told you to get out, Richard, now I'm ordering you…get out of my church."

"We're not doing anything."

"You're defaming God's temple with your blasphemy!"

But the threats didn't work. "She's not a blasphemy, that's what I wanted to tell you. She's a living human being, Jess, and her name's Violet. She was only seven when she died in a house fire outside Ballarat, Australia, in 193—"

"*I don't care!*" Jess turned, climbed onto the dais and walked to the lectern. His hands were shaking so badly he could barely grip the sides. "I don't care what its name is or what lies it told you. It's an abomination unto God and I want it and you out of my sight."

"Jess, please."

It took most of Jess's concentration to pull the cell phone from his pants pocket and hold it up. "Leave, or I'll call the police and have you arrested for trespassing."

Richard didn't move but the thing clinging to Laura started to cry and the voice of a terrified child echoed through the church.

"She died in 1932 when a fire swept through her family's sheep station. She was trapped in the house and burned to death."

Jess thumbed the nine and the one and stopped.

"I was wrong, Jess. *We* are wrong. She's not an imposter, none of them are. They're just people like us."

Jess's finger hovered above the one.

"What would you have done if it had been Jessica?" Richard took a step closer. "What if it had happened to Jessica? Would you have buried an empty coffin and pretended it never happened, like befo—"

The phone fell from Jess's hand as he charged the man who'd once been his friend. He'd never hit another man in his life, but it felt wonderful when his fist slammed into the side of Richard's jaw and sent him back a few steps.

Two voices screamed, but it was the child's that cleared Jess's head. They were the perfect image of a mother and daughter…

clinging to one another while the man who'd been his friend wiped blood from his bottom lip as he walked back to join them.

"Don't ever come back," Jess said. "God forgive you."

When the last echo of the door closing faded, Jess walked over and picked up his phone. The screen was shattered and made a soft grinding sound when he closed his hand around it.

He tightened his fist and imagined it was Richard's throat.

★　★　★

Phoenixville, Pennsylvania

Jessie jabbed a fork into the pizza and speared a curl of thinly sliced beef.

"Don't you like it?"

Jessie looked up. Mrs. Steinar seemed worried, but she'd seemed worried from the moment they walked into the house. It was a nice house, two stories done up in timber and stucco to make it look like it should have been in Stratford-on-Avon instead of a Pennsylvanian suburb. Jessie remembered living in a house with two stories, but there'd been nothing special about it. It was just a....

The cloud drifted over the memory. What was he thinking about?

The Mrs. seemed worried, but she always seemed to be something or other.

Jessie blinked. "What?"

"I asked you if you like the pizza," she said, and looked like she was about to jump up from the dining room table. "I can make you something else. A sandwich?"

"No, I do," Jessie said when the pieces of what she'd been saying came together. "The pizza. It's just hot."

"Oh, well." The Mrs. smiled and pulled her chair back in. "Blow on it."

Jessie blew on it.

"Have you ever had a cheesesteak pizza before? They were...*are* our favorite."

Jessie picked up the slice and sacrificed his upper palate for the sake of show. "Mmm."

The pizza was good, but it wasn't Beau Jo's pizza good.

"Well, if you like this, you'll love a real cheesesteak. When you're feeling up to it I'll take you into Philadelphia and get you one at Geno's."

"Pat's," the Mr. said without looking up from his plate.

"Or Tony Luke's," she said and laughed.

Jessie didn't get the joke. He didn't want to tell them he'd had a cheesesteak in the hospital and thought it was okay but couldn't compare to a thick bison burger with mushrooms and cheese.

"We can go to all three," the Mrs. said, "and you can decide which is best."

Jessie nodded. "Okay."

"What's your favorite pizza? If it's okay to ask."

Why wouldn't it be okay to ask? Abigail liked pepperoni with olives and salad peppers. Carly liked vegetarian with extra cheese. Jessica Faith had liked ham and pineapple, the classic Hawaiian. He wasn't sure what *he* liked yet so he shrugged.

"Well, you can just tell me the next time we order, okay?"

"Okay."

"You know, *we* really don't know all that much about you, Jessie –"

The pizza Jessie had already eaten turned over in his stomach. What *did* they already know?

"– so why don't you make a list of the foods you like and don't like and—" The door chimes suddenly echoed through the house. "Now who can that be? I'll get it. Excuse me for a moment."

Jessie watched the Mrs. stand up and head for the front door. The Mr. took another slice from the open box between them and took a bite. Jessie put his slice of pizza back on his plate.

Jessica Faith had been taught not to eavesdrop, that it was impolite to listen in on other people's conversations, even unintentionally. But Jessica Faith had died, he'd read her obituary and had already eavesdropped on her funeral, so what did it matter if he listened to the conversation out in the entrance hall?

Not that it would have been easy to ignore, given the volume.

The Mrs.' voice was soft, but the other voice, another Mrs. by the sound of it, was almost shouting.

"Was that Curtis in the car with you? I thought I saw him in the car when you drove up."

The Mrs. said something too soft for Jessie to catch.

"No! Really? My goodness, you mean he's home? Well, that's wonderful!"

The Mrs. was saying something else when the Mr. got up and left the dining room. "Excuse me for a moment, Jessie. Hi, Sue."

"Allan. Isn't it wonderful? Curtis is home!"

"Yes, wonderful, but he's tired."

"And we just sat down to dinner."

"Then my timing's perfect!"

"Sue."

"*Sue!*"

An elderly woman with gray hair and glasses rushed into the dining room with the Mr. and Mrs. hot on her heels. The woman was holding a plate covered with aluminum foil. When she saw Jessie she smiled wide enough for him to see the top of her dentures.

"Curtis! How are you, dear?"

"Um...."

"Curtis...." The Mrs. stepped around the woman. "Wasn't it lovely of Mrs. Ramos to stop by?"

Jessie nodded. "Yeah. Hi. I'm okay."

"What's wrong with your voice?" The old woman's eyes widened behind her glasses. "What's wrong with his voice?"

"He's getting over a cold."

"Oh dear, the things you can pick up in a hospital. There should be a law."

"Yes, there should. Oh, is that for us?" The Mrs. reached for the plate. "Thank you, so much, Sue. Why don't I just take that and—"

"Oh, don't bother, dear, let me."

The woman looked like she was in her eighties, but managed a quick sidestep and came around the table to Jessie before either of the Steinars could move.

"When I saw you...." She leaned down, her face closing the distance between them. Jessie caught a whiff of vanilla and Bengay. "My, you do look a bit peaky, don't you? Well, when I thought I saw you, I knew I had to bake some of those cookies you liked so much when I used to babysit you. You remember what kind they are, Curtis?"

"Well, of course he does, Sue," the Mrs. said as she came around the other side of the table and put a hand on his shoulder, squeezing ever so gently. "They're—"

"Let him tell me, Eva." The old woman cocked her head to one side. "What kind are they, Curtis?"

"Um...." Jessie took a deep breath and guessed. "Chocolate chip?"

The old woman looked disappointed as she straightened and handed Jessie the plate.

"Right you are. Well, I'll let you get back to your dinner. Sorry to interrupt. Welcome home, Curtis."

Jessie nodded. "Thanks for the cookies."

The old woman's eyes narrowed. "You're very welcome, Curtis."

"I'll see you out, Sue." The Mrs. took the plate from Jessie and put it on the table, then walked around the back of his chair and began herding the old woman toward the front door.

"Go on, don't let your food get cold, Curtis, Allan, I'll be right back."

They ate and no one talked for the rest of the meal.

The cookies were good.

★ ★ ★

Arvada, Colorado

Jess hadn't noticed the blood on the floor until he was about to leave and by that time it had already started to dry. Three drops, one large, two small, where Richard had been standing. The thought of bending down to clean them up made his own blood pound in his ears, but he knew he couldn't leave it.

Or could he?

The congregation might want to see how he, their shepherd, had spilled blood for them and their faith. Jess took out his pocket handkerchief and spit on it as he bent down. The blood belonged to a traitor and blasphemer who had turned his back on everything they believed and held dear. If so much as a smear remained, it would pollute the sanctity of their belief.

"One body," Jess said as he wiped the blood away. "One soul."

The blood was stubborn, almost as stubborn as the man it had come from. Jess hawked another wad of spit on the stain.

"I should have listened to you, Jessica," he said as he scrubbed at the hardened outlines. "I'm so sorry. I should have done what you asked. It would have been justified and I would have saved our friends from the sin they now commit. I should have listened to you. I should have been stronger. I should have had more faith."

Jess sat back on his heels and looked at the floor. It was clean again, free of the contamination.

"But I swear to you, Jessica, on your soul, that I'll make this right. I will bring them back into the fold and make them see to what depths their transgression had brought them. I will save them, Jessica, I swear it."

Holding the soiled handkerchief by one corner, Jess stood up and walked to his office. He had a sermon to write.

The Way. The Truth. The One Life.

"Amen."

CHAPTER TWENTY-FIVE

Phoenixville, Pennsylvania
Jessie pulled the chair closer to the window and stared down at the small greenish lights that flashed on and off across the front lawn. He'd never seen fireflies before and it was like watching a miniaturized fireworks display.

To make up for the one he'd missed.

In the hospital there hadn't been much to do at night except watch TV and sleep, so his body had gotten used to it and started yawning just after eight. The Mrs. had suggested he go up to bed – he was still convalescing, remember – and it had sounded like a pretty good idea until he saw the fireflies.

That had been an hour ago and he was still watching them.

Jessie turned when the door opened, squinting at the light that silhouetted the Mrs. "Why are you sitting in the dark?"

Jessie looked back into the room that wasn't really dark. There were enough glow-in-the-dark stars and planets decorating the ceiling that the room was almost as bright as the evening sky.

"I was watching the fireflies. We don't have any in Colorado."

The Mrs. turned on the overhead light. "Colorado? Oh, is that where you're from?"

"Yeah," Jessie said, but didn't elaborate. Both Millie and Dr. Ellison said he didn't have to talk about his life – meaning his other life – if he didn't want to. And they must have told the Steinars the same thing because the Mrs. took the hint.

"I thought you'd be asleep by now. Oh." She took a step into the room and stopped. "You're still dressed. Where are your pajamas?"

He wasn't dressed, exactly. Jessie looked down at the baggy shorts he'd found in a drawer and undershirt he'd put on instead of the pale blue cotton pjs that looked too much like the ones he wore in the hospital.

"This is okay."

The Mrs. took a deep breath. "I should have bought new pajamas, I'm sorry. It's just that Curtis used to wear those shorts when he was upset with me because he knew I hated them."

Jessie ran his hands down against the material. "I'm sorry. I'll put on the pajama bottoms."

"That would be lovely, thank you," the Mrs. said, but didn't leave the room as Jessie took off the shorts and pulled on the pajamas. It might have been really awkward if he hadn't also been wearing underwear and, fortunately, she didn't say anything about that. "I thought you were sleepy."

Jessie sat down on the edge of the bed and gently poked around the inside of his head. The cloud was still there, but only around the edges like thin mist. Maybe he was getting used to it. "I guess I got my second wind."

The Mrs. nodded and it was the first time Jessie had ever seen anyone, other than in some of those old black-and-white movies Abbie liked to watch, wring their hands. It looked even stranger in real life.

"I want to apologize for this evening, Jessie. I shouldn't have let her in and I want to thank you for playing along. Mrs. Ramos is an old busybody. She always has to know what's going on. When the ambulance arrived…after Curtis had his accident…she was the first person over here asking all sorts of questions and getting in the way. The whole neighborhood knew about it by the time we got home that night and they probably already know about this. About her telling everyone that Curtis is home, I mean, but don't worry, I'll keep her and everyone else away until you feel more like yourself."

Like that was going to happen.

"The thing is…. May I sit down?"

Jessie nodded and watched her cross the room to perch on the edge of the desk chair. She didn't look very comfortable.

"Thank you. Now, I know it's a difficult thing to ask of you, but do you think you could continue to pretend to be Curtis until we explain things? I mean, if we happen to run into anyone who knew him."

Jessie nodded. The last thing he wanted was for anyone to know about him. "Sure."

The Mrs. exhaled and her hands finally went still. "I know this isn't your home, Jessie, but we want you to feel comfortable here, so if there's anything you need just let me know."

"Okay."

"Okay." The Mrs. stood up. "Well, it's still a little early for your medication, so...would you like to come downstairs and watch TV with us?"

Oh hell no. Jessie forced a yawn. "Maybe I'll just read a little or something."

She smiled. "I'm afraid Curtis was only interested in science and math, he was a genius, you know, but I think there might be a few fiction books in the shelves. And we can always order whatever you like."

Jessie looked at the bookcase. He'd already checked out the titles and opened a few and they were all science and math books, just like the Mrs. said, but they were written for kids, grades four to six. If Curtis was a genius like the Mrs. said, where were all the real textbooks?

Not that Jessie cared. He'd never been all that great at math, or science either.

"Can I use the laptop?"

"Why?"

Jesus, did she think he was going to look at porn? "To play games. You know, solitaire, stuff like that."

The Mrs. smiled. "Well, Curtis did love his games, but I don't know his password. If you can wait I'll have Allan take a look at it in the morning and see if he can change it. I don't know much about computers."

"I do," Jessie said. "Can I try?"

For some reason that made the Mrs. chuckle. "Well, of course you can *try*. Just don't be disappointed if you can't do it."

Jessie wondered if she was saying that because he wasn't a *genius* like her son.

"Okay."

The Mrs. stood up and walked to the door. "I'll come back when it's time for your medication." She nodded and left the room.

Jessie nodded back to the empty doorway and walked to the desk. The room might be everything a kid playing out some future scientist fantasy could hope for – from the glow in the overhead stars to the wall posters of famous *real* geniuses (some with not very nice remarks scribbled on them) – but the laptop was top of the line.

Jessie lifted the lid and cracked the knuckles of the big, bony hands.

"Okay, let's see how much of a genius you really were."

★ ★ ★

Arvada, Colorado

Jess sat back and looked at the writing tablet on the desk in front of him.

The blood he'd spilled was gone and the handkerchief that had cleaned it burned to ash in one of the church's portable barbecues, but it had left its mark on him, and the longer Jess sat at his desk the more he realized a sermon denouncing the man and woman who had betrayed their church and their beliefs wouldn't be enough.

They had turned their backs on everything they once believed.

They had rejected The Way, The Truth, The One Life.

Their sin required more than just words, but words were all he had.

For the moment.

Jess barely remembered the drive home or acknowledging his daughter as they passed in the downstairs hall – him to his office, her toward the family room.

"You're home."

"Yes."

"Okay."

"Okay."

But he remembered sitting down at his desk and ignoring the laptop in favor of a pen and pad of lined paper.

Some words and thoughts required a more personal touch.

He'd written five pages when a tentative knock echoed through the office door.

He set the pen aside and folded his hands over the page he'd just finished. "Come in."

Abigail opened the door but stopped before actually walking in. She looked half-asleep and the skin beneath her eyes looked bruised.

"Mr. Wingate called and asked if you could call him back. He said it was important."

Jess looked down at his hands. "It's not and I don't want you to pick up if they call again, okay? Just let it go to voice mail."

She nodded and started to leave.

"Abigail?" She turned, still holding onto the doorknob. "Are you okay?"

He expected her to say she was fine even though she wasn't, that was the gentle lie they'd been telling each other since the funeral, but this time she didn't.

"I can still feel her."

"What?"

"Jessie. It's like I can still feel her, like she's out there somewhere."

Jess stood up and walked across the room. She trembled a little when he took her into his arms.

"I know, baby, and she is. She's looking down at us from paradise."

"No. She's closer."

It took Jess a moment to realize what Abigail was saying, what she meant, and he didn't react well.

Grabbing her arms, he pushed her away from him and shook her. "No! Jessica's dead and went to her grave whole, in body and spirit. She's dead, Abigail, accept it! Believe it!"

He hadn't meant to shout or hurt her, but he did both. She looked up at him, her eyes a little too wide, a little too wet, and nodded.

"Good, because I know Jessica was delivered from us whole and incorrupt. Her body returned to the earth the same way her spirit returned to Heaven and if you feel anything, anything, you feel her love, which is eternal." Jess released his grip and walked back to his desk.

He heard the door click shut as he sat down and reread the last line he'd written before picking up his pen.

What will it profit a man if he shall gain the whole world, and lose his soul?

★   ★   ★

Phoenixville, Pennsylvania

Jessie leaned back in the desk chair and blew the air out of his lungs in one long frustrated puff. This *should* have been a piece of cake. He'd cracked Abbie's password on their first joint computer – *JeSsieISaSnoop!!14* – in under ten minutes.

It was twice that now and he still wasn't any closer to cracking the Boy Genius's code than when he first started. Jessie rubbed the heels of his hands into his eyes and took a deep breath. It couldn't be that hard.

spaceship1? No.

maninmoon1? Nada.

geniusboy1? Dammit.

Jessie looked at the defaced poster of Albert Einstein on the wall above the desk.

aeinstein1 Nothing.

"*Augh!*"

Crossing his arms over his chest, Jessie stared at the screen until the screensaver popped up and a pixelated version of Wylie Coyote began chasing an equally pixelated Roadrunner.

Hmm.

Jessie reached for the mouse and ran it back and forth across the pad until the startup screen came back.

Okay, let's try lucky #52.

roadrunner Enter. No.

53: *wyliecoyote* No.

54: *whilecoyote* Also no.

Um…. What was it they always said?

55: *meepmeep*

56: *meepmeep1*

"Dammit."

57: *iamagenius.* Perfect. Nope.

58: *imagenius1*

Another swing and a miss. "Goddammitto—"

Wait.

Jessie tapped the caps lock.

59: *IMAGENIUS1*

WELCOME

"Yes!"

Jessie clicked on the internet link and had a moment of shock when he discovered a single Gmail account but no social media presence. How could anyone live without Facebook or Twitter or YouTube or Instagram or Reddit? Well, that was easily fixed.

In the boy genius's honor Jessie used the shot of Albert Einstein sticking out his tongue as a profile picture for the new Facebook account. Once established, Jessie moved the cursor to the search box and typed in Jessie F. Pathway, curious to see if Abbie had deleted the page after the funeral.

She hadn't, and it was strange to look at the picture Abbie had posted – it showed a girl who looked like Abbie but wasn't, smiling at the camera. The name Jessica Faith Pathway and the day of her death was printed across the bottom of the picture.

There were one hundred and four comments below the picture, Jessie counted them, all accompanied by either a sad face emoji or GIFs that showed flowers or candles or sunsets.

Not bad, but not as impressive as the three hundred plus comments, virtual hugs and condolences on Abbie's page.

All of which Abbie had Liked or Loved before answering.

Jessie moved his hands to the keyboard, still not knowing exactly what he was going to type until he saw the words appear in the comment box.

I'm sure Jessie's watching.

He hit *Send* just as the bedroom door opened.

Jessie could almost hear Lurch's voice as he shut down the computer and stood up. Medication time, gentlemen. Medication time.

*   *   *

Eva opened the door just enough to clear the latch. Curtis hated to be interrupted when he was on the computer and maybe his body remembered that.

"May I come in?"

There was a soft thump from inside and a pause, then the voice that didn't sound anything like Curtis said, "Sure."

He was on the bed with a pillow propped up under his head, reading. Eva glanced toward the computer, tempted to feel the case to see if it was warm. But if she did that he'd know she didn't trust him, so she smiled and looked at the book he was holding instead.

"Which book is that?" He held it up but she still had to walk almost to the bed before she could read the title. "Oh, that one. It is a bit silly, isn't it? About a space pet...no real science in it, but Curtis liked it."

He nodded. "Me too. I read *The Star Beast* when in third grade but it's still kind of fun."

Eva was trying to think of something to say – Curtis hadn't really developed an interest in reading until he was twelve – when her husband pushed past her, holding the prescription bottle and glass of water. He'd told her he was going to be in charge of Jessie's meds and she hadn't argued. Not this time.

"Excuse me, Eva. I don't know how fast these work," he said as he handed Jessie the glass and opened the bottle, "so if you have to use the bathroom...brush your teeth or anything...you'd better do it now."

Eva watched Jessie put the book down and take the water.

"I'll be okay," he said, holding out his empty hand. "It takes a few minutes."

Her husband nodded and shook a single orange pill onto Jessie's palm, then stepped back and watched until the pill was taken and washed down.

"Okay. See you in the morning." He took the empty glass and left the room.

"He's never been much of a conversationalist," Eva said and picked the book up from the mattress where Jessie had put it when he took the water and pill. "Why don't you go use the facilities and I'll just wait here until you get back."

He looked at her as he stood up and left the room and for a moment Eva forgot it wasn't her son – except for the eyes and the lack of an argument.

Curtis wouldn't have just done what she asked; he'd have asked why. She missed that.

Eva had the book back in the bookcase and the sheets folded down by the time she heard the hall toilet flush. He was dragging his feet and yawning when he came back into the room, the green eyes that weren't her son's already half-closed.

She didn't have to tell him to get into bed.

"I'll give you my Amazon password in the morning and you can order some new books and...whatever else you need. Within reason."

The corners of Curtis's mouth turned up. It looked so unnatural, but at least the eyes were closed all the way.

"'Kay, thanks."

"See you in the morning," Eva said as she shut the door, but he was already asleep.

"Good night, Curtis. Welcome home."

AUGUST

CHAPTER TWENTY-SIX
Sunday

Arvada, Colorado

It had taken almost three weeks, but as Jess looked out over the congregation he knew all his efforts and the bureaucratic hoop-jumping had been worth it.

It had been hard, though, so very hard to stand at the lectern each and every Sunday before this one and force himself to begin his sermon as he always had, with benedictions and a welcoming speech that spoke of community and loyalty and what it meant to belong to a fellowship of truth.

But his wait was over.

Jess took a deep breath. Today a new world began.

"What will it profit a man if he shall gain the whole world and lose his own soul?"

The words had burned themselves into his mind for three weeks, but now they were free, now the spark was lit. He met as many eyes as he could.

"'What *will* it profit a man if he shall gain the whole world and lose his own soul?' Do you know? Then I'll tell you…nothing. His profit, his reward is nothing. How can a man think there would be a profit in exchange for his immortal soul? How could he expect anything good to come after he has bartered away God's gift in exchange for *things*?"

A few of the congregation nodded, a few others frowned, but they all listened.

Jess pointed to the words inscribed on the arch above him.

"The Way, The Truth, The *One* Life. Those are more than words, more than a proverb, but let me say them so they'll be more meaningful.

One Way. One Truth. One Life." Jess heard the puzzled mutters from the congregation and ignored them. "Bear with me, friends, and listen. One Way – there is only one that leads us to God. One Truth – that we are created, body and soul, in his image. *One* Life – period.

"This is how it has been since man first stepped out of the primordial shadows and gazed up into the sky. Our souls are our own. Say it with me, our souls are our own."

"Our souls are our own."

"One body, one soul."

"One body, one soul."

"So then how may a man – any man – think he has the right to forfeit it? For profit? What profit could a man possibly think is worth his soul?"

The congregation sat silent, waiting for him to tell them.

Jess gripped the sides of the lectern as if he needed to feel the polished wood against his flesh. He didn't, but saw his motion imitated as members of the congregation clasped their hands in front of them.

"Is there nothing a man would forfeit his soul for?" Jess paused just long enough for the congregation to wonder. "What about a child? Would any of us not forfeit our souls for our children?" Mutters and nods. "But what about someone else's child? Would you forfeit your soul for another man's child?"

They couldn't answer that, but Jess hadn't expected them to.

"What if the child came like a thief in the night and took what wasn't theirs? What if the child was an imposter?

"*No!*"

The roar seemed to reverberate longer inside Jess's head than it had within the walls of the church.

"No, of course you wouldn't, but a man and woman have done that very thing. They have turned their backs on those words –" Jess pointed again to the words above him, "– as they have turned their back on us. They have forfeited their souls to gain nothing but the imposter that wears the body of their dead daughter."

It didn't take long for the congregation to figure out who Jess was talking about. Gasps and whispers, low and angry, filled the church, rising to the arched ceiling and creeping into every corner. They only needed him to say the names.

He obliged.

"Richard and Laura Wingate have turned their backs on us and renounced not only our beliefs but our mission, our fundamental rights as True Borns. When their daughter lay dying, we prayed with them for Carly's safe passage into death, one in body and soul."

"One body, one soul."

"But they lied. When Carly died, instead of turning their backs on the thing that stole her body, they accepted it. Still accept it and guard and protect it as if it were their own child when it is nothing but an imitation, an imposter. They forfeited their souls and gained nothing."

Jess stopped because the shouting from the congregation had overwhelmed the abilities of the lectern's microphone to rise above it. He let it continue for only a few seconds before raising his hands for silence.

"But that's not the worst of it, my friends. They came here to this church, the three of them, and tried to tell me that we're wrong...that the Travelers, the Imposters are just like us. They wanted me to believe that...here...under those words. One Way. One Truth. One Life."

Many of the congregation were on their feet, but all were shouting condemnations. Only Abigail sat quiet and still, her eyes never leaving his face.

There was only one way of getting them back. Jess leaned closer to the microphone.

"One body! One soul!"

"One body! One soul!"

"'What will it profit a man if he shall gain the whole world, and lose his soul? Or what shall a man give in exchange for his soul?' Nothing. And nothing is what the Wingates deserve. Let us pray!"

* * *

New Hope, Pennsylvania

Millie opened her eyes as the dawn breeze fluttered against the sheer bedroom curtain and the first warbles and tweets of the robins and thrushes drifted into her room.

It was her favorite time of day, the most peaceable, before anything happened. Twilight was a good time too, when the colors started to bleed away, but night always followed and sometimes her mind would fret and wander like a ghost come back to haunt the place it died.

Dawn was a start, not an end...a whole brand-new day full of possibilities. Her mama had always told her that and Millie still believed it to be true.

Throwing back the thin sheet, Millie sat up and slid her feet into slippers even though the room already felt hot and sticky. In the before time she'd gone barefoot so much the bottoms of her feet were like leather; her now time body was much more delicate.

Stretching, Millie walked to the window and pushed the curtain aside. She wasn't the only resident who kept a window open at night. Muggy heat of summer or the sharp bite of winter, an open window meant a quick escape if you needed it.

'Course being that her room was on the third floor meant she'd take a pretty steep tumble, but she'd never had to find out in the two years she'd lived at the school.

Millie knocked twice on the wooden windowsill for luck as a flash of movement below caught her eye. A mama deer and two near-full-grown fawns raced along the stone path below, heading for the woods at the end of the property, as a bobbing blue-white light followed.

If she'd seen something like that in the before time she would have screamed, but it was the now time and Millie knew it was just someone out for a morning run. Running was good exercise, they said, but Millie had done more than enough of it to last both lifetimes.

When her neighbor's alarm went off, muted by the wall between them but still loud enough for her to hear, Millie slipped on a robe, grabbed her towel and toiletry bag from the coatrack next to the door and left her room, heading for the communal privy and shower room at the end of the hall.

She wanted to be showered and dressed and sitting in her seat − second row, fourth chair, left-hand side − well before the seven a.m. service so she could watch the sun come streaming in through the stained-glass windows.

Dawn was always a special time, but Sunday dawns were a blessing.

★   ★   ★

Phoenixville, Pennsylvania

Jessie opened one eye. Closed it. Opened both and stared at the multifunction clock next to the bed until his brain woke up enough to remember what all the various colors meant.

White: Time: 6:30am	Too early.
Green: Temp: 72°F	Already?
Blue: Humidity: 63%	I hate Pennsylvania.
Orange: Day/Date: SUNDAY/8-15	

Jessie watched 6:30 become 6:31.

Once, in a different life, Sunday mornings meant a six a.m. race to the bathroom to see who got to shower while the smell of coffee and toasted English muffins – "*The girls have to eat something.*" – and their dad's "*hurry up or we'll be late*" shouts drifted up from the kitchen.

They were never late; they couldn't be...service couldn't start without them. Even after their mother died, the three of them were always early.

Jessie wondered if they still were now that there was only the two of them.

6:32

The Steinars weren't churchgoers and hadn't asked Jessie about it, so he hadn't said anything. Jessica Faith had been a true believer as well as a True Born; Jessie No Middle Name, not so much.

6:33

Jessie closed his eyes and went back to sleep.

And woke to the smell of coffee and the Mrs.' voice.

"Jessie? Are you awake?"

9:05

"Yeah. I'm up."

"Good. I'm making bacon and waffles, your favorite."

Jessie kicked the covers off and sat up. The Mrs. had started the whole 'favorite' thing a few days after he arrived – favorite foods, favorite games, favorite clothes, favorite scientific theory – as if... as if she thought Jessie was still her son and not a complete stranger wearing his skin. It had bothered him at first, her thinking that, but time and meds helped.

He was an Imposter and imposters took what they got and liked it.

What else could they do? Besides, bacon and waffles sounded good and he was hungry.

"Jessie?" At least she called him by his name.

"I'm up...I'm up."

It took less time to get ready now that he had a bathroom all to himself.

Fifteen minutes later, clean, combed and dressed in shorts and one of the Champion logo T-shirts he'd ordered online, Jessie was greeted with a smile from the Mrs. and a quick glance from the Mr. If he had to be honest, he preferred the Mr. over the Mrs.

Mr. Steinar might have accepted the situation, but he didn't want Jessie there any more than Jessie wanted to be there.

Not that Jessie had limitless options to choose from. He could live with the Steinars and make Curtis's favorites his own or he could spend the rest of his stolen life inside a mental hospital.

"Smells great," Jessie said as he took his place at the kitchen table. "My favorites."

There was a small orange pill waiting for him on his placemat.

Jessie popped it into his mouth and washed it down with three large gulps of pulp-free orange juice. At least he and the dead boy genius shared that favorite.

It was only after Jessie put down the glass that the Mr. nodded and the Mrs. slid a golden-brown waffle onto the empty plate. The bacon was on a smaller plate to the side.

Jessie slathered on butter and drizzled maple syrup as the Steinars went about their usual morning routine – ignoring him and each other. The Mr. read the paper between bites while Mrs. Steinar ate at the counter and tidied up.

Not big talkers, the Steinars.

Jessie yawned, using his napkin to cover his mouth and wipe the drop of syrup off his bottom lip. The syrup was dark enough to cover the stain left behind by the little orange pill as he wiped it off and slipped it into the pocket of his shorts.

Jessie had stopped taking the pills a week after he became part of the family and, as far as he could tell, not taking them hadn't had any negative effects. Of course, he still acted like there was a cloud inside his head and they, Mr. more than Mrs., still watched him like a hawk every time he took a pill.

Not that it mattered. Jessie had become an expert at dietary sleight of hand by the time Jessica Faith was six. She'd learned to slide the mushiest pea or slimiest piece of eggplant into the space between her upper lip and gum, finish dinner, ask for and receive dessert. Then, when no one was watching, the offending morsel would be spit into the trash or toilet.

Not that the little orange pill would receive the same fate. After breakfast it would join the others he'd collected.

Millie might not be right, especially if the cloud inside his head became a gale-force hurricane. This time he might not come back.

Jessie took another bite.

And so began another Sunday.

CHAPTER TWENTY-SEVEN
Wednesday

Phoenixville, Pennsylvania / 6:30 p.m.
It had been another Stellar Steinar Supper. Chinese food. All of Curtis's favorites from Curtis's favorite takeout place: wonton soup, pork-fried rice, and sweet-and-sour chicken. Almost as good as Red Lantern in Arvada...which was *Jessie's* favorite.

He burped. Ah, wonton.

The Mrs. had said something about going out for water ice, once dinner had settled, a philosophy that was very different from the snatch-n-grabs on game nights where he...or rather Jessica Faith...would be lucky to swallow the last mouthful on the way to the pitcher's mound or the hurry-ups before a U.C.U.A. meeting.

Jessie set down his fork. No chopsticks; Curtis didn't like them.

"Are you finished, Jessie?"

"Yes. It was great. Thanks."

"I'm so glad you enjoyed it."

Jessie burped again. Geeze, what did this place put into its wontons? "Excuse me."

The Mrs. smiled.

"The same thing always happened with Curtis." Jessie looked down at the empty bowl. Well, that explained it. "Let me know when you're ready for water ice. Unless you'd rather have something else."

"No, water ice sounds good. Isn't it time for my pill?"

"I'll get it," the Mr. said and got up from the table. They had two bottles, one upstairs and one downstairs, but Jessie didn't know where and looking for them would have been next to impossible. Unless he was in his room or the bathroom, the Mrs. always found plausible reasons for being close by. Do you need anything, Jessie? Can I get you something to eat, Jessie? Why aren't you in your room, Jessie?

It would have been easier if Jessie had found either one of the bottles, but as he discovered, you can't always have everything in this life. Or even the next.

The Mr. popped off the plastic childproof top as he came back into the dining room.

"There you go," he said, tapping an orange pill into Jessie's hand. "You have enough water?"

Jessie nodded and popped the pill into his mouth, shoved it into its hiding place behind his upper lip and reached for his water glass. He took three long swallows for show and put the glass back on the table. The Mr. walked away.

"Well, why don't you go upstairs and rest a bit. I'll call you when we're ready to go." Jessie watched her eyes shift off his face to the window behind him. "We don't have to rush. They stay open until nine."

In an hour or two or three, the long Pennsylvania twilight would have darkened into night and it'd be safer to leave the house. The Steinars and Jessie agreed on one thing; even if they didn't know it, none of them was comfortable about him being out in public.

Fortunately, according to the Mrs., Curtis hadn't been a big fan of leaving the house, although he would, on occasion, demand to go out for water ice or computer parts or wherever a genius went and the neighbors, especially Mrs. Ramos, noticed. It was also fortunate that most people had better things to do after dinner besides watching a tall, gangly kid get into the back of the family car.

Jessie carried his plate and water glass into the kitchen, even though he'd been told Curtis never bothered with menial things like that, and went upstairs.

He burped again – *ah, fried rice this time* – as he shut the bedroom door. No lock, but he knew neither the Mr. nor Mrs. would enter without knocking first. Curtis didn't like to be interrupted.

Good ol' Curtis.

Jessie spit the pill into his hand as he crossed the room to the bookcase. Years of living in close quarters with a twin sister had given Jessie an edge when it came to hiding things. Unlike Abbie's attempts at concealment, which ran to the standard hiding under the mattress (fake diary) or on the topmost shelf of her closet (second fake diary) or wrapped in a pair of panties in the back of her underwear drawer (real diary), Jessica Faith had always hid things in plain sight.

Never diaries, but the sketchpad with pencil drawings of Carly was always in the same corner of her desk and the cheap school journal filled with the love poems dedicated to 'My Own Lovely Miss C' was right in the bookshelf where anyone could have picked it up and read it.

Secrets were hidden, so no one ever paid attention to things that weren't.

Things like the boy genius's assortment of jars and vials and bottles he used for his 'experiments'. Jessie could only wonder what sort of experiments Curtis had been into, but when he first picked up one of the small nondescript amber bottles and opened it, the fumes that leaked out smelled like old piss.

Jessie had found an identical bottle that still had a plastic security cap.

Amber was the perfect color. Unless someone held it up to the light, the little orange pills were all but invisible.

Jessie uncapped the bottle and dropped in the pill, then gave it a little shake. The bottle was almost full. Whatever the dosage per pill, their combined strength should be more than enough to turn his brain to mush. No room at the inn after that, boys and girls.

Maybe instead of a suicide note he'd hang a *CONDEMNED, NOT FIT FOR HABITATION* sign around his neck. He did feel a little guilty about lying to Millie every time she asked him if he still thought about harming himself. A few times he wanted to tell her the truth, but what would that do except get him consigned to a rubber room for the rest of his *new* life?

In a little while it would all be over and the Steinars could have a water ice in his memory.

"One body, one soul," Jessie said and began to pour out the pills when a massive burp deposited a glob of sweet-and-sour chicken in the back of his throat. Jessie swallowed and felt it slide back to where it belonged. Not a good sign. If he took the pills now and vomited everything back up, it'd be a one-way trip back to the hospital.

Or designated nut house.

Jessie tipped the pills back in, recapped the bottle and put it back on the shelf before walking across the room to the computer.

He'd let his stomach settle over a few games of solitaire or mahjong and then....

A soft ding sounded when the computer booted up.

He, or rather 'Curtis', had an email.

Jessie opened it and felt the Chinese food sink lower in his stomach. It was from Abbie's Facebook account.

Thank you for your kind words, they meant a lot. I'm sure Jessie is watching. ☺

Smiley face?

Jessie brought up his/Curtis's Facebook page and clicked on the illuminated notification icon. Abbie had changed her profile picture. Instead of Abbie in her rah-rah cheer captain outfit, the picture showed the two of them at the U.C.U.A. Youth Camp in Estes Park the previous summer. They were standing knee-deep in water with fishing poles in their hands, half-turned – Abbie to the left, Jessica Faith to the right – toward the camera and smiling.

Abbie had been wearing a giant sunhat with the words *Swear, I'm not a Vampire* written across the brim and *she'd* had on her 'lucky' Rockies baseball cap. Their father had taken the picture.

Jessie clicked on the message box and began writing.

Saw the new profile picture. Great summer. Good memory.

Enter.

A set of rolling zeros appeared below the message. Abbie was online and had seen it.

Hi, Curtis. It was. Were you at camp?

Jessie's fingers hovered over the keyboard; he hadn't expected her to answer. They were halfway across the country from one another, in two different time zones, and she was sitting at her desk and saying hello to a dead boy.

Jessie hit three keys. Enter.

yes
oooooo

ooooooo *Just checked out your FB page. Wow, you're Albert Einstein? Cool!* ☺

Jessie read some of the comments beneath the picture of them and took a deep breath. There were fewer sympathy and condolence comments, more about school and the renovations to the old shopping mall, but hell, it'd been a couple months after all and life goes on.

Even when it shouldn't.

Jessie's fingers moved across the keys: *hah hah no.*

°°°°°° *Ok, well. Nice chatting with you. 'Bye.*

Right. Say goodbye. This is your chance, you never got to say it before. Just say goodbye.

Jessie took a deep breath.

'Bye, Abba-dabba

And hit Enter just as the Mrs. knocked and walked into the room.

Jessie minimized the screen but not before he saw another line of rolling O's begin under his last message.

°°°°°°*Je—*

⋆   ⋆   ⋆

Arvada, Colorado

He should have knocked or cleared his throat or done something to let her know he was about to come in, but her bedroom door was partially open so he hadn't thought it necessary. If it had been closed that would have been entirely different. She was a young woman and young women needed their privacy.

But the door was open and he'd heard music playing and...he just didn't think.

She was on her computer but jumped up so suddenly when he walked in her desk chair tipped over. "*Dad!*"

If she'd been his son instead of his daughter Jess would have thought there would have been porn on the screen, and it shamed him a bit when he looked and felt relieved when he saw she was on Facebook.

Until he noticed her profile picture.

He remembered when he took it. It was just before Jessica... no Abigail...no – why couldn't he remember which one? – caught a fingerling brook trout. He'd wanted to take a picture but Abigail...no, Jessica...Jessica had caught the fish...said she'd die of embarrassment if he did.

That had been almost a year ago to the day.

Jess looked away as Abigail picked up her chair and sat down, then very casually minimized the screen. The picture of a smiling kitten took its place.

"I should have knocked, I'm sorry I scared you, I didn't mean to."

She nodded and looked at the kitten. "I know. I'm okay. I just didn't hear you. I was just…you know…on the computer. And I'm sorry I yelled like that."

"You have nothing to apologize for. I shouldn't have just walked in like that." Jess tipped his head toward the computer. "Is everything okay?"

"What?" She glanced at him then back to the screen. "Yeah, it's just one of my friends goofing around."

"Anyone I know?"

She shrugged.

Ah.

Suddenly it all made sense and Jess felt even worse about barging in. Abigail had been e-chatting with a boy, a new one, someone Jess didn't know, and he'd walked in on it. If he didn't think it would have embarrassed her more, he would have told her that she'd done nothing wrong; it was perfectly natural for her to talk to boys…unless she thought it would upset him because it was still too soon.

Dear God, had it only been two months?

"You know it's okay to talk to friends and have fun, right?"

She nodded. "I know."

"So, if you want to go out or see anyone, that's fine. You know the rules and I trust you. And Jessica wouldn't want you to—"

"I know, Dad. Okay."

Her tone told him more than the interruption. She might be thinking about resuming her social life, but Abigail wasn't ready to talk to him about it. Girls didn't talk to their fathers about things like this; they talked to their mothers.

Or sisters.

And she had neither.

"Okay. Dinner in twenty. I need to get to the meeting a little early tonight."

"Okay."

Jess closed the door as he left. Next time he would definitely knock.

★　　★　　★

Phoenixville, Pennsylvania
Jessie?

Jessie ignored the voice and swiveled the chair slowly back and forth, remembering he was supposed to be drugged. The Mrs. smiled at him.

"Are you ready for dessert?"

Jessie.

Jessie glanced at the bedside clock (time: white). It'd only been three-quarters of an hour. Maybe he'd done something or said something or hadn't acted stoned enough that made them suspicious. If he'd just waited until his dinner settled and hadn't decided to play some stupid mind game with Abbie the Mrs. might have walked in and.... No, he wouldn't be dead, there hadn't been enough time. He'd probably only be unconscious and one good stomach pump would take care of that.

Jessie.

Jessie patted his stomach and forced another burp. That was another thing he hadn't been able to do before. Male bodies just seemed more adept when it came to certain bodily manifestations.

"Maybe in a while? I'm still kinda full."

The Mrs. frowned as she walked across the room and into his personal space. She wasn't a tall woman, barely coming up to his shoulder when they stood side by side, but standing that way, looking down, she loomed over Jessie like a mountain ready to fall.

Jessie?

"Are you okay?" The Mrs. pressed her palm to his forehead. "Do you feel sick? What's wrong?"

It took all of Jessie's self-control not to grab the woman's hand and pull it away. But that would have caused bigger problems than he already had, so he sat there and let her play mother.

JESSIE!

He flinched and quickly covered it with a yawn. "I'm okay. I was just...working."

The Mrs. moved her hand from his cheek to her throat and looked at the screen he'd forgotten to minimize. Shit. Where was that damned pixelated coyote when you needed him?

"That didn't look like work." She leaned in closer. "Who's Abigail Hope—?"

Jessie closed the page. "Nobody."

"You know that's a lie. Curtis never lied to me. Tell me who it is, Jessie, and tell me right now."

Jessie!

Think.

"Did you hear me, Jessie?"

JESSIE!

Jessie took a deep breath. *Give me a minute, Abbie.*

...... oh God......

"Jessie, I want an answer and I want it n—"

"I don't know who she is. It's one of Curtis's friends, I guess. I was just looking around and found his Facebook page and...." He forced a yawn so large Jessie heard his cheeks crack. Ow. "He had a lot of friends."

The Mrs. backed up and smiled as the low hum of psychic white noise filled his head. The connection was open but on hold. He'd almost forgotten what it felt like to not be alone.

"Well, of course he had friends, lots of friends, but do you remember what I asked you to do?"

Jessie nodded. "She thinks I'm Curtis." Well, she did.

"Good. Thank you. Take all the time you need. We'll be ready whenever you are."

Jessie had no idea what Curtis, the genius, was like when he owned the body, but just the thought that he'd had friends, including a (gasp) girl, had made his mother almost giddy.

"Just take your time," the Mrs. said again. "And say hello to all his friends for me."

Jessie nodded and gave her a parting yawn – what kind of a dweeb were you, Curtis? – as he turned back to the computer. The white noise inside his head had become words.

Oh my God. Oh my God. Oh my God.

Abbie.

Jessie. I knew it. I heard you scream. You're a.... You are one, aren't you? A Traveler. But it's okay, really it is.

Sure it is.

Jessie got to his feet and tipped forward as his stomach contracted. He was going to be sick. No, it felt like he'd already been sick and someone had shoved it back down his throat after lighting it on fire. *He was supposed to tell* her *and* she *was supposed to scream and* damn *him and* curse *him and* denounce *him for the abomination he became.*

She was not *supposed to use words like* it's okay. *It wasn't* okay! *It was anything* but okay!

Jessie? Did you hear me?

I heard you. How can you say that? I'm an abomination! An imposter!

You're my sister. I love you.

Jessie sat down before his legs gave out from under him and started to laugh. The voice inside his head hadn't changed. It didn't need to try and speak through a damaged set of vocal cords. It was still Jessica Faith's voice.

Jessie stopped laughing and covered his mouth. *I'm not.*

Yes, you are, no matter what. Jessie, please. Where are you?

This Old Man...

Knock it off!

...he had ten...

I MEAN it!

...he thought he died but came back again.

Jessie, get on Skype.

Jessie lowered his hand. *No.*

I need to see you.

It's not me, Abbie.

You know what I mean. Please.

Fine. If that's what Abbie wanted, that's what Abbie would get. Taking a deep breath, Jessie Googled the Skype site and began the process of logging in. It was one more thing Curtis had never been interested in. No wonder his mother had been overjoyed to think he actually had friends.

It took even less time for Jessie to download Skype and create an account in Curtis's name than it had to set up his new Facebook account. When the screen popped up he saw that Abbie was already on and waiting to accept his call.

Jessie moved the cursor arrow over the ringing phone icon.

Last chance, Abbs.

I'm ready.

I don't think so.

Jessie clicked the mouse and for a moment, just a moment before shock drained the color from his sister's face, it was like looking into a mirror again.

"Abigail Hope Pathway," Jessie said, "I'd like you to meet Curtis Allan Steinar."

"You're a...you're a...."

Jessie didn't go for the obvious. "Handsome devil? Yeah, I think so too."

The computer had great resolution; Jessie could see the blush returning his sister's natural rosy glow, especially across the nose and cheeks.

"I guess I thought.... Is it really you?"

Who else would it be, Abba-dabba?

The blush faded. They'd given each other secret inside nicknames so long ago Jessie couldn't remember when it first started. Abba-dabba and Jessy-wessy: the epitome of childish sophistication. They'd never told their names to anyone else or said them out loud. They never had to.

"God."

It was a good start, Abbie invoking the name of God, so Jessie took a deep breath and waited. He wasn't exactly sure what was coming and he couldn't even make himself guess. They weren't sisters anymore; they weren't anything to each other anymore. Abbie's sister was dead and buried and the thing sitting at the computer and talking to her via Skype was a stranger. An Imp Pinocchio pretending to be a real boy.

Jessie cleared his throat. "Go on. Say it."

Abbie licked her lips. "Say what?"

"Oh, I don't know.... Begone, foul spirit? Freak...." Jessie felt his lips tighten. "Freak's a good one, go on, say it." Abbie shook her head. "Well, say something. *You* wanted to talk, right? Talk."

"Okay. What's wrong with your voice? I thought Travelers were supposed to, you know, sound the same...I mean, sound like...."

"Curtis Allan tried to off himself." Jessie mimed wrapping a rope around his neck and pulling it tight. "I was better at it than he was."

"It wasn't an accident?"

Jessie shook his head.

"God, Jessie, why?"

Does it matter?

It's weird to hear your voice. Abbie touched her forehead.

"You should hear it from this side. So…have you had a good enough look at the freak?"

Jessie grabbed the edge of the desk and leaned forward until his face, Curtis's face, filled the screen. "Can I go now?"

Jessie leaned back in the chair. Abbie's eyes never left his face.

"Just tell me why, Jessie?"

"Why I'm like this?" He pretended to think for a moment. "Because it's punishment for my sins, why else? And while we're on the subject, why the hell aren't you…hysterical or something? It's not every day your sis…sibling turns into a monster."

"You're not a monster, Jessie."

Jessie pushed the chair back from the desk and extended his arms so she could get a better view. "What else would you call this?"

He lowered his arms and scooted the chair back in, looking out the window next to the desk. The sky had darkened to a deep purple. In Colorado the sky would still be a pale blue, the sun just beginning to disappear behind the Front Range. Different skies, different time zones, different lives.

"Look, I gotta go. I just wanted to say—"

"No."

Jessie looked back at the screen. Tears glistened in Abbie's eyes, but they didn't fall.

"I'm not going to let you say goodbye so you can kill yourself again."

Jessie felt the blood drain from his face and wondered if it had gone as pale as Abbie's had been. "What?"

"I know you, Jessie, we're the same inside."

"Not anymore." Jessie reached out and broke the connection.

TURN IT BACK ON!

Jessie stared at the blank screen.

TURN IT ON OR I'LL TELL DAD YOU'RE ALIVE!

Jessie's hand was shaking when he reconnected. "Don't. Please."

It was almost like looking in a mirror again, except Abbie was angry and Jessie was afraid.

"You wouldn't really tell him, would you?"

Abbie stared at him through the screen but didn't say or think anything.

Abbs, please.

I won't if you promise me you won't do anything.

Abbs.

"Because if you do, I'll know it. I felt you die the first time and I never want to feel that again." Jessie's body went cold as Abbie leaned back in her chair. "You asked me why I wasn't hysterical when you made the big reveal; that's why. I already knew what happened. Sort of."

Jessie still couldn't move, so Abbie nodded for him.

"I can't explain it but I felt it…you, being alive, I mean. At first I thought it was, you know, just me not wanting to let go but even after we buried you…your body, the feeling didn't go away. And then when I heard you scream I knew what happened. What you were…so I've had a little time to process it."

Oh, God. "Abbs."

Abbie sat up straighter and glared at the screen as one tear finally broke free. "So promise me now you're not going to do anything or I will tell him."

Jessie crossed his heart. *I promise.*

Out loud.

"I promise…I swear."

Abbie wiped her eyes. "Okay." Then she glared at him again. "Why did you wait so long to let me know?"

"I've been…busy?"

And for some reason they both laughed.

"You haven't changed, you know," Abbie said. "Not inside."

Jessie knew. "But the outside sure has."

"I love you." Everything went still and quiet. There were no words, inside or out, no sounds, nothing until she spoke again. "You're still my…Jessie and you always will be."

When Jessie shook his head, Abbie's image leaned closer to the monitor and whispered into the speakers.

"Yes, you are. Listen to me for a minute and stop being so hormonal. Okay, that doesn't work anymore, lucky you, but just cool it. You're transgender, right?"

Jessie cocked his head to one side. "Was."

"Well, yeah, okay, was…but that meant that one day I'd lose my twin sister and get a twin brother. And now I have one. It just happened a little differently than we both thought it would."

"Jesus Christ, Pollyanna, gender reassignment is normal and natural, dying and then waking up in somebody else's body is an abomination unto God! I'm an Imp, Abbie, a Traveler, I'm—"

"You're Jessie, my brother. And would you stop with the rhetoric, please?"

"Excuse me?"

"You heard me. Like I said, I had some time to think about this and…what if Dad and the U.C.U.A. are wrong? What if one body, one soul means the *right* body for the soul? I don't know, Jessie, but your soul was always a boy and now you have a body to match. You still have one body and one soul. Hi, Curtis."

For a moment it felt like a wild hamster had gotten loose inside Jessie's chest and was running laps wearing combat boots, but then the hamster slowed down or died or something and Jessie was able to take a deep breath so he could shout or curse or beg Abbie to take back what she just said, to please take it back or—

Jessie exhaled and wiped his nose off on the back of his hand.

"Eeew, you really are a guy." Abbie hadn't even tried to hide the disgust in her voice.

Jessie wiped his hand on the leg of his shorts and nodded.

"So what's it like? I mean, you don't have to tell me, if you don't want to."

Jessie took a deep breath and let it out. "It's…weird, but I…it sort of feels the same, you know? Like it's always been my…. Well, not my body, but…."

Abbie nodded. "Yeah. Do they call you…."

"Jessie, yeah."

"Good, because you don't look like a Curtis."

"Really? Then what do I look like?"

His sister thought a moment.

"Walter," she said. "Definitely a Walter."

"Screw you."

They both laughed. Abbie stopped first.

"Where are you?"

"Pennsylvania. And I'm older than you are."

"You always were."

"More. I'm twenty. Twenty-*one* next month. I can legally get drunk."

Jessie watched his sister's eyes narrow. "You better not!" She stopped glaring and forced a laugh. "Well, I always did want a big brother." Hah. Hah. Hah. "Are you okay?"

The *now* was implied and he nodded. "Better."

"And you promised."

"I promised."

Abbie suddenly turned away from the screen and looked over her shoulder. *Shh!* Jessie heard their father's voice in the background and felt every muscle in his body tighten.

Dinner. I'll talk to you later, okay?

Jessie nodded. *Thanks, Abbs.*

Any time, big brother. "Gotta go," she said/shouted. "I'll talk to you later, Walter!"

Bitch. "Okay," he said/shouted back. "Sweet cheeks."

Abbie stuck out her tongue as they simultaneously turned off their computers.

Jessie sat back and stared at his reflection in the blank screen. He was smiling. One body, one soul – a matched set.

Finally.

Jessie stood and walked over to the bookcase for the bottle of pills. He put it in the pocket of his shorts as he left the room. The television was on downstairs, some prime time comedy. The canned laughter followed Jessie down the hall to the bathroom.

The bathroom smell of lemons and Lysol intensified as Jessie closed the door. Turning on the light, he stared at the face in the mirror – *Hey, Walter* – and opened the pill bottle. The pills turned the toilet's blue-tinted water a putrid shade of green, the color deepening when Jessie peed on them. Standing up.

There had to be a first time for everything and even though his aim was a bit off and accuracy still needed a little work, Jessie knew he'd improve with practice. He had time. Abbie made him realize that.

Jessica Faith Pathway was dead and buried and would be remembered on holidays and the birthday she'd shared with her sister, but Jessie was still alive.

And wanted dessert.

Zipping up, Jessie walked over to the sink to wash his hands and smiled into the mirror.

"Congratulations," he said, "it's a boy."

★   ★   ★

Arvada, Colorado

Walter? Jess thought for a moment. He didn't know any Walters. His family must belong to another U.C.U.A. chapter. And whatever happened to Nigel?

Jess rapped his knuckles against the door. "Did you hear me, Abigail?"

"Yeah. Be right there, Dad."

Jess turned and walked down the hall. He'd ask her about Walter – and Nigel – later, but for the moment he offered up a silent prayer of thanks. Abigail was going to be all right.

CHAPTER TWENTY-EIGHT

Phoenixville, Pennsylvania

Eva knew there was going to be a crowd, there always was in summer, but she hadn't expected to find a sea of people, including most, if not all, of her neighbors. When she saw it, she'd almost told Allan to drive away, to turn around and head for Petrucci's, but Curtis preferred Rita's water ice so she had no choice.

The crowd, she discovered once they'd found a parking spot across the street and joined the mob, was there in support of the fundraiser for the Phoenixville Phantoms. If she had also known that, she would have suggested they come on a different night...not that she had anything against the local team, but Curtis had never liked sports so she'd never really followed them.

But he'd come downstairs looking so happy, smiling – which was something she was still getting used to seeing – that she couldn't say no.

And that's why she hadn't said no when he turned wide-eyed toward Uncle B.'s BBQ instead of the red-and-white awning and milling crowd.

"You're hungry?"

He smiled at her again. She'd never truly appreciated how handsome he was.

"It's barbecue," he said as if that were an answer, and the people nearest them laughed. He was talking too loudly, people had noticed him. "And it smells so *good!* Can we get something?"

"Sounds like a good idea," a man in the crowd, a stranger, said.

Jessie was too animated, too enthusiastic. For some reason the pill hadn't started working. She'd have to increase the dosage when they got home. Eva reached for his arm but her husband got to him first.

"Would you like something, Jes— Curtis?"

His grin widened. Curtis never used to smile like that.

"Yeah!" More people laughed and he looked around, as if finally noticing the crowd. "I mean, we already ate and everything."

"That's okay," her husband said. "If you're hungry, you're hungry." He shrugged. "It's just...barbecue, you know."

Her husband nodded as if he did. Eva stepped closer. "Instead of a water ice?"

More people laughed when they both turned and looked at her as if she'd lost her mind.

"Okay, fine. You two go get barbecue and I'll stand in line for water ice. What kind do you want, Curtis, the usual?"

"Sure," he called back, following her husband around the edge of the crowd toward the eatery. "Surprise me!"

"Growing boys, right, Eva?" The voice was familiar, the question uncalled for.

She turned away from it and got into what she hoped was the line for Rita's and not some kind of pep squad event. With luck they'd be back before she reached the order window.

★   ★   ★

Arvada, Colorado

"Dad, can I talk to you for a second?"

Jess stepped out of the doorway and back into the hall. The meeting room was filling up quickly and he didn't want to keep everyone waiting, but the look in his daughter's eyes made everything else unimportant. They were shining and bright, alive. Whoever Walter was and whatever they'd been talking about earlier that night, the young man had brought Abigail back. They'd definitely have to have Walter and his family over for dinner soon.

And find out what U.C.U.A. chapter they belonged to and if they'd consider becoming members of his congregation.

Jess took his daughter's hand and led her to the small alcove that once housed the church's landline pay phone. They'd left it and the phone, disconnected, of course, because the children in day care loved playing with it.

"How's this?"

Jess watched his daughter take a long, slow breath. "I was thinking about Jessica."

He squeezed her hand gently. "Of course you were and I miss her too, baby, but she wouldn't want us to suffer in our grief. I think she'd be happy you found someone you could...talk to."

"What?"

Jess lifted her hand and kissed it. "I have a confession to make. I heard you and Walter talking. Is he someone...special to you?"

Her eyes widened. "Yeah."

"Can I meet him?"

"Maybe. He's not from around here. He lives in Pennsylvania."

And for some reason that made Jess feel better. "Well, I'm glad you're friends. So, what did you want to tell me?"

His daughter looked up at him. "That Jessica's happy, she's finally happy."

It was a very odd thing to say and Jess was about to ask what she meant by it when a figure suddenly filled the open doorway and they both jumped.

"Excuse me, Jess, but we have a situation."

"Greg, I'm in the middle of something."

"I know and I'm sorry, but...." He looked back toward the meeting room. "You need to see this, Jess. Right now."

Jess looked at his daughter and let go of her hand. "We'll talk more about this later, okay?"

She smiled and stepped back to give him room. "If you want."

Another strange answer.

"Okay, let me just see what's going on and I'll be right back."

But he wasn't.

★   ★   ★

Phoenixville, Pennsylvania

Two girls wearing bright purple Phoenixville Phantoms T-shirts were walking down the line, one handing out bright purple *GO PHANTOMS* stickers, while the other shook her pom-poms. Eva didn't know either of the girls.

"Thank you for your support," the first girl said as she handed Eva a sticker.

"Go Phantoms!" the second girl said.

Nodding, Eva shoved the sticker into her purse and continued to watch the front of the BBQ shack. She'd been in line for almost five minutes and they still hadn't come out. How long did it take to order barbecue and leave?

Eva jumped when the girl with the pom-poms yelled again. "Go Phantoms!"

She was getting a headache. If they didn't come out soon she'd....

If they didn't come out soon she'd go ahead and order water ice – mango for Allan, root beer was Curtis's favorite and chocolate chocolate-chip for herself – like the good mother she was.

"Go Phantoms!"

Eva sighed and took a step as the line inched ahead.

★   ★   ★

Arvada, Colorado

Jess could feel the tension in the room the instant he walked in. It snapped around him like static electricity.

Only a few of the congregation were sitting, huddled together near the front of the room. The rest were on their feet, a few pacing, most standing still. Each and every one of them was staring at the all-in-one computer someone had carried in from the media room.

The only voices Jess could hear came from the computer monitor. *"...this afternoon down Colfax past the State Capitol and culminating at Civic Center Park. It was estimated to be one of the biggest demonstrations in recent months. An estimated...."*

Jess followed in Greg's wake as the man cleared a path. "Excuse us. Pardon us. Sorry. Move, please. Jess needs to see this."

When he finally got a clear view of the screen, Jess thought it was just another pro-Traveler march. Although they'd never be as commonplace as U.C.U.A. marches, or as respected, the very fact that they were allowed just proved how liberal the government – local, state and federal – was becoming on the matter. The time stamp on the scrolling text at the bottom of the screen showed it was a broadcast from earlier that day.

"What is this all about?"

"Just wait," Greg said. "I didn't believe it until I saw it. Here, it's right here."

Jess leaned forward as the camera moved in for a close shot of the banner at the head of the march – *Our Lives Still Matter!* – and the people carrying it.

"Oh God."

Hands gripping the blue-and-yellow banner, Richard and Laura Wingate stood on either side of the Traveler that had taken their daughter's body. They were smiling. They looked happy. They looked like a family.

Jess thought he was going to be sick.

"A friend of mine in the Denver police department recorded it," Greg said. "He was out there on crowd control and knows Rich and Laura are members of our chapter—"

"Were," Jess corrected.

"Were. Anyway, he thought we'd like to see it." Jess heard the rattle in the man's throat when he sighed. "I can't believe it. I'm looking right at it and I can't believe it. They're True Born. How could they do this to us, Jess?"

"They did it to themselves, Greg. Will everyone please take their seats?"

Jess turned off the computer but kept his back to the congregation even after the room quieted. When he turned around they were all seated except for his daughter, who still stood at the back of the room. He caught her eye and nodded.

"They did it to themselves," Jess repeated softly, not needing to shout. "They turned their backs on us and the truth to follow a graven image that is as hollow and profane as the one crafted during the Exodus. They have turned their backs on us and the True Way. They have fallen and are lost."

Jess clasped his hands together and closed his eyes. "'What man of you, having a hundred sheep, if he has lost one of them, does not leave the ninety-nine in the open country, and go after the one that is lost, until he finds it? And when he has found it, he lays it on his shoulders, rejoicing. And when he comes home, he calls together his friends and his neighbors, saying to them, "Rejoice with me, for I have found my sheep that was lost." Just so, I tell you, there will be more joy in Heaven over one sinner who repents than over ninety-nine righteous persons who need no repentance.'"

"Amen."

"Is it not up to us, as good shepherds, to go and bring back our lost sheep?"

"Yes."

"But what if that sheep is a wolf in disguise and the moment we reach out to help it rips open our throats?"

The congregation waited for him to tell them.

"Then isn't it wiser that a shepherd carry a stick with him to defend himself?"

"Yes."

Jess unclasped his hands. "There are wolves everywhere and we've just seen two of them. We took them at their word that they were like us, but would True Borns turn their backs on us and everything they believed? Would True Borns not only accept but nurture the creature that stole their child's body?"

"No!"

"No, a True Born would not...so it's up to us, as good shepherds, to drive the wolves back into the darkness where they belong."

"*Yes!*"

Jess opened his eyes just in time to watch his daughter turn and walk away.

"Amen."

★ ★ ★

Phoenixville, Pennsylvania

The two of them showed up just as Eva reached the window. Jessie was holding the remains of a pulled-pork sandwich and there was a smear of sauce on his left cheek. Eva grabbed one of the paper napkins from the dispenser on the counter and wiped it off, anger making her hand shake.

But not at him, never at him.

She turned it on her husband. "What took you so long?"

"We had to wait. They make everything fresh. We'll have to go back when it's less crowded."

"Yeah!"

"Don't talk with your mouth full, Curtis, you know better."

He swallowed, mumbled "Sorry" just as the girl working the counter offered Eva a tired smile.

"Hi. Welcome to Rita's. Go Phantoms! How can I help you?"

Eva cleared her throat. "Three mediums, please. One mango, one chocolate chocolate-chip, and Curtis will have root beer."

"Okay, that's one mango, one chocolate chocolate-chip and one—"

"Hang on a minute."

Shoving the last of the sandwich into his mouth, Jessie took a step closer and scrutinized the list of flavors the same way he scrutinized everything: head cocked to one side, eyes half-closed as if he could actually see the chemical formula of each flavor. It wasn't until Eva began hearing grumbling from the people still waiting behind them that she reached out and tapped his shoulder.

"Pick one. People are waiting."

He looked at the counter girl and smiled. "What do you think?"

There were louder groans.

"Um, I like chocolate chocolate-chip the best."

"Okay, chocolate chocolate-chip, please."

The girl smiled back. "One mango and two chocolate chocolate-chips. That'll be $8.85, please."

Eva handed over a ten dollar bill, put the change into the slotted lid of the purple Phoenixville Phantoms bucket that had been conveniently placed on the counter, and was reaching out to take his arm when one of the medium chocolate chocolate-chip water ice arrived.

"Special delivery," the girl said to Jessie and he smiled when he took it. Eva had never seen him smile so much.

"You look flushed. Why don't you go back to the car and wait?"

He nodded and disappeared into the crowd as her husband stepped up to pick up his water ice and drop another ten dollars into the booster bucket.

"Go Phantoms!"

"I already put money in," she said when he handed her the last cup.

He started to say something else when the shouting started in the parking lot. Eva began moving toward it when someone grabbed her arm.

"Eva!"

Oh God, another neighbor. "Hi, Leah."

"I just saw Curtis."

Eva forced a smile. "Yes, he's doing wonderfully. Kids are very resilient."

"Aren't they? Sue told me she—"

Eva shook her head, pointing to her ear with her free hand. The crowd noise was getting louder. Maybe it was an impromptu pep rally, but Eva couldn't hear what the woman was saying and didn't care.

"Right. Go Phantoms. I really have to go, Leah, they're waiting."

But when Eva tried to step around the woman she blocked her. "We prayed for him, Eva." The woman had to shout to be heard over the other voices. "I want you to know that, we *prayed* for him."

"How nice. But I really have to go."

Eva finally managed to sidestep the woman when another hand, small and cold, grabbed her arm and pulled her to a stop.

"Who is he, Eva?"

When Eva turned, Sue Ramos, chocolate-chip cookie baker, ex-babysitter, busybody, frowned up at her.

"Who is he, Eva?"

"I don't know what you're talking about, Sue." Eva pulled away and felt the old woman's nails scrape against her skin. "I have to go."

There was another voice rising above the noise. Her husband's. "Eva!"

"See, they're waiting."

"We know it isn't Curtis!" the older woman shouted. "We know! A friend of mine works at Transitional Care in Haverford. She was there, she saw what happened. We know it's not Curtis!"

"*Eva!*"

"*Who is it?*"

"I don't know what you're talking about." The cup of water ice slipped out of her hand and fell, spattering her sandals and toes as Eva turned and began to push her way through the crowd. "Leave us alone!"

"He's one of them!" the older woman screamed after her. "You brought him into the neighborhood."

"Abomination," the first woman who'd accosted her, Leah, shouted. "We don't want his kind here, Eva."

"Eva! Hurry!" Her husband sounded frantic.

Eva elbowed and shoved and pushed her way through the wall of people as the women followed, bleating like sheep.

"*Not here, Eva!*"

"Abomination!"

"*Imp!*"

Her husband was standing at the far end of the parking lot, at the edge of the crowd, clawing at backs and arms and shouting at them to "Move. Leave him alone," only to get pushed back. Eva recognized some faces in the crowd, not others, but the one face she couldn't find was Curtis's.

"*Eva*, help me get Jessie out of here!"

"Jessie," another voice, a strange voice, shouted. "Its name is Jessie!"

Sue's voice shrieked, "A Traveler!"

"Imposter!"

"Get out of here, Imp!"

"Abomination!"

"Go back to where you came from!"

"Yeah, the grave!"

Laughter followed.

"Freak!"

"*Hey!*" A new voice, louder and deeper, echoed over the parking lot and everything stopped. "Knock it off before I call the cops!"

Eva recognized the big man from an article she'd read in Phoenixville's *IN Community* magazine. Uncle B. stepped out onto the parking lot, arms folded across his white chef's coat and sauce-stained apron, and stared at the crowd until it broke apart and drifted away. Eva was still a few yards away when her husband put his arm around Jessie's shoulder – *Jessie, his name's Jessie* – and began pulling him toward the crosswalk. The collar of Jessie's T-shirt was ripped and the right side of his shorts was covered in melting chocolate chocolate-chip water ice, but otherwise he looked fine...terrified, but fine.

The big man followed until they reached the corner, putting himself between the crowd and the three of them.

"Do you need any help?" Uncle B. asked.

"No," Eva said. "Thank you."

"No problem. Take it easy, kid, and you're welcome to come back anytime. Okay?"

"Yeah. Okay. Thanks."

The big man nodded when the light changed but didn't move until the three of them were safely across the street. He was gone by the time they reached the car and most of the crowd had gone back to standing in line, but there were a few who still watched.

They really should have gone to Petrucci's.

Go Phantoms.

CHAPTER TWENTY-NINE

Arvada, Colorado / 9:00 p.m.

It shouldn't have happened.

Jess could feel the heat start to blister his skin but he couldn't move.

It wasn't supposed to happen.

"That's him."

Hands grabbed his arms and pulled him back into the cold night, but it didn't help; he could still feel the heat of the fire against his face and chest, still hear the screams above the roar and crackle of the flames. He could still hear the screams.

Dear God, what have I done?

One of the hands gripping him spun him around. "State your name, please."

Jess blinked and gasped. His eyes felt like they'd been sandblasted. "It wasn't supposed to happen like this."

"I said state your name. Please."

It was a police officer. Of course it was. Two squad cars had accompanied the fire engine and ambulance. Jess had placed the 911 call himself because he was responsible. Not for the fire; he never agreed to nor condoned that. It just happened. They weren't vigilantes or some crazed mob out for blood. The fire had been an accident. It shouldn't have happened. It wasn't supposed to happen.

Jess had chosen only twenty to accompany him and sent the rest of the congregation, including his daughter, who had been sitting alone in one of the classrooms, home with instructions to pray. He had decided against calling the U.C.U.A. office in Denver, knowing that if he did it would become a public spectacle instead of the private matter that it was supposed to be.

Richard and Laura had been part of his flock and it was up to him to deliver a just retribution for their blasphemy. Jess needed to see the look of shame and remorse on their faces when he condemned them for their heresy and told them to get out, to pack up and leave. To burn in the fires of hell.

That was all that was supposed to happen.

"Sir. Your name."

"Jess Pathway. Reverend Jess Pathway."

"Reverend." The officer glanced past Jess to the smoldering remains of the house. "Fire and brimstone, huh? Well, you got the fire part right."

Jess could feel the heat against his back. "It wasn't supposed to happen."

"Then what the hell were you all doing here? I talked to some of the neighbors and they said you and your group showed up and started shouting and behaving in a threatening manner."

"We were praying."

"Right. Neighbors also said you were trespassing."

Jess took a deep breath and tasted smoke. "We were standing on the sidewalk, which is a public right-of-way, and we weren't threatening. We were just looking at the house."

"Just looking?" The fire was out, but the coals were still sufficiently hot to provide more than enough light for Jess to see the man walking toward him. He wore a dark suit and white shirt, open at the collar, no tie, and held out a gold badge in a black case. "Detective Kurtz. So let me ask you, why were all of you just standing on the sidewalk and looking at the house? Are you a band of wandering real estate agents?"

"That's not funny."

"No, Reverend, it's not. So why were you here?"

Jess turned around and looked at the smoldering remains.

Laura had seen them first.

Jess saw a curtain in one of the upstairs windows move and was still looking at it — the two of them were standing together, Laura with her arm around the Traveler's shoulder, watching — when the front door opened and Richard stepped out onto the porch.

"Get out of here, all of you, or I'm calling the police."

"Try it," a voice behind Jess said. "We're not doing anything."

"I mean it. Get out of here and leave my family alone."

"His family...did you hear that?"

Jess took a deep breath and closed his eyes. "'For the living know that they will die, but the dead know nothing, and they have no more reward, for the memory of them is forgotten. Their love and their hate and their envy have already perished, and forever they have no more share in all that is done under the sun.'"

"She's not dead, she's—"

"Blasphemer!"

"Backslider!"

Jess raised his hand again and the voices behind him went silent.

"'For it had been better for them not to have known the way of righteousness, than, after they have known it, to turn from the holy commandment delivered unto them.'"

"Go home, Jess, we don't want any trouble."

Jess opened his eyes as Richard left the porch, walking out of the light and into the darkness. Laura and the other one were still in the window.

"Trouble? 'He who troubles his own house will inherit the wind, and the foolish will be servant to the wise hearted.'" Jess looked at the shadowed face in front of him. "How could you choose that over everything you once believed?"

Richard shook his head. "It's not that simple, Jess. It wasn't real before. There were just images and faces of strangers. It's different now."

"How is it different, Richard? She's still one of them."

"That's what I wanted to tell you before, when we came to you. Yeah, she's a Traveler and she's not Carly, we know that. God, don't you think we know that? But she's real, Jess, and she's alive and she deserves to live in peace."

"She's an abomination like the rest of them!"

"We were wrong, Jess," Richard said. "We were so wrong about them. They're just people."

"No, they're not. They were once, Richard, but their time has come and gone. They don't belong here and you know it." Jess heard the muttering as he reached out to the man who'd been his friend, but it didn't stop him. "Please. Get rid of it and we'll welcome you and Laura back without reservation. All will be forgiven."

Richard backed away before Jess could touch him. "And all Laura and I have to do is walk away and pretend it never happened."

"Yes."

Richard leaned in. "Like you did with Monica?"

Jess hit him and all hell broke out.

"I won't ask you again, Reverend, why were you here?"

Jess looked past the detective to where two EMTs were putting

Richard into the waiting ambulance. Uniformed officers had already interviewed the men and women who'd come with Jess and put them into a police bus. It was idling in the middle of the street, washed and rewashed with blue and red lights as it waited for him.

"To hold a vigil. They were members of our church and suffered a terrible loss."

The detective nodded. "I know about the losses both of you suffered. And about the organization you both belong to—"

"They left," Jess corrected.

"Is that why you broke his jaw? Because he left?"

Jess didn't answer.

"Okay, how about this: did you throw the fire bomb?"

"No, and it couldn't have been one of us. This was a peaceful demonstration."

"I thought you said it was a vigil."

When Jess didn't immediately answer, the detective took his arm and walked him toward the bus. "You have the right to remain silent. Anything you say can and will be used against you in a court of law. You have the right to an attorney and to have him present with you while...."

The ambulance began to pull away as they passed. Jess watched it and the police car that followed. Laura was staring at him from the back of the patrol car. There was a dark smudge on her left cheek. The Traveler was sitting next to her but never looked in Jess's direction.

"...Do you understand what I just told you?"

Jess nodded and stepped onto the bus.

★   ★   ★

Thursday

Phoenixville, Pennsylvania / 12:43 a.m.

The television woke him up.

Jessie rolled over and tried to open his eyes, but it took him a few tries to remember how to do it. It must have been the hot cocoa – with cut-up marshmallows – Eva made him drink after he'd taken a shower and changed. She kept telling him how hot cocoa always made him feel better and hovered over him until Jessie drained the cup.

It was fortunate Curtis liked his hot cocoa lukewarm or it would have scalded Jessie's already ruined throat.

He didn't think a lukewarm cup of anything would help calm him down after the confrontation, especially since he'd been the one being shouted at – "*Get out of here!*" "*Go back to where you came from!*" "*Yeah, the grave!*" "*Freak!*" – but it'd worked.

He actually started to feel calmer almost immediately. Who knew cocoa could do that? It was amazing. He felt light and free and barely managed to toe off his Skechers before falling back into the pillow and....

Jessie didn't actually remember falling asleep but he couldn't have been asleep long because the television woke him up and he knew the Mr. and Mrs. didn't stay up late. Jessie yawned. God, what were they watching? Must have been a war movie or some kind of SF alien invasion flick by the sound of it...all loud, angry voices shouting words he couldn't quite make out. If he wasn't so sleepy, he'd get up and ask them to turn it—

Thud.

Something hit the window next to his bed and Jessie's eyes opened on their own. It didn't sound like snow or sleet...maybe hail, but you never knew what kind of weather you're going to get in Colorado. Another thud hit the glass. No, definitely not snow or sleet and he wasn't in Colorado. He was in Pennsylvania and it was summer and they'd gone to get water ice and he had a pulled-pork sandwich and then the crowd surrounded him...and started yelling and grabbing at his clothes and....

Jessie sat up and held on to the mattress when the room spun a quarter turn to the right.

Thud thud crash.

The window shattered, spraying glass as a dark object crashed to the floor. The voices weren't coming from the television.

"They're in the back yard!"

"Abomination!"

"Get out! You're trespassing!"

"I'm calling the police!"

"Try it!"

"Go away!"

"We know what it is!"

"Imposter!"

"What are you doing? Stop it!"

"Imp!"

Besides those of the Mr. and Mrs., the other voices sounded familiar, sounded similar to those he'd heard shouting in the parking lot.

He was trying to stand up when the bedroom door opened, flooding the room with yellow light.

"There! It's in there!"

More rocks hit the house and took out what glass remained in the window. The Mrs. screamed from the doorway as the Mr. ran into the room. Jessie heard glass crunch as he swung his legs over the side of the mattress.

"No! Don't move!" the Mr. said. "Here, put these on."

Jessie fell back onto the mattress while the Mr. shoved shoes onto his feet.

"Kill it!"

"Send it back to hell!"

"One body! One soul!"

"Can you stand up?" the Mr. asked but didn't wait for an answer. He pulled Jessie to his feet and half carried him out into the hallway. "Eva, take him."

"I have you," the Mrs. said, pushing/pulling him down the hall to the bathroom. "It's all right, I have you."

Jessie squeezed his eyes tight when the bathroom light came on and shivered when he sat down on the closed toilet seat.

"Stay here," the Mrs. said, "Curtis, did you hear me? Stay here. Understand?"

Jessie leaned back against the tank.

"Curtis, do you understand what I just said?"

Jessie blinked. "What?"

"Stay here."

"Yeah. Okay."

"Good, good boy. You'll be safe here. I won't let anything happen to you ever again. Just stay here."

The door closed with a softer thump than the rocks and bottles hitting the house.

Jessie closed his eyes – bad mistake – and had to grab the edge of the sink when he opened them to stop the sensation of spinning. It didn't help much and the cold porcelain against his palm started a shiver that ran straight up his arm to his belly.

The sound of rocks hitting the house and shouting voices were muffled, but Jessie could still hear them. And he sat there, shivering and listening – *Send it back to hell! It doesn't belong here! Abomination! Imposter! One Body. One Soul! Freak!* – until the contents in his stomach had had enough and decided to leave.

Fortunately, the bathtub was only a quick fall to the side, and the pain of landing on both knees against the tiled floor cleared his head enough to make sure he was leaning into the tub and not next to it when the contents of his stomach gushed out.

Goodbye, wontons. Goodbye, pulled pork. Goodbye, water ice. Goodbye, spleen.

It didn't take long, but by the time Jessie started dry heaving the bathtub looked like something had crawled into it and exploded. He hadn't wanted to look at the mess, let alone smell it – *urp* – but he was too weak to look away and afraid to close his eyes in case the room felt like dancing again. So he sat there, curled up in a semi-upright fetal position, arms hanging over the rim of the tub, staring down into the coagulated morass as his eyes refocused on a tiny speck of blue amid the various shades of reds and cocoa-brown.

Blue?

Holding his breath, Jessie leaned forward and felt his stomach quiver. Still cocooned in the gummy, semi-dissolved marshmallow piece, the blue pill was bigger than the orange ones he'd dumped down the john and even though his stomach acids had softened it, he could still make out the cute little heart shape in the center he remembered from health class. Valium. The Mrs. had slipped him a roofie. No wonder the lukewarm cocoa calmed him down; it had help.

If the True Borns had decided to come just a little later he might have slept right through the shouting match and never heard a thing.

Unless they got in…and maybe not even then.

Jessie felt the muscles in his arms and legs tremble as he leaned back far enough to rest his forehead on the tub rim. It was cool, but the smell of vomit was making him sick again and he had to sit up. Another rock hit the pebbly glass in the small bathroom window above the tub and splintered it.

"*One body! One soul! Begone, imp!*"

They were the same words, the very same he'd said...no, not him, her...Jessica Faith, the sweet, naïve, myopic little girl who believed everything she'd been told about the Travelers and never thought to question it. And for a moment he was outside, standing with them, shouting up at the house because there was a thing inside that didn't belong, that went against the laws of God and man. For one moment he was Jessica Faith again...and then she was gone.

"*Abomination!*"

"No, we're not."

Jessie used the tub and sink edge to lever himself to his feet. It took longer getting up than it did going down, but when he finally was able to hold himself upright and look in the mirror he didn't like what he saw.

The face looking back had shadows under his eyes and stubble on his cheeks and chin and upper lip. The face looked tired and a bit stoned, but it also looked grown up, like it had matured a lifetime in the last few minutes.

"We're just people," Jessie told the young man in the glass, "just like Abbie said."

Taking a deep breath, Jessie left the bathroom and walked down the hall to his...to Curtis's bedroom. The shouting seemed louder in there, the voices angrier, the hot, muggy air pouring in through the broken window almost too thick to breathe. Jessie had to stop in the doorway to catch his breath.

"*Get it out of h—*"

WHOOP!

Flashing red and blue lights decorated the sudden silence that followed and made the soft crunch of glass under Jessie's shoes as he crossed the room sound like thunder.

Jessie stood to one side of the window and looked down. There must have been forty people standing in the Steinars' front yard, maybe more. Jessie didn't want to count, but he recognized Curtis's old babysitter and baker of cookies right away. She was the only one looking up at his window; everyone else was watching the two officers in riot gear as they walked onto the porch.

Jessie heard a second *whoop!* from the front of the house.

The cavalry had finally arrived.

Jessie watched the old woman's face as the red and blue lights washed over it.

Is that what I used to look like?

A low wave of voices began again and Jessie wasn't the only one who jumped when the officers blasted another beep from the siren. The crowd went quiet and backed away, as the officer who had been driving leaned across the top of the door and lifted a mic to his lips.

"Okay, it's over. Go home, people."

"What do you mean, it's over?"

Jessie saw the Mrs. run toward the officer as the crowd began to walk away. The Mr. followed slowly.

"Arrest them!" she screamed. "Why aren't you arresting them? They tried to kill us!"

Jessie leaned closer, wanting to hear what the officer said.

"I don't think so, ma'am, but we'll take their names. There was no real harm done and I'm sure your insurance will cover it."

"What?"

The officer glanced toward the window and Jessie backed up.

"You should have known better than to bring one of those into the neighborhood. One body, one soul. Call your insurance company and let them handle it. That'll be the best for everyone."

Jessie could hear the Mrs. still attempting to argue, and the Mr. trying to calm her down, as he left the window and walked to the desk.

The chair protested loudly when he collapsed in it. He couldn't stay there, God knows, but he couldn't go home, and that left only one option.

Jessie pulled out the desk's unused keyboard tray, didn't need one with a laptop, and reached under it for the two business cards he'd taped to the underside. Sometimes hiding in plain sight *wasn't* the best plan.

He laid both cards down in front of him and ran a finger across Dr. Ellison's, trying to press out the crease he'd put in it when he folded it. He hadn't folded Millie's. Jessie's original plan was to leave both cards in his pocket after downing the pills so the proper authorities could be notified.

God, what a stupid idea.

Jessie heard the patrol car drive away as he turned on the computer.

Jessie, I need to talk to you.

Jessie smiled and sat back as the screen came on. *I was just going to PM you. Guess it's true what they say about great minds thinking ali—*

Dad's in jail!

What?

"Curtis!"

What do you mean, Dad's in jail?

Jessie slipped the cards into the pocket of his shorts as the Mrs. ran past his room.

"Curtis! Curtis? Where are…. Oh my God, what happened? *Curtis!*"

It was terrible, Jessie!

"*Curtis!*"

Jessie could hear the hysterical edge to his sister's inside voice. It sounded a little like Mrs. Steinar's.

Hold on a minute, Abbs, okay?

Hold on? What?

Something happened…just hang on. "In here."

Jessie closed the laptop as the Mrs. ran into the room. "You got sick! What happened?"

"It doesn't matter."

"What do you mean it doesn't matter, Curtis? Of course it matters."

Jessie!

In a minute.

He hit Mr. Wingate and broke his jaw.

What?

Jessie started when the Mrs. grabbed his arms. "Why did you throw up? What happened?"

What happened?

CHAPTER THIRTY

The Mrs. tightened her grip on Jessie's arms. "Answer me, Curtis! What happened?"

Mr. and Mrs. Wingate were on TV, at a Travelers Rights March and Dad thought.... He said it was just supposed to be a rally, but....

He broke Mr. Wingate's jaw?

– – –

Abbs? What else?

– – –

The Mrs. sank her nails in deeper. "Curtis! Curtis, why were you sick? Why didn't you stay in the bathroom like I told you? Curtis!"

What else, Abbie?

There was a fire. The house...it's bad, Jessie.

The Traveler...the girl, did she—?

No. They're okay...Mrs. Wingate and the girl, but they could have died.

I know the feeling.

"Curtis!"

Why? Did something happen?

I can't stay here.

"Answer me, Curtis!" the Mrs. screamed and slapped him. "What happened?"

The slap didn't hurt, much, but it was enough to pull Jessie out of his head and back into the room just as she was raising her hand for another strike.

Jessie grabbed her arms, stopping her. "You want to know what happened – those pills you drugged me with upset my stomach. *I'm not Curtis!*"

And then he pushed her away...forgetting he was much stronger than Jessica Faith had ever been.

The Mrs. managed two stumbling steps backward before her foot hit a vertical shard of glass and she fell, screaming.

Jessie! What's going on?

The Mr. rushed in and stopped. "What happened?"

"She fell."

The Mr. took a step toward Jessie. "What did you do to her?"

"*No!*" The Mrs. stopped screaming and tried to push herself up. The Mr. rushed to help. "It was an accident. It was just an accident. I stepped on some glass."

Jessie watched the Mr.'s eyes as he helped the Mrs. to her feet.

"Come on, Eva," he said, "let's take a look at that cut."

I need you to do something for me, Abbs.

Okay.

I'm going to give you a phone number and you have to tell the person who answers to come get me. Okay?

Okay. What happened, Jessie?

The same thing that happened there, almost. I'm not hurt, but you're wrong, Abbs, my kind will never fit in...there are too many who won't let us.

Okay. Who do you want me to call?

Jessie took the cards out of his pocket, looked at both then refolded Dr. Ellison's card and tossed it onto the desk. He couldn't ask his sister to talk to the man they'd been taught was the devil incarnate.

At least not yet.

Jessie stared at the phone number on Millie's card until it glowed with a reverse color halo.

The lady's name is Millie and she's really nice. Tell her I'm okay, but I can't stay here.

Okay.

"Can I talk to you, Jessie?"

Jessie turned as the Mr. walked in. *And tell her to hurry. Gotta go, Abbs. Thanks.*

I love you, Jessie.

Same here. "Sure."

"This shouldn't have happened, Jessie, and I'm sorry it did."

"I know."

"But...."

Jessie closed the distance between them just enough to hand him the card. "It's okay, Mr. Steinar. I've taken care of it. She should be here soon."

★   ★   ★

New Hope, Pennsylvania / 2:14 a.m.

It wasn't the strangest call Millie had ever gotten since becoming a Newcomer counselor, but it was right up there near the top of the cream level.

She'd been all tucked in and asleep when her room phone chirped and the next thing she knew she was sitting up in bed and listening as a girl explained that Jessie had asked her to call because he needed to leave and wanted Millie to pick him up. The girl didn't give her name or where she was calling from or explain how she knew Jessie – the Caller ID screen just showed it as an *unknown caller* – or say why Jessie hadn't called himself.

Those questions were still buzzing around Millie's head when, a moment after she'd hung up the phone, it rang again.

And this time it had a number she recognized.

"Ms. Guzman…um, Benezet? This is Allan Steinar. I'm sorry to be calling at this hour, but can you come pick up Jessie? I'm afraid it's just not working out."

Millie didn't ask. "Of course. I'll be there in an hour. Will you see that Jessie is packed and ready. I'll bring the necessary release papers for you and your wife to sign. I'm sorry."

The call ended without another word.

Millie threw on clothes – loose blouse and pull-on skirt that looked sufficiently professional – at the same time she shoved the release forms into her toting sack and made calls to both the school's head administrator and housing co-ordinator. Neither were overly concerned by the lateness of the hour; it wasn't the first time Millie'd had to retrieve a Newcomer.

With a few minor exceptions, the staff at New Beginnings were used to working long and irregular hours.

She decided she'd call Dr. Ellison when she got back and had more information.

Usually the thirty-nine-mile trip from New Hope to Phoenixville took about an hour, but with little traffic along 202 and a near-constant speed hovering between 70 and 75 mph, Millie pulled up to the Steinar house in just under forty-two minutes.

And wished she'd been there sooner.

Millie scuffed the curb and turned off the engine.

The house reminded her of others she'd seen during and after the war to free the slaves. Most of the windows were broken and the plants that lined the walk trampled flat. There were scrapes and gouges in the paintwork and front door that reminded Millie of bullet holes. And she prayed to God they weren't. Bright yellow ribbons of police tape decorated the porch columns, illuminated by a hanging bare light bulb. A police car sat in the driveway, silent and dark until Millie pulled up, then the passenger-side door opened and Jessie got out.

She'd just seen him the week before, but he looked older somehow, fragile yet sturdy at the same time.

The officer in the driver's seat must have said something to him because Jessie bent down and nodded, then opened up the back door and pulled out a large red duffle bag. Millie saw him smile as he slung the duffle over one shoulder and started down the drive toward her.

She grabbed her toting sack off the passenger-side seat and got out of the car, unlocking the doors as she did so. Millie was just stepping onto the sidewalk when the scarred front door opened and Mr. and Mrs. Steinar came out, followed by another police officer.

"But it was an accident!" Mrs. Steinar said. "Curtis, come here, please."

Jessie kept walking until he reached the car and Millie opened the passenger-side door. "Are you okay, Jessie?"

"Yeah. Thanks for coming."

She looked over his shoulder at the house. Mrs. Steinar was still calling her dead son's name.

"I'm so sorry, Jessie."

He nodded, then turned and looked at the people on the porch.

"Curtis would never hurt me! It was an accident. Tell them, Curtis. Tell your father it was an accident!" Mrs. Steinar started down the front steps but Mr. Steinar stopped her and pulled her back onto the porch. "Curtis, please!"

"It'll be better for her if I go," Jessie said as he turned back to Millie. "I can, can't I? I don't have to stay, do I?"

Millie thumped her hand against the top of the door hard enough to clear the lump that had suddenly filled her throat. "No, honey, you don't. Now, you climb inside and get comfortable, just throw that in the back, while I go talk to them, okay?"

don't. Now, you climb inside and get comfortable, just throw that in the back, while I go talk to them, okay?"

"Curtis!"

Millie closed the door and started up the walk. She'd seen grief in both her lifetimes and it always took something away that could never be replaced. Hope and joy mostly, but sometimes, like now, reason. Mrs. Steinar had lost her son again and that kind of grief didn't go easy.

"Curtis!"

Mr. Steinar moved his wife back to give Millie room. "Eva, stop. It's for the best."

"Let me go! Curtis, I'm sorry. It was my fault. I'm sorry. *Curtis!*"

Millie reached out and took the woman's hand. "Hush, now, hush. You'll be fine, just hush. That's right."

Mrs. Steinar looked at Millie without seeing her. "It was an accident."

"I'm sure it was. Now why don't you go back inside with this nice officer and rest a spell while I talk to your husband?"

Mrs. Steinar nodded as the officer took her arm and walked her back into the house. "Curtis is a genius, you know."

"Yes, ma'am."

"Mr. Steinar, I'm—"

"Just give me the damned papers," he said, "and get that thing out of here."

Millie handed him the forms that legally relinquished any and all responsibility and obligations to Jessie and even managed a soft 'thank you' when he handed them back.

Didn't matter who or when, some things never changed.

Jessie was almost asleep when Millie got into the car. "All done?"

"All done," Millie said and started the car. Mr. Steinar was still on the porch, waiting for them to leave. Millie pulled out a little too quickly, squealing the tires against the road. "Sorry."

"It's okay. Are you taking me back to the hospital?"

Millie stared at the road illuminated by the headlights. She hadn't even given it a thought and she should have. She knew Dr. Ellison was worried about Jessie's mental state and all, which meant she should take him back, but....

A pair of green eyes almost the same shade as the boy's sitting next to her flashed in the darkness by the side of the road, reflecting the headlights. A cat or fox.

"No," she said, "I'm taking you someplace a whole lot better. Can you fetch that big sack of mine in the back seat? You know, the one I'm always totin' around?"

Millie slowed the car to almost the speed limit as Jessie twisted around and pulled the bag onto his lap.

"Got a whole new bag of peppermint sticks in there, 'case you need one."

Millie kept her eyes on the road and listened to him rooting around. "Found them. Want one?"

"Oh, yes, please. Think I need one." He unwrapped one part way and handed it to her. The bright flavor instantly cleared out the cobwebs. "Aren't you having one?"

"Naw," he said as he dropped the toting sack down next to his feet. "I'm kind of tired."

"Well, you just go to sleep if you want, but the first thing you need to do when we get to where we're going is call your friend, the girl who called me."

Jessie yawned and huddled down in the seat.

"It's okay," he said, "she's already knows."

Jessie was asleep before Millie had a chance to ask who *she* was.

★　　★　　★

"And you're just calling me now?"

"I wanted to get Jessie settled first. Was that wrong?"

Barney yawned and tried not to look at the illuminated clock on the microwave. Amandine had mumbled loudly and kicked him, without actually waking up as far as he could tell, when his phone buzzed across the nightstand, and continued to mumble and mutter and kick until he got out of bed.

"I'm sorry, Dr. Ellison, I should have waited to call you later this morning."

Leaning back in the kitchen chair, Barney rubbed the sleep from his eyes. "No, it's okay. I'm just glad you got him out of there. The mother sounds like.... Well, that might suggest a genetic predisposition for schizophrenia."

Millie made a noncommittal sound.

"You don't think he is?"

"I don't know. He was kind of cloudy when I spoke to him before."

"And tonight?"

"He seemed fine."

Barney rubbed the back of his neck and wondered if he should make coffee or try to end the conversation as soon as he could. The next yawn settled the matter.

"Schizophrenics have moments when they seem perfectly rational, but he's okay and all tucked in for the night and thanks to him, I do have a good many frequent flyer miles I can still use. I'll text the center when I get my flight and ask if they can send someone to pick me up."

"I'll do that," Millie said. "It's the least I can do."

"I'd argue if I was awake, but since I'm not...I'll see you later today."

Her sigh echoed against his ear. "Thank you, Dr. Ellison."

"But try to keep him away from the general population. I mean, don't make him feel like he's being isolated and keep him comfortable, but...you know, for the safety of the others."

This time it was Millie who yawned. "I will. G'night, Dr. Ellison."

Barney left the phone on the kitchen table and decided it might be easier, and safer, if he spent the rest of the night on the living room sofa.

CHAPTER THIRTY-ONE

New Hope, Pennsylvania
The earliest flight he could get had him landing just before lunch, which allowed him to justify his frequent sampling from the platter of assorted pastries Millie had placed between him and Jessie on the cafeteria table.

Before leaving them alone to talk.

Barney knew she'd give them at least an hour. And an hour might just be enough.

Maybe.

Through his sources, he'd read the police report on the incident only to discover Jessie wasn't the only Pathway who had been involved in a spontaneous confrontation. It was almost too strange to be coincidence, but Barney's definition of coincidence had changed considerably.

"Pretty good, huh?" he asked and tried not to smile when Jessie brushed the crumbs off the front of his shirt. The kid had put on some weight, thank God. "My favorites are the scones."

Jessie nodded. "Yeah. Bear claws are good too."

Put on some weight and making small talk. Things were looking up.

Barney smiled. "Yeah, they are. So, how do you like this place?"

Jessie shrugged. "It's nice. I stayed in one of the visitors' dorms last night and Millie showed me around this morning. Pretty big place."

"That it is. Think you might like to stay here?"

Jessie leaned back in his chair. "Isn't that up to you?"

"Well, only partially. I am sorry about what happened, Jessie, but you remember I didn't think it was the best idea to send you home with the Steinars."

"No, you wanted me to go to a nut house."

"A more controlled environment," Barney said slowly.

"A...nut...house," Jessie replied even slower.

They stared at each other for a moment and Barney broke first. "Were you always a smart-ass or is this something new?"

"What do you think?"

"I think you must have been a handful." He meant it as a joke, but knew he'd made a mistake when Jessie's face hardened. "Sorry."

"It's okay. I am a smart-ass and I'm not crazy." Jessie sat up straight and crossed his heart. "Promise."

"I believe you, Jessie, but it's not that simple," he said. "The chemistry of a schizophrenic brain is different than a normal brain. You might feel the same way you did before, but your consciousness is inside a brain that—"

"Was drugged most of the time. Yeah, okay, Curtis might have been a genius, but I don't think so. I don't even think he had a normal IQ. I didn't know the guy so I can't say for sure, but the books he had and the science stuff...they were meant for a kid half his age. So if he wasn't as bright as his mother thought and I'm still...whatever IQ I am...isn't that proof?"

Barney stopped dismantling the pastry and looked up. "Proof of what, Jessie?"

"That I'm still me, one hundred per cent smart-ass and not crazy."

"But you wouldn't know, would you?"

"Wouldn't know what?"

Both of them looked up to see Millie standing next to the table. She could be very quiet when she wanted to be.

"About me being crazy," Jessie told her.

"Dr. Ellison, what a thing to tell this child!"

"I didn't—" Barney stopped himself. "Millie, why don't you join us?"

She took the chair to Jessie's right. "Did Jessie tell you?"

"About last night, yes."

"Jessie, you need to tell Dr. Ellison all of it."

Jessie slumped back against his chair.

"Tell me what, Jessie?" When Jessie didn't answer, Barney turned to Millie. "Tell me what?"

"About the girl who called me last night," Millie said and reached out to touch Jessie's arm. "Go on, tell Dr. Ellison what you told me this morning. Go on."

"It was my sister, Abbie."

That surprised Barney. Given what Jessie had said when he first understood what had happened to him as well as the 'education' he'd gotten, thanks to his father, the fact that he'd reached out to his sister was...remarkable.

Still, being a doctor, Barney needed to prod the wound just a bit more. "I thought you didn't want her...or your father to know."

"She already knew."

Barney looked at Millie with raised eyebrows, but Millie only smiled like the cat that ate the canary. There'd be no help there.

"Okay, I'll bite," Barney said. "How did she know?"

Jessie took a deep breath and looked Barney in the eyes. "She felt me die."

Maybe schizophrenia did run in families; they were twins, after all. "Ah."

"See," Jessie said to Millie, "I told you he'd think I'm nuts."

"Hush that talk and tell him about the song."

"The song?" Barney felt like he'd suddenly stepped into a play without having been given the script. "What song?"

"'Bring Him Home'," Jessie said, "from my funeral."

When he phased out, Barney remembered, the auditory hallucination. "You mean.... No."

Millie nudged Jessie's arm. "Show him, like you showed me."

Jessie sighed, long and loud as if he'd been asked to stand up and recite. Barney had no idea what was going on, but it was obvious something was.

"Look, Jessie, if there's something you want to tell me...."

Jessie pulled a napkin from the dispenser and slid it across the table to Barney. "Write down your cell phone number."

"Why?"

"It's a magic trick, Dr. Ellison. Just write it down."

Barney reached into his breast pocket and took out his pen, then wrote down the number.

"Show me." Barney turned the napkin toward Jessie. "Where's 805?"

"Simi Valley, California."

"Cool." Jessie raised his hands in a flourish. "Abracadabra."

"Jessie, what's going—" 'Ode to Joy' began playing from his coat pocket.

No way.

Barney pulled the phone from his coat pocket and looked at the unknown caller listed on the screen.

"Well, aren't you going to answer it?" Jessie asked.

"Hello?"

"Dr. Ellison?" The voice was soft and hesitant. "God, you're him, aren't you?"

"Yes, I am, and who may I ask are you?"

"I'm Abbie. Abigail Hope Pathway, Jessie's sister."

Barney looked at Jessie. Then at Millie. Then back to Jessie. "This isn't possible."

"Neither is dying and coming back in someone else's body, Dr. Ellison," the girl, Abbie, said, "but it happens."

"How?" And Barney didn't care who answered.

"We've always been able to talk to –" Jessie said from the table before Abbie continued on the phone, "– each other in our heads since we were little." Then both together. "It's a twin thing."

Barney was very happy he was sitting down. "I've read studies suggesting the possibility…but I've never had the opportunity to witness it firsthand. It's amazing. Does your father know you can do this?"

"No," they said simultaneously.

"Why didn't you tell me, Jessie?"

Jessie looked him straight in the eye. "Because you already thought I was crazy."

"I'm sorry." Jessie nodded and Barney watched his green eyes go distant. "Are you two…talking to each other right now?"

"Yes," Abbie answered for them.

"I can't…I still can't believe it."

Jessie smiled as Abbie's voice whispered in Barney's ear. "Jessie said you should wipe the cheese off your tie before it stains."

Barney looked down and laughed at the small cream-colored drop on his blue-and-yellow plaid tie. "Thank you, Abbie, Jessie, my wife would never forgive me. She bought me this tie."

"Well, I have to go now," Abbie said, her voice becoming more formal. "It was nice talking to you, Dr. Ellison."

"You too, Abbie. Maybe we can do it again sometime."

The line went silent.

"That was amazing," Barney said and suspected he probably had the same look on his face that Millie had. "Okay, so maybe I was wrong about you hearing voices that weren't real. And I'm serious about hoping the three of us can talk.... Jessie, what is it? Did Abbie just say something to you?"

Jessie nodded. "She has to go pick up our father," Jessie said. "The U.C.U.A. posted bail, but he needs to be remanded to a family member."

"I'm so sorry."

"And she thinks I should talk to him."

Barney held out the phone.

"No, face to face."

"You want to fly to Colorado? I can take you."

Jessie's green eyes actually bulged. "No! I can't. Maybe on Skype or FaceTime, but not in person...not yet."

"We can do that too. They have a pretty good computer department here, with private study rooms. When you're ready."

"Okay."

Barney put his phone away. "I'm sorry I thought you were...."

"Fruit loops?"

"Sometimes we fall in love with the easiest explanation and don't go beyond it." He shook his head. "You'd think I'd know better."

"Well, we can't all be geniuses."

They both laughed, but only for a moment. "Thank you for telling me the truth, Jessie. I know it was hard, but truth is hard sometimes."

"I guess."

"But it's still better, isn't it, even if it's hard?"

Barney watched the boy sit up straighter. "I don't know. What truth are we talking about, Dr. Ellison?"

"One that was kept hidden from you and your sister."

Jessie's laugh was forced and not very convincing. "What truth? That we were adopted? Nope, we look too much like him."

Barney flipped a mental coin. It came up heads.

"The truth about your mother, Jessie."

The unconvincing laughter stopped and Barney watched

the muscles in Jessie's face and body tense. "She died in a car accident. It was my fault. She was coming to pick me up. Are you saying she didn't die?"

"No, I'm sorry, no, she's not alive." Barney busied himself bringing up the PDF file he'd downloaded to his phone to keep from seeing the horrible look of relief and sorrow in Jessie's face. *God forgive me.* "Monica Pathway, your mother, Jessie, died from shock as a result of a hit and run despite the attending surgeons' best efforts to save her life. Her time of death was 4:37 p.m."

"Go on."

"At 4:41 p.m., the heart began to beat and a woman named Nina Clare Andrews woke up. She lives in Norristown, Pennsylvania, and works as a church secretary. Norristown isn't that far from New Hope if you'd like to—"

"No." He hadn't shouted and that made it worse. "It wouldn't be my mom and she...the woman wouldn't know who I am. I'm not even me anymore."

"I'm sorry, Jessie, but I thought you should know, in case you ever run into her. It's possible."

"Yeah."

"Are you okay?" The question got a shrug, which was more than Barney expected. "Are you going to tell Abbie?"

The tears in Jessie's eyes glistened when he shook his head.

"You can keep secrets from each other?"

"Sometimes. Dr. Ellison, did my dad know...about my mom?"

"Yes. His name is on the release."

Barney prepared himself for shock, rage, or hysterics in any or all combination, but all he saw was a slight tightening of the face and body.

"You know, Dr. Ellison," Jessie said, "I think I would like to talk to my father, after all."

* ★ *

Jessie covered the mouse with his hand and took a deep breath. The 'ringing' receiver icon meant his father was waiting for him to connect. Abbie had set it up, lying to their father, telling him Jessie was a young man in crisis, which was true enough, and promised not to listen in – inside or out.

Jessie moved the cursor over the icon.

When he clicked it his father would smile and ask what he could do to help. He would look kind and benevolent, the way he always looked when he spoke to a troubled soul...but then, after Jessie told him, the look would change. Jessie wasn't sure which emotion would appear first or in what order, grief or shock, but he knew what the last one would be: disgust.

How dare you say something like that? My daughter died whole in body and spirit.

Okay, Jessie, he's waiting. I'm leaving now.

You promise?

Cross my heart. This is between you and him.

Jessie licked his lips and clicked the mouse. His father smiled at him.

"Hi, I'm Reverend Pathway. My daughter said you needed to talk. How can I help you?"

Jessie swallowed and looked into his father's eyes. *What do I say? Hi, Dad, it's me, Jessie? I know about Mom. Are you going to lie about me too? One body, one soul, right, Dad?*

"It's all right, son," his father said, "you can tell me anything. I won't judge."

Jessie took a deep breath – "Sorry, wrong number" – and ended the call.

I'm sorry, Abbie.

What happened? He said you hung up? Call him back. Tell him.

I can't.

Why?

I love him.

Abbie's voice went quiet.

I'll talk to you later, okay, Abbs?

Okay. Give him some time, Jessie, maybe he'll change.

"Sure, Pollyanna."

Jessie turned off the computer and sat staring at the blank screen until Dr. Ellison popped his head in. He didn't ask and Jessie didn't tell. Neither of them needed to.

"Picnic's starting," he said, "and afterward Millie'll show you your new room. Welcome home, Jessie."

OCTOBER

CHAPTER THIRTY-TWO

New Hope, Pennsylvania

Jessie looked where Millie was pointing and nodded. The girl was sitting on one of the park benches that dotted the playing field – shoulders hunched, her arms tucked into her belly, and staring down at the patch of ground at her feet.

What Jessie called 'The Newcomer Hunch'.

She looked so small sitting there all alone...alone and scared, hiding behind the curtain of long blue-black hair that hung down her back and hid her face. If he'd had to guess, Jessie would have put her age at nine or ten, but Millie said the donor had been fifteen.

Just small for her age, Millie said. Jessie didn't ask about how the donor died; that didn't matter. He was supposed to help fix the person inside.

One body, one soul – Part Two.

"What's her story?"

"Her name's Moira Doyle," Millie said, reading off the brand-new tablet Dr. Ellison had all but shamed her into accepting, "from Dublin, Ireland, and the last thing she remembered was running across a street in April of 1916. I checked the date and we think she died in...I'm not sure how that's pronounced."

Millie turned the tablet toward him and Jessie squinted at the italicized words *Éirí Amach na Cásca*. "Dunno."

"Well, the history books call it 'The Easter Rising'. Anyway, that's Moira's story. She's frightened and very confused, so you'll have to go slow and easy."

Jessie looked at the small girl on the bench. "Well, shoot, what's there to be confused about? I mean, so you died and woke up in a whole new body, big whoop."

Millie gave his arm a not-so-soft swat. "You think you're so funny, don't you?"

"Yup. Think she'd like to see the library?"

"I think she might, why don't you go find out. She's expectin' you."

"Moira, huh?"

"That's right," Millie said. "Lovely accent too. G'on now."

Jessie took a deep breath and felt the familiar sensation of the butterflies in his stomach taking flight. It'd been a couple of months since he'd become a Traveling Companion – the school's gag-me-now name for its peer support/mentor/helper buddy system – but he was always a little apprehensive about these first meetings. He never knew how a Newcomer would react. Sometimes there'd be tears, sometimes there'd be silence so heavy and cold Jessie would feel like he was back under the ice, but he'd only been punched once, nothing personal, so the odds were still in his favor.

And Moira didn't look like a hitter.

Jessie squared his shoulders and gave Millie a thumbs-up when he was still a few feet from the bench because he knew she'd still be standing there, watching.

The sun was low and to his back, so he let his shadow arrive first, cutting across the leaf-dotted ground in front of the girl, but she still jumped when he cleared his throat.

"Sorry." Jessie stopped and raised his hands then quickly lowered them when the shadow looked like it was reaching for her. "I didn't mean to scare you."

She was dressed in a dark blue jumper and gray leggings and had pulled the bulky white sweater she was wearing so tight around herself it looked like a blanket. Sweater or not, she wasn't dressed nearly warm enough for the chill in the air. Jessie stuck his hands into the fleece-lined pockets of his jacket.

"My name's Jessie. Hi. You're Moira, right?"

The blue-black hair shimmered like a black waterfall when she shook her head. "Ah was, ah dunno who ah am now."

Millie was right about the accent. It was almost musical.

"Is it okay if I sit down?" The girl scooted to the far end of the bench, giving Jessie more than enough room. "I know how you feel. I wasn't always this handsome."

The curtain of hair shimmered again as the girl turned her head to look up. She looked like Princess Jasmine from *Aladdin*...only prettier. Her face was narrow and her skin the color of rose gold, which made her large blue eyes stand out all the more.

"Jessie Pathway. I'm, uh, here, ah...."

She looked away.

"Are you...?" She shook her head.

"Like you? Yeah."

The wind circled around the bench, driving the leaves before it. She said something that was lost in the rustle. Jessie moved closer.

"What?"

"I said I dun't understan'."

"Nobody does."

She nodded. "The doctors, when I...woke up said it just happens s'times. Does it...to everyone, ya think?"

"Not everyone."

Moira pulled the sweater tighter around herself. "Do you think it coulda happened with m'brothers?"

"Maybe. We could check."

She pushed her hair back over one ear as she turned to face Jessie. "Could we? Could we find 'em?"

"We can ask. They keep really good records, so yeah, we can look for them."

"But they wouldn't look the same, would they?" Jessie watched the tears well up along the ebony lashes that framed her eyes. "I don't, they wouldn't know me."

"Not at first, but you're still the same inside."

The tear on her cheek sparkled in the last rays of sunlight as she nodded. "Yeah, I am."

Jessie stood up and held out his hand.

"Come on, let's go find out about your brothers. We can use one of the library computers."

Her hand was very small and very cold, but it fit into his perfectly. "What's a computer?"

Jessie smiled. "Magic."

EPILOGUE

Barney glanced at the man on the bed through the door's small, wire-reinforced glass window. The Traveler, according to the information already gathered, was Alois Mayerling, age eighty-four.

> Birthdate: April 20, 1889.
> Last date remembered: January 16, 1973.
> Birthplace: Braunau am Inn, Austria.
> Interned Auschwitz Concentration Camp: 1940-1945/# 21361A.
> Immigrated to United States: 1949.
> Naturalized citizen: 1954.
> Family: N/A. Last residence: Brooklyn, NYC.
> Last memory: N/A.

The man was asleep, recovering from the trauma suffered by the body of Zach Caine, a twenty-seven-year-old Huntington Beach surfer, after being body-slammed by rough surf and drowning.

There was a red sticky flag in the upper right corner of the file in Barney's hand, indicating that the donor's family had relinquished all rights and obligations to the Traveler that now inhabited their loved one's body.

Barney studied the handsome, clean-shaven face and took a deep breath. "What makes you think so?"

"He lied."

Barney turned toward the psychology resident and smiled. They were all so eager to make names for themselves in the new field of dysphoric identification disorder that sometimes their imaginations got away from them.

That month alone he'd had to shatter the hopes of one young doctor whose patient turned out to only be an Elvis impersonator.

"People lie, Irene."

"Not Travelers," she said, "not about who they are. Not when they first wake up."

"No, but he survived Auschwitz, remember. It's very possible that he's still suffering from PTSD."

The doctor shook her head. "It didn't sound like it. He was very calm when he answered my questions, but it felt rehearsed, Barney, like he was reciting lines he'd learned. When I finished I cross-checked the ID number he gave us against the lists compiled by the Auschwitz Museum and ID # 21361A doesn't exist. It was never issued because it's a made-up number."

"It was a long time ago. Maybe he forgot the number." The minute it left his mouth Barney realized how stupid that last comment was. He'd worked with camp survivors and not one of them had forgotten or would have removed the number tattooed onto their flesh. "Sorry. But what evidence do you have, besides conjecture and gut feeling, that the man in that room is Adolf Hitler?"

She smiled. "The birthday, April 20th, is the same."

"I'm pretty sure there are about a million other people who share that same birthday." Barney shook his head. "Not good enough."

But she didn't stop smiling. "The birthplace, the year, the same first name as Hitler's father, the way he spoke, in German, when he came to. He was shouting, Barney, and it was the same voice I've heard in those old newsreels on the History Channel."

"Wow, proof positive! Come on, now. A man's voice sounds similar to one that was recorded…God, some eighty-odd years ago and you jump to the implausible and slightly hysterical conclusion that he's Adolf Hitler." Barney handed her back the file. "I thought I trained you better than that."

She sighed and hugged the file to her chest. "You did, and that's why I didn't call you until I was sure. He was kept under sedation and monitored for the first forty-eight hours according to protocol. When I was given the go-ahead, I entered his room along with his attending and two nurses, to explain what happened. His reaction was unusual."

"What did he do?"

"He laughed, Barney. I told him what happened and where he was and he laughed and it wasn't hysterics. He was happy…thrilled, and I don't remember hearing about any other Traveler that did that."

Barney felt a cool breeze against the back of his neck and moved away from the air-conditioning vent. "Okay, that is a little unusual, but remember he suffered in a concentration camp...."

"But he didn't die in one." She patted the file. "He died at the age of eighty-four in Brooklyn, New York."

Barney felt the breeze again.

"When he stopped laughing he looked at us and said something. That's when I knew, because it was the same thing he'd said on one of the newsreels."

"What did he say?"

"He said, '*Wer sagt, dass ich nicht unter dem besonderen Schutz Gottes stehe?*' I have the translation if you need it."

"I don't." Barney stepped closer to the door and looked through the window. The man on the bed was awake and looking at him with bright, ice-blue eyes. The man smiled.

Who says I am not under the special protection of God?

"It is him, isn't it?"

Barney turned and began walking down the hall toward the nurses' station. He could hear the squeak of the resident's rubberized soles against the floor as she followed.

"How secure is this room, Irene?"

"I don't know."

"Okay, no problem. Sedate him until we can move him into an isolation ward and put on a twenty-four-hour monitored watch. No one is to see him or talk to him except the two of us."

Her head bobbed up and down. "Okay, I'll order the sedation and check on the room, but do we call the national committee or the FBI or who? What do we do?"

Barney stopped and looked back down the hall to the room. He knew what he'd like to do. He'd like to make him pay for the atrocities committed in his name, to shoot him between the eyes and send him back to hell.

"Adolf Hitler was supposed to have died from a self-inflicted gunshot wound and his body burned on April 30, 1945, so what we do is find out what the hell he was doing for those next twenty-eight years."

"And then what, Barney?" When he didn't answer, she touched his arm. "Dr. Ellison, what do we do then?"

Barney looked at her and shook his head. "I don't know."

AUTHOR'S NOTE

I want to thank Brian Howell, Uncle B. himself, for allowing me to use his name and establishment in the novel.

Uncle B.'s Bar-B-Q can now be found at 435 Bridge Street in Phoenixville, Pennsylvania.

FLAME TREE PRESS
FICTION WITHOUT FRONTIERS
Award-Winning Authors & Original Voices

Flame Tree Press is the trade fiction imprint of Flame Tree Publishing, focusing on excellent writing in horror and the supernatural, crime and mystery, science fiction and fantasy. Our aim is to explore beyond the boundaries of the everyday, with tales from both award-winning authors and original voices.

•

Other titles available by P.D. Cacek:
Second Lives

You may also enjoy:
The Sentient by Nadia Afifi
American Dreams by Kenneth Bromberg
The City Among the Stars by Francis Carsac
Vulcan's Forge by Robert Mitchell Evans
The Widening Gyre by Michael R. Johnston
The Blood-Dimmed Tide by Michael R. Johnston
The Sky Woman by J.D. Moyer
The Guardian by J.D. Moyer
The Goblets Immortal by Beth Overmyer
The Apocalypse Strain by Jason Parent
Until Summer Comes Around by Glenn Rolfe
A Killing Fire by Faye Snowden
The Bad Neighbor by David Tallerman
A Savage Generation by David Tallerman
Ten Thousand Thunders by Brian Trent
Night Shift by Robin Triggs
Human Resources by Robin Triggs
Two Lives: Tales of Life, Love & Crime by A Yi

Horror and suspense titles available include:
Thirteen Days by Sunset Beach by Ramsey Campbell
The Influence by Ramsey Campbell
The Haunting of Henderson Close by Catherine Cavendish
The Garden of Bewitchment by Catherine Cavendish
Black Wings by Megan Hart
Those Who Came Before by J.H. Moncrieff
Stoker's Wilde by Steven Hopstaken & Melissa Prusi
Stoker's Wilde West by Steven Hopstaken & Melissa Prusi

•

Join our mailing list for free short stories, new release details, news about our authors and special promotions:

flametreepress.com